SCOTTISH
MAGIC

Savor the fantasy!
Hannah Howell

Stobie Piel

Hannah Howell

Elizabeth Ann Michaels

Mandalyn Kaye

SCOTTISH MAGIC

Four Spellbinding
Tales of Magic and
Timeless Love

KENSINGTON BOOKS
http://www.kensingtonbooks.com

KENSINGTON BOOKS are published by

Kensington Publishing Corp.
850 Third Avenue
New York, NY 10022

Library of Congress Card Catalog Number: 96-80349
ISBN 1-57566-182-9

First Printing: September, 1997
10 9 8 7 6 5 4 3 2 1

Printed in the United States of America

Contents

*To Joyce Flaherty—who knows the value
of tilting at windmills, following stars, chasing clouds,
and believing in magic*

*Stobie Piel
Hannah Howell
Elizabeth Ann Michaels
Mandalyn Kaye*

LILY

Stobie Piel

Chapter 1

Loch Fyne, Scotland
A.D. *850*

LILY tiptoed to the last mushroom on the left, and it still wasn't close enough for good viewing. A shaft of sunlight broke through the copse of pine and low shrubs, piercing her eyes as she strained to see around the mushroom's trunk. Lily angled her left wing up and forward to shade her eyes.

Duncan MacLachlan dove deeper into the dark water of Loch Fyne, and swam farther from shore. Lily emerged from the cover of her mushroom and sighed. He was magnificent. He swam with long, firm strokes, his dark skin glistening as his arms propelled him through the water.

In the water, his curse was lifted, temporarily. In the water, the Unseelie spell couldn't touch him. Here, his perfect strength remained untarnished. As it should have been. As it would be, if not for Lily.

She reminded herself that an Unseelie's duty is to place appropriate curses on designated humans, preferably within the first three days of life. She had done so, many times. And each time, she had cheated her queen by utilizing a lesser spell.

Not deathly pox, but a persistent stutter. Not madness, but dim vision. And for Duncan MacLachlan, the curse of his forbearers. Clumsiness. A frown tightened Lily's face as she watched him reach the small island in Lachlan Bay and circle back, swimming again toward shore.

It wasn't his fault. He was innocent. It was the fault of the one called De Dalan who had tripped and stumbled his way from Ireland to Alba. He had found a hill of faerie gold, and chose to favor the Seelie queen with its location. A mistake on his part, for it angered the Unseelies who cursed the rest of his body with a clumsiness a hundred times worse than that already plaguing his feet.

Lily tried to muster outrage on her species' defense, but it didn't come. Unlike her sisters, she had no fondness for gold, for the magic within that tripled the power of magic. Her vice was envy, jealousy of the sweet and beautiful Seelies, who cast spells of forgiveness and hope, who granted wishes and were adored by mortals.

The Seelies must have blessed Duncan MacLachlan with uncommon beauty, for such a man doesn't come about without help.

And she had made him a tripper. A beautiful, utterly magnificent . . . tripper.

Duncan reached shallow water and rose from the glittering surface like a king. Lily's breath caught in her throat. Though she had spied on him here many times, each time was as the first. Her wings quivered as he shook water from his hair, droplets catching fire in the sunset.

She longed to flutter from her hiding place, to lodge herself on his shoulder. To speak with him, and tell him how very much she admired him. It was impossible. On occasion, a Seelie was known to befriend a human, but to the Unseelies, mortals were objects of scorn and derision, to be used and manipulated, but never befriended.

The sight of an Unseelie such as herself would disgust a human, anyway. She was evil. Lily knew it. She was too afraid of her ugliness to seek a vision of herself. The sight of her grim countenance would cause terror, even in a man as brave as Duncan MacLachlan.

For this reason, more than the laws of her people, Lily had kept herself hidden. Hidden as she watched him in childhood, and hidden now, as he became a man of such glory that he stole her breath.

For years, she had told herself it was to watch the results of her curse, to see how he handled the awkwardness inflicted from outside himself. From her. She knew better, and had from the first. She had hovered by his cradle, knowing her duty, and feeling so pure a strength in the infant that she couldn't bring herself to place upon him even the least of curses.

Until Nathara, the Unseelie queen, demanded her reasons, and threatened to apply the curse herself. So Lily returned and inflicted the fate of his ancestors. Clumsiness. De Dalan was supposed to have been attacked by a deathly pox. Instead, because Lily sympathized with the Unseelie's Irish enemy, he tripped and stumbled well into old age.

No doubt, his grandson would be the same.

Duncan's dark skin glistened with moisture as he pulled on braies and tied his low boots. He stood with his back to her, facing the loch. Lily squinted to better view his bottom. A brief flash of embarrassment flared, but an Unseelie should have no sense of decency. She banished hers and sighed heavily as Duncan pulled on his tunic, covering his dark skin from her vision.

She knew she should leave, that she had already lingered too long. Still, she remained beside the mushroom, watching as Duncan raked his fingers through his long hair, untangling it. Lily's fingers twitched as she imagined herself at that task.

He turned and started up the rocky bank toward the path. Lily chewed her lip. She couldn't fly from the copse now without catching his eye, but she could creep through the shrubs and return to the netherworld unnoticed.

Instead, she positioned herself beneath a bunch of bluebells, and held her breath. She was greedy for the sight of him, for just a moment near him.

Duncan started westward along the path that ran between the rocky shore and the hill. The afternoon's rain had left a marshy spot at the path's center. Duncan walked around it, passing toward Lily's position between bluebell and mushroom.

Lily gulped and scrambled from mushroom to mushroom. A quick, breathless flight took her from the copse of pine to the far side of the path. She stopped again beneath a thick, green fern, and glanced back.

Duncan had stopped, but he wasn't looking her way. He stood beside the ancient Rocking Stone, gazing west as the sun lowered over Loch Fyne. Lily watched, wondering what filled his thoughts. She felt his deep longing, as she had since he was a boy.

I want to speak with you. Lily's chest ached from within. The longing grew, year by year, moment to moment. Since his boyhood, she had fantasized about befriending him. Perhaps because she had no real friends among her Unseelie sisters. Perhaps because no other had Duncan MacLachlan's tender charm.

Duncan stood silently, motionless, watching the orange rims of sunset fade over Loch Fyne. His black hair dried softly around his wide shoulders, rippling in the evening breeze. Tears welled in Lily's eyes.

He was alone. She was alone, too. Together, alone. But it pleased her to have shared this moment with him, however unknowing he might be. She'd seen him free. It was worth the pain of eternal separation to know he was strong enough to be free, if only for a little while.

The sun disappeared beneath the horizon, and Duncan turned back to the path. Lily ducked beneath a patch of violets. Moving now would be risky. She would wait until he passed down the path to the Lachlan hamlet, then make her way back to the netherworld's secret entrance.

Lily pressed her lips together to keep herself from alerting him to her presence. Her impulses were often difficult to repress.

Duncan was looking up through the dark green canopy of rowan branches, a slight smile curving his sensual lips. Lily's wings quivered. He was probably remembering the bliss of his swim. She felt his pleasure.

A stab of apprehension distracted her. Duncan was looking up. That meant he couldn't be looking down . . . or watching . . . Oh, no!

Lily's gaze shot to his feet. Time held for the inevitable. She saw his right foot plant on the earth, his left rise. The toe came down . . . smack onto a tree root. Lily groaned. He tripped.

Duncan caught himself, cursing. He didn't curse her, his true enemy. He cursed himself as he stumbled forward. He tripped again. Lily's eyes grew wide. She gasped. She closed her eyes tight.

Branches crashed. Violet blossoms crushed, surrounding her with a faint scent. Something bumped her head, and Lily sank into blackness . . .

Duncan lay face down on the forest floor, just to the right of the path. It had to happen, after the ease of his swim. Duncan sighed and braced himself up. At least, no one was there to see his fall. Small comfort.

Duncan sat on his knees, head bowed. For one horrible instant, as he was falling, he'd been sure he heard someone scream. "No, stop . . . Oh, help!" A tiny voice, like that of a bee.

But a speaking voice.

He'd seen something flutter. Reluctantly, he looked around. He'd crushed a sprig of violets. And yes . . . a butterfly. A large, beautiful insect with purple and green wings. Wings translucent in their delicacy. And he'd crushed its life . . .

The insect stirred, struggling to right itself. Duncan winced. It might be kinder to squash the creature, to end its misery. He picked up a stone and aimed.

The butterfly rolled to one side, flipped onto its back, and screamed, "No!" Duncan held the rock aloft as the creature struggled to escape. He couldn't breathe or move, not even to lower his weapon.

No insect was this. Instead, a tiny woman peered up at him with blue eyes of terror, and perhaps embarrassment. One of the fair people. And he had crushed her. Duncan drew a long, weary breath. Such a crime would yield unimaginable repercussions. To anger them in the smallest way, for breaking a new flower petal, a man might find his crops cursed, his livestock languishing.

For this . . . Duncan closed his eyes. He steeled himself against his latest error, then forced himself to face the faerie. She was still staring at him, motionless. One wing was bent backward, twisted. Broken.

She appeared shocked, though he saw no pain on her small face. She was beautiful, as he knew all faeries were, but in a more female way than he had imagined of her race. Not ethereal, but curiously human in appearance.

"Forgive me, small maiden, and allow me to pay some homage to you and your fair folk . . . ." Her eyes widened in even more surprise and his voice trailed.

"Are you not in awe of me? Are you not terrified?" She spoke as if stunned.

Duncan wasn't sure how to answer. Her voice was small, but clear. A clear bee speaking. It was sweet and melodious, and perplexed. "I am surely in awe . . ." His voice trailed again.

"But not terrified?" She lay on her back, staring at him, tiny lips parted.

Duncan hesitated, unsure what she wanted to hear. "I am not terrified, no."

Her brows arched. "You are indeed brave, Duncan MacLachlan."

"You know me?"

"Of course . . ." She coughed. "All is known to my species."

Duncan nodded. She sounded imperious. He wondered if his question had insulted her, but she didn't appear angry. Instead, her tiny face knit as if . . . as if she were scheming.

"Have I injured you grievously, small maiden?"

She started to sit up. "No . . . yes!" She completed the task of sitting upright, though her left wing drooped dramatically. "I am near death, and unable to assume a correct flight posture."

"Can I help you?"

"Yes . . ." She looked guilty, her eyes averted. "No." Her head drooped. She seemed to be fighting inwardly. Her chin lifted as if in defiance. "Yes. Yes, in fact, you can."

Duncan's brow angled. He'd witnessed a strange battle, of a faerie against her own impulses, good and bad. He wondered which side proved victorious. "In what way, small maiden?"

She was very beautiful, more than he'd realized at first glance. Her hair fell in golden brown waves, nearly to her tiny knees. Her wings quivered, almost as if in excitement. Her legs poked from beneath a green and purple dress, which matched the color of her wings.

Pretty legs. Small, but shapely. Her tiny feet were bare. Her legs were splayed outward, which she noticed, and she quickly tucked them beneath herself. She tapped one finger to her lip, considering his offer.

"It is necessary that you transport me."

"Where do you wish me to carry you?"

She considered further, eyes narrow, wings quivering. "You have injured me, and grievous woe comes to he who injures one of my kind."

"That I know." Duncan steeled himself against his fate. It could be no worse than he expected.

"Should I return to my kind thus injured, that woe would surely fall upon you."

"It is as I deserve."

"Not so!" She rose to her feet and faced him, hands on hips. Her injured wing straightened momentarily, which she didn't notice at first. Her eyes widened, she bit her lip, and the wing drooped into its former injured position. She coughed to clear her throat.

"Should you allow me to recuperate, in your company, I can return to my sisters healed, and no one will be the wiser."

Something about the way she spoke in a rushed, nervous voice incited his suspicions. "Won't they miss you?"

She shrugged. "No. I am often gone from our burgh for long periods of time, as a matter of course." She paused and sighed as if in regret. "It is my duty to travel far and wide."

Duncan nodded. "Spreading goodwill and magic, I know. It is a task for which mortals are ever grateful."

Her eyes opened wide, her mouth dropped. " 'Tis the duty of the Seelie you speak of!"

"It is."

She shook her head vigorously. "But I am not! I represent the night of the Seelie, their dark cousins. I am an Unseelie."

Duncan laughed. Fair folk were fond of jest, of playing tricks. He hoped she would stay with him awhile. She might distract him from his own failings.

"I am Irish by blood, small maiden. We know of the wee folk. Seelies are sweet and fair. Their cousins are grotesque and evil."

"I am!" She squinted slightly, studying his face. "I didn't miss and damage your vision, too, did I?"

"What are you talking about?"

She paled. "Nothing! Nothing at all."

"Your jests please me, small maiden."

A tiny frown twisted her face. "For my race, I am considered tall. My wing span is great." She started to flare both wings, caught herself, and extended her uninjured wing instead. "Do you see?"

Duncan repressed a smile. "Impressive."

She nodded. "For this reason, the title 'small' is not entirely appropriate."

"Were you to tell me your name, I would have no reason for the title 'small.' "

"I am Lily. It is a fair name, I know, and one I do not warrant, but that was the name of my birth. I would have preferred 'Violet,' as those are my favored petals . . ."

" 'Lily' suits you."

She looked askance, lips curved to one side. "You flatter me lest I destroy you . . ." She paused and sighed. "Continue to do so." Her face softened into a wistful smile. "I like it."

Duncan laughed and held out his hand. "How shall I carry you, Lily?"

She cast a thoughtful glance along his body. "You will need use of your hands." Her gaze fixed on his shoulder. "I will perch upon your left shoulder, where I will hide in your hair. It is necessary that no one of your kind knows I have befriend . . . joined you."

Her cheeks flushed. Even on her little face, it was obvious. A strange warmth flooded Duncan's chest. "I should warn you, small maiden . . ." He caught himself at the error, but she smiled.

"I have decided to allow you the term 'small maiden.' It is spoken with affection, and might be considered an endearment. I will consider the term 'small' to be such, and not a reference to height, or possible imagined lack thereof."

Duncan wasn't sure what she said, but he nodded. "I will temper its use."

She seemed to consider the matter settled. "Shall I lodge myself on your shoulder at this point?" She seemed eager. Her wings quivered.

"Not before I warn you of my shortcomings, Lily. My fall today, that which injured you, was not uncommon. It may happen again. I am loath to injure you further."

She looked both sympathetic and guilty. He had no idea why. "We won't worry about that just now. In fact, I shall act—temporarily, of course—as your guardian. I shall warn you of impending bouts with awkwardness, and you shall henceforward avert those occurrences."

Lily was long-winded. He liked her. "If you can do that, small maiden, I am forever after at your service."

"I can, of course." She eyed his outstretched hand and maneuvered herself closer. "I shall instruct you, Duncan MacLachlan, in the art of agility. I am an expert in agility."

Her back stiffened; she looked him straight in the eye. "In this, you have my word. By the end of our tenure as companions, you will be known as Duncan the Agile."

"The offer alone is kind, small maiden." Duncan sighed. "I wonder if you know the task you take upon yourself?"

Her face revealed utmost sympathy. "I know, Duncan. I know better than anyone."

"How so?"

"Never mind. Suffice to say this task is one I consider duty. Duncan the Agile you shall be, known far and wide for the deftness and skill of your movements . . ."

She climbed into his palm and secured herself by gripping his thumb. "Elevate me."

He lifted her to the level of his shoulder and she seized a portion of his hair. He sighed in admiration as she swung herself to his shoulder. She patted his muscle. "It is well you are so firm. It is a secure position."

Duncan rose carefully to his feet. Lily maintained adequate balance, and he started slowly along the path toward the hamlet. "Does my stride discomfort you, Lily?"

"Not at all." She paused. "Is my weight troublesome to your shoulder?"

"No." He kept his voice serious, but her weight was comparable to that of a small bird. He felt her presence, but it was no burden to carry her. She seemed happy.

"This spot at the edge of your shoulder is precarious. If you have no objections, I shall maneuver into somewhat closer proximity to your neck."

"As you wish, small maiden."

Lily squirmed closer to his neck. He felt her fingers in his hair. "I am making a spot of comfort for myself . . ." He felt a small tug. "Curses!" Another, firmer tug followed. She sputtered to herself, and he glanced at her from the corner of his eye. She appeared entangled.

"Halt!"

Duncan stopped and waited. Lily tugged frantically. He winced. She braced her feet against his neck and pulled to free herself from his hair. He felt a sharp yank, and she popped loose, but she didn't fall. She drew a long breath. "I'm forced to report the loss of several prime strands of hair."

She sounded grave. Duncan fought a smile. "I noticed that."

She leaned forward and cranked her head to look directly into his face. "Have I caused you pain of a serious nature?"

"No worse than that I caused your wing."

An expression of relief crossed her face. "Oh, if that's all . . ." Again, she caught herself and coughed. "Let us move on."

Duncan walked onward, pleased with her company. She bent her legs to brace herself and leaned forward, watching the path ahead. "Take care of yonder rock, Duncan. Approximately three of your strides ahead."

Duncan noticed the rock and stepped around it. "Thank you."

"You are welcome for my effort on your behalf." She looked left, then right. "There is also a fallen rowan branch which might cause you some difficulty if ignored."

Duncan took note of the branch, too, and gave it a wide berth. "Again, I thank you."

"And again, it is my pleasure to serve you in this capacity."

Duncan glanced at her. She sat straight, looking alert and happy. "You don't have many people to speak with, do you?"

She eyed him intently. "Why do you say that?"

"You like to extend a small phrase to its utmost." Maybe he'd said too much, but Lily didn't seem offended. Instead, she took it as encouragement for further discussion. She seemed to relish explanations.

"My Unseelie sisters do not enjoy conversation, unless it's what I'd term 'crafty' conversation. How to supplant our cousins the Seelies in power in certain sectors of the forest, how to win power on various shores of nearby lochs. At present, we—the Unseelies, creatures of evil and darkness—control the eastern side of Loch Fyne, and the Seelie queen . . . By the way, she is called Titania . . . She and her daughters control the western side. The area just west of Loch Awe, however, is up for contention."

"Why? And what do you do with the land when you've secured it?"

"The matter of faerie gold, and a hill thereof, is of interest to us both. Source of power, as it were. Titania has hidden it from us for . . . oh, well, time immemorial, and we want it. At least, my queen wants it. I can't say it's a pressing issue for myself personally."

As Lily spoke, she crossed one leg over the other, relaxing against his neck. " 'Tis a pleasant sight, to view the land from this height.

We normally fly low to the ground, except at night, and not much can be seen during the nightly hours." She drew a quick breath to fuel further conversation. "Have you a mount nearby?"

"I lent my horse to my brother, Struan. He went to meet Laren Campbell, the girl he wishes to marry."

"Yes, I know. They meet in secret often."

Duncan chuckled. "Apparently, not as 'secret' as they imagine."

"I wasn't spying on them. I was watching for . . ." She stopped, aghast. Her lips formed an O. Duncan felt certain the word "you" was on her lips, but she cleared her expression. "Watching for insects who might misuse nearby flowers." She drew a quick breath. "You say Struan took your horse. Where is his own? As I recall, he has a fine, strong gray with good speed."

Her explanation came rushed and seemed implausible, but Duncan allowed her to alter the subject. "Struan's mount is lame."

Lily's eyes narrowed. "Lamed for a known cause, or unexpectedly?"

"I don't know of its cause, only that his usual mount came up lame this morning, so he took mine."

Lily sighed heavily. "Then it was most likely lamed by my kind. The winds blow ill against your brother."

Duncan stopped and turned to study her. "My brother is strong and well, soon to be laird of our clan. There is no other his like. Yet you speak ill. Do you know of some dark fate befalling him?"

She bowed her head, and the question was answered. "I can say little on this subject. Your brother is not cursed, so there is no reason his life will not be long."

"Yet there is something."

She tried to straighten her expression, but without full success. Duncan's heart ran cold. The MacLachlans needed Struan. Without him, they were left with only Duncan as protector. Duncan the Clumsy, who would do more harm than good.

"If my brother needs my aid, you must tell me, Lily."

"There is nothing you can do."

"Lily . . ."

She peered into his eyes, earnest and sweet. "If I could help, or by telling you, help, I would."

"Lily . . ."

"I can say no more. Please speak to me of your horse, and promise me that you will take me for a ride on its back. I've always admired horses."

Duncan resisted the urge to pursue the subject of Struan's fate. Lily might be stubborn, yet with gentle prodding, over time, he might learn more. He would have to keep her with him long enough to find out.

"I would think you'd be accustomed to riding dragonflies."

She eyed him dubiously. "Have you ever tried to reason with an insect?"

Duncan shook his head. "No . . ."

"I thought not. A horse can be reasoned with, it is willing to be a vessel of transport. They are unselfish creatures, horses. Dragonflies, on the other hand, are notoriously selfish . . ."

Chapter 2

DUNCAN spent the remainder of the evening walking with Lily, and her conversation never ceased. He learned the nature of birds, of plants and flowers, and of the indignities suffered upon them by thoughtless mortals. He took roundabout paths, because he liked her speech. She didn't entangle herself in his hair again, although she occasionally fingered it, as if she liked the feel.

He found himself wishing she were human. Mortal. A woman like to himself. He'd never known a woman so friendly, so pleasing. Her innate grace and beauty contrasted with his clumsiness and the strength of his body. He took little pride in his strength, for it lent no measure of agility. He'd built his condition to prime readiness for nothing. He still tripped.

They reached the edge of the Lachlan hamlet, and Duncan stopped. "It is my duty to soon take a wife. Perhaps you might aid me in that task."

Lily didn't answer. He glanced at her. She looked pale. "Why do you want a wife?"

"All men desire a wife at some point." He paused, recalling Irsa the Frail who never did want a wife, and incited rumors among both the Scots of Dalriada and Pict. "Most men desire a wife. My father has requested that I make the choice soon."

"It isn't his affair."

Lily appeared stubborn, her small jaw set hard, and slightly to one side. Her eyes narrowed.

"It is his concern, Lily. He is an old man, and ill. It would give him peace to know that his sons have produced heirs, and that our claim here is secure."

"Already, the Picts have chosen a Dalriadic Scot for their king. I see no need for your 'claim' to be pressed."

"Kenneth MacAlpin is High King of Dalriada, but the position of lesser chieftains remains precarious. Although my brother and I were born here, we call this land 'Dalriada,' in memory of our homeland."

Lily huffed. "The Picts call it Alba, but that is inaccurate also. This land is Caledonia."

"Nonetheless, my children will be born here, and our claim to this land will be complete."

"You have no real claim, of course. It is a weak concept, of value only to man. The land is owned by no one."

"It is a concept valued by the Picts, and they won't fully accept us, sons of Irish kings though we be, until our blood rises from this soil."

" 'Tis a foolish notion."

"Nonetheless, I require a wife. You are wise. You could help me select a worthy female."

Lily frowned. "No." Her face knit into her scheming expression. "Yes. Yes, I will also serve in this capacity. I will inform you of the subject's worth."

She looked guilty again, but she didn't retract her offer.

"Thank you. I think."

A wife, indeed! Duncan MacLachlan was too young to choose a wife. The earth had enjoyed his presence little more than a score of years. Too few for him to be bonded to a female. Lily's face tightened into a dark frown.

A man doesn't "choose" a wife. The fates bring together two of like heart, and love makes its own way. So it was for Seelie lovers.

Lily had often envied the Seelies their capacity to love each other. A faerie prince, his devoted bride. Another beauty denied the Unseelies.

At least Duncan was interested in her approval. Should he find a suitable woman, one with all qualities of grace, and none of selfishness or darkness or envy . . . Lily stopped her thoughts. All those qualities applied to her. She was selfish and dark—this was proven by her trickery in securing position with him. And as for envy . . . it consumed her. Especially when she thought of him choosing a wife.

She banished the sharp pangs of guilt for her subterfuge. This evening was the happiest in her life. She casually fingered his hair. Beautiful hair, nearly black. Smooth. Like his skin. She lowered her hand to his shoulder and pretended to steady herself. She felt his skin beneath her fingertips and her wings quivered violently.

"Are you chilled, Lily?"

"Why do you ask?"

"Your wings are trembling."

Lily's blush soaked from her chest, up her neck, and to her cheeks. "It's not that I'm cold, exactly. Wings are sensitive things, you see. One can never be entirely sure of their actions . . ."

Duncan's brow angled, but he made no further comment. Wings were more sensitive than skin, because they weren't part of her body, but visible extensions of her soul. They bore her between worlds, between dimensions.

Which made her subterfuge all the worse. Her wing wasn't broken. It was ajar only because her soul was so shaken by her encounter with him. And she had deceived him.

It was all part of evil. No point in repressing her true nature. She wanted, greedily, to be near him. She wanted to touch him, to speak with him. She had done so, and she would continue to do so until he found her out. He would learn, eventually, that she had tricked him. Maybe he would guess that she was the one who had cursed him in the first place.

But not before she'd satisfied her ageless yearning for his company, and perhaps taught him a few things of the world, and assisted him in finding balance. And convinced him that he was much too young to take a wife . . .

They reached the end of the path and Duncan stopped. The Dalriadic Scots built their round houses and halls near the water, on a hill overlooking the bay. Lily guessed they considered it a safe position from which to withstand attacks, although it seemed far more exposed than her underground home.

Duncan folded his arms over his chest as he watched the hamlet darken before them. Lily seized the opportunity to study his neck. His tunic revealed a portion of his chest, smooth and strong. She lengthened her right leg, but she couldn't quite reach that spot of him. She drew a regretful breath. Duncan didn't notice.

" 'Tis a fair sight, Lily, this hamlet of my people. I never saw Ireland, the land of my grandfather's birth. Though it is said that he came here as a young man."

Lily averted her gaze from his chest to his face. "Do you refer to De Dalan the Clumsy?" She winced at his dark expression.

"De Dalan was my grandsire, yes. The title bestowed upon him was not inaccurate, but I have often considered it an unnecessary addition to his name."

"Because it was likewise bestowed upon yourself?"

Lily gulped. She'd said too much. He would, rightly, toss her from his shoulder, with an angered *"Be gone!"* She deserved it. But Duncan just sighed.

"That is true. For that reason, De Dalan has my sympathies. He was not favored along these shores, though he loved it here. His tales brought my father's clan here to settle."

"I know." Lily hesitated, wondering how much of the truth she dared share with him. "De Dalan wasn't always a tripper, you know."

Duncan eyed her suspiciously. "How do you know?"

She drew a short breath. "Faeries know things." He seemed to accept this, so she continued. "He was once quite agile, I believe. And proud of that fact. Unfortunately, he angered my people, the Unseelies . . ."

"How?"

Lily bit her lip. "That, I cannot say. Not in full." She paused. "On the other hand, it was not so grievous a crime as some." She paused again. "I suppose I can reveal a portion of the story to you, leaving out the critical elements."

"It would please me to know the source of his incapacity."

"Well, as the story goes, De Dalan became infatuated with the Seelie queen, Titania."

Duncan's brow angled. "And this angered her?"

"No. It angered the Unseelie queen, Nathara. Nathara was annoyed that De Dalan admired Titania, and not herself. Also there was the matter of De Dalan's knowledge . . ."

Lily caught herself and gulped.

"Knowledge of what?"

"Of nothing! Absolutely nothing!"

Duncan shook his head and laughed. "If you will continue the tale, I will pretend to believe you."

"Agreed." Lily cleared her throat. "Titania was merely amused by your grandfather's attention, but Nathara vowed vengeance. There has always been a battle for power between the two queens. I trust you are keeping these details of hierarchy straight."

"No, but go on. What has this to do with De Dalan's clumsiness?"

"He was cursed, naturally."

"By this Unseelie queen?"

Lily's face drained of blood. "Well, no. By one of her minions. A minion, incidentally, who had no choice, and was supposed to affect him with a deathly pox . . ."

"Clumsiness was worse."

Lily's breath caught. "Do you think so?" Her voice came very weak.

Duncan uttered a brief laugh. "No. 'Tis only that I have more experience with the latter. A deathly pox would be a far worse affliction."

She breathed a sigh of relief. "So I thought myself."

"Then I guess De Dalan's curse was passed onward in his blood. To me."

Lily's face twisted to one side as guilt swept through her. "That is somewhat the way of it."

"It eluded my brother, and my father. They are well skilled. Struan is unmatched at swordplay."

"You also revealed skill as a boy." Lily caught herself, but he didn't seem to notice her intense and prolonged study of his life.

"Until I . . ." He paused to sigh. "Until I tripped and severed the side of my father's hut, and barely avoided severing him."

"He overreacted, I thought."

"My sword made contact with his backside."

"Yes, but it didn't truly injure him."

"He couldn't sit for a long while."

"It did him good. Your sire sat too much."

Duncan smiled, and Lily's heart warmed. "Nonetheless, it wasn't my first accident. He was well advised to forbid me further lessons."

"And did you obey him, Duncan MacLachlan?" She knew he hadn't. She'd watched him practicing with a "borrowed" sword, slashing at ferns, at tree branches.

Duncan's eyes twinkled. "I obeyed him in his presence, and since he commanded that I was to cease being a threat to his life, I felt, if done in private . . ."

"There are times you also 'extend a phrase to its utmost.' I think you do it to avoid a direct answer."

Duncan laughed. "I think you're right. But I had my brother's permission . . ."

"And his sword?"

"And his sword. He advised me, and displayed correct posture . . ."

"You love him very much."

"I do. He is kind and strong, and all I wish to be. For this reason, I would know his fate is untarnished by . . . external elements."

"No one's life is untarnished, Duncan. You probe, I think, for what I know of his fate. I know nothing of his fate, as I told you."

"You know something."

"There are many dark clouds passing in the sky, and not everyone's dreams come true. That is all I can say."

Duncan's eyes met hers and held. For a moment, they were the same. Duncan didn't measure up to his dreams, and neither did she. They both wished for more.

Lily peered down at him, squinting to better view his face in the darkness. A faint light illuminating from her wings shone on his high, strong cheekbones. Lily sighed, increasing the light. Duncan eyed her doubtfully.

"You're glowing."

"Yes, I know." Lily tried to keep her expression straight. "It is, of course, necessary for night travel. Faeries, both light and dark, have adequate night vision, but . . ."

"You look like a firefly." Duncan smiled and Lily's heart fluttered. "My little firefly."

" 'Tis an insect." Her voice quavered. He spoke with such gentle affection, but his words caused an alien pain within her. "I recall this term 'firefly' . . ." Her face puckered. "But I do not recall the source. It is as if it was once a term of affection, similar to your usage of 'small maiden,' applied to myself."

"There is sorrow on your face, Lily. For what reason?"

"I don't know . . ." She looked into Duncan's warm, brown eyes and her heart eased its sorrowful pull. "I find joy in your company."

"And I, in yours." Duncan glanced toward the hamlet. "You say I am to keep you hidden. Can you dim this glow?"

"Of course! I only did that to better see . . ." She coughed and sputtered, then shook her head. "For insignificant reasons which would be of no interest to you whatsoever."

"I see." He didn't. Lily felt sure of that. He had no idea how she treasured this time in his company. How much she wanted to look at him, closely, in good light.

She admired him more with each stride, with each gentle, thoughtful word from his perfect lips. Lily cast a sly glance at his lips. Well-made lips, curving easily into a smile. Emotional lips. Lips worthy of soft kissing.

"Again, your wings vibrate." Duncan chuckled. "And they tickle my neck."

Lily fanned herself with her outer wing, forgetting it was supposed to be broken.

"Doesn't that hurt?"

"No. Why would it . . . ?" She caught herself. "Oh, that. Movement doesn't cause pain, if done carefully."

Duncan didn't appear convinced, but he didn't press the issue. "I must meet with my brother to take the evening feast. There will be songs afterward, then I return to my hall. It is a minor hall. No doubt, ill-equipped when compared to the halls of the faerie queen."

Lily sighed. "The halls where Titania rules are fair, 'tis said. I have never seen them firsthand, of course, being of the dark race. But I have seen them in my dreams. All is light where Titania is queen. There is joy and music, and much laughter."

Duncan studied her thoughtfully. "You speak as if in earnest, Lily. Yet I cannot believe you are of the dark race."

"Why not? Evil radiates from my core. Perhaps it is not obvious to mortals. I am pleased of that."

"To my eyes, you are beautiful. I cannot imagine a more beautiful creature."

Lily's brow angled. "You obviously have not seen a true Seelie."

"Have you seen yourself? Perhaps if you viewed your reflection. I have a looking glass, inlaid with silver . . . You might make use of that."

She shook her head vigorously. "I dare not! And I never will." Lily paused, and a long, deep sigh poured from her soul. "I have dreams, you see. Dreams of what I might be, of how I wish I were. I will not lose that for the sake of reality. Please, do not speak of it again."

Duncan didn't respond. He watched her, both confusion and tenderness in his dark eyes. "If it pains you, I will not. But I think you deny yourself a pleasant surprise."

"I deny myself only the death of my dreams."

Lily forced her gaze from Duncan's beautiful face. Her eyes misted with tears, and the evening mist rose from the earth in response. He was so much better than she, so far above her. He was truly good. A man cursed, who did not give up, who did not turn bitter. He tried and failed, while his older brother gained admiration of both Dalriadic Scot and Pict, yet Duncan never submitted to envy.

Unlike Lily.

I will not think of that now. I will enjoy my time with him, and I will face the calamity when it comes.

Lily raised her chin and gazed over Duncan's hamlet. "We were human once."

"Faeries? Do you refer to the Unseelies?"

"All faeries."

"I thought your kind was above mortals."

"We are, of course. In a way . . ."

"The Picts say the Magic People are the souls of the ones who came before. Those defeated in battle for control of this land."

Lily puffed with pride. "We weren't 'defeated,' of course, which you would know if you were better learned in the Realm of Faerie . . . My ancestors were considered primitive, but we were not. We lived in caves, near the water. We make our homes in these places still."

"Faerie burghs. In Ireland, your kind are called the Daoine Sidhe, the Tuatha De Danann."

"That is correct." Lily assumed a posture resembling a sage. She braced her small finger under her chin. "It was in Ireland as in Alba. When the Celtic people came, the Ancient Ones took new forms." Lily paused. She gazed wistfully into Duncan's face. "Truth be told, many did blend by marriage with the Celts. But the strong ones, the magic users, they refused."

"What became of them?"

"It depends on which faction you address. There are many kinds of faeries. The Gnomes of Ireland, the Pillywiggins in Wales. In Alba, we have Pixies and the Glaistig, among others."

Duncan grimaced. "I have heard of the Glaistig. Half a fair woman, half a beast. And they are said to devour men."

Lily smiled as if this weren't a terrifying image. "But they are fond of children. Faeries, of course, are capable of any number of wonders. Not all are pleasing to the human eye. Some, such as myself, are evil."

"I find that difficult to believe."

"Only because you don't understand the nature of the Seelie and Unseelie courts. They came from the same ancestors, as I mentioned. They used their magic and became as you see me now, neither pure spirit, nor mortal flesh. They were light and dark then, too."

"Yet to the Picts, and to my Scots, Unseelies are feared, while the Seelies cherished for the good they do."

Lily sighed and then sighed again. "The Seelies chose to lend beauty and wisdom, but the Unseelies tried, and try still, to control and influence the invaders. It is a rhythm that never ceases."

Duncan's dark gaze intensified. "Does this mean you were once human, too?"

Lily tried to read the meaning of his expression, but it eluded her. "I am somewhat human now. But no, I was born thus. More accurately, spawned. Only the Seelies give birth in the traditional manner. Unseelies such as myself are more or less created by the Unseelie queen. She is Nathara, a being of great vengeance and spite."

She stopped and cleared her throat, then looked furtively over her shoulder. No one was listening. No one overheard her blasphemy, but she never felt completely at ease, even alone. Duncan noticed her attention. "Are you afraid of being overheard?"

"No!" She bit her lip. "A bit. Yes. One can never be entirely sure who is listening." Her brow furrowed as she considered the matter.

"I know no Unseelie follows me. I know them all, you see. Their sounds, the sounds the earth and wind and water make when one is near. But sometimes I feel . . ." Her voice trailed into uncertainty.

"As if someone watches you?"

Lily nodded. "I feel as if someone is watching me, with exceeding attention to the choices I make."

"Perhaps it is the workings of your own inner mind." A smile flickered on Duncan's lips, and Lily's eyes narrowed in suspicion.

"What do you mean?" His smile deepened, but he didn't answer. Lily's eyes opened wide. "You mean I may feel a certain amount of guilt for various elements of my actions, don't you?" Her voice had turned shrill. *That was it.*

"It was only a suggestion, to help you locate the source of your discomfort."

Lily stiffened, and peered at him with a regal expression. "That is not it. Not at all. Someone watches me. And it is not a comforting sensation."

Duncan watched her intently. Lily relished his attention. She had been almost this close to him many times, while he slept. More so when he was a boy than as a man. For a reason she didn't fully understand, his ascent into manhood made her nervous and . . . agitated. Her wings quivered too much, and she tended to glow in his presence. An inconvenience for such personal viewing.

Duncan looked thoughtful, but Lily couldn't guess what he was thinking. "I, also, have felt this sensation you describe. That of being watched. But for myself, it was reassuring. I felt . . . protected. I told my brother, and he said someone who cared must be watching me."

Lily's face flamed. In darkness, he might not detect her radiant blush. Unfortunately, her glow deepened, and her wings vibrated in embarrassment. A slow, too-knowing smile formed on Duncan's sweet mouth. He didn't say anything. Lily fought to appear casual and at ease, as if nothing of her secret heart had been revealed.

"You see, Nathara—our queen—isn't entirely pleased with my deportment." Her voice came rushed, and very high, higher than a bee. She tried to steady herself, but her wings twitched and she elevated slightly from his shoulder. She seized a lock of his hair and settled back down.

She sensed that Duncan repressed humor, but he made no derisive comment. "Nathara? Your mother?"

Lily frowned. "I would not call her such. She is my queen. I do not disobey her." Lily paused. "Except in small ways."

Duncan's eyes twinkled. "Such as in our association?"

"That would be one example of a small disobedience on my part."

Duncan's grin widened. "It will be our secret."

"Good. Because the Unseelies do, in fact, take spies on occasion, among mortals. Weak-willed individuals who are easily coerced, manipulated, into doing our service. I do not want one of these spies to report to Nathara on my disobedience."

"What would happen to you, should such word reach your queen?"

"She would force me to darker tasks. The curses I must plant might grow more cruel, more . . . fatal."

"I can't imagine you placing a curse, Lily."

Lily looked at Duncan for a long while before answering. "Can't you? I will advise you, Duncan, and I will do my best to serve you in the capacities which I have mentioned previously. But never forget that I am dark. I am not worthy of your trust."

"You are worthy of my affection, if only for the pleasure of your company, Lily. I will ask nothing of you that you cannot give."

It was a tender promise. Lily's eyes filled with tears. "Nor I of you."

They fell silent, watching each other. Lily's heart ached with affection. "If you would care to conceal yourself, it is time we enter the hamlet."

Lily tried to contain her excitement, and failed. "I have long imagined taking part in your festivities. True, I shall be unknown, except to you . . ." She didn't finish her thought as she squirmed close to his neck and arranged his hair around her body.

Even his hair seemed powerful, sleek and soft, fresh from his swim, clean. Lily breathed deeply of his warm, masculine scent.

"My cape is hooded so I will conceal you there. It will be a misty night, so it will appear natural that I am garbed thus." Duncan pulled his flaxen cape over his wide shoulders, and positioned his hood carefully over both his head and Lily. "Is this comfortable for you, small maiden?"

"It is." Her voice trailed. She was in bliss. She felt his pulse against her shoulder, warm and swift. Strong. She leaned her head closer to his skin. "I am well hidden, Duncan MacLachlan. Proceed."

Chapter 3

HE was hiding a faerie. He had no idea why, or what she wanted. Lily spoke of herself as a vile creature, yet she seemed to want nothing but his company. She loved to talk, to explain. Yet what he wanted most to know, she avoided. With Lily's capacity for speech, Duncan knew he'd learn the secrets she held soon.

Maybe he couldn't aid Struan in battle, but he could surely warn him if a faerie curse threatened his happiness. If he pressured Lily now, she might flee, and his only chance would be lost. He felt her close to his neck, trembling. Her little toes curled beneath his tunic. He wasn't sure when her feet went beneath his tunic, but she seemed almost part of his own flesh.

She wasn't injured. She'd slipped enough to convince him of that. Her wing was fine, though it seemed less tangible than the rest of her body. The colors deepened and faded, and glowed. As if seeing a visible soul. A beautiful soul.

He wondered why she deceived him, why she desired his company. Why not one of the native Picts, distantly related to her own people? Why not a heroic man such as his brother? Maybe she was playing some sort of trick, as faeries were rumored to do. Bored, perhaps. Seeking excitement by teasing a gullible human.

Duncan didn't care. He liked her. It couldn't last. She would tire of her game and leave, and he would probably never see her again. They would live out separate lives. A distant sorrow touched his heart at this. But the world was unfair. He had accepted that truth long ago.

Torches burned outside the heather huts and round halls. Despite the steady mist, music of the flute and lyre filled in rhythm. Soft voices sang. A drunken man laughed and called for more mead. A young wench delivered the nectar, singing, too.

Duncan entered the circle. No one noticed his arrival. His father sat in a chair close to the central fire. His raised dais had been carried outside. Tearlach MacLachlan had been born as a king's son. He lived like one still. A hued blanket of deep blue and red covered the old man's knees, but he sat straight and proud. He didn't notice Duncan's approach.

"He is rude." Lily's whisper startled Duncan. He tripped. A small, stifled squeal burst from Lily as she grappled to steady herself.

She remained hidden in his neck, clinging to his hair. Tearlach looked up in time to see Duncan recovering from the near-fall. Tearlach gazed heavenward and shook his head.

An old, dull ache surfaced in Duncan's chest, but he proceeded dutifully to his father and bowed. Tearlach responded with a brief, weary nod.

Tearlach glared upward into the mist as it turned to a light rain. "Curse this rain!" He diverted his attention back to Duncan. "You are late returning, boy."

Duncan clenched his teeth. He was long passed boyhood. But he had disappointed and embarrassed his father, and the price paid was long. Duncan opened his mouth to explain, but Tearlach frowned and uttered a disgusted sigh.

"I would guess you were lost in the wood. Or did you fall and knock yourself senseless?"

A tiny, but ferocious growl stirred Duncan's ear. Lily tensed in anger. Her wings froze stiff against his neck. He wondered if she would forget her need of secrecy to send a bolt of faerie energy at his father.

Duncan resisted his own anger. "As you requested, sire, I have studied the southward paths along the loch, and sought out possible routes across the water. It is my judgment that these areas are indeed weak, and require some method of defense lest we fall under attack by another clan."

Tearlach dismissed Duncan's advice with a shrug. "The Campbells were our only real concern, boy, and Struan has found a suitable method of suppressing their threat."

"How?"

"By marrying Iain Campbell's daughter."

"I know that is his intention, but how will that serve against assault? Iain has long resented our power in this region."

Tearlach waved his aged hand in annoyance at the reminder. "His own father and mine were allies when we came to this shore. But Iain is a weak fool, and dishonors his worthy sire by his contentious behaviour."

"He may be weak, but he has amassed warriors among both his clan and the Picts, who see us as supplanters."

Tearlach scoffed. "When Struan takes his daughter to wed, his contentions will disappear. He has offered a hefty bride-piece. He has agreed."

"He is not a man who warrants trust, sire. He may pretend agreement—"

"You fear overmuch, boy. A result, perhaps, of your own inability to defend your clan. I hear no such worries from your brother."

Lily braced. She trembled and twitched. Duncan reached casually to his shoulder and placed his hand over her small, furious body. She stilled in response, but held herself very stiff.

"My brother is a wise man, but his attention is diverted. He has won the woman of his heart, and he thinks of little beyond."

Duncan heard a deep, hearty laugh, and he turned. Struan stood tall behind him, tall and strong and utterly confident. His grin spread across his face, joy emanated from deep within him. Duncan had never seen him so happy.

Tearlach started to rise to greet his adored son, but Struan clasped his shoulder and eased him back down. "Take ease, sire, and enjoy the night."

Tearlach frowned at Duncan. "Tell your brother, boy, of your fears, and that you think him fey at heart for a woman. Blind to the dangers presented by the loch's water."

Duncan didn't respond. Tearlach seemed to want Struan's anger directed toward Duncan. Perhaps because Struan's kindness amid his strength made Tearlach seem unyielding.

But Struan only laughed and slapped Duncan's shoulder. "My brother is well informed, sire. I am fey, and nothing save my wedding will change that mood. If Duncan warns of threat, hear him. If he says our defenses are wanting, they are."

Struan didn't wait for his father's compliance. He motioned to his thegns. "My brother suggests a watch be placed on the loch's pathways. See that it is done. Any boat must be reported, and watched."

The thegns bowed and departed, and Duncan relaxed. Struan might be distracted for love's sake, but he was wise, as always. Struan turned back to Duncan, still smiling. "You have heard then, brother, that I am to take a wife?"

Duncan smiled, too. "I don't need to hear, Struan. It shows. What day has her father given? By your expression, I would guess it is near."

"Near, indeed! It is three days hence, and it is an eternity."

"Three days!" A faint, low disquiet formed in Duncan's heart, though he wasn't sure why. Lily sighed, and his disquiet grew. "Iain has been unwilling, yet he gives you Laren in three days? For what reason?"

Tearlach grumbled, then stomped his feet. "Do you see my point, son? The boy fears all, no matter the cause."

Struan's smile faded. "Perhaps Iain grew tired of contesting our will. Perhaps he saw the wisdom in compliance. I would not have these final days marred by doubt . . ."

Duncan touched his brother's shoulder. "Then let them not be marred. There is no need. My trust in Iain Campbell is lacking, but you are right. He has more to gain in our alliance than to lose. His daughter's happiness must count for something."

Lily snorted in derision, and Duncan coughed to disguise her noise. Struan eyed him doubtfully. Duncan forced a weak smile.

"Laren's happiness meant little enough to Iain until now. It is my charge to see that the full glory of her joy is fulfilled." Struan was smiling again, and Duncan smiled, too, though the disquiet refused to abate.

Tearlach caned himself to his feet. "Tonight, we celebrate your wedding, my son, of whom I am boundlessly proud." He paused to cast a disparaging glance Duncan's way. "By your union with a Campbell daughter, you have positioned us for full control of this region, and brought us much honor."

Struan seemed uncomfortable with his father's praise. "I have gained myself the sweetest treasure, and my heart's content. That is all a man can pray for, and I am ever-thankful for this blessing."

Lily sniffed, and Duncan suspected that Struan's tender sentiment had moved her heart. A strange reaction for a "dark" being. Struan placed his arm over Duncan's shoulder. Lily scrambled aside just in time. "And now that I am gifted with a wife, perhaps it is time my brother make his choice, and bring us greater honor still." Struan's eyes twinkled. "There are many who favor you, Duncan."

Duncan felt weary. Women admired him, and pretended indifference to his clumsiness. Perhaps they sought position by marrying the lesser brother of a great man, since Struan had long ago chosen Laren Campbell. Perhaps they sought access into a clan of wealth and power. Not for a moment did he believe they valued him.

Lily tensed on his shoulder, expectant. Lily valued him. He wasn't sure why, but her affection seemed genuine. Tonight, he didn't feel alone. A tiny being of power and beauty and ultimate grace perched on his shoulder, ready to defend him.

Tearlach's gaze darkened as he studied Duncan. "You must do something to bring honor to our clan. Battle is out of the question, though you might serve as some sort of advisor to Struan when he becomes laird—should he have need of you, which I doubt. Choose a wife, boy. I will have the announcement proclaimed at your brother's wedding, so that all this land will know the MacLachlan clan will forever make this the Land of the Scot."

Duncan bowed. "As you wish, sire."

"And make the choice a good one, boy. Select a strong woman, one with enough grace to lend my grandsons the agility you lack."

Lily's breath came as small puffs of fury against his neck. Duncan snapped his hand back to his shoulder and pinned her down. She struggled to free herself from his grasp. Duncan clamped down with a firmer grip and she stilled.

Struan noticed the gesture and looked confused. "Does an insect bother you?"

"In a way . . ." A small "huff" alerted him to potential danger from an insulted faerie. "Cramp. In my shoulder." Duncan eased his hand off Lily. "It's nothing."

Struan seized a goblet of mead from a serving woman, and passed it to Duncan. He smiled at his father, though the expression seemed forced. "Rest, sire. 'Tis a pleasant night."

Tearlach obeyed, grumbling, and Struan directed Duncan from the old man's presence. "Our father's words are aimed bitterly, Duncan. It is infirmity, the pain of his creaking bones, that inspire him to speak thus."

"Were I a better man, his 'creaking bones' would perhaps be directed at another."

Struan shuddered. "At myself, perhaps! Better you, Duncan. You are strong enough to remain aloof to his words."

Duncan recognized the gentle placation. It had always been thus. Tearlach resented his younger son's failures. Struan encouraged and praised Duncan anyway. "I am well used to his opinion. Yet I cannot rid myself of the desire to change it."

"He is an old man set in his ways. His words are no more than the creaking of his bones."

Duncan gazed back at his father. "If I didn't admire him, I might indeed forget to care. But Tearlach MacLachlan is a great man, and wise."

"You love him."

Duncan sighed. "I do."

Struan gripped Duncan's shoulder. "He loves you, Duncan. You remind him of his father. He recalls the pain De Dalan faced, and he is loath to see you suffer likewise. He is blind to the strength within you. But I believe he will come to see your value. It may be, one day, that his life will be in your hands. And that day, you will not fail."

"Foresight?"

"Maybe." Struan gazed upward toward the new stars. "Tonight, no magic is beyond me. Tonight, I am a man charmed."

Duncan smiled, but he couldn't respond. Struan walked away, a man in bliss. Duncan's disquiet grew.

"He is a good and pleasant man." Lily's voice didn't startle him this time. He was accustomed to her comments.

"He is a great man."

"You are a great man, too, Duncan. Maybe you don't know how great."

"And you are a kindly soul to speak thus, Lily."

He felt her hand on his face, tender and soft. Despite her tiny size, the warmth of her touch penetrated deep to his heart.

He felt a soft touch, though he couldn't be certain of her action. It almost felt like a kiss.

"By the time I must leave your side, Duncan MacLachlan, you will know you are the greatest man I have ever seen. In this, you have my word. Here, and here only, the word of an Unseelie minion is equal to that of an angel."

Duncan brought Lily to his hut and set her to the rough-hewn table. Two oil lanterns burned on opposite walls, casting a warm glow on her small body.

She looked around the room, a frown on her face. "You have not placed pleasing adornments in your chambers. In other halls, I have seen silver bowls more for viewing than for drinking. I have seen impressive displays of swords and shields. I have seen blankets hung on the wall woven of many colored thread."

Duncan picked up an old flax blanket. "This is enough for warmth in the night."

Lily grimaced. "You do not live as a laird's son."

"When I have done my father proud, I will honor myself with more 'pleasing adornments.'"

"If he had sense, he would be proud now." Lily tapped her foot, her arms folded over her chest. "I suppose he hasn't presented you with a sword."

"Not since he seized my first wooden sword and forbade me to touch one again, no."

"Humph."

Duncan smiled and shook his head. A small defender had come to his side. He felt warm despite the cold rain outside. Lily was still assessing his room. Her gaze fixed on his low pallet. "You sleep on the floor. It looks less comfortable than a mushroom."

"That, I could not say."

"No adornment there, either."

Duncan unlatched a worn trunk and pried it open. "As it happens, small maiden, I am in possession of a few treasures." He fished around in the box, casting aside broken knives, Saxon brooches, and jeweled sword handles until he found what he was looking for. He glanced over his shoulder to see that Lily was still watching him intently, then brushed off the mirror.

"I found this while unearthing an old Roman site south of here. They didn't forge strongholds in Alba as they did in the south of this land, but their treasures can be found in many holds."

"What is that?" Lily sounded both suspicious and intrigued.

"You'll see." Duncan seized a cloth and polished the silver around the mirror, then glanced at himself to be sure the image wasn't distorted. His face appeared regular. A surge of vanity told him it was a handsome face.

Duncan turned around, but he hid the mirror behind his back. Lily's eyes narrowed to slits. "What are you hiding?"

Duncan just smiled as he took the lanterns from the wall and placed them beside her on the table. He adjusted the light so that it sent a warm glow on her face.

"You will confess your intentions, or I will . . ."

Duncan pulled the mirror from behind his back, and her face drained of blood. "I know what that is."

Duncan held the mirror up. She shook her head and backed away. "I begged you . . ."

"Not to mention this. I have not."

"Treachery! You could teach the Unseelie queen new tricks!"

"Lily . . . do you trust me?"

"No!" She paused, looking shamed. "Yes."

"Then trust me now. Please look."

She peered at him, then hesitantly at the mirror. "I am afraid."

"I know." Duncan sat on the edge of his table and held the mirror facing her. "Look anyway."

She closed her eyes as if in prayer, her chin quivered. She took a step toward the mirror, drew a deep breath, then opened her eyes. She looked at her image, then at Duncan. Then back again. She stepped closer to the glass, then leaned in toward it.

"My head is bigger than my body!"

Duncan leaned down to look in the mirror, then laughed. "Because you lean your head closer. He adjusted the mirror's position. "Stand straight. Now what do you see?"

Lily didn't answer at once. Her head tilted left, then right. Her lips curved to one side as she contemplated her image. She took several thoughtful breaths. She made a slight smacking noise with her lips. She shifted her weight, then held her arms out and up. She turned to one side, then the other, examining her profile.

She faced herself again and studied her image for a long while. At last, she sighed and nodded. "I have appeal."

Duncan laughed again. "You do."

Lily fiddled with her hair. She moved it to fall over her right shoulder, then her left. Then she flipped it back, trying different postures. She combed it through with her fingers. She adjusted her dress.

Duncan watched her admiration of herself increase, and his heart warmed with affection. "Now, small maiden, was your image worth ages of fear?"

"No. No, it was not. Do you know, if I were of a somewhat larger stature, I might appear human?"

Duncan cleared his throat. "I've noticed that."

"Have you?"

"Other than the wings, and the size, you resemble a human. But isn't it preferable to be a faerie?"

Lily diverted her attention back to her image. "It depends on what you want."

"What do you want that a faerie cannot have?"

She glanced up at him. Her expression altered from self-satisfaction to one of sorrow. "Don't you know?"

"I can imagine nothing the mortal world offers that the Otherworld can't better."

Lily watched him for a while without answering. She tilted the mirror toward him, and she smiled. "I'm not the only one who doesn't see."

He waited for further explanation, but she seemed embarrassed and turned to look around his room again. "Where do we sleep?"

"Do faeries sleep?"

"It prevents dark circles beneath our eyes." Lily pointed at the mirror and chuckled. "For us both."

"If you are weary, then we sleep on the pallet. I could make you a small bed near mine."

Lily hesitated, chewing her lip. "That's not necessary. I shall sleep near you, for the sake of warmth."

Duncan eyed his narrow pallet. "It is a small space, Lily. If you are too near, I might roll on you in the night, crushing you. Again."

She looked impatient. "Should the occasion arise, I will scream with great power into your ear, and alert you."

Duncan hesitated, then shrugged. He pulled off his saffron tunic and boots, but he stopped at his leggings. Lily watched him with an expression of utmost curiosity, and no shyness. He smiled weakly and left his leggings in place. He picked her up and placed her on the upper corner of his bedding, then lay down carefully beside her.

Her brow furrowed as he lay back, arms folded behind his head.

She stood at the corner of his pillow, looking down into his face. "You sleep clothed?"

"On occasion. It's a damp, chill night."

She appeared suspicious and doubtful, but she didn't argue. He never slept clothed. Her reaction indicated she knew this, too.

Lily seated herself close to his head. "I, too, am chilled."

Duncan wondered why. It was a warm night, despite the rain.

"I shall now make use of your blanket." She didn't wait for an answer. She squirmed beneath a corner of his blanket and positioned herself just above his right shoulder. She tucked herself in closer, smiling.

"I am at ease." She paused. "Are you?"

"Until I roll over and flatten you, yes."

"Have no fear. I can withstand pressure."

Duncan looked over at her. She lay on her side, facing him. Her eyelids lowered as she gazed into his face. The lanterns sent a warm glow across her hair, turning the gold to fire, and the brown rich with light. He touched her hair with one finger and she smiled.

For an instant, he imagined kissing her. He remembered their respective sizes, and caught himself. "I am direly in need of sleep. The mind plays tricks . . ."

Lily's eyes drifted shut and she breathed deeply. "Sleep well, Duncan. Tonight, my dreams are real. . . ."

"Sleep well, Lily." He wanted to say more, but she appeared already asleep. Her breaths came even and slow, a tiny smile curved her lips. She moved closer to his neck, into his hair. He felt her breaths as little puffs against his throat.

Chapter 4

LILY spent the entire night tucked close to his neck. She woke to the first morning's light and drew long breaths of pure happiness. Duncan's pulse moved slow and rhythmic, close to her ear. The sound of his heart.

Duncan murmured in his sleep. His low voice sounded sensual. Lily's wings quivered, her heart seized extra beats. He murmured again, then rolled. Lily's nose squashed to one side beneath his ear. She struggled. He didn't respond.

"Duncan." Her voice sounded odd, constricted thus. "Duncan!"

Still, no response. Air came short. She drew the deepest breath possible, gathered her strength, and tensed all muscles. "Duncan MacLachlan!" Very loud, this time.

Duncan shot up like an arrow, brown eyes wide in shock. Lily smiled at her success, then straightened her wings, and her dress. She remembered to give her left wing a slight droop.

Duncan shook his head and ran his hand over his eyes. "I thought you were a dream. Until . . ."

Lily sat up. "It was necessary that I screech in order to remove your weight from my body."

"I understand that." He paused. "It is hard to imagine that something so small can be so loud."

"Thank you. How shall we spend the day?"

Duncan eyed her blearily. "If the day is fair, I generally begin mornings by swimming in the loch."

"Yes, I know. Yesterday was an exception."

Duncan's sleepy eyes widened. One brow rose. "It was you, wasn't it?"

Lily blanched. She'd been so careful, hiding her deceit, hiding her fascination for him. And now she casually disclosed her knowledge of his daily activities.

"Who?"

"You are the one who followed me." His voice softened and lowered, and his expression altered from amusement to tentative wonder. "Who has always followed me."

Lily closed her eyes as embarrassment swept over her. She sank back abruptly to her bottom and both wings drooped. She couldn't answer. She bowed her head and nodded.

He touched her. Very gently, he lifted her. *Oh, no!* To eye level! She couldn't face him now.

"Why?"

Tears formed beneath her lashes. He had discovered her most guarded secret. She had been a fool to think he wouldn't. His finger touched her cheek, then her chin. He would force her, gently, to reveal her deepest heart . . .

She looked at him, wide-eyed, her secret torn open and exposed. She tried to speak, and failed. She shook her head. A gentle smile formed on his mouth, his brown eyes revealed tenderness. She averted her gaze. "Because I like you."

It was the most she could say, without telling him he filled her dreams. Without telling him she loved him.

"You are a sweet guardian, Lily. I wish I had known of you long ago. I would have enjoyed your companionship."

Lily peered up at him. He misunderstood the nature of her devotion. He couldn't know how human she was, that she bore human desires, and human weakness. Perhaps that was for the best. She tried to smile, as a being of power smiles at a mortal. Somewhat condescending, benevolent. Not a woman in love.

"That is how I know you are a great man."

Duncan's head angled to one side as he studied her, his brow furrowed. He toyed with another thought, and Lily held her breath. She knew, as if she saw the inner workings of his mind, that he wondered if she might care for him in a more . . . personal way. She saw when he dismissed that notion as implausible.

They sighed at the same time.

Duncan dressed, and Lily pretended to avert her eyes. She stole a furtive glance as he pulled on a fresh tunic, and another as he tied his leggings and braies. Her face felt a little warm when he turned around, but she kept her expression both casual and innocent. Still, she felt certain that Duncan was again repressing humor.

She angled her chin at a defiant anger, daring him to broach the subject of her peeking. He didn't, but his smile widened. He held out his hand. "Will you join me for a morning swim, small maiden?"

Lily hopped onto his palm, and he lifted her. "Faeries, of course, are excellent swimmers, though I favor skimming the surface."

Duncan looked grave. "But in your injured state, is that not impossible?"

"What 'injured state'?" Lily blanched, but Duncan laughed.

"It would be easier for us both if we choose to spend these days together. You can make use of your wings, and I need feel no guilt for wounding you."

Lily blushed, but a smile formed on her face despite herself. "It has been somewhat of a trial to maintain this level of . . . inaccuracy."

"I assume it has. Let us go."

Lily positioned herself on his shoulder, and he pulled his cape over his tunic. "I shall conceal myself in the folds of the hood. Wearing the hood might raise suspicions among your clansmen."

Duncan shrugged. "They'll just think I've stooped lower, and now fear the rain."

"We will not permit them to think that." She fiddled with his hair, and covered her body in his hood. "There. I am suitably concealed. Proceed."

They left the hut, and Duncan headed for the path to Loch Fyne. His father appeared on horseback, leading a procession of three young women. Duncan sighed without pleasure, but he bowed. "You are about early, sire."

"I was up before dawn, boy." Tearlach waved his arm in the general direction of the women behind. "I have collected several daughters of worthy lairds, and you shall select among them a bride."

Lily issued a small hiss. "Now?"

Tearlach hesitated. "You have two days, until your brother's wedding." Tearlach turned in his saddle. "Females, step forward. As I told your respective sires, you are to spend the day in my hamlet. Make yourselves useful, and my son will judge which of you makes him a good wife."

The young women whispered and blushed. Lily's heart moved like ice. Angry ice. She didn't like any of them. She didn't need to see more. "Let's go."

Duncan ignored her as he scanned the young women. He was actually considering obeying his father's ridiculous command. Lily ground her teeth together in irritation. "What about our swim?"

He still didn't answer. Tearlach positioned his horse to one side and pointed at the first girl. "This is Gavina MacKinnon. Good, solid girl."

Lily coughed. "You can say that again. She has the legs of an aurochs."

Duncan adjusted his shoulder to disbalance her. Lily tightened her grip, feeling her first anger toward Duncan MacLachlan. Gavina wasn't a pretty woman, although she wasn't blushing or looking shy like the others. "It is my joy to make your acquaintance, Gavina."

Gavina rolled her eyes. "We've met before, when you bought one of our cows . . ."

Lily chuckled. "What did I tell you?"

"Ah, of course. You are much matured since then, Gavina."

"It was last month, but thank you."

Lily decided she liked Gavina. She felt certain this wouldn't be Duncan's first choice. "She's good enough. Pick her, and let's go."

"I don't think so." Duncan spoke aloud, and Lily warmed with pleasure. Gavina looked confused, and Duncan cleared his throat. "I meant, I didn't think it was last month."

Tearlach appeared annoyed. "Next. Cailleach . . ."

Lily hummed. " 'Cailleach.' It means 'hag.' Fitting, don't you think?"

Duncan groaned, then stopped himself by another fit of coughing. "Cailleach MacDuff, I know well. You are a beautiful dancer."

Cailleach looked up and smiled brightly. "You are kind to say so."

Lily felt irritation to the core of her soul. Cailleach was ill named. She wasn't a hag. She had beautiful red hair that fell in tight waves around a decidedly pleasing face. She would be a perfect mate. Except . . . Lily sensed something about the girl. Something . . . double.

Lily leaned close to Duncan's ear. "She's in the throes of motherhood."

"What?" Again, aloud.

Cailleach looked confused. "I said, you are kind to say so."

"And I . . ." Lily spoke in a delighted hiss. "Said she's pregnant."

Duncan huffed. "You can't expect me to believe you."

Cailleach's eyes widened. "I meant it! You *are* kind!"

Duncan was thoroughly agitated. Lily leaned back comfortably, one leg crossed over the other. "Ask her."

"No." Duncan clasped his hand to his forehead. "I mean . . . No, that's not what I meant . . ." He gathered himself together while Lily hummed like a bee. "You are sweet to accede to my father's request, Cailleach. But I felt certain another owned your heart. A man who most certainly wishes for your hand himself."

Cailleach brightened like a star. "Do you think so? I haven't seen much of him since . . . Oh! Parlan!"

Tearlach eyed the girl in utmost suspicion. "Parlan MacDougall?" She nodded vigorously. "One of my own thegns?"

"He is." Cailleach sounded dreamy.

"He will marry you at once. Dismissed."

Cailleach wandered off, singing. Lily beamed.

The third girl stepped forward without Tearlach's prodding. Lily scrutinized her appearance for flaws, and found none apparent. She had light blond hair, a sweet, even face. She was younger than the other two, and her eyes sparkled with decided admiration for Duncan MacLachlan.

Lily's entire being convulsed with envy. It hurt. He would marry this one. No question.

"Laird Duncan . . ." She sounded shy. Sweet. Lily fumed. "We haven't met, though I have seen you from afar."

Lily snorted, but Duncan bowed. "I have seen you also . . . Alpina
. . . MacKay, isn't it?"

The girl blushed, a sweet smile on her lips. "She has thin lips,
her eyes are too small, and . . ." Lily struggled for something more
significant. "And she's a Sassenach!"

"Sassenach?" Duncan drew a long breath at his latest slip.

Tearlach braced into ripe indignation. "Not a Sassenach . . . Not
in my clan."

Alpina started to cry, and Duncan moved to take her arm. Lily's
fists clenched. Pity. It was a danger to a kind heart. "I didn't mean
to suggest you are of Saxon blood, Alpina. Only that you have beauty
I thought reserved for their loveliest queens."

Lily issued a retching noise, loud enough for Alpina to hear. "What
was that?"

"A frog. Come, Alpina . . ."

Lily puffed her chest and croaked. It was a good imitation. And
loud. She sat back and enjoyed Alpina's confused expression, and
ignored Duncan's repressed fury.

"It sounded like it was coming from your . . . hair."

Tearlach bowed his head and slumped in his saddle. "It wouldn't
surprise me."

"The nearness of the loch does strange things to sound." Duncan
reached to casually adjust his hair. His fingers nudged Lily, deliberately.
In response, she pinched his shoulder. He winced. "But there are many
biting flies in this area. One must take care."

Gavina, ignored while Duncan lavished attention on the lovely
Alpina, snorted and thumped her foot. "You should see the flies in
the cow pen."

Alpina smiled, a patronizing smile, then beamed sweetly at Duncan.
Lily's envy reached a pinnacle. If this was the woman he wanted, she
should wish him well, charm his union. Bless his children. Children.
Her eyes welled with tears.

Duncan had never been in love before. Lily had watched him carefully to be sure of that. But he'd never met Alpina MacKay before,
either. He'd just "seen her from afar." A nauseating pronouncement,
if ever there was one. She had no right to interfere.

"She's insincere, deceitful, and manipulative. That's why she's so nice. She's trying to hide her true nature. And her beauty will fade once she reaches true womanhood. And!" Lily's whisper came in a whirring rush. "And she'll be hard and domineering in the extreme."

"She seems very sweet."

Alpina's lovely expression faded for a moment, revealing just the expression Lily described. Lily hoped Duncan noticed, but he seemed to miss it entirely. "Who?"

Duncan gulped. "You, of course. I was . . . thinking aloud."

Tearlach adjusted his position in the saddle. "Good. You've got a prospective. Females, disperse and make yourselves useful."

Alpina clasped Duncan's arm. "I am so pleased to have finally met you, face to face."

Lily snarled. "'Face to face.'" She mimicked what she considered an extremely simpering tone. But Duncan just smiled and placed his hand over Alpina's.

"It pleases me to see you are as lovely as you appeared from afar."

Lily couldn't think of a suitable comment. She made a vile noise with her tongue and Duncan eased back from the girl. "Frogs again. Must be any number of them this morning. If you don't mind, sire, I will attend the loch."

He didn't wait for approval. He bowed to the women, then hurried toward the woodland path.

Duncan tried to dislodge his small bee, and failed. She clung with fists of fury. He stopped abruptly and pulled off his cape, catching Lily in the folds. He glared down at her. She glared up at him. She was so beautiful. When angry, her wings went stiff. Her blue eyes blazed. Her tiny lips formed a tight O.

His body reacted. His heart drove pulses of desire to his groin. Lust. For a faerie. A woman small enough to fit in the palm of his hand. For a reason he didn't understand, this fanned his anger.

Duncan shook his cape, but Lily's face knit into a tight pout of equal fury, and she fluttered up and hovered before his face. "You attempted to dislodge me. You attempted to squash me." Her voice came lower than usual. Gravelly. It aroused him. "And . . ." She stopped, took a breath, then aimed her tiny fist at his nose. "You called me a 'frog.'"

Duncan's eyes watered. His chest rose and fell as he tried not to laugh. His lips curved upward. He took two short breaths to stop himself.

"If you dare utter the smallest peep of a humorous outburst . . ."

Duncan laughed. He laughed until his stomach hurt, until tears fell to his cheeks. Lily glared with such pure indignation that his laughter escalated beyond control. She fluttered and buzzed around his head. She tugged his hair.

"Cease!"

Suddenly, without warning, Lily laughed, too. She sank to the ground and settled on a mushroom, still laughing. Duncan sat beside her on the ground. They looked at each other. Their mirth stilled into silence.

"Are you going to marry that girl?"

"Which one?"

"The pretty one."

"They were all pretty." Duncan hesitated. "Gavina perhaps is too contentious to be viewed as such . . ."

"You know which one I mean. The one that wasn't pregnant. Are you going to marry her?"

Duncan hesitated. Lily peered up at him. Her hands clasped the mushroom on either side of her legs. Again, he noticed her well-formed legs, her small, narrow feet. "My father desires that I marry. Alpina is fair. I suppose that I will marry her."

A faint mist rose around his feet, around the mushroom. He sensed what this meant. Lily was trying not to cry. She looked down, hiding her tears. His heart felt swollen in his chest. He had caused her pain, yet there could be nothing between them, a faerie and a mortal.

"Did you like her very much?" Lily's tiny voice sent splinters into his heart. She was trying to be brave, to act unconcerned. It was worse than crying.

"I saw no reason to dislike her." Duncan paused. "In other circumstances, I would find her beautiful."

Lily peeked up at him. "What 'other circumstances'?"

"Had I seen her in other company."

"I cannot believe Alpina paled in comparison to the other two."

"Not them, Lily. To you."

Lily laughed and shook her head. "Again you flatter me. I told you to do so." She paused and sighed. "I still like it."

"I'm not flattering you. You are beautiful."

"Your mirrors says that I have appeal. But you must know that I am an Unseelie, creature of darkness and evil."

"There is no evidence of that. You are sweet, lovely . . ."

"Ha! Only because you are so good can you possibly think thus. No evidence? Then you didn't see the contents of my thoughts when your father brought forward your 'brides.' You didn't know the darkness of my heart." Lily stopped and stared at him. "I am not truly beautiful, nor sweet, nor any good thing."

"Lily . . ."

Tears glimmered in her bright eyes, and the mists rose as a soft veil around her. She reached as if to touch him, then lowered her hand back to the mushroom. "Say nothing, Duncan. You do not know the depth of my evil, nor how much I have hurt you."

"You haven't hurt me, Lily. You make life . . . challenging at times, but . . ."

"Duncan . . . I do not speak of today."

He waited, he didn't speak. She had changed. He wasn't sure how.

"It was I who placed the curse on De Dalan, Duncan." She hesitated, but her eyes didn't leave his face. "It was I who placed the curse on you."

"I am not cursed."

She smiled, and for the first time, he saw that behind her young face was a being who had seen many, long years. "Do you truly believe a man as strong as yourself could stumble for no reason? Do you think a man as intelligent as you could overlook a tree root in his path? Unless that portion of his being was clouded by a spell. A dark spell."

Duncan stared at her. His friend, and his enemy. He saw the years of humiliation, of trying until his muscles ached from strain, and failing. His saw his father's shame, and his brother's pity, and his own anger directed at himself. When it should have been directed . . . at Lily.

"Then all this time . . . you followed me to see the results of this curse? Tell me, did it amuse you?"

Her tiny face blanched. Her hands clasped over her heart. A tear fell to her cheek. Caught by the shards of new morning light, it glittered like a diamond, and the mist turned to soft rain.

"No ... I followed you because ..." Her voice caught and she stopped, staring as if her heart had been torn asunder. "Because I care for you."

Duncan's throat constricted until it burned, his chest throbbed. "So much that you would damn me thus, and leave me a fool?"

She bowed her head, and her tears slid down her cheek. Her small back hunched, her hair fell forward over her face. Her wings were pale now, almost translucent. "I cursed you because that is the duty of an Unseelie minion. Nathara ordered it, because De Dalan's heirs still hold her anger."

She looked up at him as if facing final judgment. "I have cursed many babies. I have made small concessions to my own will by utilizing lesser spells. Alistair MacKenzie's daughter, for instance, has dim vision rather than seizures, but it is still dark work on my part. Muir MacInnes must deal with a slight stutter. But they're doing well, both of them. Tavia MacKenzie stitches the finest blankets ... Muir just married a very good girl ..."

"You followed them, too?"

"I check on them occasionally."

"Why?"

Lily shrugged her tiny shoulder. "To see that they fare well, despite me."

"Because you care." Tears blurred Duncan's vision. "How can you be evil, yet care, Lily? Have you never wondered?"

"Nathara says it is weakness."

"Nathara is wrong."

Lily sniffed and dried her cheeks. "Have I earned your hatred?"

"You are a force of nature, Lily. Human or not, we are all that. Our ills and good fortune are things we must deal with as they come. Whether from within or outside ourselves, it matters not. I believe you are my friend."

Duncan touched her face and she clasped his finger. "Your kindness will see your way into heaven, Duncan MacLachlan."

He wanted more. He wanted to know that he was special to her. More than just a baby she had unwillingly afflicted. He wanted to know that she felt some portion of what he felt. He knew nothing of the personal side of a faerie's life. Maybe they didn't have such desires.

"I made you a promise, Duncan. I said I would instruct you in the art of agility. If you allow it, I will keep that promise now."

The rain stopped, the mist abated, yet a sorrow remained between them. Because he couldn't really have her, nor take her as a woman. Because they were together, with limits. "If I am cursed, then I see no point in trying to overcome the affliction."

Lily flew from the mushroom to his shoulder, landing with perfect ease. "You must understand the nature of a curse. It is not a matter of simply making you clumsy. It is a matter of blocking your natural tendency. I blocked that portion of yourself which knows instinctively when to look, when to avoid certain obstacles."

Duncan sighed. "It's true. I never see it coming."

"Then you must learn again, over the curse. I blocked your surroundings from your instinctive mind. Tree roots, rocks . . . that sort of thing. Now, you must learn to see them for yourself."

"How?"

"Rise!"

Duncan laughed at her commanding tone, but he rose to his feet and awaited her instruction. Lily perched on his shoulder, contemplating. "It might be wisest for me to lodge myself elsewhere." She looked around. "I shall perch on a branch."

She flew to a branch overhanging the path. "Can you hear me from this position?"

"Your voice carries with surprising force."

"Meaning 'yes'?"

"Yes. I hear you well."

"Very good!" She stood on the end of a forked branch of an oak tree, her arms folded in front of her chest, her wings splayed. If he married, he couldn't keep her with him. Yet he couldn't imagine Alpina to be such good company. No woman would ever be truly interesting again, not after Lily.

She tapped her small, bare foot. "As I instruct, you will do, while sighting the area on your own. When I say 'run,' you will run. When I say 'leap,' leap. 'Right' and 'left' are obvious commands. 'Flip' . . . We'll work on that when we get there. Are you ready, Duncan MacLachlan?"

"I am."
"Proceed."

"Leap again!"

Duncan bounded forward. He saw a rock, and he avoided it.

"Stop!" He stopped.

"Right! Left!"

He was conditioned well. Otherwise, Lily's instruction would have killed him.

"Flip!"

Duncan stopped and eyed her with misgivings. She shrugged. "Back or forward, it makes no difference. I should have been more specific." She paused. "Flip backward!"

Duncan gazed heavenward and sighed. He was used to falling. He took a few steps forward, then propelled his body back and over. And landed on his feet.

Lily clapped and cheered. "Now tell me you are clumsy!"

Duncan grinned, walked toward her, and simulated a stumble. Lily gasped and fluttered to his shoulder, concern molding her small face. "Are you all right?" She looked deeply into his eyes. For an instant, he felt as if he looked into her soul, and saw himself.

"Lily . . ." He caught himself before he said too much. "Thank you. It was a morning well spent. I won't soon forget your instruction." He slapped his thighs. "Nor will my body."

"You are fit. There is no fat anywhere on your body. All parts of you are proportioned perfectly."

Their eyes met. Her mouth parted and dropped. Her cheeks turned bright pink. She had been watching him the morning they met. When he swam in the loch. Naked.

His loins stirred again. Perhaps their desires were closer than he had imagined. Yet what could he do about it? "Shall we swim, small maiden? It would please me to see you 'skimming the surface.'"

"That sounds pleasurable. The water will be cooling to your flesh."

Duncan sighed. "I hope so." Otherwise, Lily might discover a "proportion" of his body much altered by desire.

*   *   *

He swam in his braies. There was no other way. The water was cool, but not quite cold enough to banish his desire. He kept himself waist deep to avoid shocking her. Lily flew like a hummingbird, darting over the dark blue surface of the loch, stopping to dabble her toes. Sometimes, she would float on her back and gaze at the sky.

Duncan dove and swam to greet her. She hovered above the water, a wide smile lighting her little face. "A pleasant morning has been spent. I have not bathed thus for many years."

Duncan held out his hand and she perched on his palm. "How old are you?"

"I don't know. Many years. Faeries age very slowly."

Her damp hair fell around her shoulders, but it didn't conceal her small breasts beneath her dress. That was wet, too. Duncan drew a quick breath. "I have lost my mind. My father was right. 'First the body, then the mind.'"

"What are you talking about?"

"Lily, I want to kiss you."

Her eyes opened so wide that the blue mirrored the quiet loch.

"I want to kiss you, and I can't. My lips would squash your face." Duncan forced his gaze from her to the calm, blue sky above. She still didn't speak. She just stared. Whether in horror, or not, he couldn't tell.

"I'm supposed to marry, and I want to be with you instead." He looked at her again. Her expression hadn't changed. "This isn't part of the curse, is it?"

She shook her head slowly.

"Perhaps in this I follow De Dalan, also. You said he became infatuated with a faerie queen."

"Infatuated?" Her voice was so small and so surprised that he barely heard her.

"I can give it no other name." He tried to smile, to appear casual about his admission. "I hope it is not an offense. I cannot imagine that another man would react differently to your company."

"Infatuated?" Her voice was smaller still.

Maybe she didn't know what it meant. Maybe it frightened her.

"It means I care about you." No, it meant more than that. "And that I find you beautiful, and . . ." He couldn't tell her he desired her. That *would* terrify her. "I am smitten."

"You are smitten with me, too?"

He hesitated, unsure of her meaning. Perhaps another man had already succumbed to her charm. " 'Too?' "

"As I am with you." She spoke as if this were an established fact. Obvious. He swallowed hard to contain a new emotion, one that threatened to overtake all rational thought.

"We're talking about the same thing, aren't we?"

Her face puckered. "I am not certain. It is a romantic feeling, which reveals itself in an intense interest in a person . . . In this case, yourself . . . Not only in their physical selves, but in their words and feelings. In the feel of their skin, in the texture and color of their hair . . ."

"I shouldn't have asked. We're talking about the same thing."

"Good." She puffed a quick breath. "Good."

They stared at each other. Duncan cleared his throat. "Now what?"

"Now that we have discovered that we are mutually infatuated?"

He nodded. "Yes. You are a faerie . . ."

"And a bad one at that."

"That point is debatable, but the fact remains, I am a mortal man, and you are an immortal being."

"You want to kiss me." She sighed.

"I want to keep you with me always." The joy of his admission turned to pain. He wanted her, and he couldn't have her. "And I can't."

Lily's expression darkened, too. "This has never happened in my dreams. They never got quite this far. I never expected you to return my admiration."

"Only because you deny yourself the knowledge of what you are."

"I know too well what I am. But I do not know what to do. I don't have magic enough to create a transformation spell, to become human, nor to turn you into one of my kind. It is said the power of faerie gold, in some form which I don't know, has this strength . . ."

The water surrounded him, motionless. No wind blew. The sun cast a steady light on the calm surface. No tree branch creaked nor bowed. He wanted her, and he couldn't have her.

"I have caused you pain, haven't I?" Lily spoke in a small, strained voice, but she didn't look away. "It would have been better for you if we'd never met."

"It would have been easier if I'd never known you, Lily. But not better."

"I never wanted to hurt you, Duncan. I have admired you since I first beheld you asleep in your crib. I admired you when you fought your affliction at every turn. I admired your strength and your kindness, and your beauty. It is selfishness that keeps me at your side. Selfishness and deceit. My wing was never injured, just ajar."

He smiled, but his heart felt heavier than ever in his life. "I know."

"And you were too good to say so."

She lifted her gaze and looked into his eyes. Very slowly, she moved her wings and elevated from his palm. "I will never hurt you again."

She didn't let him speak. She placed her tiny hands on either side of his face, and bent to kiss him. Duncan held himself perfectly still as her soft mouth pressed against his bottom lip. It was so slight a touch, he barely felt its pressure, yet it sent currents of fire through his limbs.

Lily drew away, hovering beyond his reach. She placed one hand over her breast. "Always, you are in my heart. But I will not lead you to live in dreams as I have done. It is too cruel a fate."

She was leaving, and he couldn't stop her. "Don't go, not yet . . . I promised to take you riding. There is much we might yet do together, as companions."

"For what?" Tears filled her eyes, but she didn't cry. A faint mist formed over the surface of the loch. "Do we not torture ourselves with what cannot be? You have a life, and you can know happiness."

"I have heard of men taking faerie brides. Their size was human."

"They were Seelies. I am not."

"There must be a way."

"None that I know." Her face knit. "Though perhaps Nathara . . ."

"Your queen?"

"If I do not return by morning, remember me as a dream, Duncan. A dream that has no power in waking life, but leaves a pleasant memory."

Duncan smiled, though his heart ached. She was still long-winded. "I will miss you, Lily."

"There is no need. I am with you in spirit."

She lifted her chin as if fighting tears. A sorrowful smile curved her lips. Lily turned away and she didn't look back. Duncan watched as she flew west across the loch, fading to the appearance of a distant butterfly, until she disappeared. Then he swam back to shore.

Chapter 5

THE dark caverns of the netherworld had never looked bleaker. Lily had to fight her resistance as she entered Nathara's cavern. Duncan cared for her. To the point of "infatuation." That was more than her sweetest dreams ever allowed. He was tender and sweet, and the impossibility of their situation caused him pain.

If she could find some way . . . Nathara might have the power. Lily would have to ask.

The cavern darkened as Lily descended deeper into its hull. No magic lit the hall. Sometimes, she envisioned Titania's bright halls, as she imagined them to be. Lit with bright lanterns, filled with music, with laughter. No one sang in Nathara's hall.

Dark beings passed her, going out, but none spoke. She'd made no friends among the Unseelies. Few even took human shapes. They moved about as dark clouds, or grotesque creatures. Many took forms terrifying to behold, with many heads, or tentacles rather than arms.

Lily proceeded down the black corridor until she reached Nathara's chambers. She rarely came this far in the netherworld. She never met with Nathara other than when answering a summons. She had little hope her plea would be answered, but it was her only chance.

She rang a solemn bell, and the chamber door creaked open. Nathara sat encased in a red glow, surrounded by a dank, noxious odor. Lily took small breaths to avoid the fumes.

"I did not summon you, Lily. Be gone." There was no music in Nathara's voice. Only bitterness and cruel pride.

"I have come to make a request, my queen."

Nathara's face altered with interest. Lily knew it wasn't from a desire to please, but with the knowledge Lily's need created a new opportunity for control. "What do you want?"

Lily hesitated, reluctant to reveal her secret. Nathara was a vile mockery of beauty, each feature molded as if in mockery of humanity, yet each part well made. Lily disliked looking at her, for the secret fear she, too, might appear thus.

Lily closed her eyes and tried to remember the image in Duncan's mirror. The darkness in Nathara's cavern blocked her memory, leaving only darkness. But Duncan said she was beautiful. Whatever she really looked like, he thought she was beautiful. The memory of his sweet words gave her hope.

"I want you to lend me the power to make myself human."

Nathara's laugh split the dank cavern, and Lily knew she had already failed. "Why should you wish such a thing?"

If she spoke of Duncan, Nathara might harm him. Lily didn't answer.

Nathara rose from her seat, propelled by black wings. She drew close to Lily. Lily shuddered, but she didn't retreat.

"What would you do in exchange for this feat of power, Lily?"

"What do you want?"

"The Seelies keep a mound of potent gold somewhere near Loch Fyne. Find for me its exact location, and I will grant your wish." Nathara chuckled and settled back into her seat.

The darkness grew as Lily considered Nathara's proposal. This time, the darkness came from within herself. She shuddered, but if this was the way to be with Duncan, she would try.

"How?"

"Follow Titania. She will lead you to her treasure."

Lily shook her head. "That's impossible! I have no power against so great a queen. She would sense my presence, as she senses all Unseelies. I couldn't follow her without being detected."

An evil smile formed on Nathara's cold mouth. "I will give you a charmed necklace which will prevent detection." Nathara reached into a cauldron of cluttered jewels and seized a necklace, seemingly at random. She passed it to Lily.

Lily examined the necklace, but sensed no power surrounding it. She eyed the Unseelie queen in confusion. "If this necklace prevents detection, why haven't you used it before now?"

Nathara's expression darkened. "If you desire your wish granted, then ask no further questions. Do as I tell you, and my word in this will be proven correct."

"I cannot believe Titania could be so easily deceived."

"Titania is strong, but she can be tricked. I know. I've tricked her before, and stolen her dearest treasure."

"What treasure?"

"That is not for you to know."

Lily hesitated. She didn't want to do this. "How will I find her?"

"You will have little trouble locating her. Tonight, go to the north glade of Loch Fyne, where the lilies and violets bloom. When the fireflies come forth, Titania will appear. Don't let yourself be seen. When her dance is complete, she will go to her sacred mound. Find its location, and bring word to me. I will handle matters from there."

"Is there no other way?"

"None. Now be gone. I have other matters to attend."

Lily turned and left the hall. She ascended from the dark caverns and sat at the entrance. Her heart throbbed with a dull beat. She admired the Seelie queen. But she thought again of Duncan's sweet face, of the longing she had viewed in his brown eyes.

"I want to kiss you, and I can't."

There was no other way. Nathara was dark, but she made no promises she didn't keep. Lily endured a tremor of disquiet. True, the queen kept her promises, but they were often cloaked in treachery. Lily banished the thought. All that mattered was winning Duncan's love. If it was done at a portion of Titania's gold, so be it.

Lily crouched beneath a dark mushroom, watching the midnight glade. The fireflies hadn't appeared, for the night started cold and breezy. The clouds moved slowly aside, and the full moon shone on a bed of lilies and violets. The lilies quavered as if a breeze affected them, but the air was still now.

Lily felt Titania's presence before she saw her. Lily fingered Nathara's cold necklace, but still it revealed no power. She doubted it could conceal her from so strong a queen. But Titania entered the glade without hesitation.

Lily's breath caught at the sight of the great being. Titania's hair streamed in golden brown waves, framing her head like a halo. Her wings varied between purple and lavender, and glittered with white. The violets opened and bowed at her presence.

Titania flew into the center of the glade, just above the flowerbed. The fireflies circled around her, doing honor to a great soul.

Titania ceased all motion. Lily froze. Nathara's necklace had failed. For an instant, she felt sure Titania looked her way. Doom.

Even the fireflies ceased movement while Lily waited for Titania's action.

The Seelie queen resumed her dance, and Lily breathed a tight sigh of relief. For a moment, she forgot her purpose. Titania was free, she was good. Lily's envy filled her soul. Tears filled her eyes. She longed to join the Seelie queen, to tell her everything, to beg for her help.

But Titania blessed only the good, and Lily wasn't good. That she was here at all proved her evil nature beyond doubt. Lily swallowed her wistful imagining, and resumed her purpose.

Titania's dance ended, and she floated slowly from the glade. Lily waited until she progressed far enough ahead, then followed. Titania never glanced back, nor seemed to suspect pursuit. She led Lily from the forest to a meadow south of Tearlach MacLachlan's hamlet. Sheep grazed in the moonlit pasture, taking no note of the faeries' presence.

Lily hid herself behind a fat, sleeping ewe and watched as Titania flew to the high ground of the meadow. To the Rocking Stone, laid by their own human ancestors . . . an obvious resting place for the faerie gold. Lily wondered why Nathara hadn't figured it out on her own.

Titania settled upon the stone, and then lowered herself to the ground. She waved her hand, and the grass yielded, revealing a shimmering gold mound. Titania ran her fingers through the gold dust, then sprinkled it through the air. The fireflies took on a brilliant glow, and spiraled upward toward the stars.

Lily recognized the act as ritual, a thankfulness directed at the goddess of nature and to the Everlasting Spirit. Titania waved her hand again, and the grass concealed its treasure once more. Titania flew down from the Rocking Stone, and toward Lily. Lily almost hoped she was discovered, but Titania flew past her without a word.

Lily watched the Seelie queen until she disappeared as a tiny light into the forest. She bowed her head, and her own light dimmed to nothing as she returned to Nathara's dark chambers.

She waited outside the chamber door for hours. Dawn approached, yet Lily still hadn't made up her mind. Could she betray the good queen, for the sake of her love? Lily considered the matter, but reason eluded her. In all her life, she'd wanted nothing. Nothing, until she had watched Duncan MacLachlan grow from earnest boyhood into a man she treasured beyond any gold.

She could make him happy. Titania didn't need all her gold. The Seelies possessed many such mounds of hidden gold. The one by the Rocking Stone was a relatively minor hold.

Nathara only wanted to restore the balance of power. Iain Campbell had stumbled upon a portion of Nathara's well-hidden faerie gold, and stolen it, thus upsetting the balance of power between the Seelies and the Unseelies. For this reason, the Campbells were cursed, though Lily wasn't sure how they had suffered.

She had kept a watch on their clan, but so far, she had detected no ill luck befalling Iain's clan. This day dawning was the day Struan MacLachlan was to marry Laren Campbell. The Campbell curse might hamper their future, but Lily couldn't be sure.

Duncan's happiness mattered more. She couldn't affect Nathara's spells anyway. Lily started to open the chamber door, then stopped. Could Duncan find happiness if his brother suffered? And what of the land itself, if Nathara's powers exceeded Titania's?

Her decision refused to be made. "I have time yet." Lily backed away from the door. She had to think, and to do that, she needed fresh air. She headed back toward the entrance of the netherworld, then sought position high in a dead oak tree.

She tried to force her thoughts into cohesiveness, but the battle within raged without quarter. First, she saw Duncan, in love, waiting for her return. Then Titania, good and sweet, spewing faerie gold into the sky. Then Duncan again. Over and over, until she thought she might go mad from longing.

Dawn broke, and still, she had no answer. Human footsteps distracted her. A man rode along the unseen path, then dismounted. Perhaps Duncan had come for her. Her heart held its beat.

Iain Campbell appeared in the dim morning light and approached the netherworld entrance. Lily's brow knit tight. No human knew the location of the entrance to Nathara's realm. Yet Iain stood before it as if expected.

Nathara appeared at the entrance, cloaked in red darker than blood. Lily stilled her impulses to avoid detection, and she listened.

"I've come as called, Dark Queen. Our gamble is set. All moves forward."

Lily's brow furrowed. *What gamble?*

Nathara poised a slender staff and fingered it greedily. "Tomorrow, your daughter is to wed Struan MacLachlan. Your bride-piece is high, I assume?"

"I offered them no less than the hill of gold, Dark Queen."

"Laren will die, of course, before that gold is delivered." Nathara laughed, cold and cruel. Lily froze in horror at their casual discussion of a plan obviously long formed. A plan that involved the murder of Iain's own daughter.

"And in its place will come a company of my warriors. Tearlach MacLachlan will fall, and the Campbells will take their land. I will have power enough to repay you."

"You attempted to deceive me once, Iain Campbell. For that, your daughter faces a curse that shall bind her for a thousand years. She will be born over and over, every hundred years. And each time, on her twenty-first birthday, she will die."

The grim announcement made no impact on Iain. "It is the price I must pay. I assume the deed will occur in time to divert Struan MacLachlan's attention from my attack on his father's hamlet?"

"Do you question the efficiency of my design, Iain Campbell?"

Nathara rose above the cowering mortal. "My spell is flawless. The MacLachlans will wait for Struan's bride, but she will be enslaved in my trance, and instead go to the Rocking Stone. And there, she will die."

Lily fought to collect her thoughts. Nathara's spells were impenetrable, even to Titania. But every curse had one chance within it for freedom, but not even the spell-caster knew what it was. Only the cursed one could find it, and few ever did. Still, a chance remained . . .

"I have given you the chance to make amends, Iain Campbell. See that you do so. Defeat Tearlach MacLachlan, and pay me homage. Serve me well, and you shall prosper like a king. Fail, and you die a death so gruesome as to make your daughter's fate seem sweet."

"I'll not fail, Dark Queen. I'll drive the MacLachlans to the dust, while Tearlach's son grovels in misery over my dead daughter. The old man will be left with only his addled son to defend him. There is no way I can lose."

"There's a new rumor about you, little brother."

Struan's teasing voice disrupted Duncan's gloomy contemplation. He glanced back over his shoulder to see his brother grinning down at him. Struan was dressed for ceremony. His sword hung in a jeweled scabbard from his belt. A gold brooch pinned his mantle over his red and blue tunic.

Duncan looked back out over the loch. He couldn't stay in the hamlet as the MacLachlans celebrated a union of love, while dutifully planning his own announcement.

He'd waited all night, then returned to the loch's edge at dawn. Lily hadn't come.

Duncan sighed as Struan sat down beside him. "I'm not sure I want to know, but . . . what rumor?"

"It's a good one this time." Struan paused to chuckle. "They say you keep a frog in your hair, and hold conversations with the creature." Struan shook his head. "There are times I think our people more superstitious and peculiar than the Picts. A frog. What next?"

Duncan considered telling his brother about Lily, then decided against it. No need to darken Struan's wedding day with his own sad tale. "You wed at the high sun, brother. I trust you are well prepared for the event."

"The morning will be long until the hour of my bliss, but I will endure the hours of waiting. And you, Duncan. Our sire tells me you will select a bride today. Have you made your choice?"

"No."

"What of Gavina?"

Duncan grimaced. "She has the legs of an aurochs."

Struan didn't argue. "Cailleach?"

"She will make a fine wife and mother. For Parlan MacDougall. She bears his child, you know."

Struan's brow rose. "No. I didn't know. How do you?"

"A frog told me."

Struan uttered a short, dubious laugh, as if hoping his brother was joking. "And what about Alpina MacKay? She is fair and much admired."

"If you can overlook her small eyes and thin lips." Duncan drew a long, forlorn breath. "And I fear her pleasant demeanor is meant to cover an insincere, deceitful, and manipulative nature."

"I don't remember you being so . . . particular on this subject. Please tell me this has nothing to do with a frog's advice."

"Only partly."

Struan groaned. "You've been under strain, Duncan—"

A sharp cry cut him off. Both turned to see . . . Duncan caught his breath. Lily spiraled downward from the sky, uttering piercing cries that sounded like "Quick! Help!" as she plummeted. Duncan leapt to his feet, but Struan just stared, mouth agape.

She narrowly averted a tree branch as she dove. Duncan waved and held out his arm. She flared her wings and landed, panting. "Lily . . ." His heart slammed. She didn't appear injured, but she was clearly panicked over something. "What is it? What ails you?"

She couldn't catch her breath. "Duncan . . ." Her eyes beseeched him as she gasped. "Calamity arises. Oh . . ."

Struan stood. He looked at Duncan, then at Lily. "What . . . ?" His voice trailed off in wonder.

Duncan's mouth curved in a half-smile. "The aforementioned frog . . . my Lily."

"I am not . . . a frog . . ." She paused to gasp. "It is well you are both here. Struan, where is your bride?"

Struan glanced at Duncan. "Laren is with her father's clan, no doubt preparing for our marriage."

Lily shook her head frantically. "No, no! She is cursed."

Duncan frowned. "Why didn't you tell me before this?"

"I didn't know for certain. I knew Nathara had placed ill fate on the Campbell clan, but I couldn't be sure it affected Laren."

Struan's face drained of blood. "But now . . . what do you know, small woman?"

"I overheard the dark queen . . ." She turned her desperate gaze to Duncan. "I found a way that we could be together."

"What way?"

"It must wait. Nathara has entered alliance with Iain Campbell, and great woes may fall this day if they aren't stopped."

Struan shook his head. "That can't be. He has offered a fine bridal-piece."

"Only because he has no intentions of honoring it. He will come to your father's hamlet, yes, but Laren will not be with him. Instead, he will bring his soldiers, and he will fight you."

Duncan clasped Struan's arm. "We must stop him."

Struan paid no attention to the threat to his hamlet. "What of Laren?"

Lily's eyes filled with tears. "She is cursed, Struan. I heard the details, and they are vile. Today, she will fall into a trance and be drawn to the Rocking Stone. She will die there. I don't know how, nor how it can be averted."

"No . . ." Struan bolted away without warning, without thought.

Duncan's blood ran cold in fear. "Lily, what do we do?"

"Follow him. Duncan, I fear it will be too late."

"It can't be." He fought to maintain reason as his mind raced in fear. "We'll need a horse. Back to the hamlet."

Lily climbed onto his shoulder and clung to his hair. "A horse has good speed. Oh, but I fear even wings haven't the speed to reach the Rocking Stone in time . . ."

Chapter 6

Struan's gray horse galloped ahead as Duncan and Lily raced to catch him. Lily clung to Duncan's hair. It flew around her, a black curtain. Wind whipped in her face, and her hair entwined with his as Duncan's horse bounded along the forest path.

They burst from the forest, into the meadow. Struan's horse charged across the field. Disrupted ewes called to their lambs as the flock scattered.

"Oh, no!" Lily saw a woman walking slowly up the mound toward the Rocking Stone.

Duncan slowed his horse to a canter and shaded his eyes against the morning sun. "Laren!"

"If she reaches that Stone before we do . . ."

Duncan urged his horse into a desperate gallop. Struan neared the mound but Laren reached the Stone first. Lily held tight as Duncan's horse leapt and surged up the steep incline.

Struan leapt from his horse's back. "Laren! Stop!" His voice echoed across the meadow. Struan ran toward her, but she didn't notice his presence. Duncan jumped down and ran up behind them.

"What is going on, Lily? She's alone. How can she die?"

Lily looked frantically around. Her gaze fixed on a dark bush. "That shrub. It wasn't there last night, Duncan. And it has borne fruit. Dark fruit."

"Struan! The berries! Stop her!"

Laren's hand reached slowly. She was entranced, hearing no one, seeing no one. She took a single dark berry. Struan leapt toward her, but too late. She ate the berry, then turned toward him. For a brief, horrifying moment, she seemed to know him. Her face contorted, she mouthed his name, and crumpled to the earth.

Struan fell to his knees and gathered her body into his arms, sobbing. Duncan knelt beside him. Tears swarmed Lily's vision. Pure love, shattered for all time. And worse, the grim death would be repeated over and over until Laren's very soul was shattered, too.

Duncan laid his hand on Struan's shoulder, but Struan buried his face in Laren's hair. The morning sun disappeared beneath a sudden haze, and a mist fell in place of the light. Duncan and Lily waited silently as Struan held his beloved, crying.

Struan looked to Lily, his face stricken with grief. "A curse. What evil could she have done to deserve this fate from your kind?"

Anger soaked his voice, and Lily's heart racked with pity. "She did nothing, Struan. She was innocent. It was her father's doing, and that of a cruel and vengeful queen."

The wind swirled into a dark funnel. Nathara's laughter came before her appearance. "'Cruel and vengeful'? Is this what you say of your queen, Lily?"

Nathara appeared atop the Rocking Stone, awash in an evil glow. "Do you mourn her now, mortal? Then know this death is but the first."

Struan started to rise, but Duncan stopped him. "She baits you, brother. Wait." Duncan faced Nathara without fear. "You say it is the first. You can take nothing more."

Nathara's mouth curled into a mocking smile. "Can't I? Every soul has its route to follow. And this girl will be born again, into a new body. But she didn't fulfill her rightful life this time, so she will repeat its creation again . . . and again. And each time she reaches her twenty-first birthday, my curse will affect her, and hold her entranced. She will walk to this stone . . . and die."

"No . . ." Struan eased Laren's body to the soft grass, then drew his sword.

Nathara's laughter bit through the damp air. "There is nothing you can do to harm me, mortal. I am impenetrable, more powerful than anything."

"Not anything, Nathara . . ." Another voice echoed, and Titania appeared in the air beside the stone. "Much evil you have done this day, much that cannot be repaired. But no spell exists that can't be broken under the right circumstances."

Nathara laughed again, though she retreated from the Seelie queen. "What 'circumstances,' sister? Even I do not know. The girl is dead. Whatever 'circumstances' she might have found to avert her spell, it is too late."

"In this lifetime, yes. But in future lives, it is possible . . ."

Struan lowered his sword and turned his attention to Titania. "Laren can still be saved, so that she may live her full life in another time?"

Titania hesitated. "It may be . . ."

Lily emerged from Duncan's hair and peeked at Titania. "If she hadn't eaten the berry, would she have lived?"

Titania ignored Lily's question, but Nathara adjusted her dark wings, a triumphant glee lighting her eyes. "She would have lived out her life, but her curse would be unbroken. Every hundred years, she will begin again. If her spell remains unbroken after a thousand years, her soul will wither and become part of the darkness that fills the netherworld."

Duncan gripped Struan's shoulder. "She may free herself."

"I must help her." Struan faced Titania. "You can help me."

Titania's gaze flicked to Lily, then averted as if the sight caused her pain. "I cannot. It is beyond the power of a Seelie to alter the spell of her sister . . ."

Lily's brow furrowed. "You're sisters?"

Titania still avoided looking her way. "We are."

Lily forced herself to ignore the Seelie queen's dislike of her. It didn't matter now. And she deserved it. But for Laren and Struan . . . "There must be a way."

Titania didn't answer. She waved her hand, and the mound of gold appeared. Lily glanced at Nathara. The location of the gold was revealed, but Nathara didn't seem surprised.

"You knew where it was all along. Why did you send me to seek it out?"

Nathara's hard mouth knit in a frown and she refused to answer. Titania still didn't look her way, but she sighed. "It was a test, I suspect."

"A test? What kind of test?"

"That is up to you, Lily."

Titania didn't explain further. She hovered above the gold, and placed her hand in its midst. She withdrew an unadorned golden dagger, then presented it to Lily.

Lily took the dagger. It throbbed with power, so much so that she felt dizzy. "It is strong. But what do I do?"

Titania's face revealed no expression, no emotion. " 'Tis a charmed dirk. With it, you can create a single spell of great magnitude. You cannot undo Nathara's curse, nor restore Laren Campbell to life, but you can create whatever is in your heart."

Lily stared hard at the dirk. *Anything.* "It can make me human."

"It can."

Lily looked at Duncan. Tears filled his warm brown eyes. For his brother, and for their own thwarted love. "What do I do?"

"Whatever is in your heart, my love."

Lily looked to Titania, and saw an expression of both sorrow and hope. And something else. *Love.* She saw Nathara from the corner of her eye, trembling with evil expectation and impending triumph.

Lily allowed herself to see Struan, his dark face stricken with tears as he bent over his beloved. And Laren, dead before her life began, separated endlessly from her love, for no fault of her own. Laren had no choice.

Lily had a choice. She clasped the dirk to her breast, then hovered before Duncan. "I love you with all the power of my soul. I have always loved you, and I always will. But if I do not act out of goodness, my love is without worth."

He didn't respond, but one tear fell to his cheek. He smiled and nodded. He understood. Lily reached to touch his face. She caught his tear in her hand, clasping its moisture, then pressed her hand to her breast. She closed her eyes, and she saw all that might have been. Herself in Duncan's arms, kissing. Herself with his child at her breast. Herself, an old woman whose eyes glittered with sweet memory, and eternal love.

She saw herself alone, but loved. By him. And by herself.

Lily flew to the Rocking Stone. She moved before Nathara and held the dirk upright. "Struan, I cannot remove the curse upon your beloved. Only Laren can find the answer to that which afflicts her. But I can help you to save her from untimely death, if you wish it. Do you?"

Struan rose to his feet and nodded. "I do."

"The power of this dirk will last for a thousand years. As long as you keep it with you, you will have the power to save your beloved. You will awaken from the sleep I shall place on you five days before Laren's twenty-first birthday. You will know your task, and what must be done. Each time you resurrect, you will have the choice of breaking your own spell by letting her die, or continue the cycle by saving her. When you have saved her, you must return to your sleep. I have no power to give you more time."

Nathara quivered with fury. "I will not let this stand. Your spell is well placed, Lily. But I will add to it. If he fails to break the curse within a thousand years, the dirk will revert to my power, and his soul will belong to the Unseelie realm."

Struan smiled despite the threat. "I will not fail. Lily, I accept your spell, and I will find a way to free Laren. If it takes a thousand years, so be it."

Lily nodded, though hot tears streamed down her face. "Then take this dirk, and keep it with you always. If you lose it, you die, Struan, and you will not wake again. I am sorry I cannot do more."

"It is enough."

Titania moved closer to Struan, her ethereal face sweet and beautiful. Everything that Lily longed to be. "I, too, will give you something to aid your quest, Struan. 'Prove your love when the sun shines in the midnight sky, and the light will shine on your fate as well.'"

Struan shook his head. "I don't understand. What does . . . ?"

Titania held up her hand. "Ask me no more. When the time comes, you will know."

Struan accepted the Seelie queen's pronouncement. He turned to Duncan and touched his shoulder. "I love you, brother. I leave you at the edge of battle, but know that I believe in your skill." He smiled through his tears and withdrew his sword from its scabbard. He handed it to Duncan. "Find your way, and remember me."

Duncan took the sword and bowed. "I will never forget."

Struan knelt before Lily, and she placed the dirk in his hands. "Hold it to your chest, and sleep. When the time comes, you will wake, and Laren will be near."

Struan gathered Laren into his arms and gently kissed her forehead. "I will not fail you, my beloved. The power of my love will be as great a thousand years hence as it is today. And one day, no power on earth or heaven beyond will be great enough to stand in our way."

He kissed her again, then lay her gently to the soft ground. He faced the Rocking Stone, and held the dirk to his chest. It glowed with unearthly power, until the glow surrounded him and became part of him. Lily trembled, knowing the good she had done, and knowing the choice had been hers.

No longer was she the result of her circumstances. She was free.

Golden light radiated in and through Struan's body. When it eased and abated, he lay beside Laren, neither dead nor alive. Waiting. Lily looked to Titania and knew even the Seelie queen couldn't predict his fate.

The rain stilled, and the clouds parted again for the sun. Duncan knelt beside his brother, holding his hand, his head bowed. "Fare well."

Titania cast a spray of shimmering gold dust over Duncan and Struan. "When your battle is over, Duncan, lay his body in Loch Fyne. The water sprites will protect him until the time comes for him to wake."

"I will."

Duncan rose and looked to Lily. They both knew that her choice sundered them forever, yet there was no other way. He smiled, though his dark eyes glittered with tears. "I told you that you were good, Lily. Never doubt again."

"I wanted so much to be with you." Lily fought tears. "But love doesn't need fulfillment to endure. I shall cherish you always."

"And I, you." Across the southern edge of the meadow, a band of mounted warriors appeared. "Campbell."

Nathara grinned with vile delight as the warriors aimed toward Tearlach's hamlet. "He will attack your hamlet, poor mortal. This day will end in misery."

Duncan's expression turned grim, but resolute as he fingered his brother's sword. "The day ends when it ends, Nathara. I will have a say in its outcome, and what I do will come from within."

Nathara's laugh mocked his words, but Duncan ignored her. He reached to touch Lily's face. "You know what I must do. Lily, you are in my heart."

Lily clasped his finger tight. "Take me with you."

"Not to battle, Lily." He took her in his palm, then pressed his mouth gently on the top of her head. His love soaked into her soul. "You are free now, Lily. You're not bound to Nathara, nor anyone. And I will do what I must do. Because of you, I will do it knowing I hold the power of my destiny."

He placed her back on the Rocking Stone and mounted his horse for battle. Lily clasped her hands over her breast. "I love you so."

He didn't look back. The horse bounded away, and Duncan rode in pursuit of his enemy.

Lily watched him go. He was beyond her aid now. She sank to her knees and wept. Titania settled beside her. "Leave us, Nathara. You have lost this day, and the balance of power remains in my favor. I banish you from the realm of Loch Fyne. Take your mischief elsewhere."

Nathara rose in a cloud of black dust. "I will not forget your treachery, Titania. Our battle will continue."

Titania sighed. "I know that. Without darkness, there can be no light. So it was, and always will be."

"Until the darkness reigns in triumph."

"Until it comes to love the light."

Nathara departed in a violent spew of wind, leaving Lily alone beside Titania. The good queen brushed a strand of hair from Lily's cheek. "You are as I remember you, my little firefly."

Firefly. Lily gazed at the queen in wonder. "Firefly . . . I have been called that term before . . . by you."

Titania smiled. "By me. Your mother."

"That's not possible. I am a dark being, an Unseelie. I have done much ill."

"No being is without flaw."

"You are without flaw."

"Pride was my failing. Between the Seelies and our dark cousins, there has always been a struggle for power. But did that power come from within, or from the circumstances of our birth? Nathara baited my pride with an insult to my youngest daughter. To you. And I rashly asserted that Seelies were beyond affliction."

"She tricked you! She told me so."

"I know. But it was my own weakness that allowed her to gain control of you. She took you from me, and I couldn't get you back until you proved your goodness is within. Today, you did that, Lily."

"I almost didn't. Last night, I followed you. I would have told Nathara where your gold was hidden, so that she would make me human. So I could be with Duncan."

"But you didn't."

"Only because I felt I had to warn Struan."

"You waited for hours before you overheard Iain Campbell and Nathara, my dear."

Lily's mouth gaped. "You followed me last night, too!"

"I have always followed you. Love is strong, Lily. I loved you, good or bad. Just as Duncan MacLachlan loves you."

Lily bowed her head. "Yet because of my choice, he will marry another."

"You have chosen, little firefly. Now Duncan must choose for himself."

Chapter 7

TEARLACH MacLachlan's hamlet was surrounded. Duncan heard the clamor of battle through the thicket of trees. It echoed across the quiet loch, and back again. His clan was outnumbered, unprepared for assault. Instead, they were garbed for ceremony. Iain Campbell had arranged for that.

Duncan had one thing in his favor. Surprise. But a man loved by a faerie understood surprise. He readied his sword and steadied his horse. He closed his eyes and saw Lily's image. She was all he wanted, and he couldn't have her.

She loved him. That was enough.

Duncan opened his eyes, and he saw everything that stood in his way. Campbell's warriors far outnumbered Tearlach's thegns. The Campbells wore mail shirts, helms. Tearlach's thegns were half-drunk from festivities, and few had bothered with weaponry.

Duncan dismounted and released his horse to the forest. He moved through the dark trees like a hunter. No one noticed his arrival. His clan was surrounded, pressed back around Tearlach's central hall. From within, Duncan heard the terrified cries of children as the warriors clashed.

Iain Campbell was positioned behind his warriors, but Tearlach stood in front of his people, wielding a claymore with two hands. Just behind Tearlach, Irsa the Frail pummeled his opponent with a power twice his size. Beside Irsa, Gavina MacKinnon wielded a hefty club. She felled a stout warrior, then turned to another with equal fury.

They wouldn't stand long. Duncan drew his sword and leapt into the fray. Two Campbells fell before Iain reacted. " 'Tis only MacLachlan's lesser son. Take him, and the old man's line will forever die!"

Despite their leader's command, his warriors hesitated. Duncan strode toward them without fear. Some backed away. "Stop him!"

Duncan didn't scan the area for obstacles. He felt it without looking. Lily had been right. His power was within.

Duncan fixed his eyes on his father's enemies and positioned his sword. Not a battle of man against man, but one against many. And still, he had no fear.

From the outer limits of his vision, he saw his father turn. He saw Tearlach's astonishment. Duncan smiled and nodded, then faced three men wielding hatchets.

Duncan's mind worked with precision. He heard a small echo in his thoughts. *"Leap!"* Duncan leapt to one side, whirled to face his opponent, then flicked the man's weapon from his grasp. Almost casual in its ease. The warrior released a startled yelp, then scrambled back.

Two men charged, both gripping heavy lances. *"Right! Left!"* Duncan jerked to one side, then back. He turned and watched as the two men stumbled and crashed into each other. Both collapsed, stunned by the collision.

Duncan shook his head in mock disapproval, then turned to the next.

"Fools! He has tricked you!" Iain Campbell's voice shook with fury, his face burned red. Still, he remained safely encased among his thegns. "Is no one here a man of courage?"

A young swordsman took an obvious gulp of air, then stepped forward. Duncan hesitated. A child, no more than fourteen years. "I will defend you, Laird Iain."

The boy poised his weapon, and Duncan's heart quailed. A wooden sword. A child's toy, sharpened, yet ineffectual in combat. Duncan allowed the boy's tentative approach. The boy slashed too quickly, allowing an easy response. Duncan tapped the wooden weapon aside, but the boy slashed again.

Duncan sighed, then engaged a more fitting response. The boy leapt forward. Duncan stepped aside. The boy stumbled, then gathered himself up, and tried again. Duncan parried each wild thrust until the boy began to learn.

"Keep the weapon up, chest high, lad."

The boy paused, then obeyed.

"Balance. Keep your feet positioned apart."

The boy adjusted his position, then hesitated as if awaiting further instruction. The Campbell warriors eased back, content for the moment to hold Tearlach's group cornered against the main hall. They appeared stunned by the casual instruction amid their leader's battle scheme.

"Watch for an opening." The boy's brow furrowed intently as he fixed his gaze on Duncan. Duncan drooped his sword and the boy stabbed with gleeful pride.

"*Flip . . . Forward!*" Duncan flipped, somersaulting through the air and over the boy's head. He bounded once and jumped to the top of a wheat bin. The boy stared, mouth agape.

"And expect the unexpected."

The boy grinned and nodded, but Iain Campbell screamed in fury. "Take him!"

Duncan held himself ready as Iain's group approached the wheat bin. No one reached higher than his feet, so their thrusts were easily diverted. Battle became a pleasure. He could do anything.

His success heartened Tearlach's defenders. Irsa the Frail waved and shouted. Gavina struck Irsa in the ribs. "Heed the battle, little man!" Duncan laughed. In the midst of battle, he found joy.

Iain Campbell was finding defeat less pleasant. He'd made a bargain with the dark queen. Duncan vowed silently to see that Campbell's vow wasn't honored.

"Take their chieftain, force surrender!"

This seemed a more welcoming task to his warriors. They backed away from Duncan, and focused their attack once again on Tearlach. "Keep this bungling madman apart from the rest! Kill the old man."

Iain shouted orders into chaos. Duncan tried to maintain reason as he surveyed the possibilities. He'd distracted them from his father's position with success, but the fight resumed, this time in desperation. Tearlach needed a stronger defense, and Duncan was all he had.

A heavyset, red-haired warrior lunged toward Tearlach. Tearlach didn't back down. Instead, the old man charged. The warrior rammed his blunt sword at Tearlach. Tearlach deflected the blow, but his own sword shattered. And the warrior raised his weapon to kill.

Iain's warriors stood between Duncan and his father. Duncan looked down. He heard Lily's small voice echoing in his memory. *"Leap!"*

He leapt. He landed. And he did not fall. Duncan knocked the warrior back, then caught the weapon in midair. Tearlach stared, dark eyes wide with wonder . . . and perhaps shame.

Duncan bowed as he passed his father their opponent's weapon. "I will not fail you, sire."

The old man's face changed. His dark eyes softened with tears. Tears that Duncan had never seen, nor dared to imagine. Tearlach ignored his attackers as he placed his hand on Duncan's shoulder. "My son, you never have."

Duncan bowed again, then took position beside his father. Duncan's unexpected arrival heartened Tearlach. The old man fought like a youth in his first battle. The Campbell warriors moved back in retreat and threw aside their weapons, but the boy Duncan had instructed didn't back away.

He knelt before Duncan and placed the wooden sword at his feet, peering up with eyes wide in admiration. "I am Darach of the Cruithne. I am at your service, lord." The boy faced Duncan rather than Tearlach. Tearlach reached down and swatted the boy.

"You are *my* servant, boy. For the time being. Until I'm dead, which will be long hence."

The boy's eyes rounded, sufficiently reduced to fear and respect. He snapped around to face Tearlach. Duncan laughed. "It appears the Campbells are once again our allies."

Iain Campbell still gripped his weapon, hatred and fear glittering in his eyes. "Never your ally, MacLachlan. Never."

"You don't speak for your people, Iain." Duncan stepped toward him, anger surging through his limbs. "Or did your people request the murder of your daughter on her wedding day? Did they approve your secret tryst with the dark queen?"

A low gasp rose from the Campbell warriors, turning to outraged growls. They retrieved their weapons, but this time, their target was Iain himself.

Tearlach gripped Duncan's arm, his aged face pale. "Laren Campbell? She is dead?"

"She fell to a curse agreed upon by her own sire, that he be spared the death himself."

"And Struan?" Tearlach's voice came small and without force. He already knew.

Duncan drew a long breath and set his hand over his father's. For the first time, he realized how frail the old man was, how vulnerable. "Struan has chosen to follow her. But I do not believe his fate is without hope."

"I knew, when you came alone. I knew . . ." Tearlach raised his claymore and strode toward the cowering Iain Campbell. "For my son, you will pay. For your daughter, your shame and damnation are endless."

"Sire, wait. Another has a claim of more vengeance than you."

Iain looked around as if haunted, terrified by the unseen. Tearlach shook his head and frowned in disgust. "Lost his mind, he has."

A dark, vaporous cloud appeared through the forest, moving slowly toward Iain. MacLachlans and Campbells moved aside, silent, and Darach positioned himself close at Duncan's side. Gavina clutched Irsa's thin arm, the first sign of fear Duncan had seen in the stout woman.

"Beansidhe, Beansidhe! The Dark Ones, they bring death . . ." Gavina's wail turned to silence as the cloud expanded and settled above Iain. He stumbled backward, but the cloud followed him. He fell to his knees, begging incoherently.

Nathara rose from the cloud, a dark red glow around her which exaggerated her size. "You failed me. This life is lost to you, Iain Campbell. You will wither in the caverns of the Dark Burgh, until I think of a better use for you."

"No, let me . . ." The vapor surrounded Iain and became part of him. Duncan watched, horrified, yet unable to look away. It seemed to him that the darkness was drawn into Iain, rather than forced. He had drawn it to himself, created his own dark fate.

Darach shuddered and clasped Duncan's hand. " 'Tis gruesome, this power the wee folk wield."

"No, Darach. There are many powers and many fates in this world.

Iain chose his own." Duncan sighed. "We choose our own paths, and draw to us what is already ours."

Tearlach nodded. "You speak well, and truly. But it is a great man who chooses strength and courage when surrounded by darkness."

Duncan met his father's gaze, and saw for the first time, respect. Not for his victory, but for what he was. A man responsible for his own fate. Neither spoke, but the balance between them was restored.

Tearlach watched as Nathara's vapor rose, leaving nothing. "We've seen the last of him. Good."

Nathara's cold laughter echoed over the hamlet, and the black cloud lifted and moved away into the forest. Darach took a quick gasp. "Chilling sound, wasn't it?"

Duncan sighed, but he felt no fear. He saw a balance in life that he hadn't seen before. "Without darkness, there can be no light."

Tearlach groaned. "You are *not* to become a sage! My son is a warrior, a wise leader. But not a sage. No beards."

Duncan might have won Tearlach's respect and earned his pride, but Tearlach still possessed qualities worthy of a tyrant. "I have no such intentions, sire." He paused. "Not at this time."

Tearlach groaned again, but he didn't argue. The balance had shifted. Duncan smiled.

Women and children came from the central hall. The Campbell warriors looked to Duncan for reassurance, but he said nothing. Tearlach grumbled and passed his claymore to a young thegn.

Irsa the Frail was already telling an exaggerated version of Duncan's success, but Gavina rolled her eyes and shouldered her bludgeon. "Never seen one of the wee folk. Never want to again."

Tearlach sputtered in agreement. "Faeries! What kind of fool gets involved with the wee folk and expects to see the light side of night again?"

Duncan sighed. "There are good faeries, sire."

"Indeed?" Tearlach's eyes narrowed. "How would you . . . ?" Duncan started to speak, but Tearlach held up his hand. "No, spare me. I don't want to know."

* * *

Laren Campbell was buried on the MacLachlan land looking west over Loch Fyne, but Duncan took Struan to the center of the loch and laid him in the blue water. Tears clouded his vision as Struan's strong, still body sank below the dark surface. An unnatural end that was no ending.

Struan disappeared, but far below the surface came a golden-white glow. Duncan allowed his tears to fall. He watched until the glow faded and disappeared. Struan was among the water sprites, beyond Duncan's aid. He had a thousand years to find what he had lost.

Duncan rowed slowly back to shore, half expecting to find Lily waiting for him. Lily, hiding beneath a mushroom, surrounded by violets as she spied on his activities. She wasn't there. He was alone.

Duncan returned to the hamlet and found the MacLachlans and Campbells feasting together. He stood watching them, silent as they honored Struan's life and wept for Laren's untimely end. When the feast ended, Tearlach rose and waved Duncan forward.

"Our clan endures because of you. Henceforth, you will be known as Duncan the Agile—my son, and laird chieftain of this clan."

Duncan the Agile. *"By the end of our tenure as companions . . ."* Duncan looked up to the new stars and sighed. *The end.* He had survived the day. He had earned his father's approval.

"Tonight, you will take a wife in hand-fast, and the future of our claim here will be assured." Tearlach didn't wait for Duncan's response. He beamed with pride and happiness as he drew Alpina MacKay forward.

"This female is your best choice, my son. Young Cailleach seems to have another, more . . . immediate offer, and Gavina doesn't want a husband." Tearlach hesitated and cleared his throat, lowering his voice. "I wouldn't argue that point if I were you. Stout woman, she is. Capable of inflicting any number of woes upon a man."

Duncan tried to smile, but his face felt numb. Tearlach slapped his back in a friendly gesture. "Take this one, Duncan. Heard the old crones . . ." Tearlach paused and coughed. "Women, that is, of the hamlet mentioning you looked good in tandem. Dark hair, light hair. Picts like a contrast."

Tearlach had partaken too much mead. Duncan eyed Alpina. A shy smile formed on her lips. She peered up at him through lowered lashes with eyes that were . . . "Too small."

Tearlach started to smile and nod, then caught himself. "What?"

"Sire, your faith in me rewards a lifetime of wish, and does me great honor. But I cannot follow you, nor take the role you give me. You have many cousins, many nephews. Choose one of them for your heir. I cannot do as you wish."

"What?" Tearlach's voice came louder this time. "What do you mean you can't . . . ?"

"I will not marry—"

Alpina's sharp hiss stopped his words. "Sassenach! Why must I bear the shame of my mother's mindless rutting?"

"What?" Tearlach and Duncan spoke at once.

Alpina pointed at Duncan, her fair face altered by fury. "He knows. Somehow, he learned the secret of my birth, and will not stain MacLachlan blood with that of the Saxon."

"I know nothing of your birth, Alpina."

"Aye, my father was Sassenach; my mother, his whore. But she knew better than to answer his plea and return to his dismal land! A MacKay laird desired her, with far more to offer. Another lord has asked for me. I will have power in this land despite you, Duncan MacLachlan!"

Tearlach cleared his throat as Alpina spun away, fury in her stride. He faced Duncan, looking grim. "That one may not be the best choice, after all, son. Grasping. Perhaps Gavina might reconsider."

"No, sire. This night, I spend alone."

Chapter 8

DUNCAN walked along the shores of Loch Fyne, but Lily didn't come. He sat alone until midnight, but he heard no sound save crickets and frogs. The night was warm, the air still. Fireflies came one by one and sent tiny lights into life around him.

The full moon rose above the loch and glinted on the mushrooms and violets where he had first found Lily. He half expected to see her there, peeping up at him with her wide, blue eyes, but there was nothing.

"Lily, don't leave me." Duncan rose to his feet and paced through the fireflies. His mind worked in agitation. "Maybe we can't live as lovers, maybe we can't rightfully marry." He puffed an angry breath. "But a true union of bonded hearts is more than that. It has to be. You are mine. I am yours. We belong together."

No answer came on the wind. He hadn't expected it to. Duncan sat on a flat rock and bowed his head. "I want you at my side, and no other. All that I wished for, I have, Lily. My father's admiration, my clan. It means nothing if I don't have you."

Duncan stared out across the loch. In his mind, he saw her skimming the surface like a hummingbird, dabbling her toes. Chattering ceaselessly about the nature of insects and birds. "If I don't have you . . ."

"I've found you another one." Tearlach spoke behind him, and Duncan jumped to his feet. A woman stood just behind Tearlach, one Duncan had never seen before. She didn't speak, and her image was veiled in darkness. The old man didn't give up easily.

"Sire, I will not marry." He paused. There were other alternatives for a man's life. "I will become a sage."

Tearlach groaned. "You haven't looked at this one yet. I haven't learned much about her family, but she has the look of a Pict. Fine bone structure, wavy hair. You'll like her. If you'd bother to look, after all the trouble I went to . . ."

Duncan sighed. Tearlach could be persistent. Well, he could be persistent, too. "No."

The girl puffed a breath of exasperation. "If he prefers sagedom to me, then I will leave. He is smaller than I imagined, his hair appears tangled, and he speaks often to frogs."

Her voice sounded familiar. Duncan moved to look at her more closely. She turned her head away. "Do I know you?"

"I'm sure you do not. Perhaps you think you do, but you are wrong. If you truly loved me, you would know . . ." She started away and bumped into an overhanging tree branch. "These trees are so much lower than they used to be."

Tearlach sighed. "I knew when I saw her march into our hamlet that she was the one for you. Walked right in, as if she belonged there, and crashed into my door. As if she expected to fly right through it."

She huffed. "It was a small oversight on my part, brought about by the inconvenience of entering a new hamlet, as well as a certain amount of distraction via the circumstances . . ."

"Long-winded girl, I'll admit . . ."

Duncan's heart froze in his chest, his breath stopped. "Lily."

She peered around Tearlach's shoulder. "You are threatened by my new stature. That is why you don't want me, and after all . . ."

Tearlach held up his hand. "Cease, woman! Your 'stature' is minimal. And my son isn't small."

"He's smaller than he used to be."

Duncan couldn't speak. His heart thundered in his chest. He gathered himself together. Perhaps his mind played tricks, and gave him what he wanted to see. She had forfeited her chance at a human form. It couldn't be.

"Sire, if you would leave us alone together, we might find reason to alter our opinions, and consent to your wish."

Tearlach hesitated, then nodded. "I will go. A conversation between the two of you might be more than an old man can endure. Marry the girl, and you become chieftain. That means you will care for me in my failing years, and request my advice at all times before—"

"Cease!" The woman gave Tearlach a small shove and then stood back for him to leave.

Tearlach sighed with deep misery, then headed back toward his hamlet, still grumbling. "What have I done, what have I done? What if they have bairns? Unless they take after myself, of course . . ."

"He is contentious in the extreme. I suspect you will become more and more like him as you age. I do not know if I can subject myself to—"

"Who are you?"

"You don't know?" She seemed insulted. "I am not surprised."

Duncan seized her arm and positioned her so that the full moon shone on her face. Her hair was long, but not to her knees. This might be accounted for, because her legs were long.

He studied her critically, analyzing every feature the moonlight revealed. The first thing he saw was a tight, annoyed frown. She didn't like his scrutiny.

"I am not livestock for your inspection."

Duncan pulled her into his arms and stopped her words with a kiss.

She braced in surprise, then sank into his arms. Her soft lips played against his, as if she had dreamt this moment all her life. Her body pressed close to him. A woman's body, full and warm and lush.

She kissed him eagerly, trailing her mouth over his, then kissing his face, his jaw. Her breath came in shivering gasps. "Duncan, I love you so."

Duncan eased her back and looked into her moonlit eyes. "Lily, it is you."

A frown tugged at her lips. Lips he could kiss over and over. "I know that. I am surprised and not entirely pleased that you did not."

Duncan smiled. "It's dark."

"Love sees in darkness."

"You're tall."

"I have always been tall. It is a matter of perspective."

"Your hair is shorter."

"Only because my body is longer now."

"You're wearing slippers."

"The increased substance of my physical body places pressure on the soles of my feet, which I found immediately painful when encountering rubble and rocks . . ."

"Your 'new stature' doesn't reduce speech, does it?"

She paused. "No. It does not."

Duncan laughed, and his joy came from deep in his soul. "How did you find the power to transform yourself?"

"You chose to be with me no matter what."

"How do you know? And if you were here, why didn't you come to me?"

"I wasn't here. Titania watched you among the fireflies. And when she saw that you had truly chosen me, and no other, she restored me to my human form."

" 'Restored'?"

"When the Ancient Ones find a place in the world, they return to what they were, to live here as they had first intended. You are my place."

"I am your place." Duncan swallowed to contain emotion. "And you are mine. Lily, I would follow you to the netherworld if you asked it."

Lily placed her hand on his face. "You are beautiful in darkness. I think that if we went there together, it would no longer be dark."

"We carry our light within."

"Your father warned me that you've been speaking like a sage, and that it might prove trying at times."

"Did he?"

"He said also that you vaulted into combat and saved him, and that he wronged you on many counts. It pleased me that he has seen the error of his ways."

"It pleased me, too. I have you to thank, Lily."

"I know. And you will thank me in many ways. The first will be to marry me, and then see that I am pleased in such a manner as begins with kissing."

"It will begin with kissing, and it will end in bliss."

She touched his mouth, quieting him. "It will never end."

ISBEL

Hannah Howell

Chapter 1

Scottish Borders, Fall 1362

H<small>E</small> *lay deep in the wood, blood seeping from his wounds and darken-ing the leaves he had collapsed upon. The late October frost was already creeping over the ground he was sprawled on, glistening, shim-mering in the moonlight. His horse stood nervously by, its eyes white with fear, loyalty its only tether and that fraying rapidly as the night deepened. The man murmured in helplessness, and the threats that lurked in the night shadows crept even closer.*

"Nay!" Isbel cried out, sitting up. Her rope-strung bed creaked its protest at her abrupt movement.

Isbel shivered and wiped the sweat from her face with the corner of her white linen sheet. She could still see the man clearly, easy prey for the unseen enemy that inched toward him. It was a bad night for a man to be helpless and alone in the dark wood. It was a bad night for anyone to be out. She wanted to ignore her dream, but the man called to her, silently but with a power she could not fight. A soft curse escaped her lips as she got up and began to tug on her clothes.

"And what are ye about, lassie?" snapped a gruff voice from the doorway.

As she yanked on her hose, struggling to do so without revealing too much of her legs, Isbel cast the little brown man in the doorway a cross look. A brownie, being barely three feet tall, was not much of a protector, but Pullhair had assumed that role with a vengeance. He stood firm in her bedchamber doorway, stiff and narrow-eyed. She was certain that even his shaggy brown beard was bristling. It was not going to be easy to get around him.

"I have had a dream," Isbel replied.

"And it told ye to rise and get dressed, did it?"

"It told me that there is a mon who is in sore need of my help."

"A mon, eh?" Pullhair further narrowed his eyes until they nearly disappeared beneath his bushy brown eyebrows. "So, now ye are creeping off into the night to meet a mon. Dreaming about a mon too," he muttered and shook his head.

"The mon is wounded, alone, and in the woods." She patted her cat, Slayer, and started toward the door.

For one long moment she and Pullhair stared at each other. Isbel knew that, if he pushed her to it, she would physically move the little man out of her way. That could be risky, for brownies were easily offended and even more easily angered. Not only could Pullhair stop coming to her towerhouse and working all the night long, making her lonely life not only tolerable but a great deal easier, but he could well do some great mischief before he stormed away. Isbel knew she would take that risk, however. The call to go to the man was too strong. Pullhair suddenly stepped aside, and as she passed through the door, Isbel wondered if he had seen in her eyes the determination she felt.

"Ye cannae go out there," Pullhair snapped as he followed her to the great hall.

Isbel turned her back to the little man and rolled her eyes. He was fretting over her like some old woman. His agitation was affecting the spirits that roamed the halls of her towerhouse. She had left the family lands of Loch Fyne in the vain hope of escaping her gifts only to discover that they had grown stronger in her new home. In fact, she was sure the shadows of Loch Fyne were not half as populated as the ones around Bandal, her towerhouse. She often thought it a good thing that her husband had not lived long enough to realize the full extent of her gifts or just how magical his lands were.

She cursed softly as she had to wrestle her thick woolen cloak free of a ghostly hand. "Your fretting has stirred the ghosties, Pullhair," she complained. "Now even they try to hinder me." She tugged on her cloak and reached for her walking stick standing next to the heavy oak doors of the great hall.

"I ne'er thought I would side with those spirits, but I now wish them more power," Pullhair grumbled, crossing his arms over his narrow chest. "You should think on your own safety. If that mortal mon was fool enough to get himself wounded and lost in the woods, then let him rot."

"Such a hard heart ye do have. I fear I dinnae have that blessing."

"What ye dinnae have is the wit to ken what ye should fear."

"Oh, I fear. I am terrified to go out into the forest at night, but I must go. The dream has ended but its strength lingers. The mon calls to me, Pullhair. 'Tis as if he has a firm grip upon my arm. Nay, upon my heart and mind, upon the verra soul of me. I cannae ignore his need, his cries for help. I *must* go to him."

"Do ye think he has gifts, as ye do?" Pullhair asked, revealing a tiny hint of interest.

"I dinnae ken. At this moment, he has power o'er me. I sense that he doesnae ken the full peril of his position. He only fears for his weel-being, for the dangers represented by untended wounds and the cold."

"Then go. Fetch your lordling. But dinnae go blindly into the night. The Sluagh ride tonight."

Isbel shivered. The Sluagh were the most formidable of the faerie folk. It was said that they were the unforgiven dead. They battled each other throughout the long, clear, frosty nights, staining the rocks below them with their blood. Tonight was clear and frosty. If the Sluagh found the man in the forest, they would take him up and command him to follow them, making him slay and maim people for them. If such enslavement was not torture enough, the Sluagh were said to be pitiless masters; Isbel wondered if that was the danger she sensed approaching the man. She had to try and save him from that living hell. Even the Unseelie Court, the malignant faeries, could not torture a man as unceasingly as the Host of the Unforgiven Dead.

"I dinnae go unprotected, my friend," she assured the brownie. "I have my cross hammered out of iron hung about my neck. I have bread and salt in the pocket of my gown and a flask of holy water to sprinkle about if need be. I also carry my walking stick carved from the branch of a rowan tree and banded with iron. And just this morning I said prayers for protection beneath a holly tree."

"Mayhap ye forsaw this."

"Mayhap." She started for the door, inwardly shoring up her flagging courage. "Howbeit, I believe I have enough gifts. I dinnae think I wish to add the one that curses me with the ability to ken what is to be."

"It can be a help as weel as a curse."

Isbel frowned when she realized that Pullhair was following her out into the bailey. "I dinnae need an escort to the gates. I believe I can find them on my own."

"I have decided to go with you."

Isbel stopped and stared at him. Even in the depths of her surprise she found herself musing that he was probably the only person, save for other denizens of the netherworld, that a tiny woman like her could tower over. The runt of the litter was what she had always been called. She occasionally wondered if the opportunity to be of a superior height was why she was so tolerant of so many of the creatures of the spirit world.

"Ye ken that ye dinnae wish to do that, Pullhair," she said in a very gentle tone, hesitant to cause him any offense. "I ken that ye have no love of the faeries, the good and the bad, and there are a great many things lurking out in the dark that hold no great love for brownies either."

"That is all true. Let us go. The sooner gone, the sooner back." The little man took a deep breath and stepped out through the heavy iron-studded oak gates. "Why are ye hesitating?" he demanded when Isbel did not immediately follow him.

"I just wait for the spirit of my late husband's nursemaid to leave go of my cloak," muttered Isbel, stumbling a little as she finally yanked free of the unseen hand trying to pull her back inside the towerhouse.

"Ye should try harder to send those ghosties on their way," Pullhair complained as he and Isbel began to walk toward the surrounding forest. "That is why there are so many of those spirits gathered here. They seek your help."

"And I give it when I can."

"There are far too many of them gathered here."

"I agree, but I cannae do much to solve that problem."

"Ye have the gift to send them away, to show them the path they need to walk. Ye just have to use it."

"And I do, whenever I can. Aye, the spirits do seem to gather here, but not all are ready to leave this earth. They seem to be drawn here, but many are uncertain. Mayhap the path they must take is clearest in this place. Howbeit, sometimes I can help them, sometimes they help themselves, sometimes they dinnae even ken why they are here, and sometimes they still dinnae wish to leave."

"Why should they wish to stay here? Why wouldnae they wish to finish their journey?"

"Because they are afraid," she replied quietly as she held her lantern forward a little to light their way through the thickly growing trees.

"Ye arenae afraid."

"Oh, aye, I am, Pullhair. I am. All mortals are afraid of what lies beyond death. I see more than most mortals do, am privy to more of the secrets of this world, yet I, too, fear that final journey. And dinnae roll your eyes in that manner," she said when she glanced at him and caught a glimpse of his expression. "Ye cannae judge we poor mortals on this fear for 'tis not one that ye must face. Ye arenae mortal. And e'en ye and yours fear something. Every creature upon God's earth fears something, from the tiniest bug to the most fearsome of giants."

Pullhair nimbly jumped over a fallen tree. "But ye shouldnae be plagued by such mortal weaknesses. Your blood—"

Isbel made a soft, sharp noise indicating her annoyance. "Please, dinnae plague me with talk of my bloodlines. I have heard it all. The laird and the faerie, the cursed brother, the secret room, and all the rest. I sometimes wonder if one reason I left Loch Fyne was that I grew weary of being told, over and over again, that I carried the look of the wondrous Lily."

"Ye do," Pullhair said quietly. "Ye have the same delicate beauty, the same wide, beautiful blue eyes, and hair the warm golden brown of sweet honey. Aye, Lily is who I see too."

"Ye kenned who she was," Isbel said, eyeing him suspiciously.

"I have served the MacLachlan family for many years. Ye arenae the first I have blessed with my skills."

"So? What did ye ken about her?"

"Nay much. I but saw her a few times. 'Twas many a year ago. 'Ware of those brambles, lassie."

She inwardly cursed. The way Pullhair had answered her told her that he would reveal nothing. He clung to the secrecy all of his kind treasured. The faerie blood in her veins made no difference to him. There might come a time or two when he would let slip a tiny piece of information, but mostly, he would hold fast to his knowledge. After so long, the truth about her ancestors, Duncan and Lily, had faded into fanciful tales told to children in the nursery. It was annoying to know that Pullhair held the truth but would not share it.

A sudden chill rippled down Isbel's spine and she tensed, trying to peer into the deep shadows surrounding them. She could sense malevolence all around her yet could not determine its source. Something in the shadows hated them yet was held at bay by all the protections she carried. She looked at Pullhair, saw how deeply he scowled into the darkness, and knew that he sensed it too.

"I can sense the evil but not whence it comes," she said, her voice little more than a whisper.

"An Unseelie, an evil faerie," Pullhair replied, waving Isbel on. "Many of the Unseelie Court dinnae like your kind, lass. They hold a special anger for mortals who hold faerie blood. They ne'er forgive a faerie for casting them and their ways aside to embrace a mortal. 'Tis a miracle, and the result of careful guarding by ones such as I, that has saved ye all from a curse."

"Not all of us were saved. Duncan's brother was cursed."

"Aye, but that was mostly of his own choosing. He wanted to try and save the soul of his lover."

"Ah, so that much of the tale is true." She met his cross look with a sweet smile as she started to scramble up the side of a hill.

"Ye try to trick me into telling ye things ye shouldnae hear."

"I but wish to ken the truth about my past."

" 'Tis not just your truth, and the others concerned prefer secrecy." Panting a little as he followed her up the steep hill, he grumbled, "Ye didnae tell me that the fool was so many miles away."

Isbel smiled faintly as she took the last few steps to the top of the hill. " 'Tis nay miles. And the mon lies at the base of the hill, in amongst the trees."

"Did ye dream a map too?"

She ignored his ill-temper, responding to his testy words as if they were a simple question. "I told you that he pulls me to him. He has guided me here."

"He isnae dead yet?"

"Nay," she replied as she started down the hill. "And ye may as weel cast aside the disapproval I can see in your every glance and hear in your voice. It willnae turn me back. I may not understand the how or the why of how I came to be here, but I am verra sure that I walk fate's path now."

"Are ye truly certain that 'tis fate guiding ye?"

"Such suspicion ye hold." She smiled briefly. "I may twist the truth from time to time, but I have ne'er lied to you, Pullhair. Aye, 'tis fate. It would be kind if fate told me why I must see this mon, but she is a mischievous mistress. Howbeit, every drop of blood in my veins tells me that my destiny lies but four yards ahead inside that group of trees. Are ye prepared to meet it at my side?"

"Aye, I have naught else to do this night."

Chapter 2

A FAINT crackle of leaves caused Sir Kenneth Davidson to tense. He dragged himself free of the heavy stupor caused by the cold and loss of blood. Groping along the ground at his side he finally found his sword, clutched the hilt tightly, and prayed that he had enough strength to strike at least one telling blow before he died. A little afraid of what he was about to see, he slowly opened his eyes and gaped.

It took Kenneth a full moment to accept what he saw. Crouched at his side was a beautiful young woman and a glowering little man. A strange thought wafted through his mind as he studied the little man from his shaggy brown hair to his tiny brown boots, but Kenneth quickly pushed it aside, blaming it on the pain and loss of blood. Brownies did not exist. They were but fanciful creatures who populated the tales nurses told children.

"Who are ye?" he demanded, startled by the weak unsteady sound of his own voice. " 'Ware, I am armed."

"Sir, ye may be a great warrior," said Isbel, "but I doubt ye could cut a weel-stewed rabbit just now. I am Isbel MacLachlan Graeme, lady of Bandal, and this is my friend Pullhair."

"Pullhair? 'Tis an odd name. Of what clan?"

"Mine. We have come to help you." She cautiously edged closer to him and began to examine his wounds, wincing in sympathy when she tried to lift his jupon and he groaned in pain.

The pain caused by her gentle attempt to administer to his wounds caused Kenneth to sweat. He then began to shiver so fiercely that his teeth clattered together as the cold air dried the sweat on his body. Harsh words flooded his mouth, but before he could spit them out, the girl and the little brown man suddenly tensed and peered into the shadows that encircled them. He looked too, but could see nothing. Despite the lack of any visible threat, however, he felt the tight grip of fear.

Suddenly, the girl stood up, took a leather flask from inside her voluminous black cloak, and sprinkled water in a wide circle around them. Kenneth glanced at the little brown man and caught a look of horror and anger on his small unattractive face. When the girl sat back down, Pullhair glared at her.

"Is there something out there?" Kenneth asked her.

"There are many things lurking in the dark and the shadows, sir," she replied. " 'Tis best if ye dinnae see them. I have protected us for now."

"Aye," snapped Pullhair. "Ye and this fool are protected, but I am trapped. None of the evil out there can cross the line ye just dribbled o'er the ground, but I cannae either."

"I will get you out," Isbel assured him. "Now, sir, may I ken who ye are?"

"Sir Kenneth Davidson of Glenmal, just this side of Edinburgh," Kenneth replied, struggling to speak clearly yet not use up too much of his waning strength. "My clan was on a border raid. I was chosen to guard the rear. A few Sassanachs were reluctant to allow us a share of their goods. A few miles back I fought them and won, but I suffered a few wounds."

"And your people just left ye behind?"

"The rear guard is chosen to take that risk for the sake of the others."

"For the sake of the loot they scramble home with, ye mean."

"Could ye argue with the mon later?" said Pullhair. "Ye said ye came here to save him. 'Tis advisable that ye get about the business of doing so. All ye came here to rescue him from is still out there and the others draw ever nearer."

"I need a litter," Isbel muttered, reluctantly accepting the wisdom of Pullhair's words.

"Ye will need to step outside the circle and I cannae help you this time."

"I have ample protection."

Isbel grabbed the length of rope curled around Sir Kenneth's saddle horn, took a deep breath, and stepped out of the protective circle. She felt the malevolence all around them edge closer but clung to her faith in her protection against it. Nevertheless, she moved quickly as she gathered what was needed to make a littler for the wounded Sir Kenneth. She smiled to herself as she removed a small hatchet from her belt, for she did not even recall looping it onto the wide piece of leather around her waist. The fates were certainly using a strong hand in directing her. They not only had forced her to meet Sir Kenneth, but had done all possible to make sure that she could help him when she found him.

As she worked to lash together saplings and branches with Sir Kenneth's rope, she thought about the man she had rushed into the night to save. He was pale, dirty, and helpless, but she found him breathtakingly handsome. He was tall, lean, and strong. Although it was a little hard to see clearly in the poor light of her small lantern, Isbel was sure that he was dark-haired and dark-eyed. Such particulars did not really matter, however. Isbel knew that she would like them no matter what their true color proved to be.

She grimaced as she tugged the completed litter back to Kenneth and Pullhair. She did not think she was going to be allowed to be too particular. The moment she had set eyes on Sir Kenneth, she had known why she had been drawn to his side, pushed and pulled by him and the fates that ruled them all. This man was her mate. It was a startling realization, but in her heart, mind, and soul, she knew it. Instinct told her that even her brief marriage to the ill-fated Patrick Graeme had been no more than one step in her journey to Kenneth Davidson. It had brought her to Bandal so that she could be close enough to aid him now. The next step was the hardest, and it depended almost solely upon her. Somehow she had to make Sir Kenneth understand and want to be her mate.

And the fates had decided to make that very difficult indeed, she mused as, with Pullhair's help, she settled Kenneth on the litter and hitched it to his horse. Everyone told her that she was lovely so she supposed it must be true. However, she was not fulsome and men liked fulsome women. Her own husband had made a number of less than flattering remarks about the lack of meat on her delicate bones and had often tried to force her to eat more. She did not have the sort of purse a man of any standing looked for in a mate, having both a very modest wealth and equally modest land holdings. Sir Kenneth's fine attire and equally fine mount told her that he was probably a few rungs above modest or came from a clan that was. Knights from a wealthy clan were expected to marry lasses who could add to that wealth and the power it brought.

She inwardly cursed as she did what little she could in the dark to temporarily bind Kenneth's wounds and make him comfortable and warm. As if her looks and near poverty were not enough to turn him away, there were her many gifts. "Gifts," she decided, was an odd word for her strange skills as they often felt more like curses to her, especially when someone turned from her in fear. Even though her husband had thought that he could use her skills for gain, he had still feared them, even hated them at times. She often thanked God that Patrick had not had the time to realize the full extent of her skills. Her own family had occasionally found her a little intimidating, despite their own history and acceptance of such things, and her gifts had strengthened since she had left them. She dreaded seeing Sir Kenneth's reaction when he began to understand and see the truth of her many gifts. Fate could at least have picked a man who understood, perhaps even shared, her peculiarities, she thought crossly.

"I cannae cross that circle, lassie," Pullhair said, his gruff voice interrupting her thoughts.

"Aye, ye can," she replied as she grabbed the horse's reins. "Get on top of Sir Kenneth, but please be careful of his wounds."

"Ye want me to get on that fool?"

"Aye. His body will be your shield. 'Tis but a swift crossing and it should serve to protect you."

"Are ye certain?"

"Weel, I *feel* it will work."

"I dinnae suppose anyone means to ask me if I want this wee mon lying atop me," Kenneth said, his deep voice little more than a raspy whisper.

"If it puts ye at ease, I swear that it will be for no more than a heartbeat. He doesnae weigh verra much and I will be in sore need of his help to tend to you when we reach Bandal."

Kenneth stared at the little man when he sprawled his small, brown body on his chest. Pullhair flashed him a broad grin as Isbel started to urge the nervous horse forward. The little man had a set of very white, very pointed teeth, Kenneth mused. Although he continued to deny it, vehemently, everything about the tiny fellow bespoke a brownie, one of those creatures of whispered tales and dreams.

"Why couldnae ye just walk out of that circle?" Kenneth asked the man, a little nervous about the answer he might receive.

"Because of the holy water she sprinkled about, ye great fool," Pullhair replied then he chuckled. "Ye ken what I am."

"I ken what ye remind me of and that ye are a little mon who, mayhap, carries too many superstitions in his head."

The moment they were outside of the circle, Pullhair scrambled off Kenneth but paused at the man's side to glare at him. "Just because ye dinnae choose to believe doesnae make them superstitions. I also ken the thought stuck in your head that ye cannae shake free. I am just what the wee voice in your mind keeps insisting I am. And since I am one of those wee creatures your wet nurse told ye tales of, ye might better spend your time asking yourself why ye can see me. Most of the rest of your kind cannae." He laughed at Kenneth's sour look and moved up to walk at Isbel's side.

"Are ye tormenting that poor mon, Pullhair?" Isbel asked, after a brief look back at Kenneth revealed the man's expression of mild annoyance.

"Me? I dinnae torment people," Pullhair protested, his air of insult too overdone.

"Aye, ye do and we both ken it weel. Ye often tormented Patrick."

"He deserved all ill that befell him."

Isbel inwardly grimaced at Pullhair's sharp response. The brownie had always detested Patrick and the feeling had been mutual. Patrick's biggest complaint about the little man was that he had never been able to catch him or really see him. Pullhair had plagued Patrick with small annoyances and curses, restrained in his actions against the man only because she was married to him. At times she wished she had paid closer heed to the way Pullhair, her spirits, and a myriad of denizens of the netherworld had reacted to Patrick. None of them had liked the man. If she had taken a minute to look beyond his handsome face and the sweet charm he had shown her before they were married, she might well have hesitated then ended the betrothal. Instead she had married the man and, within days, realized that she had made a serious error in judgment. The fine courtier she had been wooed by had quickly disappeared, leaving in its place an insulting, greedy, and often cruel man.

She finally gave in to temptation and softly asked Pullhair, "What do ye think of this mon?"

"That he is a fool."

"Why do ye call him a fool?"

"What else might one call a mon who nearly gets himself killed for the sake of a pack of thieves running back to their nest with a few skinny cattle?"

"Weel, 'tis true that I dinnae ken why men must steal from each other and certainly not why they must constantly fight and kill each other. Howbeit, if that makes him a fool, then most every land with men on it is full to overflowing with fools."

"Aye, it is." Pullhair bit back a smile when she cast him a disgusted look. "The mon can see me."

Isbel took a moment to fully understand the import of his words. When she did, she was so startled she nearly tripped. Few people saw brownies. Even fewer talked to them. Kenneth had done both.

"But he doesnae believe in such things, does he?"

"He doesnae want to, but the belief is there. He fights it as hard as he fought the Sassanachs."

Isbel felt her heart skip with hope. "Do ye think he has gifts akin to mine?"

"He has a sympathy, lassie. He feels, deep down he believes, and he isnae as afraid as he would like to be. I think he is also bonded with you in heart, soul, and mind so tightly that he precariously shares your gift."

"Oh, dear. That could make Bandal a most upsetting place for him.

I had hoped for time with him, time for him to soften towards me ere he confronts the full truth of Bandal and me."

"Ye may still have it. This could be the only night that he has the skill to see me and mine. He has been weakened by his wounds and the veil that usually covers a mortal's eyes could have slipped a wee bit."

"And so it may fade as he grows stronger. I pray it does, that this sight he has is but a short-lived gift. Fate has chosen him for me, Pullhair. I was pulled here because that mon is my chosen mate. 'Twill be most difficult to make him see that if he learns too much about me too soon."

"Ye cannae hide what ye are forever, lassie."

"I ken it. I but ask for a little time, enough time to touch his heart ere his fears send him hieing for the hills."

Chapter 3

A LOW, steady rumble stirred Kenneth from his sleep. As he woke, memories of his rescue flooded his mind. He clearly saw the lovely young woman and her tiny brown companion and felt a lingering ache from the pain caused by their administrations. They had carried him up some narrow, winding stairs, placed him on a soft bed, sponged him down, and stitched his wounds. There was also a confused tangle of partial memories, but he shook them aside for he could make no sense of them. He slid his hand over the bandage on the right side of his waist and on his right leg. He was warm, comfortable, and despite the lingering pain, felt confident he would heal.

He opened his eyes and gave a soft cry of surprise. A huge gray cat was staring him in the face, its green eyes almost level with his. The source of the low rumble, he mused, as he cautiously lifted his hand and scratched the animal's ears. He smiled at the look of pleasure on the animal's face and at how the noise it made grew increasingly louder. It was unusual for a cat to be so friendly, so clean, and so well fed, and the animals were rarely allowed access to the bedchambers. Recalling the strange pair who had rescued him, he decided he should not be surprised that an animal most people scorned or feared would be made a pet.

"Slayer doesnae usually approve of people so quickly," said a soft, husky voice from the foot of the bed.

Kenneth started slightly, wondering how she could have entered the room so quietly. "Slayer?"

"Aye. Nary a mouse nor a rat dares poke its pointed wee nose onto my lands." She idly scratched the cat's ears when it moved to sit in front of her, rubbing its head against her stomach. "Ye are in the bed he has claimed as his own. Each morning the sun comes in that window to your right and shines o'er the bed. He warms himself in its light until it moves on."

"Ah, so that is why he was so friendly to me."

"Nay, not completely. He is most particular about the ones he chooses as his friends." She moved to the side of the bed and lightly felt his forehead and cheeks, relieved to find no hint of a fever. "How do ye feel?"

"I am still a wee bit weak, but I feel confident that I will heal. I do feel verra rested."

"Ye should. Ye have slept for nigh on three days." She smiled faintly at his shock. "I gave ye some herbal drinks to make ye rest. That is why ye slept for so long. I believe most strongly that sleep is the best cure for most illnesses and wounds."

"Aye. I believe so as weel. That does explain the pieces of memories I can make no sense of. A glimpse of a face or a few words, no more."

"Ye did rouse a bit now and again."

"I owe ye my life. Ye and that odd wee mon. Where is he?"

"He will be here as soon as the sun sets."

Isbel almost smiled when Sir Kenneth frowned, his expression telling her that he ached to ask a few questions and was fighting that urge. Pullhair was right. Kenneth knew what her little friend was, could see him clearly. The man either had a gift or two he was unaware of, or because they were so closely bonded, he had slipped beneath the cloak of her own.

Her delight over that faded abruptly. It was not really important why he could peek into the shadowed worlds. What mattered was that he could see all she had to deal with, and would quickly know exactly how magical Bandal was. That was not necessarily a good thing. The way he fought to deny the truth about Pullhair told Isbel that this was a new skill for him. Sir Kenneth Davidson was about to be privy to nearly everything most people were afraid of or, at best, simply preferred not to know about. That meant she would not have any time at all to win his heart before he discovered all of her secrets.

She inwardly battled with an almost overwhelming sense of defeat. Even if the fates were not using such a heavy hand in directing her, she knew she would have wanted Kenneth Davidson from the moment she set eyes upon him. He was breathtakingly handsome with his glossy, thick black hair and eyes of a deep rich brown. His smooth skin was a light shade of swarthy, as if he spent a great deal of time standing naked in the sun. He was long and lean, muscular in an attractive, subtle way. His features were cleanly cut, just sharp enough to be extraordinarily handsome, and unmarked by scars. The bottom lip of his well-shaped mouth was slightly fuller than the top. Several times as she had nursed him she had struggled against the strong urge to touch her lips to his. She was almost embarrassed by how badly she wanted him.

Cautiously, she reached out and covered his strong, long-fingered hand with hers. Patrick had bedded her only a few times before he had died, and she had found no pleasure in it. In truth, Patrick's manner of lovemaking had left her feeling bruised and ashamed. Every part of her told her that, if she and Kenneth became lovers, she would finally know what the poets and minstels spoke so eloquently about, and she desperately wished to know. If nothing else went as the fates wanted, she prayed there would be at least one chance for her and Kenneth to make love. It was probably a shameful way to think, but she did not care.

"I shall fetch you some food if you wish it," she said quietly.

"I think I would yet I wouldnae trouble yourself too much. I am no stranger to wounds and healing and I suspect I willnae eat very much the first few times food is set before me."

"Nay, ye willnae. Ye are right about that. The trick is to eat a little as often as ye can. I will fetch ye a little hearty broth, some bread, cheese and wine. Will that do?"

"Aye, that is most kind."

The moment the woman left the room, Kenneth expelled a long, slow breath. He looked at his hand, still feeling the tingling warmth of her touch. He was not surprised that he wanted her for she was beautiful. Small and slender, she moved with the subtle invitation of a far more fulsome woman. Her thick, fair hair hung in long waves to her tiny waist. The most startling and alluring feature of her small face was a pair of wide, incredibly blue eyes rimmed by thick, long, pale brown lashes. Although her full mouth was sorely tempting, he always saw her eyes first. Each time she leaned close to him, he caught himself breathing deeply of her scent, the smell of clean skin touched with lavender.

Kenneth inwardly groaned as he felt his desire stir. Despite his pain and weakness, she could stir his blood with the slightest of touches or a brief, sweet smile. He would sternly remind himself that she had saved his life and that lusting after her was a poor way to thank her for that, but it did little to stem the longing. It made him feel ashamed of himself but he knew he was going to try and bed her before he left to return to his family's lands.

Isbel returned, smiling shyly as she sat on the edge of the bed and set a tray of food before him. Wincing, and silently waving aside her attempt to assist him, Kenneth sat up straighter against the pillows she had set behind him. In his current state of near arousal, the last thing he needed was to feel those soft, small hands on his body.

"You live here alone?" he asked before she filled his mouth with the warm, hearty broth.

She only hesitated a moment before nodding. In his weakened state he could do her no harm. Neither could Isbel believe that the fates had brought them together just so that he could hurt her. She had already endured one cruel, frightening mate. She could not believe fate would be so cruel and push her into the arms of another like Patrick.

"These are my husband's lands," she replied.

"Ye are married?" Kenneth could not believe how deeply disappointed he was.

"I was once, nearly a year ago. I am a MacLachlan from Loch Fyne and I married a Graeme and moved here. But months after Patrick brought me here, he drowned in the river just a mile north of here."

"Why did ye not return to your kinsmen?"

"I wished to remain here. These are my lands now, small though they might be. There were also things at Loch Fyne that I wished to run away from. I was not fully successful in evading my heritage, but I prefer the fact that I am alone now."

"I think I have heard of the MacLachlans of Loch Fyne." When she stuffed a large piece of bread in his mouth, stopping his words abruptly, Kenneth wondered if she was trying to veer him away from the subject of her family.

"They are not without power and wealth. I havenae heard of the Davidsons of Glenmal, however."

"And ye willnae hear much from me if ye keep stuffing food in my mouth." He tried to smile as he turned his head to the side, silently refusing another spoonful of broth.

"Ah, I see. It was not much, but 'twill do for a start."

Kenneth opened his mouth to thank her for her trouble then tensed. In the far corner of the room he was certain he saw someone, an older woman in a stained gray gown. Even as he looked straight at her, however, what he had thought was a woman became no more than a glimmer of light.

"Now that was a wee bit odd," he murmured, meekly allowing Isbel to help him lie back down.

"What was odd, Sir Kenneth?" she asked, tucking the blankets over him and forcing herself to stop lingering over the chore.

"I thought I saw a woman over there in the corner, near the chest."

"There is no one at Bandal save myself, Pullhair, and Slayer."

"But I am sure—"

" 'Twas just a flicker of the sun's light," she assured him as she stood up and collected together the remains of his small meal.

"I suppose."

Kenneth frowned as he watched Isbel scurry out of the room. Her leavetaking carried the strong scent of a hasty retreat. He looked all around the room but saw nothing. Sighing, he relaxed and closed his eyes. He wanted to believe her explanation but a small voice in his head told him there was great deal Isbel MacLachlan Graeme was hiding. Kenneth vowed that, as soon as he had regained his strength, he would search out a few answers.

"Curse that woman," Isbel muttered as she scrubbed out the bowl that had held Kenneth's broth.

"What woman?" Pullhair asked as he set a pile of wood by the kitchen fireplace.

"Mary, my late and little missed husband's nursemaid."

"What has she done now?"

"Appeared to Sir Kenneth. He caught a glimpse of the woman in the corner of his bedchamber."

"I suspect she just wished to take a closer look at the mon ye intend to replace her sweet Patrick with." Pullhair sat on the stool in front of the huge stone fireplace and looked at Isbel.

"Patrick Graeme ne'er had a sweet bone in his wretched body," Isbel said as she sat on the sheepskin rug in front of the fire. "Mary was just too blind to see the evil in him. I think she saw the wee boy she nursed whene'er she looked at him and ne'er really saw the angry, bitter mon he had become."

Pullhair nodded and poked at the fire with a large stick. "He treated the old woman most unkindly in her latter years, but she ne'er ceased to care for him. Mayhap she feared that if she looked too closely, she might discover that she had had a hand in making him the wretched fool he was."

"Weel, next time I see her, I shall scold her soundly."

"I dinnae think that will do much good. The woman does as she pleases. What I find of interest is that Sir Kenneth saw her at all."

Isbel sighed and nodded. "He sees too clearly. Soon he may weel begin to believe in what he saw. Even if I twist my tongue into knots, I will not be able to change his mind about what he sees. I tried to be most clever in dismissing Mary as no more than a bit of sunlight dancing upon the wall."

"He will not long accept such explanations."

"I ken it." She stood up and moved to scrub the heavy wooden table set in the middle of the room, needing the hard work to try and ease her agitated state of mind. "I always thought it would be nice to have a mon who kenned the things I do, who saw at least some of what I did. It would mean I could cease to be so careful. Now, howbeit, I see the difficulty it could cause. If he had been born with such gifts, it could have served me well, but he was not, or the gifts set in his his heart and mind quietly, ne'er troubling him. For him to suddenly discover such things is no good at all, for he will fear these revelations and will certainly blame me for their arrival."

"Dinnae fret so, lassie. If ye are fated to be with this mon, then ye shall be."

She smiled at Pullhair. "Thank ye kindly for that attempt to cheer me, but we both ken the truth of the matter. The fates may have chosen Kenneth as my mate, but I am the one who must win him. I dinnae believe that showing him that all the frightening tales he was told as a child are not tales at all, but the truth will do that. All I can do is pray that the fates have not brought the mon to me just to snatch him away. For all I complain about my gifts, I have really hated having them. If they cause Kenneth Davidson to run from me, however, I may weel begin to loathe what I am."

"Nay, lassie. Ye have proud blood in your veins. Ye cannae think of turning against your own heritage."

"Pride and a great heritage willnae warm my bed or give me the bairns I crave, Pullhair."

"And ye would cast all that aside for that mon?"

"Aye, in a heartbeat."

Chapter 4

"WHAT are ye doing out of bed? Are ye mad?"

Kenneth wiped the sweat from his brow with a trembling hand and, clinging tightly to the bedpost, glared at Isbel. She stood in the doorway of the bedchamber, her delicate hands on her shapely hips, and a chuckling Pullhair lurking behind her. Kenneth was not sure what annoyed him more, his own weakness, or the open delight the little man seemed to take in his helplessness.

"I am weary of lying in that bed with naught to look at but the ceiling and your twice-cursed cat," he snapped. "I have been stuck abed for a fortnight."

"And ye shall remain stuck in that bed for a few days more if ye have any wits at all," she scolded him as she helped him back into bed, Pullhair reluctantly moving to help her.

"What I should be doing is trying to regain my strength. If I dinnae use my leg, 'twill stiffen. I cannae be left a cripple."

"A wee bit of stiffness in your leg willnae make ye a cripple. And using your leg too soon can be as harmful as not using it at all. Ye are healing weel but ye must nay rush things. Ye have been verra fortunate. Be pleased with that." She briefly checked his wound, knowing that there was little chance he had opened any of his injuries, yet unable to quell her concern for him.

"Ye dinnae need to fuss so o'er me," he muttered. "I hurt nothing save for my pride, just made myself so cursed weak that I couldnae take another step, neither to the door nor back to this wretched bed."

He scowled at Isbel as she soaked a cloth in a bowl of cool water. When she gently bathed his face, he reluctantly admitted to himself that it felt very good. The brief attempt at walking had left him so weak that he was shaking. Even as he felt stirred by her tender ministrations, he was infuriated by his own helplessness.

"I cannae abide this idleness."

" 'Twill pass, sir. Endure this for but a wee while longer. The rewards are weel worth the price."

"Aye, mayhap."

"The fool accepts the truth with wondrous grace," Pullhair murmured as he sat on the end of the bed.

"My name is Kenneth," he said through gritted teeth, weary of the little man's constant insults.

"Weel, pride begins to pinch ye, does it? Fine then, *Kenneth*, ye had best heed the lassie. The art of healing is but one of her many skills."

Kenneth caught sight of the cross look Isbel sent the little brown man. She did that each time Pullhair referred to her skills or her gifts. She clearly did not want them speaking about such things. After so many days within the walls of Bandal, Kenneth knew the reason for her reluctance to talk. Bandal was a very strange place, filled to the parapets with a multitude of spirits and creatures he would prefer to remain ignorant of.

The moment Isbel hurried away to get him some food, Kenneth fixed his full attention upon Pullhair. Although he desperately wished to cling to his disbelief, he could no longer deny what the little brown man was. A brownie was not all that Bandal was cursed with either. He had fought hard to ignore it all, but that had proven to be impossible. Just because he could not see the spirits clearly did not mean that they were not there. At times he had overheard Isbel speaking to the ghosts who haunted her keep and at other times he had heard Isbel and Pullhair speaking of such things. It was far past time for someone to start telling him the truth, he decided.

"The two of ye hold tight to a great many secrets," he said, meeting Pullhair's steady gaze and not flinching.

"Now why would we be wishing to keep anything secret from such a brave knight of the realm?" asked Pullhair.

"Your tongue is nearly as sharp as your teeth." It pleased Kenneth a little when Pullhair scowled, revealing that the soft insult had struck home. "Let us cease to play these games. Aye, I have fought to deny what my wits and my eyes tell me so plainly, and ye make game of me because of it. Ye are a brownie. I dinnae understand why I should suddenly be able to see you, but that doesnae concern me just now. What troubles me is how much else I have been seeing. Either I have gone mad and dinnae ken it, or Bandal crawls with spirits of all shapes and sizes."

"And why should that concern you?"

"Because I am stuck in the midst of it. So is Isbel."

"Isbel is safe. She is weel protected."

Kenneth wisely bit back a smile of amusement over the way the tiny man puffed out his chest and tried to appear intimidating. He had never heard of a brownie taking on the role of a mortal's protector, but then he had ceased to heed the tales told of such creatures at a very young age. What little he could recall, however, told him that there were many things a brownie could not protect anyone from. His memories also warned him to be very careful not to anger or offend the tiny creature.

"Come, let us talk as men who share a concern over a tiny woman," he said gently. "Although I have ne'er glimpsed such things as brownies and ghosts before I met ye and Isbel, I cannae believe every place is as crowded with such beings as Bandal. Near to every corner of this towerhouse has something lurking in it. Why so many and are they a threat to Isbel?"

"I think Bandal is a place of passage," Pullhair said, glancing at the doorway to be sure Isbel had not come back and caught him being so forthright.

"Passage? To where?"

"To the land of the dead. Many mortals who have died find their way here. Most of them journey on, either right away or after but a short stay. And Bandal is a sacred place for my kind and others of the netherworld. There are several faerie mounds but a short walk from here."

"Faerie mounds?" Kenneth sat up straighter, tense and wary. "They could take Isbel away. That is what they do, is it not? They carry off mortals."

"Not as often as your kind would believe. They willnae touch Isbel, however. Oh, aye, there is a faerie or two who would love to do her ill, but she has too much protection, and I dinnae mean me or the things she carries about with her such as that cross pounded out of iron."

Kenneth winced slightly and rubbed his temples. "I begin to think I erred in beginning this talk. Ye are telling me more than I can fully understand."

"Foolish mon," Pullhair said in a gruff, faintly angry voice as he moved to stand at the side of the bed. "Ye weary what few wits ye have worrying o'er things that dinnae matter. Ye shouldnae concern yourself o'er why ye can suddenly see me and the ghosts that roam the halls. For some reason ye have suddenly been granted the gift of sight. 'Twould seem to me that ye are meant to do something with it. That is what ye should be trying to understand."

"If Isbel is in no danger, then there is no reason."

"There is always a reason for things that happen. There is also always some price to be paid for the gift ye now have."

"I must pay for something I didnae ask for and dinnae really want?"

"Aye. That is the way the game is played out, my pretty knight. Ye may just have the gift because ye are close to Isbel, bonded by a debt of blood. Howbeit, I repeat that ye may have been given it because ye are meant to do something."

Kenneth shook his head. "If I am meant to do something, I think I should have been given some hint of what that is when I was given these strange gifts."

Pullhair shrugged and started for the door. "That would be far too easy."

"Just tell me this then. I am not mad?"

"Nay, not in any way I have yet kenned."

"Then I am truly seeing ghosts and the like."

"Aye."

Before he could discuss the matter any more, Pullhair slipped away. Kenneth slumped against his pillows. He had not really found out much. In truth, he could not really depend upon Pullhair's assurances that he was not mad, that he was truly seeing what he thought he was seeing. After all, that brief talk to Pullhair could easily have been some delusion born of madness.

"Ye dinnae look to be very happy," Isbel said as she entered the room and shyly approached the bed. "Would ye like to play some chess?"

"Aye, that would pass the time nicely," he replied.

Isbel set the chessboard between them on the bed and carefully placed the small, hand-carved wooden pieces in position. It was going to be hard to keep her mind on the intricate game while sitting so close to Kenneth, but she knew she had to try and hide her deep attraction for the man. In all the time he had been at her keep, Kenneth had not revealed any hint of desire for her. Until he did, she intended to keep her longing for him as hidden as possible.

His agitation and ill temper had stirred her sympathies, however. She had occasionally been tied to her bed by illness or injury and knew well how maddening it could be. Although she could not spend that much time with him for she had chores to do, Isbel decided that she needed to make more of an effort to keep him occupied.

It did not take long before Isbel realized that she was outmatched. She had enough skill at the game to give him a reasonable challenge, but she doubted she would beat him, certainly not until she had had a great deal of practice. Reluctant to just give up, however, she struggled to do better than she ever had before. It did not really surprise her, however, to be checkmated by him.

"Ye need not look so proud," she murmured, smiling faintly as he set the pieces back in place, clearly intending to have another game. "One should try and win with a little more grace and humility than ye are showing."

"I shall endeavor to do so the next time I win."

"Of course. That would sound a more honest promise of improvement if your voice had not held the conviction that you will beat me this time too."

Kenneth laughed softly, then slowly grew serious as he studied her. She sat cross-legged on the bed and somehow managed to look both adorable and alluring. He scolded himself for even thinking of something as sly as the idea that flashed through his mind, but easily shook aside his brief attack of guilt. He fixed his gaze upon her full mouth and decided he was healed enough to try for a little more than her pleasant company.

"How about a wee wager on this game, Lady Isbel?" he asked even as he made his first move.

"How wee a wager?" She studied the board and prayed for a moment of inspiration.

"A kiss if I win."

Isbel was so startled that she dropped her chess piece. Kenneth glanced at her then pretended that she had not made such a serious error. Her heart pounded so hard that she was sure he could hear it. Since she was certain she would lose again, she hesitated to accept his wager. It seemed a little scandalous. The temptation was too strong, however. She had ached to experience his kiss since the moment she had seen him. At least this way she could get her wish yet feign innocence.

"And what do I get when I beat you?" she asked.

"What would ye like?"

"One day where ye stay quietly in your bed and allow your poor battered body to heal."

"That is a high price indeed, but fair enough."

The whole time they played, Isbel forced herself to be calm. She ached for the game to be quick, for her defeat to come swiftly, but knew she would be deeply embarrassed if Kenneth guessed that. When, for one brief moment, it looked as if she would get checkmate, she nearly made a foolish move. It took all of her willpower to continue to play as if she wanted to win. She breathed an inner sigh of relief when Kenneth made his move and effectively cut off any chance she had of victory.

Even as he said the word "checkmate," he pushed aside the board and tugged her into his arms. Isbel could feel herself trembling faintly with anticipation and prayed that he would misread it as shyness or even a touch of fear. She tensed slightly as he framed her face with his hands. Suddenly she was afraid that his kiss could never match her expectations and the very last thing she wanted him to do was disappoint her.

" 'Tis but a wee kiss I mean to take, Isbel," he said in a soft, husky voice. "Ye need not look so frightened."

"I am but a wee bit nervous."

"Ye are a widow. Ye cannae be a stranger to a kiss." He began to brush soft, teasing kisses over her face.

"I am a stranger to yours," she whispered.

"That is something quickly and willingly changed," he murmured against her lips.

The moment his mouth touched hers, Isbel knew the kiss would be all she had imagined and much, much more. She slipped her arms around his neck and allowed him to pull her fully into his arms. Warmth flared through her body as his mouth moved over hers. He prodded at her lips with his tongue and she quickly parted them, welcoming the slow, intimate strokes inside her mouth. Her breath grew swift and uneven as he smoothed his hands over her body. His kiss began to grow fiercer, more demanding, and she shuddered with the strength of her need for him.

Suddenly the force of her own feelings for him terrified her. She broke free of his hold and stumbled off the bed. "I think ye have fully collected your wager," she said, her voice thick and hoarse.

"Isbel," he said, reaching out to her.

She stepped away, out of his reach, and then began to back toward the door. Every part of her cried out for her to return to his arms, and she decided that was a very good reason to get far away from him for a while. Isbel had known from the start that she desired Kenneth Davidson, but the feeling she had now could only be called a deep, almost overwhelming craving. She knew she had to remove herself from further temptation until she could gain some understanding of what she was feeling. She opened her mouth to say something, then gave in to cowardice and fled the room. As she ran to the safety of her own bedchamber, she prayed that Kenneth had no idea what had sent her running.

Chapter 5

IT was a simple chore but Kenneth did not think he had enjoyed it more. He took a deep breath of the warm stable air as he rubbed down his mount. Wallace had not been ridden for days, did not really need a rubbing down, but it was one of the few things Kenneth could do. A lingering weakness, despite three long weeks of rest, made it almost impossible for him to do anything but the least strenuous of chores. It was highly irritating, for he felt well enough to do anything until he tried to really exert himself. Then his weakness revealed itself.

Knowing that it was only a matter of time until his strength returned, he decided to turn his mind to other things and was not surprised when his thoughts settled on Isbel. She had been in his thoughts almost constantly since they had shared a kiss. He had never experienced such a fierce and immediate passion. Since his youth, those days when he had just begun to learn the delights a man and a woman could share, he had never really ached for a woman, but he ached for Isbel. He could do nothing about it, however, for she had stayed well out of his reach all week.

That puzzled him, for he would never have guessed that Isbel was a coward yet she was acting very much like one. At first he had thought that her rapid retreat and obvious agitation was because he had moved too quickly or made his desire for her too obvious. That made no sense, however. She was a widow, no innocent maiden, and although he had not hidden the strength of his desire, he had not attempted to ravish her. Although he feared he could be thinking somewhat vainly, he could not stop wondering if her flight had been caused because she had experienced her first taste of passion. Her husband could well have been a poor lover, indifferent, unskilled, and hasty. If Isbel's passions had never been stirred by her husband yet had come to life in his arms, she could well have been startled, afraid, or even ashamed.

Kenneth cursed himself as a fool, even as he absently walked around the specter of a small ragged boy that had suddenly appeared by his horse's right flank. It did him no good to puzzle over Isbel's actions, for he had no facts or real knowledge to enable him to answer any of the many questions he had. The only things he knew about Isbel were that he desired her more than he had ever desired anyone, she was beautiful in an ethereal way, and she was odd. He simply did not know enough about her to understand why she did what she did.

There was something else to consider as well. All he could offer Isbel was a love affair. It would undoubtedly be fierce and sweet, but Isbel was not a woman a man married, certainly not a man in his position. His family was wealthy and powerful but he was third son. His father had been more than generous, giving a small largesse to all of his children, but Kenneth knew he was expected to add to that wealth through an appropriate and advantageous marriage. Isbel not only had little money, but her land holdings were very modest and packed with all the things most people ran in terror from. He also knew that making Isbel a leman would hurt her, even insult her, and he realized he could not do that to her.

Enough musing and wondering, he said to himself as he started to walk out of the stable. Kenneth decided that the only way he could stop his mind from spinning in all directions yet solving nothing was to talk to Isbel. It could not hurt to ask why she had run from him and why she was staying away. The worst she could do was refuse to answer.

He found her near the chicken coop, blindly scattering seed to the birds. For a moment Kenneth stood a few feet away and just watched her. She looked as confused and as caught up in her own thoughts as he had been. He cautiously approached, not wanting to startle her too much, but needing to get close enough to grab her by the arm or the hand to stop her when she tried to elude him.

"Isbel," he called softly and prepared to catch her when she whirled around looking very much like a terrified rabbit. "We need to talk."

"I fear I am much too busy," she said, and gave a soft squeak of alarm when he gently but firmly grabbed her by the arm as she tried to walk away from him.

"Ye have been very busy for a full week. I ken that there are many things one must do before winter settles in, but I believe ye can spare me a moment or two without courting starvation."

Isbel inwardly grimaced and tried to still the tight nervousness that had gripped her. She knew they had to talk, had even planned out several conversations in her mind, but each time she caught sight of him, she gave in to her own cowardice. Even reminding herself that they were destined, that she had work to do if that destiny was to be fulfilled, did not help. It was not so much what he might say to her that she feared, but what she might say to him. She knew the feelings his kiss had stirred in her were born of far more than passion. Love had already found a place in her heart. That was not a secret she wished to reveal, however, not when he had showed no sign of even beginning to feel the same.

"What do ye wish to talk about?" she asked timidly as he tugged her over to a rough wooden bench set beneath a tree that was struggling to reach its full height.

"That kiss."

"It was very nice," she muttered as he sat down and tugged her down at his side.

"Such flattery."

"I suspect ye dinnae need pretty words and assurances from me, that ye hear plenty."

"I doubt I hear as many as ye obviously think I do. And I have not come to seek flattery or even sweet words. I seek some answers."

"About what?" She inwardly cursed, for her voice was tiny, little more than a timid whisper.

He sighed and ran the fingers of his free hand through his hair. "Ye fled from me that night as if I had just grown horns and a tail."

"Ye exaggerate."

"Nay. One moment we are sharing a verra fine kiss, a sweet and passionate embrace, and the next ye are leaping from my arms and scurrying out the door. What did I do wrong?"

She sighed and stared down at her feet. He had a right to a few answers. She had been enjoying the kiss, and revealed nothing but willingness, then had abruptly changed toward him and run away. The hint of confusion she could hear in his voice was probably heartfelt. Isbel was not sure what to say, however. She was not even sure why the passion he had roused in her had scared her so.

"Ye did nothing wrong," she finally said. " 'Tis me. When ye wagered a kiss, I thought that would be nice. I confess that I had already thought of kissing you a time or two and was more than willing to satisfy my curiosity. What I had not expected was that it would be as, weel, as stirring as it was." She was not sure how she should read the brief, compulsive squeeze of her hand.

"I was stirred as weel," he said quietly. "Could ye not feel that I was?"

"Aye, and yet, to be honest, what ye were and were not feeling was not of any great concern to me at that moment." She finally gained the courage to look him in the eye. "My husband was not a particularly good man. He certainly never made me feel as ye did with but a kiss."

"Your husband has been dead for a year. Ye should feel no guilt that your passion didnae die with him."

"Oh, I dinnae. In truth, my passion wasnae stirred by him at all. For a while I suffered a deep guilt about that, but as I came to ken the mon he was, I realized that he did not notice that he was the only one gaining any pleasure from our coupling and that he probably wouldnae have cared had he kenned that I was cold to his touch. I thought I loved the mon, but soon realized that I had fooled myself as completely as he had fooled me, and he didnae marry me for love anyway." She shook her head. "Nay, I will say no more against him. 'Tis bad luck to speak ill of the dead."

He gently took both of her hands in his. "Did ye feel shamed that I made ye feel what he could not?"

"Nay. But can ye nay see? Aye, I am a widow, but in some things I am still a great innocent. The only mon I have e'er been touched by in my life left me cold. It sometimes puzzled me how the poets and minstrels could speak so eloquently of something so, weel, so cold. I decided that either something was wrong with me or they prettied up with soft words a necessary part of marriage." She caught a fleeting look in his fine dark eyes and smiled crookedly. "Nay, dinnae pity me."

" 'Twas not truly pity, more regret. Ye deserved better."

"Mayhap. And it was probably not all Patrick's fault. He found me too thin and I think, despite all his claims to the contrary, he feared my gifts."

"Ah, your gifts." She had been so truthful thus far, painfully so, and Kenneth briefly wondered if that would continue as he asked, "Ye and Pullhair oft mention your *gifts* but neither of you explains what ye mean."

Isbel stared at him. She knew that telling him the full truth about herself was not the way to make him love her. It could also end all hope of becoming his lover, even if for one brief night. Instinct told her, however, that she had to be truthful, that complete honesty was the only way she could deal with Kenneth Davidson and have any hope at all of a future with him. She knew now that her plan to hold fast to her secrets until she could find a place in his heart would never have worked. Kenneth would have seen that as a betrayal.

"Ye willnae like this," she warned him, wondering if she was also trying to remind herself of the consequences of telling him the whole truth.

"I believe I may have already guessed a great deal of it. I am not sure why but—shall we say?—my vision has become far more acute since meeting you and Pullhair."

"As I have told you, I was born into the clan MacLachlan of Loch Fyne." She took a deep breath and told him about Lily and Duncan. She was not encouraged by his widening eyes or his increasing frown.

"And so the MacLachlans of Loch Fyne believe they have faerie blood in their veins?" he asked gently.

"They do and the special gifts so many are born with seem to prove their claim. Every generation one is born who is said to look like Lily. This time it was me. And with those looks comes an added serving of skills. I can see all that lurks in the shadows, am privy to many of the secrets of the netherworld. I ken that ye have seen some of the ghosts who haunt Bandal's halls."

"I have seen something now and then," he reluctantly admitted, not wishing to elaborate for that seemed like an admission of belief and he still clung to his need to deny it all.

Isbel smiled faintly. She knew that Mary had been his first sighting and that, after her, Kenneth had seen more and more. The ghosts had begun to appear to him with the same frequency and freedom that they appeared to her. He wished to deny that particular truth, however, and she decided she would not argue with him. What she was telling him was clearly upsetting him enough. She saw no gain in adding to that by insisting that he was just like her.

"Weel, ghosties like me, and when I came to Bandal, I discovered that 'tis a gathering place for them. I can help them step onto that final path, ye see, and one of those paths appears to be right here. At times I also have a wee touch of the sight, such as when I came to help you."

"I did wonder how ye had found me."

"A dream warned me of the danger ye were facing from your untended wounds and from, weel, other threats. I simply followed where I was led."

She could tell from the look on his handsome face that he did not like what he had heard. He had come to her wanting to speak of what they had shared, perhaps even to try and share a little more. Isbel could tell that each word she had said had killed his inclinations. He might yet be her lover for a little while, but she was certain he would never ask her to be his wife. If nothing else, most people would not wish to risk passing on such *gifts* to their children. Her only consolation was that he looked more uncertain and discomforted than afraid.

Kenneth slowly stood up. He did not know what to say or what to do. He had come to her to try and soothe any insult or ease her fears and, he admitted, to see what chance there was of gaining a fuller taste of the passion she had revealed in her kiss. Instead she had filled his head with truths he did not want to know. He did not know what to do next, what to say, or even what to think and believe. There was a shadow of pain in her brilliant blue eyes, and he deeply regretted it. At this moment in time, however, he knew he could not soothe it. Now he had to put some distance between them.

"I am not sure what to say," he murmured. "This was not the discussion I had planned to have. I do appreciate your honesty and I pray ye take no offense when I, too, speak the truth. I must consider this." He shook his head then bowed slightly as he started to back away. "I fear I no longer ken what I seek or what I am willing to accept."

"At least ye are not fleeing from me in terror," she said quietly.

"Nay, and yet my lack of fear only seems to add to my confusion." He lifted her hand to his lips and brushed a kiss over her knuckles then walked away.

Isbel fought the sudden strong urge to weep. She had not chosen to be what she was, had not willingly accepted the strange gifts that caused so many unease. It seemed most unkind of fate to give her skills that ensured she would always be alone.

A small flicker of hope came to life in her heart, but she forced it aside. While it was true that Kenneth had not shown the fear so many others did, that did not mean he would fully accept her gifts. He had said he needed to consider the matter. If she allowed herself to hope that, after some thought, he would come and take her in his arms, she would only end up hurt and disappointed. The saddest thing, she mused, was that she would now be denied the chance to know true passion and would have to keep her words of love locked away in her heart.

Chapter 6

"WHY dinnae ye take the idiot his food?" grumbled Pullhair as Isbel set a heavily ladened tray in his arms.

"Because I believe he would rather I didnae," she replied, and sighed as she watched a grumbling Pullhair walk up the narrow steps to Kenneth's bedchamber.

For three long days she had seen little of the man. The few times they had inadvertently confronted each other, he had been polite but distant. Isbel found that not seeing him at all was easier to bear than that. It was beginning to look as if he had decided that he would simply stay away from her until he was well enough to return home. Fate, she decided, could be even crueler than she had imagined. She had the mate she was destined for within the walls of her home yet he may as well have been a hundred miles away.

"Here is your food, ye great, pretty fool," snapped Pullhair as he slammed the tray down on a small table near the arrow slit in the wall.

"I thought that we had agreed ye would call me Kenneth," Sir

Kenneth said cautiously as he moved to sit at the table. The little man looked furious and he was well aware of how dangerous an angry brownie could be.

"Ye told me to call ye that. I dinnae recall that I agreed. And e'en if I had, I would still be calling ye a great fool now."

"I have offended you in some manner?"

"Nay and aye. Ye havenae insulted me, but ye have hurt the lass and that amounts to the same thing."

"I havenae touched the lass."

"Aye, and that be part of the problem."

Kenneth choked slightly on the wine he had been sipping. "Are ye saying that ye wish me to dishonor Isbel?"

Pullhair swore and stomped around the room for a moment before glaring at Kenneth. "I begin to think ye are worse than a fool. Ye are also stupid. Nay, I would ne'er ask that. But I see what has happened. The lassie tells ye the truth about herself, confides in ye things that she rarely tells others, and ye turn your back on her."

"She asks me to accept some verra odd things, things most people live in fear and trembling of."

"Ye believe in me."

" 'Tis hard not to when ye are standing there yelling at me." He slathered butter on a warm slab of bread and was a little surprised when Pullhair laughed.

"And ye have seen the ghosts."

"I have seen something. It could be just the shadows flickering."

"Ye are verra good at lying to yourself considering what a honest mon ye are and all."

"Heed me, please. I like Isbel. Curse it, I lie abed at night aching for her. I also owe her my life. Howbeit, she is a good womon, one who deserves a mon to wed her and give her children. After she told me the full truth about herself, I kenned that I could ne'er be that mon. The best thing to do, for both of us, was for me to step back ere we stirred more up between us than a fiery lusting."

"Did she ask ye for more?"

"Nay, but she isnae one that is meant to be naught but a leman."

"Laddie, I believe I have lived a few more years than ye." He lifted one shaggy brow when Kenneth laughed. "Isbel is what she is. In truth, her gifts have helped make her the woman she is now. True, she needs to be a wee bit stronger, a wee bit more certain of her own worth, but she is no innocent maid. What gives ye the right to decide what she will and willnae accept? Mayhap she has no interest in wedding you. E'er considered that? And how can ye listen to truth and immediately decide that ye cannae accept it? 'Tis almost cowardly. Ye heard something ye didnae like much or didnae understand and ye ran away and hid."

"That is an unfair accusation. I see no gain in opening my heart to a lass I can ne'er take as my wife. I certainly would consider it a great cruelty to try and win her love kenning that I will leave her."

"Then dinnae try and win her heart."

"I thought brownies were supposed to be such moral fellows."

Pullhair stood up straight, squaring his narrow shoulders. "We are. Ye arenae wed and neither is she. She is no sweet innocent ye are trying to seduce out of her maidenhead. Did ye not see the hand of fate in your meeting? I am nay one to argue with fate."

Kenneth shook his head. "I dinnae ken what game ye play."

"No game. I but see the lass all sad-eyed and mournful then come into this dark room and see ye acting the same. So mayhap what ye might do if ye allow yourselves some freedom would not be seen as moral by some and willnae lead to a marriage and bairns. Howbeit, for a wee while ye would both be a lot happier."

"Aye," Kenneth murmured, his thoughts going to Isbel as they had so often in the last three days. "Aye, we would be, but there could be a high price for it."

When Pullhair left, still grumbling about the idiocy of mortals, Kenneth concentrated on finishing his meal, but his mind refused to be stilled. After Isbel had told him the truth about herself, he had spent many an hour trying to call her mad, but it had not worked. If she was mad, then so was he, for he too saw the brownie and the ghosts. He had then tried to think of what would be if he gave in to his lusts, and slowly fell in love with her. The future looked to be a whirl of ghosts, brownies, faeries, and all that goes bump in the night and it would not stop with her. Any children they had would suffer from the same curse. No matter which way he looked at it, it still seemed that the safest and kindest way to go was to keep his distance

until he was well enough to leave Bandal. He just wished that, once
he had made that decision, he could have ceased to want her.

"Ye used to smile once or twice," murmured Pullhair as he watched
Isbel scrub down the large table in her kitchen.

"Dinnae worry o'er me, Pullhair," she said, and gave him a sad
smile. "I will survive this. I but beg your pardon if, for a wee while,
I suffer the occasional melancholy moment or regret."

"So ye stay here and sigh and he stays up there and sighs. It makes
no sense to me."

"Sir Kenneth is sighing?" she asked, unable to hide her intent
interest.

"As near to it as any mon allows himself."

"He kens where I am. If he wants for company, he can come and
find me."

"Ye are as stubborn as he is. The fates have chosen him for you
yet ye avoid each other as if ye have some plague. How can ye win
his heart if ye ne'er speak to or see him? How can ye make him want
ye if ye stay far away from each other?"

"Pullhair, ye didnae see his face when I told him about me, about
what I can do, and about the history of my family. I dinnae think
there is anything I can do to make him wish to stay with me."

"But ye arenae sure, are ye?"

Isbel sighed and sat down on a stool near the huge kitchen fireplace.
"Nay, I am not *sure*. Howbeit, the mon has turned away from me.
Am I to chase after him?"

"Aye. Dinnae look so shocked, lassie. We are talking about fate
and destiny, nay some base lusting. If he is fool enough to spit in the
eye of fate, so be it. The consequences will fall on his head. Ye cannae
be so foolish. Ye must do all ye can to fulfill the destiny chosen for
you. If that means ye must swallow your pride, weel, take a hearty
gulp, lass, and do it."

She lightly rubbed her temples in a vain attempt to ease the
throbbing in her head. "I cannae even be sure he will let me near

enough to try anything, not even to talk. He wasnae afraid, not truly, but I ken that I now make him very uneasy."

"Ye also make his blood warm." Pullhair grinned when Isabel blushed. "True enough, right now the mon thinks he will only dishonor you if he follows his desires for what ye told him makes him certain that he cannae wed you."

"Then why should I trouble myself with the fool?"

"Because, mayhap if ye lie with him, he will discover that ye stir far more than his lust. And consider this, mayhap the fates arenae concerned with love and marriage, just a bairn. They said he was your mate, but they ne'er said he would love you or stay with you."

"Oh." Isbel frowned as she thought that over and tried to decide if Pullhair was just trying to trick her into doing what he wanted her to. "If 'tis neither love nor marriage he is supposed to bring me, that leaves but one thing—a child. Do ye truly believe he may have been sent here to give me a bairn and no more?"

" 'Tis possible. Ye carry the strongest mark of Lily of any of the clan and I dinnae think any since her have had as many gifts as ye do. The fates may wish that to continue. 'Tis as if Lily has been reborn in you, and if ye die childless, then Lily dies again."

The thought of a child was temptation enough, Isabel mused. Pullhair did not really have to tug at her sense of family loyalty by mentioning Lily and the chance to continue her mark upon the MacLachans. Patrick had failed to give her a child although he had certainly made an effort to do so in the short time he had been with her. What made her hesitate was the thought of the pain she would endure if she became Kenneth's lover and he still walked away. The day he would be strong enough to leave was swiftly approaching so she would not even have much time to persuade him to stay. And if he did leave her with child, she would be alone with a constant, living reminder of how she had failed to win his love. After a few moments of deep thought, she decided a child was worth the price.

"I suppose the only thing to do is to go to him, although I dinnae ken one tiny thing about how to seduce a mon." She smiled crookedly when Pullhair laughed.

"All ye need to do is wear your prettiest nightdress, close the door behind you when ye enter his bedchamber, and smile at him."

"That sounds a little too easy."

"Trust old Pullhair, lass. The mon wants ye. His desire is so strong I could almost smell it. He is just being honorable. Aye, 'tis most good of him and shows that he has great respect for ye, but ye dinnae need such things now. Ye need a mon."

Isbel stared at the heavy door, all that stood between her and Kenneth. She knew it could also be all that stood between her and complete humiliation. Just because Pullhair said the man wanted her did not make it so. The brownie also seemed to have little regard for the state of her heart. She felt sure Pullhair knew she was already in love with Kenneth and that sharing the man's bed would only deepen the emotion, yet he urged her to march into the man's arms and risk a pain no salve or magic could cure.

She took a deep breath to steady herself and smoothed her hands down her delicately embroidered, crisp white nightdress. She had not worn it since her wedding night, yet felt certain it was right to wear it now. Her long, thick hair was secured with a wide, blue silk ribbon, for when she had looked at herself with it hanging loose she had felt uneasy. It had looked far too wanton. As she lifted her hand and softly rapped on the door, she prayed it would take Kenneth at least a few moments to guess exactly why she had come. Isbel knew she would be sick with embarrassment if he knew immediately.

The door opened and Isbel felt her breath catch in her throat. Kenneth wore only his braies. She had tried hard to forget how good his body looked, but the memories of all she had seen as she had nursed his wounds had been impossible to discard. The sight of his tall, lean figure now brought all those memories back in a heady rush. The hint of brown to his skin made it appear warm and inviting. His thick, wavy black hair fell just past his shoulders and she was eager to thread her fingers through it. Her heart pounding, she briefly met his dark gaze then stepped past him into the room and began to look around.

"Isbel," he said quietly as he shut the door, never taking his eyes from her, "why are ye here?"

Kenneth watched the thick swath of her hair sway to and fro as she moved, and he felt his insides twist with want. He also felt all of his grand intentions to be honorable seep away. He had been right to think that the only way to keep his hands off her was to stay away. Now she was in his bedchamber dressed in a sweet yet alluring nightdress. Everything about her invited him to reach for her, and if she did not leave in the next moment or two, he knew he would.

"I am looking for Slayer," she answered, not looking at him for fear he would see that she was lying. "There was a mouse in the kitchens. He should be down there hunting."

"He wasnae in here when I came in and I shut the door."

"And it has stayed shut?" She looked under the bed and idly noted that she needed to clean under there sometime soon.

He grimaced as he suddenly recalled a few incidents, ones caused by the ghosts he was still struggling to ignore and deny the existence of. "There was a brief time when it was difficult to keep the door shut."

"Oh. Sorry. I never have visitors, weel, living ones leastwise, and ye are of great interest." She stood up, brushed off her hands, and realized that he had moved closer. "I will speak to them but I cannae promise that they will heed me."

When he stepped even closer and reached out to trail his long fingers down the sleeve of her gown, she trembled. She clasped her hands behind her back, not wishing to let him see how they shook. There was a soft look in Kenneth's brown eyes that told her Pullhair was right. Kenneth did want her. Isbel prayed that she had tempted the man enough, that he would now push all of his fanciful thoughts of honor aside. A strong sense of honor would have him pushing her out the door soon and that was the last thing she wanted.

Kenneth gently grasped her by the shoulders and pulled her close, smiling faintly when he felt her trembling beneath his hands. "Isbel, did ye truly come to find your cat?"

"Do ye really wish to hear the truth?" she asked in a soft, unsteady voice.

"Aye, I have always favored the truth," he murmured and touched a kiss to her forehead.

"Nay, I didnae come to find the cat."

"What did ye come to find?" He cupped her face between his hands and brushed a kiss over her faintly parted lips.

"Another kiss," she whispered.

"Isbel, my sweet child of the faeries, if I kiss you, 'twill nae end there."

"I am nay an innocent. I ken what the kiss could lead to."

"There will be no *could* about it. It will lead to a bedding. Ye pulled away from the first kiss we shared and I let you. I cannae promise I will let ye free this time. Not unless ye put up a verra loud protest."

"I willnae put up a loud one." She curled her arms around his neck. "I dinnae think I will be inclined to even whisper one."

"Before we start to play this game, honor demands that I tell ye a few rules. I cannae promise ye I will stay—" He frowned when she stopped his words by touching her soft fingertips to his lips.

"I ken that there will be no promises made. I ask for none, save for a wee taste of the passion I felt when we kissed."

"Aye, that I can give ye easily enough. But are ye sure ye dinnae want more of me?"

"I didnae say I dinnae want more, just that I dinnae ask for it and accept that ye may ne'er wish to offer me more."

"Most lasses would want more."

She smiled and stood on her tiptoes, bringing her mouth close to kiss. "As ye may have guessed by now, I am nay like most women."

Kenneth laughed and picked her up then placed her gently on the bed. As he sprawled on top of her, he could not help but wonder if this was some dream. He had had enough of them about having Isbel in his bed, willing and eager. He could simply be having a particularly vivid one.

As he slowly pulled the ribbon from her hair and ran his fingers through the thick waves of soft hair, he decided he would ask no more questions. A dream as real as this was not one he wished to interrupt.

The moment Kenneth began to kiss her, Isbel knew she had made the right choice. If he did leave her, she would at least have sweet memories to ease her pain. Instinct told her that a passion as strong as this did not enter a person's life too often, and if she let him leave without fully tasting it at least once, she would regret it for the rest of her life. She wrapped her arms around him, met the ferocity of his kiss and equaled it, and let her desires rule.

Kenneth sighed with a mixture of satisfaction and regret as he finally eased away from the intimate embrace he and Isbel were locked in. He flopped onto his back, immediately reached for her, and pulled her into his arms. Although he was no profligate, he was not without experience and he knew he had never felt a desire so strong or found lovemaking so richly satisfying. Isbel was all any man could want in a woman. Unfortunately, she was also everything a man should not look for in a wife.

He smiled faintly when she snuggled up against him. He idly moved his hand up and down her side, testing the smallness of her waist, and exploring the gentle curve of her hip. Isbel was a woman of passion, had a quick wit, was beautiful and honest. She was poor in wealth and land, had a strange family history, had a brownie as her closest friend, and seemed to be surrounded by ghosts and all else that most people spoke of in fearful whispers. Kenneth delighted in the former and heartily cursed the rest.

"So, sweet Isbel, have ye found what ye sought?" he asked.

"Nay, ye were right, Slayer isnae here." She grinned when he laughed.

"Wench." He dragged her on top of him and gave her a quick kiss. "Ye could at least try to flatter a poor mon."

"Ah, ye need your vanity stroked."

"That and one or two other things."

"Beast. Aye, I found what I was looking for. And how fares your sense of honor?"

" 'Tis a wee bit bruised, but it will survive."

"Good, for I meant all I said."

"I believe you, and yet, 'tis odd but that makes me feel slightly guilty." He smiled crookedly when she giggled.

"Shall I leave you alone to wallow in it?"

"Try to move, my bonnie spirit, and I shall be forced to take swift and immediate—" He frowned when he suddenly noticed a faint shifting in the shadows. "I am nay admitting that I believe in ghosts, but are ye certain we have been private?"

Isbel sat up and glared at the specter lurking in the corner of the room. "Get out of here, Mary."

"Ye have betrayed Patrick." The old woman's voice echoed in her mind, and a quick glance at Kenneth assured Isbel that she was the only one who had heard Mary.

"Nay, I am a widow. Have been one for near to a year. Now be away with you." The moment the woman disappeared, Isbel assured Kenneth, "I did look o'er the room 'ere ye kissed me and saw no one so I believe we had our privacy."

Even as she spoke, she realized Kenneth was not paying her any attention. His gaze was fixed firmly on her breasts. She blushed as she became aware of how much of herself she had exposed by sitting up.

When Kenneth reached out and covered her breasts with his hands, she murmured in pleasure. "I dinnae suppose ye are doing that to preserve my modesty."

"Nay, I dinnae suppose I am."

She laughed as he pulled her to him. Her happiness might be short-lived but she was determined to luxuriate in it while she could.

Chapter 7

"I WISH ye could help instead of just watching," Kenneth grumbled at the faint image of the young boy that floated along at his side.

He picked up a piece of fallen tree branch and tossed it into the little cart he dragged along behind him. Collecting firewood was a menial task for a knight, but he had to admit that he enjoyed it. It was pleasant to walk through the sunlit forest on a crisp fall day.

It had been a fortnight since he and Isbel had become lovers, and he had almost immediately begun to help with the work around Bandal. At Glenmal he had done his share of the work but only that deemed worthy of a knight. At Bandal there were no servants to leave the less desirable chores to—only Pullhair, who arrived every day at sunset.

As he bent down to pick up another piece of wood, Kenneth suddenly found himself face to face with a very small creature. Not daring to even blink, he studied the thing floating just in front of his nose. It was a woman, a very small woman with wings. His mind told him it was a fairy, but he did not wish to hear that. The tiny woman suddenly grinned and Kenneth gaped. She looked exactly like Isbel. He gasped in shock and straightened up. For one brief moment the creature stayed right before him. Then she vanished.

He glanced at the ghost of the small boy, who smiled shyly, then back to the place where he had seen the tiny winged lady, and shuddered. What was happening to him? He was seeing things he should not be able to see. Worse, he realized with a start, he was accepting such things as if they were a normal part of life. He treated Pullhair as a friend, a man he could talk with about most anything. Ghosts flitted in and out of his sight and he did not even twitch, had even begun to talk to them. Yesterday, he was sure he had heard one of them answer. When Isbel had told him not to go outside two nights ago because the Sluagh were riding, he had accepted her words without question and stayed indoors. And now he had fairies popping up in front of him and grinning at him.

"Nay," he snapped as he threw the firewood into the cart. "I willnae be pulled into that pit of madness."

Kenneth was not really surprised to see that the boy had vanished. He was a very timid ghost. Dragging the little cart behind him, Kenneth started back to the towerhouse. His steps slowed a little as he neared the heavy gates of Bandal and he began to wonder what to do next.

While his anger had been hot, he had intended to march into Bandal, leave the firewood, and forcefully announce that he was leaving for Glenmal in the morning. He knew he could not do so, yet he also knew he had to leave. Each day he stayed with her, each day he breathed the air of Bandal, he became more deeply mired in its strangeness. If he did not get away very soon, he never would, because each day he also found himself becoming more and more willing to stay in Isbel's slender arms.

Isbel smiled at him as he entered the kitchen and he felt his heart sink. Leaving a lover had never been very hard for him. He would fill their ears with words of gratitude and sweet regret, give them some gift and ride away. For some reason he could not even consider treating Isbel that way. He knew he was going to have to be completely truthful, and for one brief moment he resented her for not allowing him to play the same game that he always had.

"I think I saw an elf," he announced, watching Isbel closely as he put the wood he had collected in a box by the fireplace.

There was a tone to his voice that made Isbel tense. She was not sure if it was anger she heard, but she was certain that he was far from pleased. A harsh curse echoed through her mind. He had accepted

Pullhair and seemed at ease with the ghosts, but she knew he still did not want to believe in it all. Now he had seen one of the truly fabled creatures of the netherworld. It had to have recalled him to the fact that he was in a very strange place seeing things he did not want to see. The fates could have chosen a more willing recipient of such gifts, she thought crossly as she began to knead her bread with more force than was needed.

"A lass or a laddie?" she asked with hard-won calm.

"A lass. I bent down to pick up some wood and there she was right in front of me, so close she could have tweaked my nose."

"Ye must have startled her from her hiding place."

"Nay, she didnae look startled and I didnae flush her out of some bramble. She just appeared. Now that I think on it, she looked curious."

"Aye, faeries can be very curious."

"And she looked like you."

He said the words in a cool, flat voice. There was no compliment intended, but no insult either. Kenneth had just been strongly reminded of her unusual bloodline and he did not like it at all. Isbel struggled against a sudden urge to weep and flee the room. She knew what was coming next—the farewell. He was going to flee Bandal before he could see or learn any more.

For one brief moment she wondered if the faeries had sent one of their own to appear before him. They knew everything that happened at Bandal so they knew how badly she wanted Kenneth to stay with her and how uneasy he was about the magic of Bandal. It would not take much thought to realize that he only needed to see a few too many of the spirit world's secrets in quick succession to be sent running home.

Inwardly she shook her head. She could not blame the faeries or the ghosts or even Pullhair. Such things had always been hard for mortals to bear. It would have been wondrous if Kenneth had been different, but she should not condemn him because he was not, nor should she try and grasp some reason, some place or person to blame.

"I am sorry ye were given a fright," she said quietly.

"Nay, not a fright really." He stepped up beside her and idly stroked the thick braid hanging down her slender back. "I was but awakened to all I have been skillfully ignoring."

"Aye, I understand."

"Do ye? Ye were born to this. I was not. Ye have probably been taught that ghosts, faeries, and all such creatures are but a part of life. I was taught that they were the creatures of dreams, nay, nightmares. Ye were taught to understand them. I was taught to fear them."

She wiped the flour from her hands and turned to face him. "I could teach you to understand."

"Could ye? I am eight and twenty and was taught my fears as a child. 'Tisnae easy to banish the lessons set firmly in one's mind and heart whilst he was still young."

"And ye arenae sure ye really want to understand."

Kenneth could see the hurt in her wide blue eyes. He could even feel it and that disturbed him. It implied that he was truly and deeply bonded to Isbel and he did not think he wanted to be that close to her, to anyone. Such closeness left one's heart bared to sorrow and pain. That was something any reasonable man would shy away from. As he stared into her captivatingly beautiful eyes, he was not sure how reasonable he would remain if he stayed with her. The only thing he could be grateful for was that she had no idea of the power she had over him.

"Nay, I dinnae think I do. Lass, do ye ken how close ye stand to the secrets death holds? Ye are knee deep in the spirits of ones who have died and e'en ken where they journey to or at least the path they must take. That alone is enough to make a hardened warrior tremble."

"Ye didnae seem too troubled by the ghosts." She was not sure she understood why suddenly all he had accepted was now unacceptable.

"I wasnae, and that worries me." He dragged his fingers through his hair and scowled as he looked around the kitchen. " 'Tis as if this place has put a spell on me. Not only do I see things I never saw before but I am beginning to treat such sightings as but a part of life. Weel, it may be a part of life at Bandal, but it doesnae exist outside these lands."

"It does. 'Tis just that most people dinnae see it."

"Exactly. I want to be one of those blind, ignorant people again."

"Can ye just forget all ye saw and learned here?"

"I can try." He could see the glint of tears in her eyes and pulled her into his arms. "Lass, 'tisnae ye I run from. 'Tisnae ye I want to push from my mind."

After briefly hugging him, she stepped out of his light embrace.

"But it is. I am Bandal. It is me. I believe I was fated to come here because this is where I truly belong. Patrick's kinsmen could have taken back the lands, for the marriage was a short one and there was no child, but they didnae. They gave it to me. Everything that has happened to me since I came here has only shown me more clearly that I belong here."

"Ye could leave. Ye could come with me," he said impulsively, then realized that he badly wanted her to. He wanted to leave Bandal and all its spirits behind but not her.

"Nay, I dinnae think I can."

"Why? Are ye trapped here?"

"In a way, for I am needed here, wanted and accepted. And this is all I own. Then, too, taking me from Bandal will change little." She smiled sadly. "My gifts werenae born here, merely strengthened."

"Ye mean to say that, wherever ye go, the same things will happen," he said quietly, disappointment sweeping over him.

"Aye, more or less. The magic is strong in Bandal, but 'tis everywhere. Faeries, brownies, ghosts, and all the rest, are everywhere. If ye must get away from such things, then ye must get away from me."

"I am sorry," he whispered and wondered if she would ever know how much he regretted leaving her.

"So the fool is running away, is he?"

Isbel looked up to see Pullhair standing beside her. She tossed aside the rag she held, suddenly realizing she had been rubbing that same spot on the table since Kenneth had walked out of the kitchen several hours ago. The pain she felt seemed to have become part of her blood, flowing through her constantly with every beat of her heart. She did not really want to discuss it but knew Pullhair would prod at her until she did.

"Aye, he is leaving in the morning. He saw a faerie today and she smiled at him. He has decided that he has had a bellyful of the magic of Bandal and cannae stomach any more."

"He is a coward."

"Nay, for he really doesnae flee out of fear. Aye, 'tis there, as it is in all of we poor timid mortals. Kenneth simply doesnae want to be a part of all this. He doesnae want to ken all the secrets this place holds. He doesnae want to see what few others ever will. He wants to return to what he was."

"And ye will just let him go."

She stood up so abruptly she knocked her stool over. "Aye. What would ye have me do? Tie him to the bed until he changes his mind? E'en if I could be so bold, it wouldnae work. As he says, this isnae his life, isnae what he was raised to accept or e'en like."

Pullhair shook his head. "I had thought him a better mon than that."

"Oh, I think he is." She smiled sadly. "He just doesnae think he wants to be. I can understand that. There are times when I heartily wish I wasnae what I am. I wish I could look into the shadows and see only shadows or walk through the forest and see naught but the trees. The blood I carry and the gifts I hold can sometimes be a great burden, Pullhair."

"That is only because your people willnae accept them."

"And what is wrong with wishing to be accepted, e'en liked, by your own kind? That is what Kenneth runs back to. He may ne'er say so, but if he accepts me, then he must accept near banishment by his own people. The choice is either me or the rest of the world. I was ne'er given that choice, but he has it and I cannae fault him for returning to all the others."

"But he hasnae e'en given ye a child yet," he grumbled.

A chill ran down Isbel's spine. One thing that had kept her from total despair was the thought that Kenneth had left her with child. Pullhair's cross words killed that hope.

"Are ye sure?" she asked, her voice tight with emotion.

"Aye. Here now," he cried in alarm when Isbel buried her face in her hands. "Dinnae start weeping. There is still hope."

"How can there be? The mon leaves in the morning." She righted her stool and sat down, knowing that Pullhair's presence was all that kept her from succumbing to her intense grief.

"There is still this night."

She gaped at him. "The mon is leaving me. Am I to go to his bed after he has said fare thee well? Surely that would mark me as little more than some hedgerow whore."

"Nay. Ye are letting your pride rule ye again. Ye became the mon's lover with no promises made nor love words spoken. In truth, ye entered his bed kenning that he might leave. I cannae see how it makes much difference now that ye ken for certain he will leave and when."

Isbel sighed and gently rubbed her forehead with her fingers. "Weel, it does. I am nay sure I can explain the why of it, but it does make a difference."

"Weel, ye had best swallow your pride again."

"Why? Why cannae he swallow his pride?"

"Because he willnae. 'Tis certain he willnae twixt now and sunrise. So, ye must be the one to do so."

"I begin to get a bellyache."

Pullhair reached out and yanked her braid, ignoring her sharp curse and easily avoiding the swat she aimed at him. "Ye want your belly filled, lassie, and ye cannae get that wish by sitting here weeping and moaning."

"I am *not* weeping and moaning. The mon might well be offended if he kenned we were using him for stud."

"Are ye planning to tell him?"

Her natural inclination to be honest welled up inside her, but she ruthlessly quelled it. "Nay, and I shall have to do a penance for that." She sighed and idly drummed her fingers on the table. "Are ye certain that, if I lie with that mon tonight, I will bear his child?"

"Now, lassie, ye ken that I shouldnae be telling ye such things."

"Pullhair," she snapped, then took a deep breath to ease her temper. "Ye are asking a lot of me and have your own purposes for doing so. I ken well that ye are my friend, but ye dinnae push me into the mon's arms solely for the sake of my happiness. For that, I think I deserve something. All I ask is some assurance that, if I go to Kenneth tonight, I will wake with child come morning."

"Aye, ye will."

"Thank ye," she whispered. "I am treating the mon most dishonestly and myself most dishonorably. Howbeit, I will do all that and more if it means I can hold a child in my arms."

*   *   *

Kenneth frowned when there sounded a soft rap at the door. He had just retired after a somber, quiet, and somewhat tense evening meal with Isbel and Pullhair. There was a good chance it was Pullhair at the door preparing to scold him or try to talk him into staying and Kenneth was certain that he did not wish to see the little man.

He opened the door and gaped. Isbel dressed in her fine linen nightgown with her hair loose and flowing over her slim shoulders was the last thing he had expected to see. For a moment he was afraid that he had not made himself clear.

"Isbel, did ye heed me at all this afternoon?" he asked uncertainly as she slipped past him into the room.

"Aye, ye are leaving when the sun rises," she replied as she sat down on the bed, clasping her hands in her lap to hide the way they trembled.

"Yet ye have come to me?"

"I do understand why ye must leave." She frowned when he shut the door but continued to just stare at her. "Why are ye looking at me like that?"

He smiled crookedly as he moved to stand in front of her. "I suppose I was feeling a wee bit unsettled because ye arenae upset o'er my leaving."

"I didnae say I wasnae upset. I said I understand. What I may have misunderstood was that ye were truly saying farewell this afternoon, setting yourself away from me right then and not in the morning."

When she stood up, he caught her in his arms, sat down on the bed, and settled her on his lap. "Nay, I am glad ye came to me tonight, more than words can say. I fear I am just confused as to why ye would do so after I have told ye I am leaving."

So ye can give me a child, she thought but bit her lip to keep from babbling out the truth. "Ye ken that I want you," she said, staring at their clasped hands to hide her blushes. "Ye saying fare thee well doesnae end that wanting. I like the way ye can make me feel and this is the last night I will e'er have the chance to savor that pleasure." She peeked up at him and felt the warmth of his gaze enter her blood. "I think no other mon will e'er make me feel as ye do and, let us face the cold, hard truth, there are none about to teach me otherwise."

The mere thought of another man touching Isbel both hurt and enraged Kenneth, but he fought to push such feelings aside. He had no right to feel them because he was walking away from her. He decided it might be wise not to think about who she might be with or what she might be doing once he was gone. The feelings raging through his body told him he could easily find himself returning to Bandal. That would be foolish since he would still be unable to stay, and also very unkind.

"I should be mortally ashamed of myself," he murmured.

"Why?"

"Ye have saved my life and ye have given me a sort of pleasure I have ne'er tasted before, yet I turn my back on you."

"I couldnae leave ye to die or be taken up by the Sluagh and I chose to come to your bed. The pleasure was also shared. Mayhaps I should be ashamed."

He fell back onto the bed and pulled her on top of him. "Then let us wallow in our shame together."

She smiled, clinging to him as he squirmed around until they were in a better position on the bed. " 'Tis always best to share such things."

Isbel cried out in amused surprise as he hastily removed his braies and her nightgown. When their flesh met, she shuddered. Their passion was so strong and so well matched. She could not understand how he could not see that, could not see as clearly as she did that they were meant to be together.

She slid her hand down his side, savoring the feel of his smooth, taut skin. Isbel knew she would not get much sleep, and if she had her way, neither would Kenneth. A greed born of desperation gnawed at her. As she touched her lips to his, she knew this would be the very last night of lovemaking for her. Kenneth might well find another. A man in his position was expected to marry and sire children. She could not do the same, could not seek out a new lover. After he walked away, she would be completely alone except for his child. As Kenneth began to make love to her, she prayed that Pullhair was right, that this was the night she would conceive a child. It could be the only thing that kept her from complete despair.

Kenneth silently dressed and donned his sword and padded jupon. For a long moment he stood at the side of the bed and stared at the sleeping Isbel. He wanted to crawl back in beside her, to hold her in his arms, despite a long night of lovemaking. He also knew that, if he gave in to that urge, he might never leave.

As quickly and as quietly as he could, he slipped out the door. Kenneth wished he did not feel quite so much like a thief in the night. He hurried to the stables, saddled Wallace, and let himself out of the bailey. The only clear thought in his mind was to get away before he changed his mind.

Isbel slipped out of bed, tugged on her night rail, and went to the window. It had probably been cowardly to feign sleep as Kenneth left the room, but she felt sure it was for the best. As she watched him ride away in the gray light of dawn, she placed her hand over her belly and prayed that Pullhair was right. If she could not have the man at least she could have some solace in bearing and loving his child.

Chapter 8

ISBEL grimaced, straightened up, and rubbed at the ache in the small of her back. As soon as Kenneth had left, she had dressed and come to the stables to clean. It was hard, filthy work, and it almost succeeded in making her forget how alone she was. She just wished she could work through the night.

As she stepped outside to draw water from the well so that she could clean off the stench of the stables, she tensed. Something was wrong. Never before had she felt afraid or threatened within the surrounding walls of Bandal, but she did now. It was as if all the magic that had protected her had suddenly been yanked away.

She kept looking around as she washed up, anxious to get back into the towerhouse and bar the door. Even as she tossed the water into the dead garden near the stables, she knew it was too late. The gates of Bandal were pushed open and two men rushed in. She knew she had no chance of reaching the safety of the towerhouse but she ran for it anyway.

The thinner and taller of the two men charged her, caught her around the waist, and threw her to the ground. The bulkier man quickly joined them and helped his companion pin her down. An icy hand clutched at her heart. She knew what they planned to do and her only clear thought was that they would not damage the child she carried.

In her mind she screamed Kenneth's name but she knew it was hopeless. He had left over an hour ago. Even if she could somehow touch his mind with her pleas, he would never be able to reach her in time. Realizing that she was truly alone, that even her spirits had deserted her, she struggled even harder. The skinny man sitting astride her raised his fist and Isbel prepared for the blow. She felt almost grateful when his knuckles slammed into her for the blackness swiftly followed.

"Kenneth! Kenneth, help me!"

Kenneth abruptly reined in his horse to a stop and looked around. He saw nothing yet fear clutched at his insides and that plaintive cry for help still echoed in his mind. It was Isbel's voice, he was certain of it. What he could not understand was how he could hear her, for he was a full hour's ride from Bandal.

"Magic," he muttered. "She tried to use her magic to draw me back, Wallace."

Even as he spoke the words, he knew they were not true. Isbel would never trick him like that. The fear in her voice had also been too real. Something was wrong. The pull he felt, the silent demand that he race home to Bandal, was not one of greed or selfishness, but one of terror and need. She was not calling for his love or his passion, but his strength and protection.

He turned his horse back toward Bandal and spurred it to a gallop. Panic rose up in him but he forced it back down. It would not take him an hour to return to her for he was traveling much faster, but he was not sure he would be in time. Was the cry for help a premonition or was it torn from her own mind because she was already in danger? If it was the latter, he knew he could never reach her in time and he heartily cursed himself for leaving her at all.

The sight that greeted Kenneth's eyes as he rode through the gates of Bandal made him blind with rage. He screamed his battle cry as his horse reared to a halt, then he leapt from the saddle. The two men assaulting Isbel barely got to their feet before he was confronting them, sword in hand.

Kenneth cut down the bulkier of the two men quickly, but the tall, thin man had managed to draw his sword by the time Kenneth faced him. The battle was fierce but short. Kenneth knew he had the greater skill, and his confidence in himself was justified in but minutes as he ended the man's life with a clean thrust to the heart.

He hastily cleaned his sword blade off on the dead man's ragged jupon, sheathed his weapon, and rushed to Isbel's side. Some of his fear and rage seeped away when he saw that the braies Pullhair had demanded she wear were still securely in place. Her clothes were torn and there was a vivid bruise already forming on her chin, but he could not see any other signs of injury.

After hastily tending to his horse, all the while keeping a close eye on Isbel in case she began to wake, Kenneth picked her up in his arms. He carried her to the bedchamber he had used. The sight of Slayer basking in the light of the sun on the blankets was oddly comforting. The cat moved to sit at the end of the bed, watching as Kenneth tended to Isbel.

First he removed her torn clothes then gently bathed her. It troubled Kenneth a little that she still had not stirred by the time he had her dressed in her nightgown. He frowned down at her, absently stroking Slayer as the cat moved to curl up at her side. He reassured himself by noting that her breathing was steady and even and her color was good.

"Ye keep a close eye on your mistress, Slayer," Kenneth murmured. "I have to clear away that refuse I left bleeding in the bailey."

The moment Kenneth stepped out into the bailey, he knew something was wrong. It took him another moment to believe what he saw. The bodies were gone and the gates were closed. He stared down at the bloodstained dirt for a long while, needing to reassure himself that he had truly fought and killed two men.

"Ye do a fine job of cleaning up after the battle," he said aloud, glancing around and not surprised when he saw nothing, "but where were ye when the lass was in danger?"

He shook his head, no longer amazed at anything that happened at Bandal. A cry from within the towerhouse drew his attention and he raced back to the bedchamber. As he hurried to Isbel's side, he noticed that Slayer had had the wit to move out of the path of his thrashing mistress. Kenneth gently restrained Isbel and talked softly, trying to pull her free of her terror.

Isbel felt Kenneth's presence before she heard him. Slowly his soft words of reassurance reached her mind. She ceased fighting his hold, her breathing steadied, and her heartbeat slowed. When she opened her eyes to see him watching her with concern, she forced herself to smile.

"Ye came back," she whispered.

"Aye." He rose to pour her a goblet of wine from the jug by the bed. "I answered your call."

She frowned at him and took a long drink of the wine he handed her. "Well, aye, I did call out to you, but ye must be mistaken. Ye could never have gotten to me in time, for I called your name but moments ago, when those men attacked me."

"But I am certain I heard ye cry out. Ye said, 'Kenneth! Kenneth, help me!'"

"I did, but ye must have heard that an hour after ye left in order for ye to return here when ye did. I was not in danger then. In truth, I was mucking out the stables."

Kenneth just stared at her for several moments then cursed. She was right. Those men attacking her could not have arrived many moments before he did. Isbel had called for him only when she had been attacked, and he had heard her cry about an hour before that attack had happened.

"I have been made game of," he said as he poured himself some wine and drank it down swiftly in an attempt to cool his anger.

"I swear, Kenneth, I have done naught."

"Nay, bonnie Isbel." He sat on the side of the bed, took her hand, and kissed her palm. "I dinnae point the finger of accusation at you."

"Then who?"

"There are many possibilities. The faeries, Pullhair, e'en your cursed army of ghosts. They wished me to return, and they did what they had to to make that happen."

Isbel sipped at her wine as she thought over his accusation. She did not want to believe it, but could not refute it either. Too many things pointed to the truth of his charge.

"But I am certain those two men were real," she finally said.

"Aye, very real. The blood soaked the earth they fell upon and it wasnae cleared away although the bodies were."

"Someone took their bodies?"

"Aye, and closed the gates after them."

"Kenneth, did ye notice anything different about Bandal?"

"Nay, 'twas the same. Aye, there was e'en that moment as I rode up to it where I wasnae really sure it was there. 'Tis as if a haze clouds it from view, but then all was clear again."

"Yet when I stepped out of the stable, I felt something was wrong, something had changed. I recall thinking that it felt as if someone had yanked away all of Bandal's protection."

She cursed and thrust her empty goblet at him. As he refilled both their goblets, she struggled to think clearly. By the time he sprawled on the bed at her side, handed her her wine, and draped his arm around her shoulders, she had come to a decision.

"Ye are right, Kenneth," she said, her anger roughening her voice. "Someone has made game of you. Aye, more than you. Me and e'en those two men. We have been naught but pawns in someone's chess game." She looked at him, saw his grin, and nearly gaped. "Cannae ye see it? First, ye hear me call out to you an hour 'ere I do so. Second, the protection around Bandal that has kept me safe for so long vanishes. Third, suddenly two men rush in and attack me. Fourth, ye ride in to slay the two men and save me."

"A true hero," he drawled and laughed.

"Are ye not furious? They play with our lives."

"Mayhap they think we are too stupid to ken what is best for us."

She turned to face him squarely. The man should be furious but he was not. He was not even faintly annoyed. It made no sense to Isbel. He had fled Bandal because he could not abide the magic, yet when that magic tricked him into returning, he laughed.

"Kenneth, have ye suffered a blow to the head?" she asked, eyeing him warily when he just grinned.

"Nay, love." He tugged her closer and lightly kissed her. "Aye, when I first realized what had happened, I was angry, but that anger was mostly because of the danger they had put you in. They allowed you to be mauled and hurt just to get what they wanted. As I waited for ye to wake, however, I kenned I could forgive them their interference—this time."

"Weel, I am nay sure I can," she mumbled as she stared down at her nearly empty wine goblet. "Now I must bear hearing ye say farewell again."

"Nay, for I willnae say it."

Isbel tensed, but continued to stare at her wine. She was afraid to look at him, afraid she was just dreaming the words. When he gently grasped her chin, careful not to add to the pain of her bruise, she almost resisted his attempt to turn her face back toward him. Even though she now faced him, she could not look at him. Isbel was terrified he would see in her eyes the hope and the love she felt for him or, worse, not notice it at all.

"Look at me, Isbel," he commanded.

She slowly raised her gaze to meet his and felt her breath catch in her throat. There was a soft, tender expression upon his face, a warmth in his gaze, that she had never seen before. Although she told herself not to let her hopes get too high, Isbel felt taut and breathless with anticipation.

"Are ye planning to stay a wee while longer?" she asked, inwardly cursing the tremor in her voice that exposed her fierce emotions.

"Would ye like me to stay?"

For the first time since he was a gangly youth, Kenneth felt uncertain. There was an expression on Isbel's face that gave him hope, but he suspected it was easy to deceive oneself in such things. He knew what he had to do now, what he needed and wanted. Despite the passion she had revealed in his arms, he was just not certain she needed and wanted the same.

"Ye dinnae like the magic that is Bandal," she replied.

"Isbel, my sweet, overgrown faerie, ye didnae answer my question. Would ye like me to stay?"

"Only if ye wish to."

He laughed, amused by her vague responses and how they made him feel—more confident. The very fact that she could not bring herself to say a simple aye or nay told him that she was feeling as uncertain as he had been. Isbel was also afraid to expose her heart for fear such emotion was not returned. One of them needed to go first, to state clearly and plainly what they felt and what they wanted. Kenneth knew it should be him, if only because he had already left her once, but he was not sure he had the skill or the courage.

"I feel as if we do some strange dance," he said. "When I first heard you call to me, I fear my thoughts were unkind. For one brief moment, I thought ye tried to bring me back through some pretense, some trick."

"I would ne'er do that. And what purpose could it serve? Ye would surely discover what I had done and just leave again."

"It took but a heartbeat for me to ken ye would ne'er do that. Then I felt your fear. It became my fear. My only clear thought was to get to you as swiftly as I could and end the threat ye were under, end your fears. That need was so strong it was nearly a madness."

"Weel, I thank ye, but I think I will be safe now. The protection of Bandal has returned and I dinnae think they will play that trick again, whoever they are. The faeries are the ones I suspect."

"Isbel, I ken that ye will be safe, safer than e'en the king. That isnae what I am trying to say. The way I felt when I kenned ye were in danger told me that no matter how far I rode I could ne'er get away from you. I am nay sure I could get away from the magic that surrounds you and is within you."

Her heart was pounding so hard and fast, Isbel was surprised Kenneth could not hear it. "Are ye saying that ye want to stay with me? That ye can now abide the spirits and all the rest?"

"Aye, I want to stay. I need to stay." He smiled when she clung to him for, although he ached to hear a few more words of love, the emotions she was revealing would suffice for now. "I kenned that ere I had passed through Bandal's gates."

"But ye kept riding." She pressed her ear to his broad chest and delighted in the steady beat of his heart.

"Aye. I am very skilled at deluding myself. I had said I had to leave and I was hard at work denying all my heart and mind told me. When I sensed the danger ye were in, I realized I played a fool's game, that I could deceive myself for a while, but only for a while. Soon the truth would come out and the truth was that I was making the greatest mistake of my life by leaving you."

When he turned her face up to his, she readily accepted and returned his kiss. She offered no resistance when he gently pushed her down onto the bed, although she was astonished at how swiftly he removed their clothes. Their lovemaking was fiercely passionate, and she reveled in it despite the occasional twinge it gave her bruises. They lay entwined for a long time after their desires were sated, and when he finally eased the intimacy of their embrace, Isbel murmured her regret. She wanted to keep him close for fear he would change his mind again.

"Ah, Isbel," he said as he rolled onto his back and tucked her up against his side. "Such passion comes but once in a lifetime. I cannae believe I was such a fool as to try and leave it behind."

"Are ye certain ye wish to leave all else behind?" she asked, terrified that he had not really considered the consequences of staying at Bandal.

"I dinnae believe I need to turn my back on all I once knew." When she started to speak, he stopped her protest with a brief kiss. "Nay, hold your warnings. I ken that few people can bear the magic of Bandal and ye have often suffered the sting of that fear, the loneliness it forces upon you. I think there may be a few of my people who are nay so timid, but if not, I willnae regret it. I will have you and any bairns we are blessed with. And though they be spirits and creatures of the shadows, there are a lot of, er, people about."

"I pray ye are certain, that ye truly ken what ye may give up, for I dinnae think I could bear it if ye left again."

"Why?"

The words stuck in Isbel's throat for a moment as she stared at him. Then she decided it was her turn to be honest and bare her soul. Kenneth had not spoken of love yet, but he had certainly been forthright, and he was going to stay.

"Because I love you," she whispered and gave a squeak of surprise and a little discomfort when he hugged her tightly.

"Sorry," he murmured, realizing how he was squeezing her. "Now I am sure we will survive, no matter how apart from the rest of the world we are, for we will have our love to keep us strong."

"*Our* love?"

Isbel knew she was trembling a little as she raised herself up on her elbows to stare at him. She was not sure which made her more unsteady, her anger or the fact that Kenneth truly cared about her. He could at least have the courtesy to say it clearly, she mused, and understood why she felt angry. Kenneth wanted the words from her but expressed his love in vague, sweeping statements.

"Ye dinnae look too loving just now, my bonnie elf," Kenneth said, eyeing her warily.

"I am nay sure I feel too loving. Ye pull the words from me, my fine knight, but I hear naught from you."

"But I have told ye how I feel."

"Aye, I ken that ye think ye have and that is what is so annoying. Ye have spoken of staying, of needing and wanting me, and e'en of how glorious our passion is. Ye have not said how ye feel about me."

"Ah, Isbel, I love ye with all my heart and soul."

Her anger fled so quickly, replaced by such a strong surge of joy, that Isbel felt weak. She collapsed in his arms and fought the urge to weep. Kenneth would probably have a difficult time understanding that a woman could cry simply because she was so happy.

"Now I am certain we will abide well together," she said.

"Ye were concerned that this happiness wouldnae last?"

"Aye, for I didnae ken that ye loved me. I dinnae think we will skip merrily through the years ever smiling, but love is needed to hold two people together. Now I ken that we have that, that our bond is strong and will endure."

"We must be wed as soon as possible."

"There is a priest but a day's ride from here."

"Then we shall travel to him on the morrow."

"I dinnae suppose Pullhair can attend."

"Nay, and I am sorry for that. Howbeit, I believe our marriage will start more smoothly if we dinnae approach the priest with a brownie at our side." He smiled at her when she looked up at him. "Now kiss your husband and tell him how much ye love him."

"Are ye going to demand that of me a lot?"

"Oh, aye, most every day."

"And may I demand the same?"

"Ye will ne'er have the need to ask, for I will tell ye in every word and every act. Ye have won me, lass. Ye have woven your magic around me."

"Nay, love has," she said and kissed him.

Epilogue

Kenneth wrapped his arms around his wife and smoothed his hands over her swollen belly. It had been three years since he had raced back to Bandal and he knew he had made the right choice. For all of its strangeness, Bandal was home and Isbel was the mate of his heart and soul. If he had not returned to her, he knew he would have never felt whole again.

He looked around the bailey and smiled with pride. There were now others living and working at the towerhouse. After being duly warned, a few of his kinsmen and their families had joined him. It had been proven that all one had to do to learn the secrets was to live and love Bandal and care for its mistress. His people had needed some time to adjust but now they, too, accepted the magic all around them, even took pride in it.

"Young Robert has become very quick on his feet," Isbel said and pointed toward their son as the sturdy boy of two ran across the bailey, a nursemaid hurrying along behind.

"May it please God to make our next child as strong," Kenneth murmured, lightly kissing the top of her head.

"And as protected," she said as she turned in his arms and smiled up at him.

"Aye." Kenneth laughed and shook his head. "I think he draws the spirits to him even more than ye do."

"He does. At first Pullhair was disappointed. He thought I was to bear another Lily and how could that be when my child was a male. It did not take him long to see that Lily's spirit is very strong in the boy."

"Very strong."

"Ye sound proud of that."

"I am."

Isbel hugged him. "I dinnae think ye can ever ken how much I love you."

"It cannae be any more than I love you."

"Even after ye decided to stay, I still feared ye would ne'er fully accept the magic of this place, that it might still drive ye away from me."

"Never." He tilted her face up to his and brushed a kiss over her full lips. "I will ne'er leave again. I realized that there was one part of Bandal I could never live without, one of its magics that was no less than the very blood in my veins. That magic is you, Isbel. Even if all the rest vanishes in the blink of an eye, Bandal will still be my home, for its mistress holds me firmly in her spell."

Isbel curled her arms around his neck and kissed him. Fate, she decided, could at times be extraordinarily perceptive.

FAERIE
PRINCESS

Elizabeth Ann
Michaels

Chapter 1

Lachlan Castle on Loch Fyne, 1818

Eyes *as deep as the loch and as brown as the richest mahogany stared at her with an intensity that burned straight to her soul. A smile came slowly, fleetingly to hard lips before they lowered and took possession of hers.*

Inside, she quivered, knowing it was to be this way, and yet not knowing what to expect. She wasn't prepared for his heat or his strength, or the way her body wanted to cling greedily to his. Nor could she have put a stop to any of it, even if she had the power or the will to do so. Both had been stripped away by forces beyond her.

His muttered words came to her in a language she didn't understand, melodic, fervent, pressed into the side of her neck and against the curve of her breast. His fingers followed his lips' path, stroking, caressing, making her arch . . .

"Krista?"

The voice seemed to call to her from a great distance.

"Krista, sweetheart."

She blinked back to the present, dazed for a moment or two as she always was in the aftermath of one of her visions. After a lifetime of such experiences, she should have been able to collect herself with practiced ease, but composure wasn't coming this time. Her vision had disturbed her greatly.

With a feeling of consternation, she looked up to find her family regarding her from their places at the dining table in the castle's solar. Mother, Father, Glenn, Agnes, and Catherine. The MacLachlans of Lachlan Castle.

"I'm sorry," she said, returning her mother's smile with an effort.

"What is it, dear?"

"Were you *seeing* things again, Krista?" little Agnes asked.

She had been. Oh, heavens above, she had been.

"It's just another of her visions." Ten-year-old Glenn dismissed the entire matter as routine and returned to his breakfast.

More curious than anything else, her father asked, "What was it this time?"

The only thing she could possibly tell them was, "Keith is bringing a guest home with him." There was no telling them that she had *seen* this guest, this man, in her bed. "He's a Russian general. A prince, actually."

Five faces registered a mingling of surprise and joy. "A Russian prince?" Catherine exclaimed, delight making her seem far younger than her sixteen years.

"If you say it's so," her mother said, "then it must be." She fingered the lace at her collar and mused, "I wonder why Keith dinna mention in his message that he was bringing anyone with him. Are you sure, dear?"

Oh, aye, she was sure. For days, she'd *seen* snippets of this prince in or about the castle, dining at this very table, lounging in front of the fire in one of the guest rooms, riding over the land. And finally, incredibly, *in her bed.*

"I'm positive." As positive as she was that her eldest brother was returning after five years. In that time he'd fought against Napoleon's armies before assuming the roll of diplomat. Now, with the occupation of France nearly at an end, he was coming home with a Russian prince destined to become her lover.

Swallowing with great difficulty, she said, "He'll be with us for a short while."

"Then I had best see that one of the guest rooms is made ready," her mother averred, already rising.

"That would be best. They'll be here within the hour."

"So soon?"

Krista couldn't have explained why she knew that any more than she could explain why for the first time in her nineteen years she had been included in one of her visions. Until now, her second sight had without fail been directed toward others, never herself.

Too tense to sit still any longer, she gave up the pretense of behaving as if she were fine. Thankfully, no one noticed. The jubilant energy of expectation was in the air. Family and servants alike were overjoyed as they awaited Keith's return.

She left the castle behind for the rocky ground patched with expansive swells of green. Loch Fyne lay nearby, its waters as familiar as the mossy hillock on the edge of the forest where she came to sit. Her faerie hillock, or so she thought of it with an easing of her spirit.

There were others. Strathlachlan boasted its share of faerie domains, marked by boulders or flowers or even rocking stones. But there was something about this particular hillock that drew her as the one in the shadows of the old castle ruins never could. She assumed it was because the faeries wanted it so. And who was she to second-guess the faeries?

There were those—misguided, unfortunate souls—who doubted that the wee magical beings lived at all, let alone within this mound guarded by a broken ring of boulders, but she had no doubts. She was proof that faeries existed and that they had bestowed their magic upon her.

How else to explain away the unexplainable? From the time she'd been a mere lass, she'd been gifted with what some called the second sight, *seeing* shipwrecks off the coast, *knowing* whether a bairn would be born a boy or a girl, *feeling* the arrival of a storm.

How else could she explain the more rare times when she had been helpless to bestow her entire emotional being on a few select people? Only faeries, with their magical powers, could have made it possible for her emotions to inundate a dying child, a crippled man, a grieving widow. One and all had been in need, and one and all had received a boundless love to comfort them.

How else to explain away her eyes? In a family whose eyes were an invariable brown, hers were a light, silvery blue. Fey eyes, some called them. She'd been told they possessed an otherworldliness that had the weaker of heart crossing themselves, and hanging branches of rowan over their doors at night in a bid for protection.

It was utter nonsense. She was a perfectly normal young woman who just happened to be blessed with a gift, as she preferred to think of her abilities. She couldn't make the clouds rain or turn someone into a toad, although on a great many occasions when she'd been younger, and Keith's teasing had rankled, she'd dearly wished he'd grow webbed toes and jump into the loch.

Thinking of him made her smile. She loved him as she loved the rest of her family. She had missed him terribly, and now he was home.

The knowledge came to her on the wings of the green and purple-winged butterfly that stopped to sun itself on her lap. At the finger she offered, it perched for a second or two longer, then went off to meet its day.

She rose to do the same, knowing Keith was arriving at that very moment. Knowing the prince was with him made her drag her feet. Virgin that she was, it was daunting to know that the man who would alter that state was waiting for her. Doubly daunting was that the whole matter seemed to be destined, as if she had nothing to say about her own fate.

Casting the hillock a damning glance, she asked of the faeries, "Why are you doing this?"

A sudden gentle breeze whirled about her, lifting the hem of her gown. "Do not play your tricks on me," she scolded. "You're up to your old mischief, only this time it isn't amusing." It bordered on alarming.

Having a man in her bed was something she had always associated with marriage to a man she loved. Making love to a *Russian prince* she barely knew was astounding, and would have been preposterous if she had cause to doubt her visions. Unfortunately, her visions were unfailingly accurate.

She wasn't certain what to expect, or how to proceed. Her vision had revealed none of that, but then, her visions always had been as frustratingly incomplete as they were involuntary and inconstant. At times, this gift of hers was irritating at best.

The sound of voices raised in laughter reached her before she even entered the castle's inner courtyard. It didn't take any special powers for her to know that the family had rushed outside to Keith, too overjoyed to remain in the castle a minute longer. After five long years, such happiness couldn't be contained. There would be hugs and kisses as well as tears.

The scene was all she imagined it to be. Her parents and siblings stood in the shadows of Keith's coach, all talking and laughing at the same time. Keith himself was a tall figure, taller than she remembered, bent low to hug Mother, with Father's arm around his shoulders as if he, Father, had to reassure himself that his eldest son was home safe and whole.

Struck suddenly by the enormity of that, she raced from the gateway across the inner courtyard. "Keith," she called out.

He turned within the tight circle of family. "There you are." Laughing, he caught her up in his arms to give her a hearty hug. At length, he held her at arm's distance. "Little faerie, let me have a look at you."

He looked his fill, noting all the changes wrought by the passage of time. "When I left, you were little more than a lass, but I come home to find a grown woman, and bonnie in the bargain."

She gazed back, taking note of the maturity fashioned by war. "And you're not the skinny, twenty-year-old laddie who left us," she teased in return.

"Still as sassy as ever, I see. *Seen* anything of interest lately?"

"She did, she did," Glenn announced in gleeful abandon. "She knew you were bringing the prince with you."

For a few blessed minutes, she'd forgotten the prince. At this reminder, she straightened, her smile splintering at the edges. Almost fearfully, she looked about and found him, recognized him, a tall figure in military garb, standing just beyond the carriage, staring at her with sheer, overwhelming intensity.

Helplessly, she stared back . . . and felt the rest of the world fade away. It was the most peculiar sensation, as if family and surroundings were gone and she and the prince were alone with nothing to guide her but the certainty of her visions.

As usual, they had been woefully incomplete, giving her mere glimpses of what was real. Reality was wide shoulders, narrow hips, and long legs to complement the height. Reality was a clean-lined jaw, high forehead, and hair a shade shy of black. Reality was liquid brown eyes she had come to know, and yes, perhaps to fear, and a mouth so amorously sculpted her stomach fluttered uncontrollably. Oh, heavens above, reality was supreme male power underscored with a raw sensuality for which no vision could have ever prepared her.

But there was another layer to reality, one far more subtle and nearly concealed behind the challenging smile and the sense of command. It was an unmistakable air of barely leashed civility, an air of a man too accustomed to the horrors of war.

She blinked the split-second impression away, its effects so unsettling she had to fight the instinct to step back. Her visions had most definitely not shown her this. A bit unnerved, she lifted her eyes to his and bit back a startled gasp. An indefinable awareness filled his gaze, a glint that spoke of a heightening of his senses. He was as conscious of her as she was of him.

From far off, she heard Keith's voice, and could have easily rejoiced for the return of reality. "Krista, may I introduce my good friend, General Prince Alexi Petrovich Kaskov. Sasha, my sister, Lady Krista MacLachlan."

Alexi. The name of the man to whom she would give her innocence was named Alexi.

By some magic, she remembered her manners and produced the necessary smile. "Your highness." There was no helping the threadiness of her voice. "Welcome to Lachlan Castle."

In spite of the wobbling of her knees, the curtsey she gave was picture perfect. Private congratulations were surely in order, she thought, until Prince Alexi lifted her offered hand and with indolent, masculine grace pressed his lips to the backs of her fingers. Then it was all she could do not to trip to her knees as heat raced up her arm.

Instinctively, she tried to pull her hand free, but he retained his hold, his gaze delving more deeply into hers.

"The pleasure is mine," he murmured with a trace of Russian accent, the sound of his voice in startlingly perfect harmony with the firm pressure of his hand. Neither should have surprised her. On some unfathomable level, she knew this man, his manner, his touch, but still, they came as a shock.

The resulting turmoil set her insides to quivering. Even if he was the handsomest man she'd ever met, she wasn't one to let herself be beguiled by appearances. Character was far more appealing to her than looks, but there she stood, trembling like a green lassie with her first suitor, feeling as if no one else existed except the two of them. Was it because she already knew their ultimate outcome, or were her uncontrollable responses meant to lead her to that very outcome?

She was still wondering long after they'd all settled comfortably in the Lord's hall. Ages ago, the great open room would have seen armaments stacked in the corners and rushes on the floor. Now, it was outfitted for formal entertaining. Krista sat farthest from the fireplace, feeling absurdly warmed from within. Little wonder there. With the heat from Prince Alexi's touch still lingering in her fingers and her mind fighting to regain full awareness, she felt in dire need of a snowfall.

"Krista?" came her mother's voice.

She forced herself to focus her attention on the group. "Aye?"

"You look flushed, dear."

"Do I?" She scrupulously avoided glancing at the prince. "It must be all the excitement."

"But I thought you knew the prince was coming," Catherine said.

"Ah, ha," Keith laughed. "*Saw* him, did you?"

"She did, she did," Glenn assured him. "She had one of her visions at breakfast and *saw* the prince as clear as day."

"She's a faerie, you know," Agnes announced for Alexi's benefit.

"She has magical powers," Catherine confirmed.

"That's not true," Krista hastily denied in her own behalf. Unthinkingly, she turned to the prince and he captured her gaze again. Her mind filled with the image of him lying above her, and her heart began to race.

One of his dark brows arched in wry humor, but there was nothing comical about the force of his interest. She could practically feel the unrelenting power of his attention reaching out, touching her. "Do you cast spells, Lady Krista?"

If anyone was casting spells, she thought in mounting irritation at her own helplessness, it was Alexi Kaskov, stealing her composure, bestowing darkly seductive smiles that made her go weak. Seated with his elbow resting on the chair's arm and his chin propped on his raised fist, he had about him a manner of one who shaped life to suit his own purposes, where his every wish was no more than a princely command away.

He regarded her now as if his wish was to discern her every secret for his own personal enjoyment.

"No, I do not cast spells," she returned, refusing to give in to the betraying trembling in her limbs.

"But she does have 'the sight,'" little Agnes was only too happy to supply.

His gaze still pinned to Krista, the prince said, "That must make life interesting."

"It has been that," her father laughed. "There was the time—"

"Please, Father," she broke in, "I'm sure his highness isn't interested in—"

"But I am." And his expression said as much, that he wanted, no *intended*, to know everything there was to know about Krista MacLachlan.

It was all she could do to remain seated, and as her family regaled the prince with stories attesting to her fey abilities, the feeling only worsened. It didn't help that even though Prince Alexi listened to each and every word with an outward show of attentiveness, his eyes never strayed from her for very long. Again and again, those brown orbs came back to meet hers. Again and again she felt the strength of his will as he repeatedly caught her gaze . . . and seemed to make silent promises.

A bit frantically, she looked to her parents and siblings, fully expecting them to be uncomfortably aware of, or possibly even offended by, the prince's inordinate attention to her. But to a person they were oblivious, joyfully wrapped up in their stories.

"On the very night she was born, the faeries danced with joy," her mother sighed, "their smiles creating a light so loving it circled the moon in a silvery ring."

"That's why her eyes are silver blue," Agnes giggled.

Needing to extricate herself from the increasing awareness of Prince Alexi burgeoning within her, Krista came to her feet. "If you are all trying to embarrass me," she announced with admirable humor, "you have succeeded." Determinedly, she clung to a lighthearted élan she was far from feeling. "I cannot speak for his highness, but I have heard enough. I wouldn't be the least bit surprised if you have wearied five years off his life with your tales."

"On, the contrary," he said, standing to his full height. "I have been greatly entertained, but I would very much like to see the rest of this magnificent castle." He paused for half a beat; extended his hand. "Come. Show me."

She automatically began to decline, but her mother happily agreed and her father, too, before he clapped Keith on the back once again. Glenn and her sisters seemed more interested in the presents Keith had mentioned bringing.

Krista wondered if they'd all lost their minds. This man was a power unto himself, a commanding force with which she was ill prepared to deal. That aside, he was a guest whose comfort should have taken precedence. What were they thinking to turn him over to her keeping? She could only surmise they were so overcome by Keith's return they had forgotten their manners and lost their collective good sense as well.

Or it had been snatched! Silently, she railed at the faeries. In answer, sparks danced in the fireplace and skipped up the flue.

In silent defeat, she gave in gracefully, having no choice but to play escort to a man who issued his orders with no thought of ever being denied, a man who would forever change her life.

She led the way up the stairs, every step of the way feeling a great affinity for her ancient ancestor, De Dalan the Clumsy. The poor soul had been so awkward and helpless, he'd fled his home in Ireland for Scotland. She had no idea what had caused the poor man's clumsiness, but her own inclination to wring her hands and stutter was due to the knowledge given to her by her sight. This man, this bold prince among men, was destined to be her lover.

"And this is the solar," she explained stiffly as they ascended to the third story. "It's exactly like, that is, I mean to say, it's an exact duplicate . . . of the solar in the old castle. The entire castle is, for that matter. The old castle burned, you see, years ago, which makes this the new castle." She wanted to cringe at her halting speech. "But then, you can see that for yourself." Sighing in exasperation, she lamely finished. "The family's suites and guest rooms are on the floor above."

Alexi Kaskov strolled around, from all appearances more taken with this private, family room than with any other she'd shown him. At the windows, he stopped to take in the view. "So you're a faerie, are you?" He turned to lean a shoulder against the window frame, looking as if he had no intentions of moving until he was good and ready.

From her place by the doorway, she dug deep for poise, and stood precisely where she was. Without her family to act as a buffer, she needed the distance between them. "No, I'm not a faerie, but it's easier for my family to explain things in those terms."

"Ah, yes, these visions." He was clearly skeptical, his manner amusingly indulgent.

She smiled briefly in return, not at all insulted by his doubts. To convince people had never been her way. "I'm glad you find the idea entertaining."

"It's unique." He tipped his head to one side. "Rather like you, I'd say." His lips curled slowly, that knowing light entering those liquid brown eyes of his. "You don't need to stand clear across the room."

She hesitated long enough for him to lift his hand in invitation, or perhaps another of his commands. Pulled along by fate—she refused to think she was drawn by the magic of his smile—she crossed to stand before him, but for the life of her, couldn't place her hand within his. He laughed at her balking.

"Shy little faerie."

"I'm not a faerie."

"The designation suits you." His humor faded abruptly. A battle-tense look was in his eyes as she felt his gaze slide from the careless tumble of umber curls atop her head, along the slim column of her throat to the full roundness of her breasts. "And your brother was right."

With all her might, she tried to remain calm. "About what?"

"You're a beautiful woman."

Was this where it begins, she wondered in rising panic. Was this the starting point of the events that would take her into this man's arms? She couldn't help but think that it was.

"Your highness—"

"Sasha."

How was she supposed to fight this? "Prince Alexi—"

"Sasha," he repeated, this time with a slight narrowing of his eyes.

"Why don't I show you to your rooms." She pivoted only to have him catch her wrist and swing her around to face him again.

"Why don't you stay right here and tell me what has you ready to fly from me like a frightened bird."

She stared blankly at his fingers wrapped about her wrist, unable to tear her eyes away, knowing that if she looked elsewhere, she'd be lost. She would be anyway; in the end she'd be his, but it was impossible for her simply to relent. He took the choice from her, cupping her chin in his hand and raising it until she was forced to meet his gaze.

It was her undoing, but not in any way that she would have ever anticipated. From the depths of her, she felt the warm tide of emotions churn, rise, and reach out to him.

Utter peace claimed her as it had on those rarest of occasions in the past. She helplessly stood by as her physical vision dimmed and sound was reduced to the steady beating of her heart. Thought was beyond her as she gave her emotional being, her very self, to this man.

It was over in mere seconds, time seeming to have been stopped ever so briefly. Nonetheless, it took her three breaths before she became fully aware again. When she finally shrugged off the last of the lassitude, it was to find Alexi staring down at her with a dazed expression, and she realized anew what had happened. She'd bestowed her emotions on him. And he'd felt the impact. She could tell by the color gilding his cheeks and the nearly sleepy cast to his eyes.

The others in the past had looked the same way, as if a terrible void had been filled, as if contentment was theirs for the first time in their lives and their minds and bodies couldn't make sense of it all. The prince looked the same way; a needy man whose soul had been touched.

She stepped back, shaken by her thoughts. The others *had* been in need, and through her the faeries had chosen to help each person. Each had taken from her what he or she had needed most; serenity, joy, a sense of well-being. In that they were all the same, but Prince Alexi wasn't like them. Rich, powerful, handsome, life was his for the taking. What could he possibly need from her?

Images of them in her bed, writhing in passion, filled her head, and she took another step back, then another when she saw his brows slant fiercely. Unable to face him, or the inevitable, she turned and fled.

Chapter 2

U NGOVERNABLE desire had Alexi shoving out of bed and pacing naked to the fireplace. There he lingered, feeling the heat of longing as surely as he felt the heat of the flames against his skin. He wished the former felt as satisfying as the latter.

Sprawling into the nearby chair, he shoved one long leg out before him, but the move did nothing to ease the persistently dull ache in his loins. It had been plaguing him for hours, ever since he had first beheld Krista MacLachlan peering at him with her crystalline eyes.

If he lived forever, he'd never forget the moment. It was as if everything and everyone except Krista had dimmed from view. Stunned, confounded, he'd wanted to analyze the sensation, but her beauty had fascinated him to distraction.

Little faerie. The name did indeed suit her. Delicately proportioned with slender hollows and temptingly round curves, the top of her head barely reached his shoulders. Her lips were naturally pink, her skin smooth and flawless. The grace of her smile had the power to curl about the muscles of his chest, a perfect foil for the stunning impact of her eyes.

He'd never seen the like. A blend of pale blue and silver, they'd shined with her every emotion; delight at Keith's return, humor at her sisters' teasing, shyness when having to speak to him. Trepidation, too, had flashed and something else he could have sworn went far beyond mere nervousness.

And yet, again and again not only then but throughout the day and evening as well, she'd been helplessly drawn back to him, her eyes meeting his, darting away, returning, evading, returning again, as if she wanted him, but didn't know what to do about it. And against all better judgment, he had let himself be enticed. He'd let himself savor every facet of her beauty and character . . . and something more. An inner quality he couldn't define, an allure that had captivated him with hints of untold pleasures.

Pleasure had been foremost in his mind in the solar when he'd held her fragile wrist in his hand. He had been searching for the sensuality he sensed lay at the heart of the woman. Instead, he'd been blinded by a euphoric serenity that left him feeling the kind of desire he'd never before experienced, or even imagined.

Shaking his head, he couldn't dispel his profound confusion. Passion and lust were by no means foreign to him. Women were his for the taking if he so chose. Being a Russian prince did, after all, come with the benefits of power and wealth. And modestly speaking, being born with a collection of features that appealed to most women only enhanced the attraction.

He'd learned that truth at an early age and, in the ways of youth, had shamelessly overindulged in the pleasures the fairer sex seemed all too willing to share. Through the years, he'd come to appreciate the gratification found in being selective, but the world was a vast place, filled with beautiful women. He hadn't lacked for bed partners.

Hence, now at the age of thirty-six, he possessed a sexual expertise he'd been told by more than one knowing lady was unsurpassed, an expertise with which he had grown somewhat complacent. Controlling his body's responses required little effort. He chose when to become aroused and when not. It was quite simply mind over matter, or so the case had been until today. Today, Krista had him feeling as undisciplined as the intemperate boy he'd been long ago, aching and not at all inclined to wanting to deny himself.

That his mind had gleefully joined his body's mutiny was mystifying. Normally, if he marked a woman as off limits, that was all there was to it. Knowing Krista was Keith's sister should have been sufficient incentive for his brain to issue its orders of restraint. From the moment of their introduction, he should have behaved the perfect gentleman instead of trying to charm her. But there was something about her that made rational thinking impossible, something that had incited every male instinct he possessed.

He wanted Krista and damn the fact that Keith trusted him, or that Krista was a virgin.

Oh, she was definitely that. He knew an untried woman when he saw one. He'd recognized Krista's innocence in the same instant he'd sensed her as yet undiscovered sensuality. He'd wager his last ruble that she had no idea of the depths of her own passionate nature. The idea of being the man to guide her through the discovery was heady stuff.

Tempted by all manner of possibilities, he shoved to his feet, cursed his conscience, and got dressed. Minutes later, he exited his rooms and was down the stairs, his passage lit by sconces set into the walls. For a man accustomed to gratifying his carnal urges, he scorned his escape, but he damn well couldn't take his closest friend's virgin sister to bed. That was a bit much even for him.

More importantly, he couldn't use Krista that way. He sensed in her a rare gentleness of spirit unsuited to amorous games. She wouldn't be one to give herself lightly and she wouldn't know how to handle his eventual leaving.

Thinking of her in humiliated tears was enough to stiffen his resolve. He didn't want to see her hurt, and she would be if he let himself seduce her. After all the pain he'd encountered in the last years, he couldn't inflict more, especially not on one so defenseless.

He paused at the bottom of the stairway, his eyes drifting shut on an internal agony. By all the saints, he was wearied by the last years of strife and horror. The endless battles that had seen comrades fall and armies bloody themselves had struck the life from his heart and the being from his soul. Deep inside, he felt so withered there were times when he feared he'd never regain his ability to embrace life to its fullest. Keith's invitation to join him at Lachlan Castle had been a godsend.

Knowing his spirit was in need of rekindling, he welcomed this respite before going home to the inevitable responsibilities waiting for him in Russia. All he craved in life right now was the uncomplicated solace to be found in the company of friends, unlimited rest, good food, and perhaps a woman or two in his bed. Casual, experienced women. Krista was not cut of that cloth. She was a woman meant for marriage, and marriage was beyond his capabilities right now. Perhaps forever.

War had done that to him. The repeated threat of not knowing if he was going to be alive five minutes from now had changed him, numbed him to all thoughts of the future. He'd become accustomed to living for the moment, acting for the moment, and damn the consequences.

A warring mentality to be sure, one that had become second nature. Some called it selfish and reckless. Others merely considered it survival. Either way, he'd realized only months ago that he could no longer live like that. In truth, it wasn't living as he would define it. He had made a conscious effort to purge himself of this state of mind, to cleanse the stench of killing from his senses and rid his dreams of the bloody butchery.

Only then, when his heart and soul had healed, could he think of women like Krista. Only then, when he could offer himself whole and unfettered to a woman he loved, would he feel justified in taking a wife. In this, he would not be swayed.

So he would enjoy Krista's company, take pleasure in her beauty, but it would be no more than that.

Braced by his intent, he stepped outside into the inner courtyard, and came to an abrupt halt. As if thinking of the very woman whose effect had driven him from his bed in the first place could conjure her spirit out of thin air, he spied Krista no more than twenty yards off . . . alone, defenseless.

Automatically, he searched the enclosed yard, already reaching to his left hip where his sword had rested for so long. Finding himself unarmed, he scoffingly reminded himself of the time and place, and that the battle was long over.

Without weighing the wisdom of doing so, he leveled his gaze on Krista once more. He couldn't help but smile at the sight she presented—a beautiful woman strolling about a carefully tended flower garden. The sheer peace and rightness of it was a balm for his starving soul.

Preferring, perhaps even needing, to observe her undetected, he remained where he was and gave himself the pure, simple gift of watching her.

Her voice came to him in the whispered tones of a quaint melody. His smile grew. A singer she wasn't, but no man in his right mind would care. With her rich umber hair loose and flowing down to the small of her back, and her skin iridescent in the moon's light, her beauty was enhanced tenfold. Even the muted blue and red plaid of her tartan shawl couldn't hide the bounty of her slender grace.

"You could almost make me believe in faeries," he said, stepping from the shadows.

Krista gasped at his first word, startled into pressing a hand to her chest, her eyes rounding with her shock. Clearly, she'd believed herself alone. "Your highness."

"I didn't mean to alarm you," he apologized, advancing slowly in order to give her time to recover. He didn't want her to be frightened of him, even though that might be for the best. It was all too easy for him to fall prey to that indefinable quality that made her so special, that drew him and made him want to forget how to be decent. "Am I intruding?"

"No, your highness."

He frowned lightly at the formality of the address, wanting against all better judgment something more personal between them. "I thought we had reached an understanding," he cajoled.

"Did we?"

"Of course. Don't you remember? You're to call me Sasha." Knowing he shouldn't, he bent low, picked a sprig of heather, and offered it with a smile. "All my close friends do."

His charm was irresistible, his grin pure and unmocking enough to surprisingly dispel a portion of the nervousness Krista had been experiencing all day. Staring at the heather, she hesitated in accepting the innocent gift, but in the end relented, having only so much strength to deny her fate. "Thank you, Sasha."

"You see? That wasn't so difficult."

Normally, it wouldn't have been, but their circumstances weren't normal. The flower as well as his presence took her one step closer to her own seduction. Automatically shrinking from the thought, she asked the obvious, "What brings you here at this time of night?"

"I could ask the same of you."

Her shoulders lifted in a slight shrug. "I was restless. Coming here is an old habit when I can't sleep."

"Then we must be of one mind."

She was instantly concerned. "Was there something amiss with your rooms, with your bed?"

Nothing that your company couldn't cure, he thought. He caught himself at once, damned his lack of control, and then damned his conscience. Why did she have to be Keith's sister? Why couldn't she be a distant friend of the family who knew what she was about, or failing that, prune faced and uninspiring? Why did she have to be the one woman he was rapidly coming to desire more than any other?

She was a guileless wonder with her emotions flashing freely. Her innocence was as seductive as her gentle warmth reaching out to him. "No," he murmured at length, irritated at the sensation of being at odds with himself. "There's nothing wrong with my rooms. Like you, I was restless so I thought to come out here."

That wasn't true. No conscious thought had led him to this spot. The impulse to seek out the courtyard had been purely instinctive.

He shook off a ripple of curiosity. "I've never put much store in coincidence, however in this case, my faith is renewed."

Flowers swayed and bobbed as if they'd been merrily caught by a stray breeze. Krista cast them a censorious glance, knowing precisely who and what was involved and it was *not* coincidence. "If you wish to be alone, I'll leave you—"

"Stay."

"Are you certain?"

"More certain than is wise."

"I beg your pardon?"

He laughed, the sound full of regret. "Ah, little Krista, I'm waging a losing battle with myself."

"I'm sorry, I don't understand."

"And why should you? You're more magic than real." Absolutely unable to help himself, he tucked an errant lock of hair behind her shoulder, ordering himself to be content with that one small touch. "So, pretty faerie, tell me what it's like to dance with the elves."

Krista knew he was placating her, although why he chose to do so was a mystery. "You don't believe in elves or magic."

"You think not?"

"No."

"Looking at you could change my mind."

The barely concealed fire in his eyes flushed her with a rare heat. Unnerved, she sank onto the nearby bench, taking meager refuge in the defensive move when what she really wanted to do was flee. But what was the use? Her fate was set; the faeries had proven that. She'd come out here seeking escape from her worries and instead Alexi had been delivered to her as if on the proverbial silver platter.

Frustrated by her utter helplessness, she relented to a silent temper. Perhaps she should stand up and throw her arms about his shoulders and kiss him full on the mouth. Or lay back on the bench and offer herself up for his pleasure. At least then she wouldn't have to fret over the when and the how of it. At least the waiting would be over, and she would be free of the anticipation and the anxiety.

Then her stomach might not twist and coil at the sight of him, her heart might not race at his smile, her hands might not shake in excitement. Heavens above, once in his arms, she might be able to take a full breath without wanting to fill her lungs with the subtle scent of the cologne on his skin.

Peace would be hers again if only they could get on with it. Unfortunately, what she knew about seduction would scarcely fill a thimble.

"What are you thinking, little Krista?"

At the sound of his deep voice, her gaze snapped up to find him searching her face, silently probing for secrets. "You wouldn't believe me if I told you."

"Why not tell me and find out."

She considered it, but a passing cloud in the otherwise perfectly clear sky briefly blocked the moon's light. Krista understood that to tell Alexi was not the way. "Some thoughts are best kept to one's self."

"And some are best shared."

"At times."

"Will you change your mind with time?"

"I'll know in my heart if I should."

He didn't like being refused, and by nature felt compelled to bend her to his will, to know what had put that slumberous look of desire in her eyes. He could see, however, that she wasn't going to relent, and to push her would be a mistake, for both of them.

Reminding himself yet again that he had set her off limits was one of the most difficult things he'd ever had to do. He marshaled what command he could call his own and let the matter go. Although the effort cost him, he settled for teasing. "I thought faeries were all-knowing, all-wise."

"I've told you, I'm not a faerie."

"No wings?"

She was immensely glad for the shift in conversation, as well as mood. "No, no wings."

"Then why does your family believe you have special powers, that you can see the future?"

"Because I can."

Placing one foot on the bench, he leaned both forearms across his thigh, the position bringing him close, his body sheltering hers. "Then you don't deny that you have this second sight."

Comfortable with herself, she smiled. "No, and I prefer to think of the ability as a gift rather than a mystical power."

"A gift? From whom?"

It wasn't often that she related the tale, especially to someone as openly skeptical, but for some reason, she found humor in the idea. In mock primness, she peered out the corners of her eyes, her smile widening in genuine pleasure. "As doubtful as you are, I don't know why I should tell you, but if you must know—"

"I must."

"I've been blessed by the first MacLachlan bride wedded in Scotland, who just so happens *was* a good faerie by the name of Lily. She gave up her magic powers to marry her one true love, Duncan MacLachlan. Although Lily became mortal, her faerie blood still runs in the clan."

"Don't tell me there are hundreds of MacLachlans running about predicting storms."

"Of course not," she laughed, tickled by his assumption. To be able to jest with him was wonderful, and everything inside her responded—to the moment, to the shared merriment, to him. "As far as I know, I'm the only one, in the last one hundred years and you're not to ask why, because I don't know, and I truly gave up questioning years ago." She spread her hands wide, beaming up at him in carefree delight. "I simply accept my abilities for what they are."

Her capricious charm was a magic all its own, tightening all the muscles in Alexi's chest, feeding a part of him that had ached with emptiness for so long. His conscience sent out a warning to leave her in peace, but the temptation of her was beyond bearing, instantly slaughtering every one of his good intentions. *"Dushka,"* he murmured, his voice as dark and velvet as the night, "you have no ideas of what your true abilities are."

Before she could divine his intent, while the smile was still on her lips, he kissed her, and almost groaned at the exquisite relief of tasting her. Her lips already parted, he took full advantage, slanted his head to the most desirable angle, and thrust his tongue against hers.

In those few seconds, Krista's mind struggled frantically. Thoughts of alarm collided with far sweeter impulses of enjoyment and acceptance. By the time she could sort it all out, Alexi had drawn her to her feet, straightening to his full height so that he held her body flush against his.

Her mind reeled with a feeling of recognition. In her visions, he'd kissed her so often she had come to know the feel of his body and how she fit the steely planes to perfection. She'd come to know the taste of his lips and welcome the pressure of his mouth. All of it was a joyous memory and a wondrous discovery at the same time.

From chest to knees, he held her immobile while he kissed her with a magic that made a mockery of his skepticism on the matter. It was truly sublime, feeding her senses until she shuddered and kissed him back. Along the length of her, she felt his body tense as a groan worked its way up his throat. His breathing turned ragged and his mouth slanted with increased ferocity.

His desire matched hers, she realized in amazement. In her visions, she'd only ever known a wee portion of her own responses, had only guessed from the incomplete images what his might be. She knew now and happiness surged. She didn't want to be alone in her desire. She wanted him to feel the same passion for her as she felt for him. It was, she knew, the only way she could willingly, wholeheartedly accept him into her bed, her body.

The idea had her melting from the inside out. She sagged against him, but his arms supported her with ease, molding her to him as he saw fit. One of his hands tangled in the length of her hair and tugged back, arching her neck up to his mouth. His other hand quested to softer territory and found her breast.

Starting at this unexpected intimacy, she quivered, marveling at the tremors that coursed through her. For the first time since she'd begun *seeing* him, she could understand how they would eventually end up in her bed. With every brush of his lips up and down her neck, her desire flamed. With every stroke of his fingers, longing welled into a tight ache that centered itself low in her belly. The instinctive urge to curl her hips up to his couldn't be denied.

His arms tightened in response, his mouth crushing hers. A fine trembling marked the depths of his desperate need. Dimly, she recalled wondering what this man could possibly need from her. Innately, she sensed that mutual desire was only part of it, definitely not the whole. He was too practiced with women for his need to be appeased by lust alone.

So what was it that he needed from her, what was it that she was fated to give him, other than her body? Her heart? She could well imagine that. The longer he kissed her, the more deeply her emotions were touched. What had begun as desire could well turn into love.

She jerked back at the notion, staring wide-eyed up into his face, seeing lines as harsh as his breathing bracketing his mouth. "Alexi," she whispered. It was on the tip of her tongue to tell him that she didn't know this would happen, but he stepped back and ground his eyes shut, his whole body going taut as if in pain.

It was a long moment before he could draw an even breath and even longer before he managed to say, "You would tempt the saints above, Krista." He smiled without humor. "And I am no saint." Lifting his hand in a gesture intrinsically sad, he ran his fingertips over her heated cheek. "Go inside before I forget how to be noble."

She could have told him that all the splendid intentions in the world weren't going to make a bit of difference. But she remained silent, and did as he said, knowing he wouldn't believe her any more than he believed in magic.

Chapter 3

Alexi rarely made mistakes, but he knew without a doubt that kissing Krista had been the biggest mistake of his life. Now that he had tasted her, he wanted her more than ever.

From atop his mount, he scanned the rolling hills, and suppressed a grunt of frustration at the memory of how she'd responded to him. She'd come alive with all the passion he had known lay dormant within her, kissing him with sweet abandon, fitting her body against his as if she had been fashioned purposely for him alone. He had been hit by a hunger that had nearly stripped him of conscience. And when her hips had rolled toward his in silent beckoning, cradling, enticing, it had been all he could do to retain coherent thought.

Jerking away from the memory, he swore liberally. For a man who prided himself on his intellect, he was infuriated with his lack of control. Control was, if nothing else, intellect exerting itself to the fullest extent. Damnably ever since that moment in the solar when he'd been overtaken by that strange euphoria, his intellect could most favorably be compared to that of a mushroom, with apologies to the mushroom! Ever since that moment in the solar, Krista had taken up permanent residence in his mind.

Perhaps the cause of his problems lay in the fact that after all the death and carnage he'd witnessed, his response to Krista was so profound because she typified what he needed most—reaffirmation of sweet, innocent life. That was the very reason he'd come to Scotland, to seek, not the elaborate overindulgences of society back in Russia, but life's simple pleasures to embellish his spirit and replenish his soul.

On a jaundiced note, he admitted that the atmosphere and lifestyle here in Strathlachlan might be simplicity incarnate, but nothing about Krista herself was so uncomplicated. She was like a magnificent filigree intricately wrought of compassion and beauty, naiveté and seductiveness. The combined effects had him wanting to forget that she was not his usual type of woman, one who knew how to play love's games.

That was the kind of woman he should be lusting after, he reminded himself. Not one whose gaze was fascination itself, not one who didn't know the power of her own femininity. Certainly not one who tempted him until he wanted the whole woman. Judging from Krista's responses last night, he wouldn't have to press hard to have her.

Not for the first time, he gave the notion serious thought, letting his eyes drift shut in sweet, sweet yearning. By all that was holy, he wanted her. It would be an untold joy to make love to her, to feel her body sheathing his, to take all her passion and goodness and make them his. But all he had to do was recall her beguiling smile and he was reminded of the gentleness of her. He'd be damned if he would do anything to injure such a rare quality.

The only thing to do was avoid her at all cost. He could see no other recourse short of quitting Scotland at once. Krista would be left as unspoiled and innocent as she was now and he would be spared the worst of his constant internal struggle. To the best of his ability, it would be "out of sight, out of mind."

Feeling better for having reached his decision, he nonetheless scoffed in open derision. He may have charted a course, but that didn't mean he liked it. Even now, he chafed at the longing that wouldn't go away.

He set his heels to the gelding and galloped across the land, welcoming the physical exertion as a much-needed diversion from his thoughts. Under the graying sky, he gained if not relief then at least comfort from the pleasure to be found in riding for riding's sake alone. Too much of the riding he'd done for so long had been for military purposes.

And hour later, he circled his way back toward the castle, the worst of his tensions exercised away. Unfortunately, the clouds above had increasingly thickened. Rain was imminent. It was by sheer luck that he spotted a deserted cottage tucked into a thicket of trees.

He could ride for the castle just to the other side of the small bay. It would not be a hardship; riding soaked and chilled to the skin had become more typical than not these last years. And that was precisely why he chose to seek the cottage's shelter; to regain the civility of a simple comfort, to merely stay dry.

The first drops met him halfway to the cottage. By the time he had secured his horse in the makeshift lean-to behind, the scattered drops had turned into a full-fledged downpour. He sprinted the short distance to the door and burst inside on a gust of wind that seemed to come out of nowhere.

"That's quite an entrance," Krista laughed.

He spun toward the sound of her voice, halting in his tracks. For a full count of five, he stared, astounded to find her here.

"I see that I've caught you by surprise," she said, nervous laughter gilding her eyes as well as her lips. "I'm sorry."

No more so than he. No sooner had he determined to keep his distance from her than he found them very much alone and secluded.

How in the hell had this happened? And how in the hell was he supposed to resist temptation with her presenting such a fetching sight? Sitting before the fire in the grate, her hair caught up at the crown of her head, her face delicately flushed, she was so appealing he was jolted by a wave of the very same desire he'd spent hours trying to tame. Damn it all to hell!

"Your coat is wet," she told him, rising gracefully. "You should remove it so you won't take a chill. Here, let me have it and I'll hang it by the hearth so that it dries."

Trying to subdue his body's uncontrollable response, he looked from her to the fire. His frown deepened into a scowl. Flames crackled and danced, sending whorls of smoke up the chimney.

"Alexi?"

He'd seen no smoke, nor smelled any either when he'd first spied the place. From all appearances, the cottage had appeared deserted. If he'd known who the occupant was, he would have ridden on and spared himself the ordeal of having to contend with a traitorous body and a miserable excuse for self-control.

"Your wind and light play tricks here in the Highlands," he accused, his voice brittle.

"Aye," she murmured slowly, wariness entering her eyes at his tone. "They've been known to, your highness." She lowered her extended hand, visibly withdrawing.

In the strained silence, he watched her intently, still struggling to check his ungovernable reaction to her. Damn it all. She was too enticing and he wanted her too much. He should leave at once.

At the thought, rain lashed the cottage with unearthly fury.

Mentally cursing the forces of nature for conspiring against him, he actually eyed the door for a long moment, contemplating the ten minutes it would take to reach the castle.

Thunder rolled menacingly.

On a disgusted sigh, he shrugged out of his damp coat with ill grace.

"There." Krista arranged the garment over the back of a spindly chair and set it close to the fireplace. "It should be dry by the time the rain stops."

"You sound as if you know when that will be."

Over her shoulder, she shrugged with her brows. "In a way I do."

"And?"

Turning to face him fully, she sighed, "As long as it takes."

He had the distinct impression they weren't talking about the same things, but she turned for the table then, her manner suddenly that of a hostess entertaining a guest she'd been expecting.

"I was just about to have tea. Would you care to join me?" She returned with a tray laden with an odd assortment of crockery. "Or would whisky suit you better?"

Alexi raised one dark brow. To have either in this unlikely setting made him shake his head. The room could barely be called livable with the one chair and table. Windows were paned with glass, but the surfaces were filmed by grime that spoke of neglect. Strange that the wide-planked floor around them was relatively clean. Nonetheless, refreshments of any kind were improbable at best.

Taking the tray, he let her settle herself on the floor again, hesitating in joining her. A masochist he wasn't. The expectancy in her expression, however, was his undoing. Clearly she hoped he would seat himself for her impromptu picnic, and he found he could not disappoint her.

Coming down on his haunches, he made sure to put a safe distance between them. He could hardly credit was he was doing. He, Alexi Kaskov, who had seduced more women than he could count, was actually behaving like a monk.

Angry because he felt like a stranger to himself, he demanded, "What the deuce are you doing out here all by yourself? It's a lengthy walk from the castle."

"Not too terribly." A half hour, no more. Still, it could have been three times that, and it wouldn't have made any difference. She'd woken that morning to a vision of the cottage, and the certainty that she should journey to this place this very day. At the time, she hadn't understood why, but it made sense now. She and Alexi were obviously meant to be here alone.

From the look and sound of him, though, he was less than pleased about that. After the way he had kissed her last night, she would have thought he would welcome the kind of privacy they wouldn't have found at the castle.

That in itself was unnerving. She had no defenses against this man. If she ever thought she did, his kisses had obliterated that notion. Just the memory of the way his mouth had claimed hers had the power to constrict her breathing. Seeing him now caused a funny ache near her heart.

He was casually dressed. Dark trousers tucked into high, leather boots clung faithfully to every line and muscle of his legs while the black silk of his tunic emphasized the breadth of his shoulders. The strength she'd noted from the first was chiseled into his jaw. The princely air of command filled his dark gaze.

"I felt like taking a walk," she explained on a shuttered breath. Her hand hovered over the crude teapot. "Which will it be?"

"Whisky, definitely." Sitting with one leg bent and his wrist propped on his knee, he gave the tray's contents a suspicious look, as if wondering if she could have possibly known to expect him. "Did you bring all this with you?"

"Oh, no. It was here." Waiting for her in a tidily packed basket set next to a fire lit in the grate. She'd realized the second she'd unpacked the hamper that it was intended for her and Alexi. "Since no one lives here, I dinna think it could hurt to help myself." She handed him a battered cup. "And now you, as well."

He accepted the cup with seeming reluctance, contemplating first her and then the small amount of whisky by turns. In the end, he breathed deeply like a man seeking strength and took a drink.

The liquor warmed a path clear to his stomach, the flavor so gratifying he had to suppress a grunt of pleasure. A man accustomed to having the very best in life, he closed his eyes in mute appreciation.

"Do you like it?"

Gazing at her, he replied, "Very much." But that was an enormous understatement. A smokey richness soothed his senses while a mysterious piquancy had a more teasing effect. "I've never tasted anything like it."

Nor would he ever again, she knew. The faeries did have their own special recipes. "Well, if you can't come by fine whisky in Scotland, it's not to be found. Would you like more?"

Common sense said no. He had a high tolerance for liquor, but this golden brew was extraordinary stuff. The last thing he needed was its hypnotic effects dulling his better judgment or his self-restraint.

Reckless self-indulgence had him extending the cup for more.

He didn't know whether to be annoyed or pleased when the bottle yielded less than half a cup. He drank deeply, and abruptly decided it wasn't worth his worry. In fact, he determined he was damned sick and tired of worrying, period. He had been seeking life's simple pleasures, and here they were—shelter from the rain, warmth from the chill, drink to quench his thirst, and the company of a beautiful woman. It didn't make sense that he should continue to deny himself.

Leaning on his left forearm, he stretched out on his side, the cup held loosely between his palms. The shift in position put his chest near her knees, his body angled toward hers. Not for a second did he forget his decision to act the gentleman, but the knotted strain of his internal struggle seemed to have died. Oh, the war still raged. The whisky hadn't obliterated his understanding of right and wrong, but the few swallows he'd taken had shaved away the worst of his tension.

"What is this place?" Flexing his shoulders into a more comfortable position, he glanced about and gained a new perspective. There was a curious appeal he hadn't noticed earlier.

"A crofter's cottage. It was abandoned long ago."

"Why?"

The blue and silver of her eyes lightened until they sparkled with glee. "It's said to be haunted."

"Haunted?"

"So the story goes."

"Tell me."

"Oh, it's not anything you'd find interesting."

"What makes you say that?"

"You're a skeptical man."

He lifted his cup in her direction. "You mean about your faeries."

"Aye."

"That doesn't mean I don't like a good tale."

Only Krista knew it was more than a tale. "Very well, but I warn you to mind your manners. The wee ones do not take kindly to being offended."

His mouth tugged to one side in a gesture that clearly revealed a supreme male confidence. "I've survived war, Krista. I think I can withstand your faeries."

Her eyes rounded. "That's exactly what Shaw MacLachlan thought after he'd spent years with the clan fighting the MacLeans. The good faerie queen, Titania, came to bless him with seven years of good luck, but he spurned her offer and denied any belief that she was real. She cursed him for all eternity, and to this day, his spirit is confined to this house, where he plays the pipes for the faerie queen's pleasure."

She stopped to lift her brows in exaggerated warning. "So if I were you, Alexi, I'd be careful with what I said. I wouldn't want to see you turned into a shriveled-up crone or snatched away to faerieland."

"I'll be sure to act appropriately respectful."

"See that you do," she advised, her manner a beguiling mixture of lighthearted cheer and true concern. "I would feel terrible if you were to be turned into a goat."

"A goat?"

"Or something equally dismal."

"What could be more dismal than being turned into a goat?"

Tucking her chin, she peered up in impish delight. "Being turned into a three-legged goat?"

He laughed heartily, throwing his head back, his wide shoulders shaking with genuine mirth. In all her life, Krista had never heard or seen anything quite so entrancing. Like a warm magic, his pleasure swirled about her, filled her heart, her mind . . . her vision.

"If you tell me this wit of yours is a gift from the faeries," Alexi challenged, "I won't believe it—with all due respect to your 'wee ones.' " He lifted his cup, his gaze seeking hers over the rim. "Krista?"

She sat still and silent, her sight seemingly focused on something only she could see.

Instantly, he tossed the cup aside, came to his knees, and took her by the shoulders. "Krista." Head lowered to hers, he peered directly into her eyes and saw a blank, faraway look. His fingers tightened. *"Dushka,* what is it?"

To his relief, she blinked slowly at first and then more normally with each passing second. Her brows arched and she finally focused on him.

"Alexi."

"What happened?" She fell silent long enough for him to give her a gentle shake. "Answer me."

"I *saw* us." Her gaze dropped to his lips. Her fingers followed, delicately tracing the sculpted contours to reassure herself that they were real, that he was real. Her vision of him kissing her had been so startlingly clear, the edges of reality and magic were blurred.

"What do you mean you 'saw us'?" he carefully but implacably demanded. "Are you saying you supposedly had one of your visions?"

"Aye, the same one I've been having for days," she breathed in a voice that matched her expression.

It was soft, intoxicating, and it seared straight through Alexi. He felt the impact like a pleasurable jab piercing his heart.

He sucked in a breath that was supposed to be bracing, but instead, drew in the sweet scent of her. It was a mysterious, mystical perfume of woman and flowers, rife with the promise of devotion, and sensual delights. Its essence dragged on his self-control until all he could think of, all he was achingly aware of, was how much he wanted her.

Briefly, he tried to remember every good reason he knew of why he shouldn't kiss her. But then he searched her eyes and saw his passion mirrored, and trying to be noble became impossible. Whatever she had or had not seen, she wanted him as much as he wanted her.

In a gesture of tender restraint and compelling desire, he threaded his fingers through her hair until he cupped the back of her head in his palm. "Ah, Krista, I've tried to do what's right. I don't want to hurt you."

A woman's smile as bewitching as magic and as innocent as a ray of sunshine curled her lips. "You won't hurt me." She placed her hand on his chest, feeling his thudding pulse. "You can't. It's meant to be, Alexi."

With all his might he tried to resist, to exercise some last remnant of control. Alas, the lure of her was a power unlike anything he'd ever encountered. It had been from the very start.

He lowered his head and seized her mouth with all the pent-up need he'd been so desperately suppressing. It fleetingly crossed his mind to take his time and savor how her mouth fit his, but he felt her lips tremble and part, felt her yield to his tongue, felt the way she shuddered as she pressed herself against him, and the thought was banished.

On a low groan, he clamped his arms tightly about her, one hand between her shoulders, the other in the small of her back. Kneeling as they were, the pressure he exerted molded her into intimate contact, her breasts crushed to his chest, the softness of her belly cradling his hardened flesh.

"You're trembling," he muttered into the silky column of her throat.

"I know." She clung tightly to the muscles of his shoulders.

"Are you afraid?"

"I . . . I dinna know it would be like this." Her heart beating so thunderously she could scarcely breathe, her body aching and empty, her mind consumed by one thought and one thought alone—that she wanted to spend the rest of her life feeling exactly what Alexi was making her feel this very moment.

She'd told him the truth; she didn't know it would be this way. Last night she'd known what to expect; her visions had prepared her to that wee degree. His kisses had been heady and they'd made her yearn for more, but they were different today, *he* was different. She sensed in him a depth of urgent need born of a fierce struggle that waged within him. There was a possessiveness about the way he held her, a forceful element that seemed to declare that she was his alone.

There was no doubt of that. He slanted his mouth over hers again and she was lost. His tongue plunged into her mouth, withdrew, plunged again in a dark rhythm while his hand rose to cup her breast. Spirals of heat and pleasure cut a path straight from beneath his fingers to the core of her. When he slipped his hand inside her bodice to stroke over her nipple, it was all she could do not to come apart.

He kissed her again and again until she was breathless, her thoughts whirling, her mind clouded by so much pleasure she didn't realize he'd freed the buttons down the front of her gown. The feel of his hands spreading the two halves of her bodice and chemise came as a shock, but only until he lowered his head and caught her nipple between his lips. Then shock took on new meaning.

It didn't make any difference how many times she had *seen* him do this. She still was not prepared for this new assault on her senses. She arched instinctively and inadvertently increased the contact.

"Alexi!"

He raised his head, his liquid brown eyes glazed with a passion she could see ran clear to his soul. The skin across his cheeks was pulled taut, his breathing was as frayed as hers. For endless seconds that stretched the bounds of time, he stared down at her, his body wracked with tremors.

"I want you," he told her, his voice a grating whisper. "Do you understand?"

All she could manage was a weak nod of her head.

"I hadn't counted on you."

"I know."

"You were not in my plans."

"Aye."

"But you're in my blood and I can't walk away." He smoothed stray tendrils of hair back off her face.

"I don't know the why of it."

"Nor I. I've told myself to leave you alone, but I can't." He trailed his gaze from her lips to her breasts, his voice tortured, his face strained with regret. "God forgive me, I can't."

His anguish tore at her. "There's nothing to forgive, Alexi."

"There is. You're a virgin and what I'm offering you is less than honorable." His grip tightened about her. "But it's all I have to offer you."

"I haven't asked for anything."

"You should be demanding marriage."

"Would that make you feel better?"

"Hell, yes. It would remind me that you're pure and fine, that I don't deserve you."

His reply made her blink in wonder. "Why do you say that?"

"It's the truth."

"I don't believe it."

"You should. You deserve a man who can make you happy, a man who can make promises and keep them. I'm not that man, *dushka*." His voice lowered, his gaze dimmed. "I've seen too much, done . . . too much."

She could feel the utter rawness of his pain as if it came from deep within herself. And it broke her heart. He was a casualty of war, she realized, as much as any man who'd lost a limb. Only it wasn't a physical wound Alexi suffered, it was a damage done to the very heart of him.

"Oh, Alexi." What had he endured to make him feel so desolate? Tenderly, she laid her hand along his cheek, knowing now what the faeries wanted of her. This man had suffered, and she was meant to heal him.

Sunshine broke through the clouds is a blinding ray, filling the cottage with light and warmth.

The sudden shift from dismal gloom to radiant splendor came as a shock. Alexi jerked himself to his feet and crossed to the door. Krista watched him from behind, wishing with all her heart that she could alleviate his suffering that very minute. But the time and place were wrong. She had only ever *seen* them in her bed. And he had withdrawn emotionally from her as surely as he had physically.

Hands still trembling, she restored order to her clothes and rose. The sound drew Alexi around to face her. His expression closed off, it was clear he had himself under strict control again.

"This won't happen again, Krista." His voice was as rigid as his posture. "I promise."

"Alexi, don't torture yourself so."

It was as if she hadn't spoken. "Come. I'll take you back to the castle."

"Please, Alexi—"

"Now." With the single word, the wounded man was gone. The prince stood before her now, all-powerful, imperious, his regal facade in place.

She didn't say another word until she was mounted in front of him, his arms supporting her with ease. With her heart shining in her eyes, she whispered, "All will be well, Alexi. *I* promise you." She smiled. "The faeries have decreed it."

"I don't believe in your faeries, *dushka*." He didn't believe in elves or sprites or magic or good always triumphing over evil. At times, he'd come to doubt God.

His faith had been battered, and he was doing his utmost to revive it. He wouldn't allow Krista to suffer in the process. He'd be damned before he'd hurt her.

This one time, he had given in to temptation, but never again.

Spurring his horse on, he lifted his face to the horizon, and suddenly tipped his head to one side. Just as suddenly he shook off the impression of having heard the sound of Scottish pipes drifting on the wind.

Chapter 4

*J*UST *a wee get-together of the family,* Mother had said, *to welcome Keith home and celebrate Prince Alexi's visit.* But Krista knew there was nothing "wee" about a gathering of the clan. They numbered in the hundreds and were scattered all over the realm. Nonetheless, at Father's invitation, relatives enthusiastically dropped whatever they were about and came from as far away as London.

Nine days after Keith and Alexi had arrived, relatives happily filled the castle for what Mother thought of as a "wee bit of a ball." With every guest room filled and extra servants from the village hurrying about, the castle was alive with activity.

Krista herself was not quite so excited as she gave herself one last critical look in her mirror. Any glow in her cheeks was due more to tension than to anticipation. Truth was, in the past days she had grown increasingly frazzled waiting for the inevitable to happen. Oh, she'd tried to be philosophical about it, but each morning she woke wondering if this was to be the day. Every evening she questioned if this was to be the night. The constant tug of eagerness and apprehension had stretched her nerves thin.

Despite that, or perhaps because of that, she'd dressed for the evening with special care, having no delusions as to why. This was the first time Alexi would see her in her formal best. She didn't want him to find her lacking before her more sophisticated London or Edinburgh cousins. She wanted him to take one look at her and finally put an end to her waiting!

She gave the pale gold of her gown another discriminating inspection. The color should have clashed horribly with the silver of her eyes, but it didn't. Somehow the burnished yellow fabric accented the blue and silver tones, all the while draping her curves to full advantage. As reassuring as the sight was, she found little comfort in it.

"Yer lovely, yer are," her maid sighed.

"Do you think so?" Krista asked, eyeing Molly with a touch of doubt.

" 'Tis sure is I'm sure," Molly insisted. She fussed with the one lone curl that had been left free to coyly graze Krista's neck. "Not a man here will be able ta keep his eyes in his head."

There was only one man Krista wanted to impress. All others could do what they wished with their eyes, or themselves, for that matter. Nervously, she tugged at the scooped neckline of her bodice, and was instantly scolded.

"Ahck, don't be foolin' with the lay and the fall of things." Molly adjusted the neckline so that it once again displayed the desired amount of Krista's breasts. "A bit higher and they'll be thinkin' you don't know a thing about fashion. Any lower and they'll be thinkin' other things entirely." She shook her gray head at Krista's continued fidgeting. "Don't know what's the matter with you. 'Tisn't as if you've never danced in a man's arms before."

Krista had never danced in *Alexi's* arms, and before the night was over, she knew she would—protocol demanded as much. The certainty sent a giddy rush through her veins. Since the day in the cottage one long week ago, Alexi had maintained a distance from her, holding true to his promise that they never be alone again, that he never have the chance to give in to his desires for her. For seven endless, trying days, he'd treated her as politely as he did her other sisters.

His coolness stung. From their very first glance, they had crossed boundaries that put their acquaintance on a personal level. To have him withdraw so drastically hurt. Her heart had been well on its way to being captured with his first kiss. All she had come to learn of the man since then had only confirmed her heart's yearnings. Alexi was as kind as he was commanding, as honorable as he was passionate. He was a man worth admiring and loving, and she had come to care for him, deeply. In return, he avoided her as if he couldn't stand the sight of her.

In desperation she'd considered telling him the whole truth about her visions of the two of them, but what was the use? He'd made his opinion clear on the matter. He didn't believe in faeries, which in some ways could be forgiven. After all, he wasn't a Scot. He hadn't been raised amid the legends, so it stood to reason that his skepticism would be more pronounced.

More to the point, though, and infinitely more sorrowful was his tormented spirit. She ached for him, and worried daily for his happiness. Unless he could bring himself to believe in life's magic again, true happiness would not be his. Without that happiness, he would put no store in her claims of visions.

Taking him into her body was the only way. As much as she accepted that, she didn't understand it. Why? A hundred times she asked the silent question of why his healing should be fated to come through her? The only answers she ever received were the croakings of the frogs in the loch or the swirling shrouds of mist that hovered over the meadow. Those gave her no more assurance than Alexi's steely withdrawal.

To stoically accept the barriers he erected, she'd clung to the promise of her visions. She'd swallowed her dejection and acted as pleasantly immune to him as he appeared to be toward her, but she wasn't fooled. Every now and then, their gazes would lock and she was able to see the carefully banked desire in his eyes, the ruthless restraint he held on himself, and she knew that he had forgotten neither her nor their shared passion.

Thoughts of that passion accompanied her from her rooms. She would be lying to herself if she denied that she wanted Alexi. Immodest as that was, it was a truth that had become extremely frustrating, and that frustration only added to her ever increasing anxiety. She longed to have him take her in his arms and kiss her once again. How that was ever going to happen with things proceeding as they had she didn't know.

"I suppose you have an answer," she grumbled to the faeries.

From the gallery above the Lord's hall came the first lilting sounds of music.

"You're all possessed of a warped sense of humor."

She entered the hall to find exactly what she had expected, a crush of people she'd known all her life. Smiling faces and laughter surrounded her as she greeted one person and then the next, all the while wondering a bit irritably where Alexi might be. In the crowded room, it was impossible for her to tell until a very distant cousin all of the age of fifty sighed in open enchantment.

"Isn't he the handsomest man you've ever seen?"

Krista followed the lady's line of vision to the man in question. Not surprisingly, she found Alexi and her breath caught. In formal military garb, he was overwhelming. His waist-length coat of forest green was accented with heavy braid and polished brass buttons. Red and gold slashed his cuffs and high-standing collar while gold epaulettes accentuated the width of his shoulders. Almost indecently form-fitting white pants were tucked into tall, black leather boots, and around his waist was tied a dashing white sash.

He was quite possibly the handsomest man she'd ever seen, and it had nothing to do with his uniform and everything to do with the man himself. He'd been just as handsome, just as compelling, just as extraordinary that day in the cottage dressed in causal country clothes of his native land. It was the vitality and character of the man himself who drew her eye and held her enthralled.

As if feeling the pull of her gaze, he looked up and started straight at her. For one brief instant, he seared her with the force of his longing, and chills rippled over her skin. Then in the blink of an eye, he turned away, his message perfectly clear: *I want you, but my promise holds true.*

"Definitely handsome," she agreed, her voice choked in her throat.

"There isn't a woman here who isn't smitten with him."

That was obvious. A throng of women was gathered around him, each, it seemed, vying for his undivided attention. Alexi smiled and nodded his head, from all appearances enjoying himself immensely.

"I'm sure they'll find him charming company."

"*Charming?!* Why the man makes my heart race and I'm old enough to be his mother."

Krista's heart was doing its own racing, torn between longing and anguish. Somehow she managed to laugh at her cousin's good-natured infatuation, hoping to present just the right touch of unaffectedness. They may be in Strathlachlan, but in a social setting such as this, the edicts of London's *ton* still had to be observed. Casual courtesy was a must, and to that end, she set her mind.

It proved to be a difficult task. No matter whom she spoke to, they wished to discuss Alexi, as if someone had waved a magic wand or sprinkled faerie dust over their heads, rendering them incapable of any other topic of conversation.

"His actions in battle saved the lives of countless men."

"I understand he has palaces in Saint Petersburg *and* Moscow."

"He's a favored relative of Tsar Alexander, you know."

"Isn't his accent decadence itself?"

Time and again, her attention was drawn back to him. Time and again, her resolve to appear genial and unperturbed was tested to its limits. Heavens above, how was she supposed to carry on normally when the mere sight of him slapped her in the face with the memory of her visions?

It didn't help her unraveling nerves one whit that Alexi continued to keep his distance from her with a studied precision that would have done any military strategist proud. After three hours, however, even he could not prevent them from finding themselves in each other's company.

Krista's breathing turned ragged. Standing between Keith and her parents, the small group they formed somehow melded with the nearby cluster made up of Alexi and three of her ancient great-aunts. Alexi was on the verge of giving her the same detached smile he'd bestowed on her for a week when the musicians struck up a waltz.

In something close to dismay, she watched his smile freeze as he was caught in the very situation she knew he'd been doing his utmost to prevent. But with her mother's and father's and even her great-aunt Beulah's eyes turned to him expectantly, Alexi was given no choice but to act the gallant.

Inclining his head, he offered his hand. "My lady. I believe you have yet to honor me with a waltz."

No response was necessary or even possible. Her throat too tight to utter an intelligible sound, Krista placed her hand in his and allowed him to escort her onto the dance floor. There, fully aware that they were the focus of a great many gazes, she matched her pleasantly amused expression to Alexi's and kept it intact even though her lips were prone to trembling.

To be near him again, to feel his touch as he swept her about the room with commanding ease, was the richest of pleasures. To know he wished to be holding anyone else tore at her heart.

Striving valiantly for a poise she was far from feeling, she said, "I hope you've been enjoying yourself, your highness."

It was too much to hope that the glitter in his eyes was due to humor. Around a pasted smile, he stated in excruciatingly exact tones, "Don't start with that, Krista."

She didn't pretend ignorance. He wasn't pleased that she had addressed him so formally. But after behaving as if she didn't even exist, did he actually expect her to call him Alexi or the more intimate Sasha?

"You have made quite an impression on the ladies," she sniffed back, thoroughly piqued. He had no right to be irritated with her when it was he who was responsible for their mutual strain and unease. "I dinna know you were so highly thought of by the Tsar himself. No fewer than six people here tonight told me so."

The only sign he gave that her remarks had struck a raw nerve was the tightening of his jaw. That and the low grating of his voice. "And did they also tell you that you are the most foolhardy young woman I have ever met?"

"Me?" She was genuinely surprised.

"Only a fool would toy with me, Krista. Only a fool would provoke me when my tolerance is hanging by a thread."

The fierceness of his reply might have been concealed by the required socially congenial expression topped off by his own rakish air, but held as close as she was, Krista felt the full impact of his fury. Like a sizzling bolt of heat, it struck her with unexpected force, sobering her to just how precariously thin his control was.

For days he'd been holding himself in check by keeping his distance. She hadn't realized until now how difficult that had been for him. She'd known all along that he hadn't forgotten their intimacies, but she hadn't understood that in his remembering he'd suffered.

"I'm sorry," she said to the front of his jacket, her annoyance evaporating entirely. Where only moments ago she'd felt angry, all she felt now was a deep sense of remorse. "I know you wished to avoid this."

He didn't deny it. "It couldn't be helped." Though his expression remained pleasant enough, his voice was as tense as the muscles under her fingers.

She swallowed with difficulty. "If I could undo everything, Alexi, I would." Her eyes lifted to his. "I dinna mean to cause you any upset." She'd never meant for him to endure another moment of torment. He'd already borne more than enough. "I never wanted your stay with us to be ruined."

"It hasn't been ruined."

"It has, and it's my fault. You can't bear being in the same room with me—"

"Krista, don't."

"And when you are, you look through me instead of at me."

"I'm trying to do what's right."

"I know what's right for me, for both of us, Alexi, only you refuse to admit it."

A flash of pain tore across his face before it was masked with a cold ruthlessness. Just as quickly, that expression was obliterated for one of perfect social polish. "Don't do this, Krista," he ordered under his breath. "Don't make this any more difficult for either one of us than it already is."

Her voice broke. "I'm sorry."

His fingers at her waist tightened. "Stop apologizing. None of this is your fault."

No, it wasn't. Nor was it his, yet they were both suffering nonetheless. She was at her wit's end, wondering, hoping, tense and miserable, a virgin on the brink of taking one of the most momentous steps of her life while he was more rigidly under control than ever. If she doubted that, she had only to peer into his eyes to see proof that every second he touched her brought him untold agony.

Pain pierced her. How she finished the dance without dissolving into tears, she didn't know, but as soon as Alexi delivered her to her parents' sides, she wasted little time in escaping. Damn her visions, and the faeries, too. She was a mortal woman, with mortal feelings and mortal frailties.

She didn't bother climbing the stairs. Tears were already a real threat. The quickest means to the privacy she so desperately needed lay through an antechamber and from there to the servants' stairway.

Blinking furiously, she hurried through the dimly lit room. Without warning, her arm was caught from behind, and the force of her own momentum swung her around with a startled gasp.

"Alexi," she choked out.

He stood tall and indomitable, his face lined with all the anger he'd so carefully concealed up until now, his eyes dark with every bit of desire he'd fought to suppress. "What do you think you're doing? You practically ran out of the there."

Her emotions were too fragile to endure another beating, and that's exactly what would happen if she remained. After days of longing to be alone with him, she suddenly couldn't take it. "Let me go."

"Why? So you can run off and feed every gossiping tongue in the castle?"

A bit frantically, she tried to pry his fingers loose, all the while twisting and tugging to free herself. The last of her composure was about to slip and she didn't want him to witness her falling apart.

"Krista, stop."

She twisted all the harder, only to have him take hold of her other arm as well.

"Cease."

To do so seemed beyond her. Suddenly, he hauled her close and lowered his head until he stabbed her the full force of his penetrating stare.

"Be still, *dushka*, before you hurt yourself."

It was the endearment that finally snapped her self-control. Everything inside her felt as if it broke into a million pieces before plummeting to her toes. "I've already been hurt," she cried, tears and a look of pleading filling her eyes. "Don't you understand? The way you've treated me this last week has hurt me more than I can tell you." With that, she relented to the sobs that wouldn't be contained.

Alexi stared down at her averted face, shocked, disturbed. As quick as his mind was, it couldn't fathom the reality of Krista crying. She was light and goodness, a faerie who laughed like an angel. It was one of the qualities that drew him to her and yet she was weeping now, all her radiance gone, buried under a mantle of unhappiness.

Shaken, he regarded her trembling body. Echoing through his head were her anguished words, stabbing him with all the force of a saber's thrust, spearing him with the truth of his actions. He'd been trying to protect her, but without meaning to, he'd treated her cruelly, ignoring her, disavowing her very existence. In his attempt to do what was honorable, he'd wounded her terribly.

He ground his eyes shut, telling himself he should have known. He should have realized that, as sensitive and fine as she was, she wouldn't be capable of braving such callous treatment, even if it had been well intentioned. These last days, he'd seen the silent anguish in her fey silver eyes, but he hadn't known to what depths it ran. He hadn't known it went to the very heart of her.

The muscles in his chest constricted with a pain surpassing any he'd withstood in battle. He tried to brace himself against the assault, tried to endure. There was no withstanding her grief. He was the cause, and it was beyond his bearing.

Cursing himself, he caught her close, desperate to ease her suffering in the only way that felt right, with the shelter and comfort of his body. "I'm sorry," he whispered. "I'm sorry. Please, don't cry." Hating himself for giving in, for drowning in the sheer pleasure of holding her again, he pressed his lips to her forehead. "I can't bear to see you cry."

Against his chest, she quietly sobbed.

"Krista, please." He would do anything, take any torture, pain, or sacrifice rather than have her suffer such misery, a misery for which he alone was responsible. "Forgive me, I never meant to hurt you so. I was trying to do what's best."

But she was past hearing. Her delicate body shook, her tears continued to flow.

Without a second thought, knowing only that he had to wipe away her sorrow, he swept her into his arms and made his way up the servants' stairway to her rooms. A single kick to her door secured it tightly before he carried her to her bed. He gently laid her against the pillows, unable to release her. Sitting on the edge, he held her close, her head coming to rest on his shoulder.

Again and again, he whispered disjointed pleas and fragmented commands—cajoling in English, dictating in Russian—for her to please forgive him. For her to rail at him or hit him, anything to make her feel better. In the end, he had no choice but to let her tears run their course.

Long moments later, in the shadowy silence, she finally lay quietly in his embrace, every now and then an errant shudder wracking her slender figure. Alexi absorbed the tremors with his own body in an effort to take her pain and make it his.

His left hand made small comforting circles in the small of her back, his right traced up and down her neck. Rubbing his chin against her temple, he pressed a kiss into her hair, a kiss meant to comfort, but she turned her head in the same instant, and their lips met; hers soft and yielding, his warm and hard.

The universe seemed to hang suspended. Past, present, and future ceased to exist. He was spellbound by the feel and the taste of her. For days that felt like decades, he'd longed to hold her, to feel her alive and warm in his arms. He'd ached until his insides burned just to be able to kiss her, to hear her breath catch in her throat, to know he was responsible for making her melt with desire.

"Krista," he breathed. Taking in every nuance of her expression, he scrutinized each of her features. His conscience sent out one last appeal, but Krista brushed her lips over his, sweetly, innocently, and he was lost.

Almost fiercely, he covered her mouth with his own, parting her lips with a hunger that emanated from the core of him. Silently he damned himself for being less than gentle. Restraint wasn't possible, though, not with her warmth inundating his body, not with her response bewitching his mind. Sweet Jesus, not with him feeling as if he'd just found his way home after a lifetime of wandering.

"Ah, Krista, what have you done to me?"

I've loved you, Alexi, she wanted to say. I'll always love you. The words were whispered from her heart and went no farther than her mind. The time wasn't right, it might never be right, for her to tell him. That was something she'd have to face in the days ahead. For now, her visions were unfolding and it was all she could do to retain coherent thought as memory combined with reality.

He slanted his mouth over hers just as she'd *seen* countless times. His hands caressed and teased, her clothes were carefully removed, then his stripped away, her body lay under his, all in exact replay of her visions.

Eyes as deep as the loch and as brown as the richest mahogany stared down at her with an intensity that burned straight to her soul. A smile came slowly, fleetingly to his hard lips before they lowered and took possession of hers.

Inside, she quivered, knowing it was to be and yet not knowing what to expect. She wasn't prepared for his heat or his strength, or the way her body wanted to cling greedily to his.

His muttered words came to her in a blend of Russian and English, melodic, fervent, pressed to the side of her neck and the curve of her breast. His fingers followed his lips' path, stroking, caressing, making her arch . . .

The tension centered low and inside her was almost unbearable. She clung tightly to his shoulders, incoherent whimpers trembling on her lips.

"Alexi . . ." She was writhing beneath him, trembling with a need that bordered on painful.

"Not yet, *dushka*," he murmured, snatching her cries around a knowing smile.

"Please." Her whole life was meant for this one moment; she knew it with absolute certainty, and yet he continued to take his time, drawing their pleasure out, exploring her body, teaching her to learn his.

The differences fascinated her, for the contrasts were obviously intended to create a perfect balance, a harmony of mind and flesh. His angular hollows and her rounded curves, his strength and her frailty, his worldly expertise and her naiveté. They were like a rare, one-of-a-kind puzzle that had been fashioned ages ago and were only now brought together to join in exquisite unity.

The joining. She'd never imagined . . . could barely think, and when she did, it was to truly appreciate the full extent of all those differences between them.

He eased into her in slow increments, advancing farther with each careful thrust, giving her a chance to adjust to his size, to the unequivocal masculine invasion, with each near-withdrawal. Still, she couldn't prevent herself from gasping. She felt herself being stretched and filled to a point that bordered on discomfort.

"Easy, love." Above her, Alexi's face was drawn tight with the effort of keeping a brutal rein on himself. He'd purposely set a slow pace, not wanting to do anything that might shock or frighten Krista. However, he hadn't counted on how fully her passionate nature would exert itself. She more than met his ardor, eagerly, generously, fueling his passion until now, every muscle in his body quivered as he fought the unrelenting demand for release.

In all his life, he'd never experienced this wild, uncontrollable urgency to forsake all niceties, where he wanted to lay claim to Krista with a desperate, barbaric need. The urge to thrust with all his might ran clear to the marrow of his bones.

For Krista's sake he tempered the need, wanting to spare her as much of the pain as possible.

"I'm sorry, love," he whispered against her lips. He wouldn't hurt her for anything on earth, or Heaven, either, but there was no avoiding the pain to come. Clasping her tightly, he covered her mouth with his and thrust forward.

The instant transcended carnality and spirituality. It took him to another time and place, to a state of mind and being previously unknown. It filled him with peace and wonder, and a profound contentment of the soul. How long he remained still, absorbing the sensation, he didn't know. With his forehead pressed into the curve of her throat, time was irrelevant. All that mattered was this sublime feeling of having been reborn. And Krista.

He lifted his head to find her regarding him in dazed wonder, and stunned confusion, too. Amid the amazement and passion in her eyes, he could see the questions as well.

Gently, he gave her the answers she sought, and she soared. Clinging to his back, she returned his kisses and lifted herself up to meet his thrusts with unrestrained abandon. Gentleness became impossible after that.

She offered herself without restraint or reservation, half out of her mind with a yearning that expanded and grew, to what end, she didn't know. But it couldn't go on, not the way it tightened and coiled in on itself until she didn't think she could take another breath without shattering into a million pieces.

And then she did. Without warning, all the pleasure in the universe seemed to explode inside her, going on and on without end. Her entire body bowed and a keening cry broke over her lips.

To Alexi, the sounds were pure magic. He convulsed in the sweetest, most violent release of his life.

In the heavy silence that followed, it was the most natural thing in the world for Alexi to gather Krista to his side and for her to lay her head on his shoulder. As if she'd done so a thousand times before, she draped her arm over his chest, breathed in the musky scent of him, and fell into an exhausted sleep.

Happiness was hers. Until a black vision of danger woke her with a scream.

Chapter 5

LIGHTNING slashed a turbulent sky. Rain pelted, driven by howling winds. Out of the east, a man approached stealthily, sliding from shadow to shadow, his face concealed.

He came alone, consumed with rage, his intent revenge, murder. It was a madman's purpose, twisted beyond any sane reasoning or proportion. A maniacal obsession meant for Alexi . . .

Krista blinked out of the vision, lips parted, hands shaking. Confusion claimed her.

"Easy, *dushka*." Alexi's voice. "You were dreaming, but I'm here."

She found herself sitting bolt upright, Alexi's arms about her, and abruptly realized exactly what had happened. "Oh, no." Fearfully, she shook her head in denial, searching out every one of Alexi's beloved features. "Oh, no!"

"Shh, little Krista. You've been dreaming."

"It . . . it wasn't a dream."

He pressed his lips to the top of her head. "There's no need to fret."

"You don't understand." Panic began to swell, cramping her insides. Her fingers dug into his shoulders. "I had a vision. I saw danger."

"A nightmare, nothing more."

"No." She tried to squirm out of his embrace, as if that could somehow make him believe her. "It wasn't a nightmare. I saw a man, a . . . a Frenchman." She was certain of it. "He's coming here to kill you."

With ludicrous ease, he controlled her struggles. "You were dreaming." He soothed caresses up and down her back. "It's understandable. Too much has happened this night for you rest easily."

Her panic was escalating to fear. "Please, Alexi, you must believe me. You must listen to what I'm telling you. You have an enemy."

"I have many." He shrugged with negligent disregard. "It comes with war."

"But this one would see you dead." She quaked at the idea, and he frowned.

"You truly are frightened, aren't you?"

"Aye, and with good reason."

Easing her back to the pillows, he loomed over her, bracing himself on one forearm. "Little faerie, you humble me with your concern." As tenderly as a butterfly's kiss, he smoothed the hair back from her face. "I doubt that I deserve you. What can I do to convince you that you have no reason to be frightened?"

"What can I do to convince you that the vision was real?"

He smiled broadly, and heaved a sigh. "I can see that you need to be put at ease." Tracing her bottom lip with a finger, his eyes took on a seductive cast. "Perhaps I'll have to give you something else to think about."

"But—"

"Have faith, *dushka*. Do you honestly believe I will allow myself to be killed?" He tossed the words away with careless nonchalance. "Especially now when I've only just found you?"

"No, not intentionally, of course not." His fingers lowering to the pulse beating in her throat was distracting. "But you . . . you could be taken unawares."

"True. It's happened before." He studied the slope of her breast as if discovering the greatest treasure. "And I'm alive to tell about it."

He was far more interested in watching her nipple tighten at his caress than in her warnings. "Sasha, please." Her voice caught.

"Say it again."

This time the name emerged on a sigh. "Sasha."

Lowering his head, he whispered, "I'll banish your frightful dreams, love."

"Oh, Alexi, they weren't dreams, they weren't."

Again, there was the lack of concern in his voice, the sound that said he didn't, couldn't take her claims seriously. "Dream or vision, fantasy or actuality, you didn't see me die, did you?"

She thought carefully. "No." She'd only *seen* the figure of the Frenchman, and sensed his evil purpose. Nothing more.

"Then trust me to look after myself." He sipped at the tip of her breast. "And you."

Pleasure unfurled, seeking out all the little nooks and crannies of her body. Her mind resisted, trapped by dread. Her body surrendered, intoxicated by love. It was a piteous battle, one to which she didn't acquiesce lightly. She had to cling to the reassurance that she hadn't actually *seen* Alexi's death. The Frenchman might intend murder, but that didn't mean he would succeed.

In the end, she had no resistance to Alexi's magic. He wove his spell with all the skill of the faeries themselves. With special care, he carried to her the heights.

In the dim light of dawn, Alexi lay on his side, gazing at Krista's still form. She was all that was beautiful, all that was good.

Had there ever been such a woman? She had given herself to him so unselfishly, so lovingly, he'd been enchanted. Her innocence had charmed him nearly as much as her impassioned responses, and all had been underscored with what he very much suspected was love.

His eyes drifted shut at the idea. There was no other reason for her to have lain with him. She was a creature guided by her emotions. She laughed when she was happy, cried when she was sad. She loved him so she gave him her innocence.

He'd feared this very thing. It was why he'd resisted her for so long. He hadn't wanted Krista to fall in love with him; it was bound to bring her pain for he wasn't ready for love.

Or he hadn't been—he didn't know. After last night, he couldn't be sure any longer. With his first thrust into Krista's welcoming heat, something within him had changed. Even now, hours later, with the urgency of passion sated, he couldn't fathom the unearthly sensations that had claimed him. Something other than passion and physical satisfaction had occurred. He'd felt reborn, and still did, his mind and body filled with the kind of peace he hadn't felt in years.

He embraced the feeling, savoring it in much the same way he would a delicious flavor long-lost and discovered again for the first time after decades of deprivation. It felt good beyond description.

Yes, something within him had changed. The emptiness had begun to diminish. The pockets of lifelessness were no longer barren but sowed with hope. Hope, and a fledgling sense of the future.

Stunned, exhilarated, he lifted his right hand, the hand that had wielded a sword too often. Splaying his fingers, he stared at his palm as if seeing it for the first time. With infinite care he molded it to Krista's breast, emotion closing his throat.

She stirred at the touch, drawing in a long breath. Her eyelids lifted languidly, shut, lifted again. And she smiled. "Good morning."

It was a good morning. The best he could ever remember having. "I didn't mean to wake you."

"I'm glad you did." She was still more asleep than awake, her eyes struggling to remain open. Even so, she trailed her hands up his arms. Arching into a stretch, she flinched.

"Sore?" he asked.

"A wee bit."

A rakish smile curled his lips. "Should I kiss all the tender spots to make them better?" To his delight, she blushed, even in the dawn light her heightened color visible. He had to laugh as he hugged her tightly. "What a treasure you are."

Krista's answering laugh was more of a drowsy, contented sigh. "I am the lucky one, Sasha."

He couldn't resist kissing her, savoring her just as he savored the feeling of peace and hope. Her response was a sleepy albeit eager greeting that had an immediate impact on his mind and body. It took a concerted effort for him to tamp down his unruly desires.

"As much as I would like to, we can't. You're still too tender and . . ." He cast the windows a knowing look. "The castle will be up soon. I won't chance having anyone see me leaving your rooms. As it is, we may already have caused a stir. Our mutual absence from the ball was most likely noted."

"No," she murmured, beginning to sink back into slumber. "No one noticed. The faeries made sure of that."

She was asleep with her last word, dreaming, he'd wager, of winged sprites and magic. On a smile, he kissed the tip of her nose and left her to her dreams.

The sun was high when Krista woke for the second time. She sensed Alexi's absence at once and fought to subdue her disappointment.

Greed was foreign to her nature, but in one night she admitted she'd fallen victim. It wasn't enough for her to have had him near her all night. She wanted him beside her when she woke in the morning. She wanted to be able to go through her day and look across the room and find him looking back at her. She wanted to be able to listen to the sound of his voice or feel his hand in hers, to exchange secret smiles and kiss whenever the mood struck them.

She wanted . . . him. All of him, the one and only man she would ever love. Husband, friend, confidant, and yes, lover, too, for now and for all the years to come. God willing, she could bear his children. Together, they would grow old and take pleasure from their family and each other. And when they'd look back at their first night together, they would share the memory of how perfect it had been. Sublime loving, rich pleasure, the sweetest of dreams . . .

The memory of her vision came back in a rush, dispelling the joy of her reverie, rippling over her skin in chilling waves. Not all of last night had been perfect. She had indeed fallen asleep to dream and had awakened to a vision of danger.

The chill spread to her bones. In self-defense, she sat up and hugged her knees to her chest, wishing she could be hugging Alexi instead. His life was in peril, but she hadn't been able to convince him of that. He didn't believe in the magic or second sight; there would be no swaying him to her way of thinking. Not until this enemy, this fiend, arrived to exact his revenge. Then Alexi would have his proof that her visions were real, but that proof could come too late.

What was she going to do? How could she protect him? The questions tumbled through her mind as she hastily bathed, dressed, and hurried off to find Alexi. He was in the Lord's hall with Mother, Father, and Keith.

"Ah, I see you've decided to join us at last," her father laughed.

"Aye." Her smile was forced until it came to rest on Alexi. He'd risen to his feet at her approach. It was impossible to look at him and not be reminded of the night just past. She had lain in his arms, taken him into her body, and given him her love.

"The morning got away from me," she said, all too aware of the way Alexi regarded her. The intimacy in his eyes was a delicate stroke over her senses.

"For you and everyone else," her mother replied. "Only a few hearty souls have begun to stir after last night."

Keith contained a yawn. "I could return to my bed without a second thought." He studied his sister, his brows elevating. "But you look none the worse for wear. You must have slept soundly."

Krista took a seat on the settee beside her mother. "Why do you say that?"

"You're radiant this morning. What time did you quit the ball?"

Her eyelids fluttered in her effort not to glance in Alexi's direction. "I'm not entirely sure."

"What's important is that you enjoyed yourself," her father maintained.

"Oh, I did. Immensely."

"And you, Alexi?" her father went on good-naturedly. "I hope our entertainment was to your liking."

"Without a doubt."

"Splendid."

Krista bit her bottom lip, terribly uncomfortable sitting there pretending to discuss one thing when in her heart, and she knew in Alexi's as well, they were referring to other things entirely.

"I believe I'll go for a walk," she announced.

"If you don't mind my company," Alexi said, "I'll join you."

Her mother was quick to applaud the idea. "Excellent. Krista, why don't you take him over to the ruins. For some reason, visitors seem to enjoy the experience."

It wasn't until they were making their way down the sloping hill that Krista lifted a brow Alexi's way. "Does that set your mind at ease?"

"About what?"

"About our being missed from the ball."

He exhaled in open relief. "I admit, I was prepared to fabricate some tale or other."

"I told you the faeries would watch over us."

His grin pulled to one side. "It's always the faeries with you, isn't it?"

"Aye. It can't be helped. It's in the blood."

"A descendant of Lily, the good faerie." He raked a bold look from her lips to her breasts. "Somehow I have trouble thinking of you as anything other than a woman."

Krista couldn't have gained the crumbling shell of the original castle soon enough. She yearned to feel Alexi's arms about her and the old walls offered a much-needed source of privacy. The moment they cleared the outer courtyard, she turned to Alexi and he pulled her close.

"God, I've missed you," he muttered, his cheek pressed to her temple, his hands roaming freely from shoulder to hip.

"I missed you, too. I dinna like waking up alone."

"Leaving you took all my willpower. If I'd had my way, we wouldn't have moved from your bed all day."

"Will you come to me tonight?"

He caught her chin under his thumb. "You would have a devil of a time keeping me away." It took the barest pressure for him to tip her chin up and capture her mouth.

The kiss was cherishing and enticing, spiritual and wanton, that of a man not only desperate for his woman, but one meant to bind. It went on until Krista was out of breath.

"I love you," she whispered. She hadn't meant to tell him. The words just slipped out as naturally as a rainbow formed in the wake of a summer's rain.

His arms drew her closer. He started to speak, but she cut him off.

"Please, don't say anything. I dinna tell you for any purpose. I would never try and coerce you with emotion or make you feel beholden or guilty. I told you because I couldn't hold it in any longer."

"I know that, Krista."

"Do you?"

"You aren't capable of deceit or blackmail. You couldn't lie any more than you could sprout wings, faerie or otherwise."

That earned him a gently chiding frown. "Don't make light of the magic, Sasha. It's real even though you won't admit it." The worry came back to haunt her. She pressed her forehead to his chest. "You must promise me you'll be careful."

The fear in her voice drew him up short. "Are you still bothered by that dream?"

She looked him square in the eye. "I am. And if you believe that I cannot lie, then you have to believe that I'm telling the truth about what I *saw*. Someone is coming here to kill you."

Her anxiety was real, sobering Alexi when he would have preferred to have continued with their lazy seduction. He wouldn't have thought that she would put such stock in a nightmare, and it bothered him greatly that she did.

It was due to this belief she had about having "the sight," a fanciful notion perpetuated by her family. He couldn't blame them if they chose to take their superstitions seriously, but he wouldn't stand by and allow their blind convictions to hurt Krista.

"If it makes you feel better, then I promise to keep a watchful eye. But in return, you must promise me something."

"Anything."

"Promise me that you will put the matter from your mind. I will not have you upset by this, do you understand? I won't have it, Krista."

It wasn't the response she was after, but she knew it would have to suffice. He had resorted to his princely custom of issuing orders and expecting them to be obeyed without question. He would not allow her to worry, and there would be no discussing the matter further.

"I promise I will do my best." And that would have to suffice for him.

She did her utmost to hold true to her word. The day sped by, a glorious progression of hours spent in Alexi's company. Twice the fear threatened to encroach on her happiness. Twice, she forced herself not to dwell on the inevitable.

Their night together was more wonderful than their first. Now that Krista knew what to expect, she was as gloriously imperious as any

Russian princess, demanding that Alexi show her everything there was to know about making love. Laughingly, he told her it would take more than one night.

It took a great many. A fortnight later, Alexi had to marvel at the openly sensuous woman Krista had become. She marveled right back, so in love with him she wasn't certain why her heart didn't burst.

The one blemish on her happiness was the recurrence of her vision. She'd *seen* the danger two more times, and each time her certainty grew that Alexi's life was at stake. Keeping her anxiety hidden from him became more difficult with each passing day. It chafed sorely at times, dulling the glow in her eyes.

"What is it, *dushka?*" Alexi asked, visually tracing the delicate lines pulling at her brow. He was seated before the fireplace in her room, Krista cosily ensconced on his lap. In the aftermath of their loving, he was magnificently sated. "Have I tired you out? Have I been too demanding?"

Thunder rolled up from over the loch, bringing with it the wind and rain, and some element that unnerved her.

"No. It's just the thunder. It seems to bother me tonight." She hesitated in telling him that she felt each streak of lightning, a slight pain that worsened as the storm's fury grew.

"You're worn out, love." He stood with her in his arms. "Come. I'll put you to bed."

"As long as you stay beside me."

Another distant spear of lightning, another stab of pain. Huddled beneath the covers, her head on Alexi's shoulder, she fought to breathe steadily, to conquer the unreasoning fright. It wasn't to be vanquished. It riddled her nerves until she wanted to dissolve into tears. When she finally did sleep, it was a restless slumber, troubled and short-lived.

She came awake at the deafening sound of booming thunder, a scream choked off in her throat. Terrified, she took in the whole of her room in one sweeping glance and knew, absolutely knew, that the Frenchman was close.

"Alexi," she gasped. "Get up." Against the windows, the rain beat like a maddened thing, trying to gain entrance.

"What is it?" He roused from his sleep to prop himself up on an elbow.

"He's here." Swallowing past a rising nausea, she scrambled from bed. Without even realizing it, she donned her dressing gown.

"Who?" He gave the room a cursory inspection.

"The Frenchman." She spun to stare at the door, pivoted, and turned her pleading gaze on Alexi. "I know you don't believe me, but it's true. He's here. I . . . I . . . feel it . . . I know."

The sky filled with unholy light. Inside, her muscles clenched against the pain.

"Krista?" The sight of her physical discomfort drew him up.

"Sasha, *please*. You've got to arm yourself."

"Are you ill?"

He wasn't listening. "No! Listen to me, you stubborn, foolish man." The threatening tears became a reality. "I've tried and tried to tell you. Why won't you believe me?"

Annoyance pulled at his brow. "I am perfectly safe. There is no one here to harm me."

"But I tell you there is!" She could feel the malevolence reaching out to her, a vile blanket of evil, smothering in intensity.

"Come back to bed, Krista, and be done with this nonsense."

Every instinct she possessed rebelled. To go back to bed would mean certain death. She knew it as surely as if Lily herself were whispering the future in her ear.

Wildly, she shook her head. "It isn't safe here. We have to leave, now, this instant!"

Again and again the sky was slashed with light, jagged bursts connected one to the next in a continuous stream that seemed to go on forever. Krista doubled over, unable to breathe.

Alexi bolted from the bed and caught her. "By all that is holy, you're in pain."

It was nothing compared to the pain in her heart, a pain that would never cease if he died. "I would bear any pain if it meant keeping you safe."

She bolted from his arms and fled to the door. Alexi's voice echoed behind her as she raced down the stairs and out into the midst of the storm.

Chapter 6

THE rain tore her in one direction, the wind in another. Overhead the sky was tinted with a strange green glow. Krista ran, not knowing whether instinct or the faeries guided her.

Stumbling, barely able to see where she was going, she raced away from the castle, knowing Alexi was following her. In between the booms of thunder, she could hear him cursing and calling her name.

"I'm sorry, Sasha," she cried softly. "It's the only way." She didn't understand why. Logically, the castle offered the best protection. There, Alexi would have had the best advantage in defending himself. However, this was not a night for logic. The forces of good and evil were at work. She was not about to question that.

Lightning split the sky, so close she fell to the ground, screaming in agony and fright. But she didn't stop . . . she couldn't. It suddenly became imperative that she reach her faerie hillock on the edge of the forest. She realized with unexpected insight that she and Alexi had to gain the protection of the broken ring of boulders.

"Krista!"

She scrambled to her knees, her sodden dressing gown dragging at her legs, her breath coming in torn, burning gasps. She yanked at the fabric, pushed to her feet, and lurched and stumbled her way toward the trees.

The ground shook with the vibrations of thunder, the trees bent under the force of the wind. Krista turned her back in a bid for protection and scrambled backward for the faerie hillock.

"Krista, stop before you hurt yourself!"

Lightning and thunder came at the same time, the night seeming to burst itself open. The force knocked Krista to her knees. Alexi was there to catch her.

She grabbed hold of his shirt and managed to point to the broken ring of boulders. "There," she shouted over the deafening sounds.

He looked around, clearly seeking the best possible source of protection. With breaking branches careening down in the forest and the open land providing a sure target for lightning, the boulders were the best and only shelter.

Quickly, Alexi carried her to the center of the ring. Krista wrapped her arms tightly about his shoulders, her face tucked low into his chest. The urge to weep in relief was overwhelming. Now that Alexi was within the ring, he would be safe, the faeries would see to it.

He set her on the ground next to the largest stone, and used his own body as a shield to protect her. He couldn't have done so a second too soon. Without warning, the night exploded. Alexi shoved her against the stone as lightning struck the ground on the other side of the rocks. Clods of dirt spewed upward, a tree caught fire, heat and a gruesome odor of death permeated the air.

And then all was silent. Everything stilled around them. A gentle rain continued to fall like a delicate cleansing. The burning tree cast a comforting light. Slowly, breathing heavily, Alexi lifted his head and scanned the area. Krista emerged from her safe cocoon, peering around Alexi's shoulder.

At her shift in position, his hands tightened on her arms. "Are you hurt?" From under angry slanting brows, he searched her face for signs of injury.

"No." Although tears continued to make paths down her cheeks. Cupping his face between her palms, she drank in the sight of him. "Are you all right?"

"Other than having you scare a decade off my life, I'm fine." Angry beyond restraint, he gave her a shake. "What in the hell were you thinking to have come out here? You could have been killed."

Her hand fluttered weakly to his chest. "It was the only way, Sasha. I couldn't convince you that you were in danger. And physically, I dinna stand a chance of making you leave. So I ran, knowing you would follow."

"Out into the storm?" He surged to his feet, plowing a hand through his hair. "We were in more danger here than in your bed."

She had never seen him in a full temper before. She wasn't certain she wanted to now. At the best of times, Alexi was formidable. Filled with anger, he was daunting. She rose slowly, bracing herself against the rock at her back, and held silent. What could she possibly say? More of the same, and she already knew how he felt about that. Nor was she about to apologize—not for saving his life.

"You're alive," she finally said. "That's all that matters."

He spun to face her, his expression incredulous. "Alive more by chance than anything else." He swept his arm out in an encompassing arc. "Where is this supposed danger, Krista? Where is this mad Frenchman who supposedly came to kill me?"

"I . . . I don't know."

"Of course not, because he isn't here. He never was. You've let your dreams and some old superstitions warp your mind."

If he had slapped her in the face, she couldn't have been more hurt. Her entire body flinched.

Alexi swore under his breath. Heaving a tired, disgusted sounding sigh, he held out his hand. "Let's go back."

She ignored his hand, wrapping her arms about herself instead. Sidling around him, she stepped from the ring and stopped.

"Alexi."

He followed her line of vision to a body lying on the churned-up, smoking ground, no more than three feet away. The person had been struck by lightning. With one look, Alexi recognized the charred face. "Marchineaux," he whispered.

"Do you know him?"

"André Marchineaux."

That Alexi was stunned was apparent. He couldn't seem to take his eyes off the lifeless body. Carefully, she asked, "Was he your enemy?"

Alexi nodded, so amazed by the implication of Marchineaux's presence, he spoke slowly, precisely. "Yes. He was one of Napoleon's private assassins, a ruthless killer who thought nothing of slaughtering for his own pleasure. I was responsible for tracking him down and sending him to prison." He scoffed out his amazement. "He was supposed to have been executed, but he obviously escaped."

"How did he know where to find you?"

"I made no secret of my coming here."

"So he followed, seeking revenge," she finished softly.

Pivoting, he stared at her in equal parts wonder and accusation. "And you saw him," he charged, shoving each word out in disjointed syllables.

"Aye."

"You tried to warn me, but I didn't believe you."

Her brows arched in silent agreement.

His brows rose in stupefaction. "You truly are a faerie, aren't you?"

"No. I've been honest with you about that from the start. I'm as mortal as you, Sasha." She paused to tip her head from side to side. "With a wee bit of help from Lily."

He cast Marchineaux a telling look. "More than a 'wee bit,' I'd say." Sweet Jesus, the situation shook him to the core. He hadn't believed in faerie tales since he'd been a child. As an adult, he'd come to think of magic in terms of sexual satisfaction. This night's work had forever altered his beliefs, to what extent remained to be seen. He needed time to come to terms with all that had happened. For now, he wanted Krista warm and dry.

He held out his hand, and this time, she came willingly. An arm about her shoulders, he led her back to the castle.

They didn't speak privately until late the next afternoon. There had been no opportunity. When they'd returned to the castle, the whole family had been hovering at the door with questions. Keith and Father and been about to go searching.

Alexi's accounting had been honest and accurate with one omission—the fact that he had been in Krista's bed. Everyone assumed

Krista had rushed into his room to tell him of the danger, and he told them no differently.

Feeling oddly detached, Krista had watched the flurry of activity around her. Father had dispatched servants to see to Marchineaux's body. Mother had called for warm beverages and even warmer baths to be sent upstairs for her eldest daughter and Prince Alexi.

Before long, Krista had settled into bed. Mother and Molly and both her sisters had lingered to fuss, upset by the scratches and scrapes on her legs and feet. The sun had already risen by the time she'd fallen asleep, alone in her bed, wishing Alexi were with her.

Her wish was hers upon awakening. Opening her eyes, she found Alexi sitting in a chair pulled up to the bed. Happiness suffused her heart. He was safe.

"Good morning," she murmured, pushing herself up against the pillows.

"Good afternoon."

She noted the angle of the sunlight slanting in the windows, and smiled. "How long have I been asleep?"

"It's felt like forever."

"Have you been sitting there long?"

Humor glinted in his deep brown eyes. "It's felt like forever, but no, only a short while." With a thoroughness that left her breathless, he scrutinized every inch of her, visually trying to strip away nightgown and bedcovers alike. "How are you feeling?"

"Well." She gave him as thorough an inspection as he'd given her. "And you?"

He didn't answer immediately. "I'm not hurt, if that's what you're asking."

She could see how physically fine he was, but there was a slight strain about him that gave her pause. "Are you still angry with me about last night?"

"No. How could I be? You saved my life. I only wish you hadn't had to put your own life in danger for mine."

"It had to be that way, Sasha."

"Why? I could have fought Marchineaux here."

"You could have, aye, there's no doubting that. But the faeries dinna want it that way."

"The faeries," he grumbled. In the lengthening silence, the statement hung between them. "I wouldn't have believed it possible, but they're real, aren't they?"

"That's what I've been trying to tell you."

"And you truly are, as you say, blessed with second sight."

Her answer was a winsome smile.

"This is going to take some getting used to. I admit, I don't understand how these 'wee ones' of yours think. If all they wanted was to have Marchineaux done away with, they could have accomplished it in a fashion less dramatic than striking him with a bolt of lightning."

He sounded so disgruntled, she had to laugh. "That's not all they were after. I dinna understand it last night, but it's clear to me now. You needed to be given proof. You needed to see with your own eyes and believe in your heart that their power is real, that the *sight* they've given me is real."

He wasn't ready to relinquish his annoyance and it plainly showed. "I still do not like the fact that you were put in danger. They could have left me to take care of the bastard."

Loving him for wanting to protect her, she stretched out her hand in an invitation he could not resist. Facing him, her hip caressed by the hard length of his thigh, she felt at peace.

"The faeries sent us out to the hillock so you wouldn't have to fight, so you wouldn't have to kill again." She laid her hand over his heart. "You spent too many years doing that, Sasha, and it hurt you terribly. The faeries saw to Marchineaux so you wouldn't have to."

He'd asked himself dozens of times over why the situation had played itself out as it had. No explanation he'd come up with had made sense because, he realized now, his every explanation had been grounded in very human terms.

There was nothing mortal about last night's events or about what Krista had told him, but he believed her. How could he not? The faeries had indeed given him proof. More importantly, they'd brought him to Krista and she had made him whole again. He didn't need second sight to know that. He felt it with his entire being. She had given him all that she was, made him all that he could ever want to be, and he loved her.

"You're staring," she prompted in a softly beguiling voice.

"Am I?"

"It's impolite."

"I'm a prince. I'm allowed to do as I please."

At his continued staring, she laughed. "Alexi, what are you looking at?"

His gaze sought hers, tender, compelling, filled with love. "The most beautiful woman I've ever met. My future wife, the mother of my children. The woman I will love forever."

Covering her mouth with his, he sealed his vows with a kiss of infinite love. "Will you marry me?" he finally asked.

"Oh, aye," she breathed.

"You'll be a princess, you know." His very own Faerie Princess to love through all the years to come.

"I like the sound of that."

Into her mind came a lovely image, the loveliest image she'd ever *seen*, forcing the present from her consciousness. As always the vision lasted only a few moments, but it was long enough to make her the happiest woman ever.

"Krista?"

She saw his uncertainty. Now that he'd accepted her visions for what they were, he clearly was at a loss as to what to do. "It's all right to ask. Go ahead."

"What did you see?" came his cautious query.

"Children."

"What?"

"Children."

"Whose?"

"Ours."

His gaze immediately dropped to the vicinity of her belly beneath the covers.

"They're not there now," she laughed.

"They could be."

"*They?* Oh, no, only one at a time. Three boys and three girls, in that order."

He wanted to ask if she was sure, and caught himself. She was certain of what she'd *seen*, and he was certain of his faith in her. Faith. It was his again, whole and unfettered.

"Children." He felt warmed from the inside out. He couldn't remember the last time he'd thought of children with honest hope. Like faith, that was his also.

Securing Krista in his embrace, he settled back against the pillows and, for the first time, talked of the future. "I like the name Mikhail. And Levka."

"Elle for one of the girls," she countered.

"Elle?" He raised a brow her way.

"It means 'beautiful faerie.'"

He laughed. "Elle for the eldest. And Katarina, after my grand-mother."

She tested the name. "Katarina. I like it." Narrowing her eyes, she studied the feeling that came over her. "Yes, Katarina, for the youngest. She'll be special, I think."

"With you as their mother, they'll all be special," he decreed with just enough princely command in his voice to make her smile.

She wouldn't think of disagreeing with him, though. Each and every one of their children would indeed be as special as the love and magic she and Alexi shared.

BENEATH THE MIDNIGHT SKY

Mandalyn Kaye

"Prove your love when the sun shines in the midnight sky, and the light will shine on your fate as well."

Chapter 1

Beneath Loch Fyne, Argyll District, 1850

H E had loved her for a thousand years.

That explained, he supposed, why the odd sensation of waking from his slumber always began in the region of his chest.

Struan MacLachlan, of the Clan MacLachlan, waited patiently as the tingling spread outward from his heart. After so many times, he no longer felt the straining panic he once had. The breath, he knew, would come. His lungs would fill. The feeling would return to his limbs. And with it, would come the memories of her.

Laren. His beloved.

In a few hours, he would see her again. The waking always meant that the hour was at hand. For that reason alone, he welcomed it, though he knew he would endure, again, the sorrow of parting.

A first, sweet breath of the air in his secret chamber seeped into his body. As always, he used it to whisper her name. Gradually, he became aware of his surroundings. The chamber was the same. Little had changed since he'd last risen from the cursed sleep that held him in its power. Far beneath the rocky exterior of Lachlan Castle, deeper still beneath the murky waters of Loch Fyne in the western Highlands, his cryptlike chamber served as both home and prison during the long years of his slumber.

As a surge of energy made its way through his limbs, he used it to sit up on his stone bed and lay aside the gold dirk he held to his chest. The stiffness began to leave his shoulders. The heavy feeling of uselessness edged from his limbs.

In the near darkness, his gaze found the red and blue tartan, neatly folded where he'd left it, awaiting him. His white shirt, sporran, bonnet, and pin lay in precise position. Even his badge, a sprig of the rowan tree, miraculously fresh, remained as it had been when he'd last succumbed to the darkness. His chamber, like his slumber, it seemed, had not been disturbed.

A hundred years had passed since he'd last seen her. Impatience mingled with fear as he rose from his bed and began to dress. The tartan settled about his large frame in a neat array of pleats and tucks. With remembered frustration, he recalled the last time he'd been with her. Saving her had been a narrow thing. Her soul had grown more sure, less trusting, with each return. He'd almost had to abduct her to prevent her fateful journey to the Rocking Stone. She had not wanted to listen. Then, he'd felt the presence of evil more acutely, more strongly, as if Nathara, the queen of the dark faeries, in her own evil manner, was letting him know that his time ran short.

One thousand years. That was all he'd been given. In all that time, since the first afternoon when the faerie Lily had given him the enchantment, he'd never found an end to the dreadful spell. Titania, queen of the light faeries, the most powerful of the Seelies, had promised him that there was a way out, that he was not trading his hope of eternity for naught but despair.

"Prove your love when the sun shines in the midnight sky, and the light will shine on your fate as well."

He remembered her words. Still, the hope inside him dimmed with each passing. Only his memories of Laren, and the knowledge that his sacrifice had saved her, made his solitary existence bearable.

With a new sense of dread, he lifted the dirk that kept the enchantment alive in his soul. This time, he knew, would be the last. If he failed, her soul and his would wither and die. But as before, he could not force aside the sudden burst of joy that brought a rare light to his heart. Laren, soon, would be his once more. Sheathing the gold dirk in his stocking, he paused to adjust his clothes before making his way to the stone door of the chamber.

The hour had come to go to the Rocking Stone.

"Marriage," she told them, "is simply out of the question."

Not surprisingly, her assertion was met with silence. Laren Campbell dropped back among the bed of bluebells where she'd sat talking to the unresponsive faeries for the last several hours. She had been so sure they'd come to her here, in the shadow of the ruined old castle, by the enchanted Rocking Stone, despite their notoriously stubborn tendency to appear when it best suited them. Never had a person, she was sure, needed the help of the faeries as she did. Such was her desperation that even Harry the Brownie, the enchanted keeper of Lachlan Castle, would be a welcome sight.

"You must understand," she went on, "that I know a compromise here and there is what makes this world work, but you cannot be expecting me to spend the rest of my born days with the likes of Cullen MacEwan." Her fingers sifted through the pale blue flowers as she watched the sun sink between the high, rocky hills that cradled the Loch. "It's too much to ask of any woman."

Her only answer was the whisper of a chilled breeze that lifted several of her unruly reddish curls. "Och," she muttered. "What good are you then? 'Tis not a big miracle I'm asking, just something to keep my father from marrying me off to the MacEwan. And on my birthday, yet. I'd think the irony would appeal to you, if nothing else."

She lay breathlessly still, waiting, listening. No sound came from the hillock where legend held that the great faerie hall lay deep beneath the surface. She gave the mighty Rocking Stone a gentle push. It creaked on its ledge of rock as it tipped into a swaying motion. The very presence of the mysteriously placed stone had always drawn her. Here, she felt removed from the damp, lonely interior of her father's house. She found a strange peace at the Rocking Stone that made her long for the days when the old castle had still stood proudly on its rise. In her dreams she'd met the man who should have dwelled here. Lately, the dark stranger had come to her slumber more and more often. He always appeared, racing from the trees with that same anxious look on his face. She'd wanted desperately to believe it was a sign that she need not marry Cullen, that somehow, by some miracle, something or someone would intervene.

The stranger in her dream, like so many of the things in her life, compounded her own disquiet that she didn't belong in this place, in this time. Images of times past haunted her sleep. A discomfort with the world around her made her life lonely and frustrating. In her heart, deep in the secret places that she'd shared with no one, she believed she was a changeling. Long ago, she'd decided that the faeries must have switched her soul for another's, else she wouldn't long so desperately for a bygone time and the stranger of her dreams.

To the dusk, with a deep sense of despair, she whispered, "All I wanted was a small miracle. You wouldn't think I was asking so very . . ." Her voice trailed away when the shadow fell across her resting place.

Her heart leapt as she considered how alone she was near the deserted ruins. Daylight had disappeared without her notice. A sliver of fear sent her hand to the pleat of her skirt where the small skean dhu lay sheathed in its hidden pocket. Though the knife would offer her little protection, she felt better with the weight of it in her hand. She should have known better than to stay so long, but miracles, she had argued, took time. "Who is there?"

When her voice echoed in the clearing, it seemed to emphasize her solitude. "Why are you hiding in the shadows?" She hoped the intruder wouldn't hear the quiver in her voice. It wouldn't do to show him fear.

Giant rocks jutted out from the Loch like sentinels. A movement near the cluster of stones, slight, but distinct, captured her attention. His shape emerged from the darkness like a specter, as he moved toward her. "Do not be afraid," he said.

The rich burr of his accent surprised her. She wished the moon was fuller that night, so she could see the man more clearly. Only the outline of impossibly broad shoulders, and height that seemed, even from her spot on the ground, significantly higher than the norm, were visible to her. "Who are you?"

He stepped into a shaft of moonlight, and gave her a generous glimpse of him. Startled, she studied his features. It could not be.

The man in her dreams could not be standing before her, studying her. Yet she knew his features, knew his presence. Anywhere, she would have recognized the strength of his character. "I've fallen asleep," she muttered. "Fool that I am, I've fallen asleep."

"Why would you think that?"

Oh, his voice. It was as pleasing as she'd always imagined. The words fell from his lips in a seductive caress so unlike Cullen's sharp tone. "You can't be real."

"Can't I?"

"Of course not. I've dreamed of you so many times."

At that, a strange expression crossed his angular features. Placing one foot on a craggy shelf of rock, he braced his forearm on his wide thigh. The movement brought his face fully into the bright moonlight. "Glad I am to hear it." His firm lips twitched when he made the remark, as if he found her confession pleasing.

She could clearly make out his features now. Black hair, long and untamed, lay about his shoulders. On many men, his traditional garb, the pleated tartan, the woolen jacket, the plaid bonnet, would have looked ridiculous. Certainly, the fashion had enjoyed a return since Queen Victoria had made the Highlands her second home, but few Scots wore the attire outside the festivals and family gatherings. The stranger in her dreams, however, had always worn them. He'd stepped from a bygone time, and his clothing reflected it. The clothes emphasized a certain primitiveness Laren found simultaneously alarming and exhilarating. "Please," she said as she pushed herself to a sitting position, "who are you?"

With grace uncommon in a man so large, he strode forward to sink to one knee beside her. His big hand lifted a bluebell from her hair. "I am Struan MacLachlan." His voice, deep and vibrant, set off a strange tingling in her stomach.

She recognized the tartan and the family, but not the name. "Are you visiting your family, then? I had not heard your name before."

"Nay. I am not a visitor." He glanced behind his shoulder at the Loch. "I have lived here all my life."

Her brow puckered into a frown. She must be asleep after all. "That would be odd. My father knows most everyone, and I'm sure he's never spoken of you."

"Perhaps not, but he knows of me, just the same."

The breeze traveled off the Loch again. This time, it made her shiver. She pulled her knees to her chest for warmth, then adjusted the skirt of her woolen dress over her legs. "Then what's your business lurking about in the shadows like that. If you don't come as my father's enemy, you come as his friend. Why did you feel the need to frighten me?"

With alarming intensity, he scrutinized her for several long moments. When he spoke again, his voice had dropped to a rumbling whisper. " 'Twas not my intent to frighten you, Laren Campbell. Did I not hear you asking the faeries, this very night, for a miracle?"

She hoped he would not see her pale. "You may. Still, I do not see the reason for your lurking about."

"I was not lurking. I was waiting."

"Waiting?"

"For the moon rise," he explained. "Had you not heard that miracles always appear with the moon rise?"

"Miracles?"

"Aye, Laren. Miracles. Don't you believe in them?"

She frowned. How could he know about her dreams? Had he listened to her before? Perhaps she had caught a glimpse of him once, and that explained his appearance in her mind. He certainly didn't look like any miracle she'd ever seen. He wasn't a faerie, that she knew for sure. Everyone knew the wee folk were tiny. He could be, she supposed, Harry the Brownie, but Harry had always been described as an ugly, trollish sort of creature. Surely this very large, very handsome man could not be the gnarled little brownie who was said to keep watch over Lachlan Castle and its clan.

The stranger seemed to sense her confusion. "You know of me, Laren. You said I've come to you in your dreams."

"You cannot be real," she insisted.

With deliberate patience, he took her hand in his. The meeting of their skin sent a warm feeling along her limb. "Do I not feel real?"

He felt better than real. His callused palm cradled hers like a treasure. There were many things she longed to ask, but the unsettled feeling in her stomach gave rise to just one question. "How do you know my name?"

" 'Tis a long tale, one that will require your faith in its telling."

She hesitated. He was too big, too—her mind sought the right word—*present*. She should not be here near the middle of the night, much as she longed to stay and listen to his persuasive voice. "I—I should be getting home. My father will be worried. 'Tis unusual for me to remain gone such a long time."

He made no move to detain her. "I understand. I will tell you when you wish to hear it."

She rose to her feet where she brushed the flowers from her skirt. When he stood, he towered over her. Laren tried not to fidget beneath his piercing inspection. "Then I would thank you, sir, to quickly explain yourself. I've not time for a long tale."

His gaze searched her for long moments. "As I have said, I am Struan MacLachlan of the Clan MacLachlan." She didn't think she imagined the way his shoulders seemed to set beneath his jacket. "And I've come for you."

That gave her pause. "Come for me?" Her voice halted on the words.

"Aye," he said again in that rolling burr that did such strange things to her inside. "Next time you go to the faeries for a miracle, be sure you know what you ask."

With an acute sense of loss, Struan watched Laren retreat. She'd managed a startled goodbye in answer to his warning about the faeries, then hurried away from the ruins.

He'd had to force himself not to make her stay.

His time with her was so short. With just five days to accomplish his goal, he longed to spend every minute of it at her side. His first sight of her never failed to humble him. Each time, she grew even lovelier to him.

Never had there been a woman as fine to his eyes, to his heart, as his Laren. In her simple woolen dress, with her long, dark hair pulled back in a neat braid, she still looked as beautiful as the first day he'd met her. Each time, her appearance had been different, but little had changed in the way his soul responded to hers. He would know her anywhere.

Long ago, however, he'd discovered that knowing her fully was not necessary to his goal. He walked the earth for one purpose alone, and he'd learned to protect himself while protecting her. The partings were too painful if he did not keep emotional distance between them. This time, however, he felt a connection like none other. She seemed to know him as she never had in the past. The knowledge had staggered him.

In some lives, she had trusted him enough to speak with him. The partings, then, had been almost beyond bearing. The agonizing sense of loss threatened to weaken his resolve. More than once the temptation to end his own cursed existence had endangered his sense of purpose. The knowledge that he was saving Laren's soul so she could go on and marry another, find happiness in another man's arms, had wounded Struan's heart. Still, he had given what he could for her. He could not allow her to die.

So forcibly, this time as in all the others, he made himself remember his purpose. His fingers tightened into a fist as he studied the Rocking Stone. In five days, the berry bush would grow there. He would keep her from it by any means necessary. In the fifth night, if he failed to find a way from the hold of the curse, his soul would belong to Nathara, forever enslaved in the darkness of her Unseelie hall. Worse, Laren's soul would lose its light, a thought that threatened to rip him asunder.

Anger at the helplessness of it all channeled through him in a bitter river of resentment. He had traveled an ocean of time to give Laren the life she deserved. Always in his mind, the hope that had kept him sane had been Titania's promise that they would find a way.

This time he must.

With a renewed sense of purpose, he settled his large frame by the Rocking Stone to wait for Titania's nightly dance.

This time, he vowed, it would end.

Chapter 2

Laren watched in fascination as the small hillock began to glow. Struan MacLachlan sat watching the spectacle, calm and at ease. He seemed undisturbed by the strange events, but then, he had appeared to her out of the mist, making incredible claims, impossible promises. She held completely still as she hid in the shadow of the ruined castle.

In an explosion of light, a faerie, almost too beautiful to behold, burst from the hillock. Behind her trailed a shower of gold dust. Music trembled around her, as if it came from the bluebells that blanketed the hillside. When the faerie began to dance, Laren's eyes widened in wonder. The earth seemed to move with the small faerie. The waves of Loch Fyne kept rhythm, while the flowers and grasses swayed. Even the song of the crickets had melded with the faerie's lilting music.

In the glowing light, Laren could clearly see Struan's face. He watched the faerie dance with an expression of mingled respect and hope. He remained perfectly still, reverently silent, until the music stopped.

The faerie tossed a handful of the gold dust into the air, as a sort of tribute to the land, then settled upon the Rocking Stone to face him. "Hello, Struan MacLachlan. It is your time." Her voice held the same musical quality as the song of her dance.

"Aye, Titania. It is."

Laren stifled a gasp. Could it be that this man consorted with Titania, queen of the faeries? This, she knew, was a dangerous and powerful thing. Every Scot knew that faerie magic was unpredictable. Laren, like many, had spent her life respecting the unknown realm of the wee folk, while never quite sure it existed. Still, no one would dare risk offending them, just, perchance, they happened to be real.

She should not have been shocked, she supposed, that a MacLachlan would so easily find access to the faerie world. Legend held that their ancestor, Duncan MacLachlan, had wed a faerie, and that her blood still ran in their veins. Even the current chieftain's sister, Krista, was rumored to have carried the gift of second sight. Her marriage to a Russian prince, and the dramatic way she'd saved his life, were oft-told stories around the women's evening fire.

Struan's expression, she noted, had altered a bit. She saw a look of such longing in his gaze, that it stirred something deep within her. He was watching Titania with an earnest pain that made Laren long to go to him, to smooth the pucker from his brow, ease the notable tension in his large body.

"I have reached the end." His deep voice rumbled on the still night air. "I have failed to find a way from the curse. I must know what to do."

Titania seemed to consider the problem. With a shimmering flutter of wings, she raised herself until she hovered at a level with his face. "Yours is a mighty love. Tell her what is in your heart. Together, you will find a way."

"Tell her? I could not. She wouldn't believe it."

"It is her soul you seek, not the person. The soul will carry memories. If you can reach it, she will know you."

"She says she has seen me in her dreams."

"That is her heart speaking, Struan. She knows you well. You will see."

"But what of the curse? How shall we end it?"

"I can tell you no more. Go to her now." Titania waved a hand in the direction of the ruins. "She awaits you there."

When Titania disappeared back into the ground, Laren gasped, startled. How had the faerie known she watched them? She would have fled, but Struan's gaze found hers in the moonlight. She felt, at once, trapped and sheltered. Her heart, always too romantic for her own good, longed to know the secrets the faerie had discussed. For years, Laren had sat by this spot and longed for an unknown treasure. The temptation to learn of the place's magic was beyond resistance.

"Laren?" His voice beckoned her. "Please come." With the broken-sounding plea, he extended one large hand.

And she was lost.

She picked her way from the ruins, down the slope to the Rocking Stone. "I should not have spied on you. I regret it."

His lips turned into a most appealing expression. "I suppose you could say it was your due. I listened to your conversation with the faeries. No harm can come from you listening to mine."

His words warmed her. Without thought to the rightness of it, she slid her hand into his. Fingers, large and calloused, and impossibly heated, closed around her hand, making it feel small. She was certain her fingers trembled.

With a slight tug, he guided her to the slope by the Stone. "Should we sit?"

She hesitated. She had no business sitting on this hillside with a stranger, let alone one who consorted with the wee folk. If her father found her, he'd be furious. Still, the night was oddly warm, and her curiosity peaked. "I should be returning home." The words failed to convince her.

"I will walk you back once we've spoken. Nothing will harm you." He waited until she sat before lowering himself to the ground.

" 'Tis not proper for me to be here alone with you."

His eyebrows lifted. "Do you believe that?"

She met his gaze in the moonlight, hesitated, then shook her head. Her heart had always known she belonged here. Only her mind gave her pause. "No. I do not."

With a satisfied sound, he leaned back on his elbows. "I am glad." She listened to the lulling sound of the waves while she waited for him to continue. "Laren, the story I have to tell you is long and remarkable. I am not certain you will believe it."

"Is this what the faerie meant when she said you should tell me what's in your heart?"

He nodded. "Aye. It is."

"Then I will believe it. I promise."

"Be careful how you give your word. You may find it more difficult than you think."

"Start at the beginning, then. I will decide what I can believe."

He pressed her hand to his chest, and her heart began to beat faster at the light contact. He didn't appear to notice. "Do you know the legend of Duncan MacLachlan?"

"Which one?"

"The first of the MacLachlan chieftains born on these shores."

"Not which Duncan," she said, amused, "which legend."

Struan's eyes crinkled at the corner. "There is more than one?" he teased for the sake of hearing the sound of her voice.

"Indeed. The MacLachlans are very proud of their noble ancestor."

"As they should be." She felt his chest swell with the deep breath he drew. "I am speaking of how Duncan came to lead the MacLachlans in their first conflict with the Campbells."

"Aye. I have heard it. It is said that your Duncan married a faerie named Lily after saving his family."

"Aye, he did." He'd learned of Duncan's marriage to Lily the first time he'd awakened from the curse. "And it gladdens my heart to know my brother's fate."

"Your brother?"

"Aye." He glanced at her. "Duncan MacLachlan was my brother."

She absorbed the incredible statement. She knew, of course, the legend. Everyone did. Struan MacLachlan, son of the first MacLachlan to make his home on these shores, had surrendered his soul to the evil Unseelies in exchange for a chance to save his beloved's life. As the story went, his brother had given Struan's body to the water sprites, and they'd hidden it far beneath the Loch in a secret cave below Castle Lachlan. Her ancestor and namesake, Laren Campbell, had died at the hands of the faeries when her father had first battled with the MacLachlans. The feud existed, in different forms, to this day. While the Campbells and the MacLachlans had tried several times for peace, particularly in the face of the impending threat of the MacEwans, they had never succeeded. Her father hated the MacLachlans as much today as his ancestor had one thousand years ago. "You," she finally said, "are Struan MacLachlan of the legend?"

"I am."

She felt his gaze on her face. " 'Tis, indeed, an incredible tale."

"Aye. Will you let me tell it to you in full?"

A smile tilted her lips. "Having taken me this far, I'd be vexed if you turned back."

She particularly liked the sound of his laugh. It held none of the malice of her father's or Cullen MacEwan's. Instead, she found it oddly musical, pleasing to the ear. "I see you have changed little," he told her. "You are still far too curious for your own good."

Laren lay back against the cool grass. "Please, then, tell me your story."

"I was born in 825 in what we then called Dalriata. 'Tis this very place now. My family established the hamlet that used to lie a morning's walk from this spot."

"How have you learned our modern way of speaking?"

"I don't know. When I accepted her spell, Lily made certain provisions for me. Perhaps, I have always been able to communicate with you because I know your heart. The language has changed much over the years, but I have always known how to speak with you."

"Perhaps it is so. Still, I would have you continue. This tale is strange."

"And you are not yet ready to believe it?"

"I told you I would believe it. I merely want the whole of it before I accept what you've told me."

Again, he laughed. "As you wish. For years, my family struggled to secure our position here. Those were violent times, and it seemed we were constantly at war. My father longed to establish a haven for our family, and that is why he was so pleased when I pledged to wed a Campbell."

"The first Laren Campbell?"

"Aye. He saw it as a great alliance on my part. In my mind, I'd been given my heart's desire. No man ever loved as much, or as purely, as I did. We were to be wed on the evening of her twenty-first birthday."

Laren sucked in a breath. "You were?"

"Aye. You will turn twenty-one in five days, will you not?"

"I will."

His fingers tightened on hers. "Nothing should have stood in the way of our happiness. Her father had delayed the wedding a hundred times, but had finally given his consent. Even Harry the Brownie seemed to have given his blessing. He made no appearance to warn me against wedding a Campbell as he's been known to do. I walked on clouds for days as I anticipated taking her to wife."

"But she died before you wed." She knew this part of the story.

A look of pain shadowed his features. "She did. At this spot, through her own father's treachery, she died." He drew a ragged breath, as if the story had suddenly become too much for him. " 'Twas then I accepted what Lily offered me."

"The eternal slumber."

His gaze met hers. "I see some of the story has survived."

"I have always found it intriguing, particularly as it concerns the woman my father named me for. I have spent years trying to learn as much of the tale as I can."

That seemed to please him. His thumb rubbed a casual circle on the back of her hand. " 'Tis right that it should be so. Had it not been for Lily, I would have lived out my days, trapped in grief at Laren's loss. Lily told me, however, at risk to her own hope of happiness, that I could follow Laren into eternity. She chose to forsake her chance to return to her human form and marry my brother in exchange for giving me the spell. I am glad they were given a path to their own happiness."

"Is the legend true that you risked your soul when you accepted the spell?"

"Aye."

"You loved her that much?" She couldn't keep the wistful note from her voice.

"No price would have been too high. Lily gifted me with a thousand years to set right the terrible things that had been done here. Every hundred years, I wake from my slumber. If I have failed to break the curse by the end of the thousand-year cycle, I will lose my hope of eternity to the darkness of the Unseelie queen."

"Nathara." The very name made Laren's blood run cold. No one who lived on the shores of Loch Fyne was unaware of the evil faerie queen's treachery. She'd haunted the MacLachlans and their kin for centuries.

"Nathara," he confirmed.

"And each time the cycle is the same?"

"It is. During the slumber, I remain in my chamber beneath the Loch. Long ago, my brother surrendered my sleeping body to the water sprites. They shelter me in a stone chamber far beneath this spot. With time, I have altered its appearance, but it is still the cell that holds me until I awaken."

"What happens then?"

"I find you here"—with a push of his hand, he set the stone into motion—"where I lost you."

The breath stilled in her body. "You mean—"

" 'Tis you, Laren. Each time, it is you. If you search your heart, you'll remember."

"This is what Titania meant when she said I would know you?"

"Aye. The dreams you spoke of, do they not seem more like memories?"

She pondered the question. Each time she'd seen him, the dream had been the same. In it, she stood near the Rocking Stone, feeling strangely entranced by the spot. The sound of his voice reached her, and she found him, seated astride his gray horse, at the edge of the high hill above the castle ruins. The loose rock and damp earth provided treacherous footing. He raced toward her in a shower of debris. Always, an unreadable mask of intense feeling characterized his strong features. Each time, she fell to the ground just as he reached her. She always awoke to the sound of him calling her name.

Could it be that the odd dream was, indeed, a recollection? Had she known this man before, sat with him here, shared her heart with him? In the dream he seemed so very real, as if she knew him more surely, more fully, than any living soul. Impossible though it seemed, the probing look in his dark eyes found the last whisper of doubt in her heart and pushed it away. A warm feeling began to spread through her. "How many times have I known you?"

"I came to you in 950 when my ancestor Domnall was defeating the Danes of Lough Neagh by destroying their fleet. Again in 1050 when the De Dalan named for my ancestor was born and walked these shores.

"In 1150, you and I stood here as the final stones were laid on the old castle. In 1250, when Lachlan Mor, the younger, paid Alexander's tax by sending his moneybags on the horns of the roebuck, I came for you. Thirteen-fifty was the year Harry the Brownie appeared to warn a MacLachlan chief about the Campbells. In 1450, Donald MacLachlan confirmed our family's grant to the Blackfriars of Glasgow.

" 'Twas 1550 when our clan first began to hope that the crown would give us a permanent charter for these lands. Archibald MacLachlan, I later learned, finally earned the charter twenty-fours years later. Sixteen-fifty brought tragedy to the MacLachlans as we saw Oliver Cromwell defeat the Covenantor army, and with it, many of my clansmen who supported Charles I.

"Then, the last time I walked these shores, in 1750, this castle was destroyed because of our defense of Charles II."

"You do not know, then," she questioned, "what happened after the bombardment of the castle?"

"Nay."

Laren exhaled a slow breath. "The MacLachlan Chief, along with a hundred and fifteen MacLachlans, rode into the battle at Culloden and lost their lives defending Charles's position. The Campbells aligned with the royalists, and it's one of the reasons that enmity still exists between your family and mine."

A look of pain crossed his expression. "I feared the worst would come."

She indicated the new castle where it stood a few leagues away. "Your family rebuilt here. Keith MacLachlan is chieftain now. He is a good and honorable man."

Struan rolled to his side so he could prop himself upon an elbow and gaze at her. "I am glad that my father's descendants live on, but I confess after so many years of waiting, their welfare is not the present desire of my heart."

His tone had enslaved her. She lay upon the ground, transfixed by the expression on his face. " 'Tis not?"

"Nay, Laren Campbell. There'll be time enough to ask you later what has happened since my last breath. Tonight, I have but one question."

"You want to know if I believe you."

He laid a hand on his heart. "I want to know if you see yourself in my eyes, Laren. I want to know if you feel any portion of what's in my heart for you."

Awareness flooded through her. With trembling fingers, she traced the fine planes of his face. Her thumb dipped into the cleft of his chin. The pad of her index finger trailed the firm line of his full upper lip. Aye, she knew him, had known him. Though it seemed impossible, she suddenly understood the irresistible pull of this place, the yearning emptiness that had plagued her soul. She'd known for most of her life that something was missing. He was the lost piece of her. This man was no stranger at all. Her dreams had always known. "Aye, Struan MacLachlan. I've known you in my dreams—I know you in my heart."

With a smothered cry of joy, he bent his head to cover her lips in a kiss of tender, aching triumph.

Unbridled joy filled him as he moved his lips against hers. She was unfailingly soft, warm and strong, beneath his mouth and hands. He found himself starved for her taste. All the times he'd known her, she'd never seemed so much like the woman he'd lost to Nathara's evil. This time, however, she'd stolen his breath at first sight. "Laren." His voice was a hoarse whisper, as if he'd run a very great distance. "Dear God, how I love you."

When she shivered, he wondered if his declaration had frightened her. The worry disappeared when she moved closer to him. "I have loved you always, haven't I?"

He pressed a tender kiss to her forehead. "It is my fondest wish."

"I have." Her voice was filled with wonder and confidence. "I have loved you from my soul's beginning."

He moved to kiss her again. Rubbing his lips back and forth across her mouth, he exulted in her surrender when her mouth parted for him. "Don't let me frighten you," he whispered against her lips.

"You could not." One of her hands, strong and tender, captured the back of his head. "You could never frighten me."

He pressed her more fully into the grass as he sought to relearn her shape. His hands skimmed the line of her body where he found changes. Fuller breasts pushed against his palms. A waist, a bit thicker, but still perfect for his hands, flared to hips that fit against him in tantalizing, intoxicating perfection. She was all he remembered, and so very much more. Then, she'd met his passion with a carefully banked fire. Now, she answered him with a flame of her own that had his blood singing.

In times past, he'd avoided touching her. This time, however, he would disallow nothing. If he had just five days to end the wretched existence that bound him, he could not deny himself her warmth.

The moment she'd touched his face with her butterfly light caress, she'd sealed his fate. He refused to acknowledge the warnings that echoed in his mind. He ruthlessly thrust aside the way his conscience insisted that he was taking advantage of her innocence. This woman was meant to belong to him.

"Greed," said a small voice, tight and pinched and very near his ear, "has long been the undoing of your kind."

When the tone sent a chill through him, he stilled. He would know the voice anywhere. The stench alone would give away Nathara's presence.

"Struan?" Laren, her lips swollen and moist, her eyes slightly hazy, gave him a beseeching look.

He lay a finger on her mouth. "Still." When she seemed to heed the quiet warning, he moved to shield her with his body. "Show yourself, Nathara," he insisted. "I know you are lurking."

A glimmer of reddish light caught his attention. In a burst of foul-smelling smoke, she appeared on the Rocking Stone. "We meet again, MacLachlan." Her tone mocked him. "Your time is near."

"I have not lost yet, Nathara." He hated the sudden fear he felt when Laren pressed her body near him. "Lily gave me a thousand years to do my deed. I have five days, yet, before you can claim victory."

She leaned back on her hands, her tiny body radiating a kind of smug wickedness that made him ache to crush her. "Each time you have failed to end the curse. You will fail again."

"Lily said there is a way from every curse."

"Lily said." She practically spat the words. "Lily said, Lily said, Lily said. Do you really think it matters to me what that insignificant little fiend said?" A small firefly crossed before her vision. She squashed it with her tiny hands. "It depresses me to think of how she betrayed me."

Something dangerously close to hate lodged in his chest. Mentally, he flailed about for refuge. Titania had warned him, at least a dozen times, not to let the hate win. With a feeling of heaviness, he gently edged away from Laren so he could help her sit. The expression on her face gave him the anchor he needed.

She was watching Nathara with a look that said, all too clearly, what she thought of the evil little Unseelie. Laren, obviously, had quickly grasped the depth of Nathara's role in their unhappiness. Like many a wronged woman, she wanted immediate, and preferably bloody, vengeance. He smoothed the pucker from her forehead with his thumb. "She will not win," he promised in a low whisper. "I will not bear it."

Laren searched his expression, then seemed to relent. "Be done with her, Struan, please. Her presence disturbs me."

"I will." He turned back to Nathara. A small pile of dead fireflies now lay at her feet. "You cannot touch me," he told her, "and you know it. I still have the five days Lily and Titania gave me."

She heaved a disgusted sigh as she gathered her red cloak around herself. "My sister Titania is a fool. She has always had a weakness for your kind."

"If you seek to provoke me, Nathara, you have failed."

She considered him for long moments, before her lips turned into a nasty interpretation of a smirk. "That may be so"—she indicated the castle ruins with a sweep of her hand—"but I imagine my servant will have better success."

She disappeared as she had appeared. In her wake, a tainted mist settled about the base of the Rocking Stone. An eerie silence—one that stopped even the night song of the crickets, the gentle babble of the nearby stream, and the lap of the waves on the rocky shore— made Struan's body tense.

"Struan?" Laren watched him with widened eyes. "What does she mean?"

He released a pent-up breath. "Only that we have much to do." With soothing fingers, he brushed her hair from her forehead. "It is past time I walked you home. Your father will be worrying."

A cloud passed over her expression. "I don't want to leave here. I don't want to leave you."

"I don't want it either, but I need time to prepare."

"Prepare?"

"The enchantment is at its end, Laren. Nathara is determined to win."

"She won't. We can't let her."

"Nay." He pressed a soft kiss to her forehead. "I have not waited this long to lose you now. Will you come to me tomorrow? Here, at the Stone."

"When can I come?"

"As early as you wish. I'll be waiting."

"I'll be here at first light."

Surging to his feet, he extended his hand to her. "Then come with me. I'll see you safely home."

Chapter 3

THE next day was a day like none other.

Laren couldn't remember a time when she'd felt more content. From the moment she'd seen Struan's dark head, tipped against the Stone where he sat awaiting her, unbridled joy had filled her. After he'd walked her to the edge of the glen where she lived, he'd given her the gentlest of goodbye kisses. It had taken some convincing on her part, but he'd finally agreed not to walk with her to the door. She'd have found it difficult to explain the presence of a thousand-year-old man to her father.

Still, she'd felt the lingering touch of his gaze until she'd slipped into her father's home. By sunrise, she half believed the extraordinary events had been a dream after all. She'd approached the Rocking Stone with a mixture of hope and trepidation. Her heart wouldn't bear the knowledge that he wasn't real.

When she'd seen him, happiness had flooded through her. His gaze met hers, and once again, she found it easy to ignore the warning in her head that his story must be trickery. While her mind argued that he couldn't possibly be telling her the truth, her heart knew better. This man was her soul's mate. She could never doubt it.

They spent the day learning again the pleasure they'd once known in each other's company. Struan talked to her about the land, about the times he'd known her, about the days past when she'd been free to sit with him here at this spot.

She told him how her heart had longed for him, how she'd always known he existed for her.

And they lay for long hours in the cool grass, simply enjoying the nearness of each other. He taught her to fish. She instructed him in the waltz. He showed her how to wield his sword. She wove a wreath of bluebells for his hair, which he wore just to please her.

With each passing moment, her heart grew more sure that here was where she was meant to be. She loved him fully and completely, as he loved her, and by day's end, she believed that nothing could separate them ever again.

As the sun began its slow descent into the Loch, Struan seated her by the Rocking Stone. "The moon rises, Laren. You know what this means?"

"You told me miracles always come at moon rise."

His lips curved into a slight smile. "So I did. I'm wise that way."

At his jest, she poked his ribs. "And vain."

He settled on the ground beside her. "I cannot help the vanity. It comes from knowing you love me."

Her eyes misted. "You say the most remarkable things."

"My time with you is short"—when she would have interrupted, he pressed a finger to her lips—"we should be prepared for that. I find that I don't wish to waste my hours with you. I have ten lifetimes' worth of things to tell you. Jesting comes hard to me."

Her head settled naturally against his shoulder. "Last night," she prompted, "did you find a way from the enchantment?"

"Nay. I fear I cannot solve Titania's riddle."

"Tell it to me again," she prompted. "Perhaps we have missed something."

He drew a deep breath. "When the sun shines in the midnight sky, and you have lost what you treasure most, then will you be free."

"What could she mean by your greatest treasure?"

His fingers threaded into the auburn brown of her hair. "You need ask? 'Tis you, Laren. There is nothing I treasure more."

"There must be a way. Perhaps if we ask Titania tonight—"

"I have tried. Each time I have begged her for the answer, and each time she has told me I have to find it myself. I fear"—his hand tightened on her shoulder—"that Nathara will win after all."

"She won't," Laren insisted.

"I will ask Titania again, tonight. I will beg her if I must."

Laren knew what the promise cost him. He was a proud and honorable man who had already given so much for her. She couldn't bear the thought of him humbling himself, even to the faerie queen. "Why can't I ask her?"

He paused. "The risk is too great. I can't allow you to speak with her."

"This isn't 850, Struan," she said with a soft smile. "I'm not sure I'll give you the right to disallow me anything."

"Don't be difficult in this. You don't understand the magic of the faeries. Even Titania is unpredictable. I have seen her anger more than I wish. She is kindly enough, but there are thorns waiting to prick an unsuspecting hand. It is dangerous, Laren."

"You consort with her."

"I have no choice."

"Neither have I." She leaned back to study him in the paling light. "You have shared your heart with me, Struan. I will not lose it now."

He opened his mouth to respond, but shut it again when he heard the heavy fall of horses' hooves on the narrow path to the ruins. The sound held the unmistakable threat of disaster. Nathara's rage was unleashed. He sensed it.

Laren touched his arm. "Someone's coming."

"I know." He covered her hand with his. "Laren, do you trust me?"

"I do." She said the words with a quiet certainty that thrilled his heart. "With all of me."

He paused to press a hard kiss to her mouth, then rose to his feet. "Then stand with me. We'll face them together."

"Who?"

He waited until a dark-cloaked rider crested the hill. "Cullen MacEwan."

Laren's hand slipped into his. A second figure rode into sight. "And my father."

They approached in silence. Even at a distance, Struan felt the darkness radiating from Cullen. The form had changed, but the soul remained the same. Nathara had recalled Iain Campbell, the very man who had first sacrificed Laren for his own gain, in order to thwart them.

Iain's soul lived in Cullen's person.

Struan's body shook as he realized the extent of Nathara's evil. Before him was the soul of the man who had orchestrated his destruction. As Laren's father, Iain had traded her life to Nathara. Because of Lily, and the unselfish act she'd performed to counter Nathara's treachery, Iain had failed to conquer the MacLachlans. Now, however, he lived again as the man Laren was now promised to wed.

Struan waited until Cullen and Laren's father reined in their mounts. Except for the tightening of her fingers on his, Laren showed no sign of her reaction to their arrival.

Cullen spoke first. His eyes blazed with an unnatural fire as he raked an insulting gaze over Laren. "It seems we've found her, James. You'd assured me you could control her."

James shifted in his saddle. "Daughter, come away from that man."

"I will not."

"You seek to shame me, then, just days before your wedding, by consorting here with this stranger?"

She glanced at Struan, before leaning into him. "He is no stranger to me, Father."

With an angry bellow, James dismounted. "I can see Cullen was right. I have allowed you too much freedom."

He would have stalked toward her then, but Struan held up his hand. "Stay there." James halted, an expression of stunned disbelief on his face.

Cullen's laugh echoed in the night. "I see my bride-to-be has found a champion." He glanced at Laren. "Is he prepared to fight all your battles, or only the one for your innocence?"

At the insulting remark, Struan lost what remained of his temper. "Enough, Cullen MacEwan. Dismount and face me, or I'll strip you from that horse like a lamb's wool in shearing season."

Cullen continued to regard them both with disdain. "What is your business here?"

Struan withdrew the impressive sword from his belt, then thrust its point into the ground in open challenge. "I am Struan MacLachlan."

He guided Laren in front of him so he could wrap both arms around her as she faced Cullen and her father. "And I have taken this woman to wife."

Struan felt Laren tense beneath his hands as she absorbed his incredible claim. Cullen MacEwan swung down from his horse with a growl of disapproval. "What game are you about, MacLachlan?"

Struan watched his measured approach. He would not allow Cullen to touch Laren, not under any circumstances. He sensed the danger in him, sensed the evil. " 'Tis no game. I assure you."

James advanced several steps. "Laren, what is the meaning of this?"

Her hands moved to cover Struan's. "Father, if you will just—"

Cullen laid a restraining hand on James's shoulder. His eyes never left Struan's. "I am to wed this woman. Keith MacLachlan cannot think to form an alliance, now, by marrying off his family to the Campbells. Promises have been made. The land will still be mine."

Struan narrowed his gaze. "MacLachlan has no knowledge of my marriage."

"No one has knowledge," James insisted. "They are lying, Cullen. Surely you can see that."

"Quiet," Cullen roared. His gaze went to Laren. "What is afoot, Laren? What are you doing?"

Laren's hands fluttered. "What he says is true, Cullen. I am his wife."

At the declaration, James sucked in a sharp breath. "Saints in heaven, if she wasn't before, she is now."

Cullen's brows drew together in a sharp frown. "You think to take what is mine by means of an interchange of consent?" he asked Struan. "Such a marriage has not held in the courts for over a hundred years. The marriage contract has already been made for Laren to be my bride. It's just as binding, just as firm, as this sham of a union."

" 'Tis legal," Laren insisted. "The law allows man and wife legal marriage by means of mutual pledge. While I would not have chosen you as my witness, Cullen, the deed is now done. I am Struan's wife." She glanced over her shoulder at him. "He is my husband."

Struan's heart swelled to near bursting. While he would not have had it this way, given his choice, the knowledge that Laren had trusted him so fully nearly sent him to his knees. He had not planned to wed her, not until he had broken the spell and could give her forever, but the moment he'd faced Cullen's anger, he'd known they had no choice.

Nathara was evil enough, determined enough, to have brought Iain's soul back from death—a feat that would have required an enormous risk and sacrifice on her part. The balance of power in the faerie world was delicate indeed. Titania never would have allowed such a remarkable feat without an incredible bargain with Nathara. The two faerie sisters, one evil, one pure, held the power of the other in perfect check. Neither, to his knowledge, had ever been able to actually raise a soul without the permission of the other.

Now, with time running out, and Nathara's desperate ploys stacked in the balance against him, he had crossed the forbidden line and made Laren his wife. If he spent an eternity in Nathara's hell for it, he would not regret the decision.

At last, she was his.

With a sudden urgency born of the knowledge that every second brought them closer to the end, he wanted to be done with Cullen. Longing, acute and intense, to show Laren his enchanted chamber, welled within him. Drawing a deep breath of the damp air, he waved a hand at Cullen and James. "You cannot be done with this tonight," he announced. "If you wish to challenge my claim, you will have to do it on the morrow before the court. Tonight, she stays with me."

James looked appalled. "*Stays* with you? You can't be serious."

Struan lifted his large sword from the ground. "Deadly serious."

Turning to Cullen, Laren's father pointed a crooked finger at his daughter. "What do you intend to do, Cullen? You cannot let this stand."

Cullen was watching Laren through slitted eyes. "Lest you forget, Laren, I've paid your father for your favors. We have a contract. I intend to have it honored."

Struan saw the way Laren's body tensed. She didn't look at him as she answered Cullen's claim. "If my father has taken money from you, he's done it without my permission."

James snorted. "I didn't need your permission."

Ignoring him, Laren continued, "You cannot hold me responsible for his actions."

"It's your actions that concern me." With his dark cloak swirling about him, Cullen mounted his horse. "I don't like to be tricked. You'll have to learn that the hard way, I suppose. I'll see to it that I have my due."

He rode away without a backward glance. Virtually shaking in his rage, James stood, still staring at his daughter. "How could you do this? Do you have any idea what this means?"

"You took money for me?" Laren's voice broke on the shameful words. "How could you? How could you sell me like some piece of livestock? 'Twas not fair, Father. Not fair at all."

"Fair? With the landholders gradually losing all they have to the taxes from the Crown, you speak to me of fairness? At least I'm not having to evict our tenants. Don't you realize that your marriage to Cullen was the last chance we had?"

"You should have discussed it with me."

"Why? To listen to more of your complaining over why you don't want to wed him." James wiped a hand over his gaunt face. "I've heard enough of that to last me a lifetime." He took a step forward.

Struan, seeing the anger in the other man's eyes, placed himself between Laren and her father. "You will not touch her," he said.

James met his gaze. "And you? What right have you, a MacLachlan"—he spit on the ground—"to intervene in my affairs. If I wished to take her home and beat her, you'd have no right to stop me."

Anger, fierce and deep, burned within him. "You have only to lift a finger against her, and you'll lose your miserable life."

James absorbed the lethal-sounding threat. "When Cullen is done exacting his due from me, I might as well be dead. No telling what he'll demand for this."

"Father"—Laren laid a hand on Struan's arm in gentle restraint—"we can find a way to—"

"No." He shook his head. "No, we can't. At your mother's insistence, I've allowed you too much freedom, Laren, and now you've used it to destroy me." With a bitter laugh, he pulled his horse around so he could mount. "I should never have listened to your mother. She insisted that I should let you persist in those ridiculous daydreams of yours. Now you've dishonored yourself, and me, and probably brought ruin on our entire family. I owe Cullen more than I can ever pay."

"Father, please—"

"Enough." He mounted his horse. Struan felt Laren's fingers tighten on his forearm. "It is over. You and I," James told his daughter, "we are over. Do not bother returning to my home, Laren. Ever. I will claim you no more." He jerked his horse around and disappeared into the night.

Laren made a tiny sound in the back of her throat that threatened to lay open Struan's gut. He was simultaneously torn between his desire to hunt down Cullen and her father, and his need to comfort her. When he looked at her, she was staring at her father's retreating form with a grief so acute, he felt it rip through his blood. " 'Tis over," he told her.

She shook her head. " 'Tis just beginning. They will come back. Cullen means to have the lands my father promised him."

"There is nothing to stop him from taking them. Your father can still fulfill his bargain."

She shook her head. "The lands are mine, passed to me by my mother. I have no brother, so I am my father's heir. Cullen wanted it all, not just the parcel my mother left me."

For a long moment, Struan considered the consequences of the night's events. Already he had passed beyond so many of the barriers he had set for himself. Once more, he thrust the point of his sword into the ground. "Do not let them sorrow you, Laren. You are my wife now, in the eyes of the law and in the eyes of God. I will not let them harm you."

She raised stricken eyes to his. "You want me now, a woman cast aside by her family, with nothing to bring you but the humiliation of knowing that her own father sold her like a flock of sheep to the highest bidder?"

His heart ached for her. "There is no humiliation in what you could not control."

"You heard what he said to me. How could he trade me for money? How could he?"

He could not bear the thought of telling her that this was not the first time her father's treachery had wounded her. Instead, he thrust the haunting thought aside as he concentrated on offering her comfort. "I have chased you through time for a thousand years, Laren. Do you think I have come so far to fail you now?"

She hesitated, then slowly crossed the short distance to him. "I have nowhere to go, Struan. You married me tonight to avoid a fight with Cullen and my father. Don't think I'm not aware of it."

"I married you because I have waited to do so for as long as I have lived."

"You could have killed them, but you knew it would distress me."

"I knew it would make me little better than they are. Is that what you wanted for me? Their blood on my hands?"

"Of course not."

"Then don't go finding heroics where there are none. I sacrificed nothing tonight. I gained my heart's desire."

She searched his face for long moments. "When you first had the chance to wed me, would you have done it if there had been no lands, no money?"

"I would have wed you even if it had started a war. I loved you then, Laren, as I love you now. Nothing could have kept me from you." He pointed to the Rocking Stone. "Not even death."

"And in all that time," she said, her tone laced with hurt, "I have offered you nothing. Just like now. I have nothing left but a shamed reputation."

He held out his hand, palm up. "All I have is now yours. Trust me this much. Come with me, and let me show you."

She placed her small hand in his. "Where are we going?"

With a soft smile, he led her toward the rocks. "Home."

She glanced around the large chamber with an odd sense of disquiet. Being here, deep beneath the Loch where Struan had spent so many years, made the entire experience seem startlingly, almost terrifyingly real to her. He seemed to sense her mood. "I've frightened you?"

"No. Not really. I'm overwhelmed." She managed a slight smile. "I hadn't planned on having my wedding today."

"I wish it had been different. I would have liked to marry you with ceremony. I planned it that way, once."

"It's all right. I would have married Cullen with ceremony and been miserable." She tore her gaze from one of the ornate tapestries. When she looked at him, she saw the worry in his eyes. "I'd rather be here with you."

"You should have had flowers."

She walked to him so she could pluck what remained of the bluebell wreath from his hair. "I did."

He studied her for long moments. "I have longed to bring you here."

"Show me this place," she prompted. "Tell me about it."

"Over the years, I have worked to make it seem more like a home and less like a prison."

She glanced around the stone chamber. "Where does the light come from?"

"I don't know. It's always here."

She pointed to the comfortable-looking feather bed. "You sleep there?"

"Nay. I thought I would."

At her raised eyebrow, he laughed. "It was one of my earliest additions to the chamber. Getting it here was difficult. I had to bring it through the caves in pieces, then assemble it."

"But you don't sleep there?"

"I found that I couldn't. A hundred years is a long time to spend sinking into a mattress. I use it only during the five days I'm with you."

Her gaze found the large stone table. "There?"

"Aye."

Slowly, she approached the platform. Her heart squeezed when she thought of him there, asleep as if dead, waiting for her. Reverently, she ran her fingers over the smooth surface. "Are you comfortable?"

"I am unaware," he admitted. "At the end of my time, I come here, I lie on the stone, and the slumber claims me."

"Oh." She felt small, suddenly, and overwhelmed by the knowledge of the sacrifices he'd made for her.

"The rest of it," he said with a sweep of his hand to indicate the comforts in the room, "I have added with the years."

She met his gaze once more. "Struan, do you ever regret—"

He crossed to her in two quick strides. "No. I never regret. I could never regret. What we've been given, few humans ever have. In her generosity, Lily gave us a second chance at the happiness that Nathara stole. Why would I regret it?"

"Because you have to live here, away from the sun, away from people. You gave up everything for me. I am the cause of your fate."

"It was my choice, Laren. You couldn't have stopped it." He cradled her face in his hands. "You were deceived by your father, through no fault of your own. Don't be laying blame where there's none."

She glanced around the chamber with saddened eyes. "This is all you have left of your family. Of your brother, your father, these are memories, aren't they?"

"Aye."

She wrapped her arms around his waist so she could press her face against the soft wool of his tartan. "What could I give you that would make up for this?"

"You're my wife, Laren. I have all that I have ever wanted."

She struggled with the enormity of the situation. A deep and terrible sense of foreboding filled her as she considered that Struan's sacrifice might be for naught. If they could not break Nathara's curse, he'd lose his soul. He would have given up all that had once mattered to him simply to give her a chance at life. "I am humbled, Struan, that you should love me so much."

"There was selfishness in the act, too," he insisted. "I left my family in the midst of a terrible crisis in order to follow you. I was thinking of myself, of my own hope for happiness. Do not doubt it."

"This place, is it enchanted?"

"I don't think so. Except for the light, it seems a usual enough spot."

"If you weren't here during your slumber, would you survive?"

In answer to her question, he removed the gold dirk from his stocking. "This keeps me alive. Titania gave it to me to protect me from Nathara's evil. As long as I possess it, I cannot die."

"Until the spell is ended."

"Or until time runs out."

The words made her shiver. He had borne the burden alone, for so long. She could not let his choice be in vain, nor did she want to. If they had just three days left, she would spend them showing him how much she loved him.

Determined, she pressed a kiss to his throat. He stiffened, but remained still. "When you wed me tonight, did you do it to protect me from Cullen?"

"Nay. I did it because I wanted you for my wife."

"Do you? Do you really?"

He gazed at her as he rubbed his hands up her back. "You doubt it now? After seeing this?"

"No. I want to understand, though, to be sure, that you want me here as your wife." She hesitated. "As I want to be your wife."

His hands stilled on her shoulders. "What are you saying to me, Laren?"

"Once, we would have shared a wedding night, and you would have taken me to your home and claimed me as your own."

"Aye."

"With time, I'd have borne your children, and we would have grown old watching them grow."

"Aye." His voice sounded hoarse.

"I want that now, Struan. I want to be your wife. In every way."

With a slight groan, he set her from him. "You cannot know what you ask."

"Do you not still want me?"

His eyes blazed at her. "With everything in me."

"Then let me love you."

"Don't you see? In three days, my soul could be sucked into Nathara's hell. What will I have left you with?" He swept his arm to indicate the chamber. "A stone cave full of useless trinkets?"

"The memory of knowing I was your wife."

"What if my babe lives in your belly? How will you care for it? I can leave you money—I have plenty—but I can't give you honor or my protection."

She shook her head. "Please, Struan, I cannot stand to spend the time we have together worrying about its end. We don't know, either of us, what will happen. I need you. I need to show you I love you." She sensed his hesitation. "Please," she said again as she wrapped her arms more tightly around him. "My soul has waited a thousand years to belong to you. Please don't turn me away now."

Long, agonizing seconds passed while he stood, motionless. She stopped breathing as she tried to absorb the internal battle he fought. A fever seemed to burn behind his eyes. Warily, Laren laid a hand on his face. The featherlight caress seemed to break the slender rein on his self-control. With a soft exclamation of surrender, he scooped her into his arms. "Laren, you have bewitched me."

It felt so incredibly wonderful, so right, to be where she belonged. She hugged him tight against her. "Struan, love me. Please."

His lips found hers in a heated kiss that conveyed a thousand years of longing. When he'd kissed her the night before, there had been a certain urgency to it, as if he'd felt pressed by the passing of time. Now, he simply explored her mouth in the tenderest of ways. His hands cradled her face. His tongue laved at her lips with intoxicating precision.

Laren could no longer wait to touch him fully. Her hands learned the planes of his back, the width of his shoulders. When she found the pin that held his tartan secure, she tugged at it. Her fingers felt leaden and weak. The blood singing through her body slowed her movements. At the sound of her frustrated moan, Struan set her gently away from him. "My love, I find I have no wish to hurry." His lips were turned into a slight smile. "I had believed that a thousand years would sharpen my appetite. I was wrong."

She frowned. "You're not stopping, are you?"

"Nay." His hands moved to the buttons of her dress. "I'm savoring."

She watched, mesmerized as his fingers slowly worked open the buttons of her simple dress. He was looking at her so intently, his gaze felt like a caress. If she were the proper lady her father wanted her to be, she should be embarrassed, she supposed, that Struan was removing her clothes. There didn't seem much point in that. His nearness seemed to have wiped away all need for convention.

To her surprise, she felt no embarrassment at all as she waited for him to lower the dress. Finally, his gaze returned to hers. With intoxicating slowness, he slid his hands inside her dress and pushed it free of her shoulders.

Struan's body ached.

Above the thin cotton of her chemise, her breasts rose and fell with each breath. The way she stood, quietly waiting for him, was far more arousing than any deliberate seduction. He should have known she would not cower before him like a frightened virgin. Laren's spirit was stronger than anyone he'd ever known. It pleased him to know the same determination, the same strength of will and purpose, lived in her still. "You are beautiful."

She swayed a bit toward him. "You make me feel beautiful."

Using the tips of his fingers, he brushed the swell of one breast. A tiny row of goose bumps spread over the soft flesh. Laren sighed in pleasure. "Do you know how good it feels, Struan?"

He couldn't resist a quiet smile. "It feels wonderful." He flexed his hand for emphasis. "Soft. Tender. Wonderful."

For a moment, she studied him with confused eyes. When understanding dawned, her laugh warmed him like a summer breeze. "To me. Do you know how wonderful it feels to me?"

"Tell me." The sound of her voice aroused him. He wanted to hear her telling him how he made her feel.

"I feel strange. My insides feel warm. My flesh tingles when you touch it."

He bent his head to replace his hand with his mouth. "Now?"

She gasped. "Heat."

He pressed a kiss to her nipple. "Now?"

Laren leaned into him with a soft moan. "Fire."

"Ah, love, I have wanted you so long." He picked her up to carry her to the bed. The soft feather tick wrapped her in a comfortable cocoon when he laid her on the cushions.

Laren caught at his arm when he would have moved away from her. "Don't leave me."

"Never." He kissed her again, thoroughly, then rose to remove his clothes.

Fascinated, she watched as he peeled away his garments. Each glimpse of his flesh sent shivers along her skin. In the odd glow of the chamber, his dark hair gleamed. The expression in his eyes had her trembling in anticipation as she thought of the night ahead. When the last of his clothes dropped to the floor, Laren stared at him in unabashed delight. He was perfect. Sculpted muscles rippled beneath smooth skin. The strength in him probably should have intimidated her, but it didn't. Struan would never hurt her. She knew, instinctively, that he was not like her father, and Cullen, and the other men she knew. He wouldn't use his strength to prey on weaker folk. She could trust him implicitly. Wanting to feel his touch, she held out a hand to him. "You're the one who is beautiful," she told him.

Struan's warm laugh echoed on the stone walls. "You're the only woman to ever think it." His hand covered hers.

Guiding him to the bed, she waited until his naked body lay stretched beside her. "There'd better not be any other women seeing what I'm seeing to tell you so, either."

He bent to nuzzle her ear. "Are you jealous, my Laren?"

Squirming beneath the wicked foray of his lips, she ran a possessive hand along his spine. "I did not think so before, but I am finding that I wouldn't like to share."

When he raised his head, an impassioned flame lit his gaze. "I have waited a thousand years to make you my wife. There could never be another woman."

In her soul, she knew it was true, and the admission stunned her. Never in her wildest imaginings had she thought she'd be loved so completely, so wholly. Tears stung at her eyes as she thought of the depth of his commitment to her. She sent up a silent prayer of gratitude and thanksgiving as she turned to align her body with his. "I love you so completely, Struan." She pressed a kiss to his throat. "Show me how to love you."

With a low groan, he stripped away the rest of her garments.

He lingered over her endlessly, learning all the places where her body gave her pleasure. Lover's curiosity drove his hands, his mouth, as he explored her. Her tentative caresses grew bolder. Her fingers found his center and paid a slow, tortuous tribute to the part of him that ached for her.

When, finally, she lay breathless and panting beneath him, her frantic little moans echoing the insistent thunder in his heart, he slid into her.

Laren gasped as she clung to his shoulders. "Struan."

Instantly, he stilled. "Am I hurting you?" He'd felt the fragile tearing as he'd entered her. Though his body screamed for release, he couldn't bear the thought of her pain.

Her head tossed back and forth on the pillow. "Nay." Her hands clung to his shoulders. "Nay. I feel so full. So wonderful. Where are you taking me?"

With a gentling kiss, he began to move within her. "Follow me."

He gathered her close as he started a slow, easy rhythm. He had not waited this long simply to see her pleasure denied. He wanted to feel her body closing around him, ached to give her the kind of joy he'd always known they'd find together.

Restlessly, she began to stir as he continued the slow strokes. Soon, she met his pace, raising her hips to take each one of his thrusts more deeply. Sweat sheened his skin from the effort of holding himself in check. His body thundered for a quick release, but he watched her face in the dim light as he waited.

Higher and higher they climbed until Laren felt a strange coiling sensation begin to tighten and constrict in her lower body. When she thought she could bear it no more, she called his name. He pressed his knees into the soft mattress and plunged into her until all of his hardness filled all of her softness.

Her body convulsed around him like a tight fist. She screamed his name. He spilled himself and gave her his soul.

Chapter 4

In the aftermath, Struan held her to him in a fiercely protective grip. He couldn't have known, couldn't have imagined, how intense the experience of making love with her would be. The last vestiges of his civility were stripped away. In the last thousand years, the world had changed.

People had changed.

In his time, men took what they desired and damned the consequences. When his father had first seen the shores of Loch Fyne, he'd claimed them as his own. If anyone stood in his way, he fought for what he wanted. But those times were gone. Struan had seen warfare replaced by diplomacy. Strength on the battlefield no longer mattered as much as wealth and political power. He felt unsettled and ill at ease as he considered the magnitude of his decision to marry Laren.

Should he fail to break his curse, his life was forfeit. As his wife, then his widow, she would have to establish a new life for herself. In his selfishness, he'd taken the one thing that gave her security. She was no longer a Campbell. Should he die three days hence, he'd leave her alone and unprotected.

His mind searched in vain for a solution to their problem. Like a knife to the gut, he considered the consequences of losing her. The thought tore at him until he felt his hands tightening on her shoulders.

She lay, soft and warm, against his side. The sensation sent fear spiraling through him as he thought of the days ahead. With just three moon rises left, he was no closer to an answer now than he had been before.

Her hand moved along the line of his chest. "You are thinking of Nathara." It wasn't a question.

With a heavy sigh, he turned to face her. "Yes."

She smoothed away a deep furrow in his brow with her thumb. "I thought I made it clear that I would not have other women on your mind when you share this bed with me."

Thankful for her levity, he pressed a kiss to her palm. "You need not worry on that count. My mind would never stray when I already have perfection."

She laughed. "You flatter me, Struan. I find that I like it."

"Shall I do it some more?"

She stayed his roving hand. "Now that the subject of Nathara has been introduced into our bedchamber, you've diverted my attention."

"Shall I divert it back?"

"Too late. You have me thinking now."

"A thinking woman. The bane of man's existence for as long as I can remember."

"Stop your teasing. I wouldn't wish to retaliate."

"You can't tease me. There's nothing to tease about."

"No? Perhaps I should remind you of your less than illustrious history."

"The MacLachlans have a fine history."

"Except that your ancestor De Dalan led them here to avoid the ridicule he faced in Ireland over his clumsiness. De Dalan the Clumsy, they called him, possessed of unwieldliness that only worsened a hundred times over once he reached Loch Fyne. You call your lineage illustrious with a story like that in its past?"

To her delight, he laughed. "De Dalan was a poor cursed soul, and my ancestors have long made up for his faults."

"Is that so?"

"It is."

"Then perhaps you'd like to tell me why your brother was known as Duncan the Agile, but you have no such title?"

Struan felt a swelling pride when he thought of his younger brother.

"After Duncan distinguished himself in battle against the Campbells, our father honored him with the title, Duncan the Agile, and named him laird chieftan of the clan."

"I am pleased for him, but you still have not answered my question. Your brother's valor aside, are you certain you didn't inherit some of your grandfather's clumsiness?"

With a leer, he loomed over her. "Shall I show you again how agile I can be?"

She chastised him with a poke to his ribs. "Have you always been so vain, Struan?"

His expression turned suddenly serious. He found he had little patience for jesting when their situation was so urgent. Solemnly, he answered, "Since the day you first said you loved me."

With a soft sound of distress, she kissed him gently. "We will find a way. I know we will find a way."

Struan was still clinging to the promise when he emerged from the chamber several hours later. Laren lay sleeping, quietly exhausted. During the long night, he had made several decisions, and saw no point in delaying their action.

She must come first. Above all things, he must ensure that she'd be well protected, cared for, when he was gone. Despite her insistence, he was not prepared to risk her safety should they fail to break the curse. Under no circumstances would he allow her to fall beneath Nathara's power on the fifth night. If he died in the process, he would ensure that Laren had the rest of this life to walk upon the earth.

That thought in mind, he determined to go first to Keith MacLachlan. Laren had told him that the new MacLachlan chieftain was an honorable man. Struan would persuade Keith to offer the protection of the clan to Laren. She was, after all, his wife. She was now a MacLachlan, and entitled to their kinship.

Once he'd secured Keith's promise, he'd find Laren's father, then Cullen MacEwan. He had just three days left with her; he would not allow them to mar the happiness he and Laren had finally found together.

She awoke alone. Glancing around the chamber, it took Laren several minutes to orient herself. Memories of the previous night flooded in. With a contented moan, she stretched languorously in the soft bed.

She was Struan MacLachlan's bride.

Bone-deep satisfaction filled her at the thought. Had she doubted, even slightly, the fantastic story he'd told her, the night had chased it away. In a homecoming too long delayed, her heart had soared at Struan's first touch. In the night, she had felt his worry, knew he was concerned about the coming confrontation with Nathara. Her mind traveled to his conversation with Titania. Laren was not yet ready to believe that the faerie queen couldn't help them. There was a secret to the riddle. She believed it lay in Titania's realm.

Determined, she shoved aside the tartan blanket. She would not while away the day when she could spend her hours securing her future with Struan.

By the time he returned to the chamber beneath the Loch, his spirits were revived. He'd spent a productive morning with Keith MacLachlan. At first, the laird had not wanted to believe Struan's claims. Though he'd heard the legends, he was ill prepared to believe that the spell of the thousand-year slumber was real. It had been, in the end, his niece who had swayed his opinion.

Visiting from Russia, Katarina Kaskova, MacLachlan's niece, had gently persuaded him to listen to Struan's story. In Katarina, Struan had sensed a kindred spirit. He remembered Laren's story that Keith's sister, Krista, carried Lily's faerie blood in her veins. Katarina seemed to share the trait and, clearly, held a special place in her uncle's heart. Keith had finally yielded and offered Laren the protection of the MacLachlans. At Struan's request, he'd deeded them a small cottage on the eastern part of the estate where Laren could comfortably live out her days should he fail to defeat Nathara.

His visit to James Campbell had been less civil, but equally productive. Using some of the considerable fortune he'd discovered in the cave upon his first awakening, he'd paid James a bride-price that had quickly squelched his complaints of Laren's betrayal. The money, just one of many gifts from the faeries, had been more than enough to amply pay the debt owed Cullen MacEwan, as well as secure James's own claim to the land.

His confrontation with Cullen, on the other hand, still left a foul taste in his mouth. Once again, he'd sensed Cullen's evil, felt Nathara's spell lurking about him like a second skin. Cullen had shown only mild reaction to Struan's warning, but Struan gave the matter little thought. A final confrontation would come, he knew, and when it did, he'd see to it that Cullen no longer posed Laren a threat.

He returned to find her carefully rolling the tapestries from the walls of his chamber. Most of his possessions were packed in the cotton sacks lined by the door. He dropped the cleaned pheasant he'd netted for their dinner on the stone table. "You've been working."

She slipped the last tapestry into a bag. "We're moving."

"Are we?" He strode to the hearth where he'd lit a fire that morning to ward off the chill of the room. He was pleased to see she'd fed it during the day so it burned still. "Don't you like my chamber?"

" 'Tis not a question of what I like, Struan, 'tis a question of why you stay here."

"It's my home."

"It's your prison."

He glanced at her. "You feel strongly about this."

"I do. You have told me that you do not need to stay here to survive."

"That is true. As long as I possess Titania's dirk, I live."

"All these years, this has been the sanctuary that protected you. Now, you no longer need it."

He paused in the act of putting the pheasant on a spit. "No longer need it?"

"No." She met his gaze squarely. "In three days, the curse will be ended. You won't be returning here. I see no point in staying here now."

The quiet words sent a shaft of joy through him. Dear God, how he loved this woman. How was it possible that she knew his heart so well? This place had been home to him for ten centuries. In that time, he'd realized its necessity, and come to resent its purpose. He'd spoken of his ill feelings toward it to no one. But Laren had known.

Laying the spit across the fire, he rose to go to her. "How did you know?"

"I just knew. Do you need to know how?"

From his belt he withdrew the deed to the stalker's cottage. "I saw Keith MacLachlan this morning."

"I found your note after I woke. Did he receive you?"

"He did. It took a good bit of persuasion on my part, and I couldn't have done it without his niece, but he gave me this."

Laren took the paper. Her eyes lit when she read it. "I know this place," she told him. "It sits just across the bay from the ruins. We'll be able to see them from the bedchamber."

"Keith MacLachlan seems to think it's haunted." Consorting with faeries as he did, he found the notion whimsical.

"It is." She sounded so certain, he couldn't hold his smile.

"You think so?" he teased.

"I know so. Shaw MacLachlan, one of your ancestors, haunts the place. In the dawn and the twilight, you can hear him playing the pipes."

He groaned. "I shall never escape the sound of them, then?"

"Never."

"And I assume that pleases you?"

"Almost as much as the knowledge that you'll never escape me." Her gaze met his. "That's why I wanted us to have a home."

He swept her hair away from her face, then cradled her chin in his fingers. "Should anything happen, Keith has agreed to let you live out your days there." She would have spoken then, but he stopped her. "Hear me out, Laren. It must be said."

"I don't like to speak of it."

"Neither do I, but it would be unwise to doubt Nathara's power. I've failed each time."

"But surely—"

He pressed a finger to her lips to quiet her. "I have settled your debt with your father, and let Cullen MacEwan know of my intentions. If the sun rises four days hence, and I have ceased to walk this earth, I will die knowing I have cared for you. Keith has accepted our marriage. You are a MacLachlan now, and they will protect you as long as you live."

"I couldn't bear it without you."

"And please God you won't have to, but all I've ever wanted is your happiness. If I can die knowing I've given you that, it'll be enough for me."

With a quiet cry, she flung herself against him. "It isn't fair. We have to find a way to break the spell."

"I will speak with Titania tonight," he promised. "Perhaps she will have answers." He didn't mention that he'd tried before, or that he'd given up much of the hope he'd once had.

"She must." Laren clung to him. "She must."

"I pray she will." That was the best he could give her.

They spent a busy two days moving Struan's possessions into the stalker's cottage by the Loch, and making the place into a home. Moving their bed, alone, took the better part of the morning.

Struan called the house a little larger than cramped and a bit smaller than huge, but to Laren, it seemed perfect. With wide windows that overlooked the water, nestled in a copse of trees, it was just the location she would have chosen. The land, she knew, had been disputed for some time, but the MacLachlans had finally laid claim to the little cottage and its surrounding woods. It stood within viewing distance of the new castle. Best of all, to her way of thinking, the main bedroom overlooked the ruins and the Rocking Stone.

Together, they cleaned away the cobwebs and the dust. Laren scrubbed the floors and walls, while Struan repaired the shutters and furniture that had weakened with age. She laid out new linens. He wiped the dirt from the glass windowpanes. She aired the rugs. He cleaned the chimney. The labor of love helped take their minds from the relentless ticking of the clock on the mantel.

Struan went to the Stone each evening. Despite Laren's pestering, he would not repeat his conversations with Titania. He'd made it more than clear that the faerie queen wouldn't appreciate her interference, and Laren had reluctantly agreed to stay away from the enchanted spot. Struan seemed determined to keep her from the Stone. He'd warned her in the strongest way about the dangers of the place. A dozen times he'd told her about her first death there, how she'd been tricked into eating the fruit of the berry bush. Then, because he seemed to fear that his warnings might not be enough, he'd begged her not to venture to it. Because she loved him, she'd reluctantly agreed.

Each night when he returned, he made love to her with a kind of desperation that frightened her to the core. He had given up. She knew it.

That knowledge pained her like none other. Struan seemed to be determined to make some kind of noble sacrifice on her behalf. He had readily accepted that the curse would end, and that his life would be forfeit in the process. She felt him preparing for the time when Nathara would claim his soul. She found herself hating the evil little faerie queen with a raging passion.

When she awoke alone on the morning of the fifth day, she felt an acute sense of panic settle into her soul. Facing the last moon rise, they were no closer to a solution. Struan's lovemaking had been heartbreakingly tender during the night. With each caress, each kiss, she'd felt him telling her goodbye. When he'd finally claimed her, she'd wanted to weep. How, she wondered, could God have been so kind to give her this man—her life's mate—only to take him from her in such a horrible way?

The thought had her begging before her feet touched the floor. At Struan's request, she'd stayed away from the Rocking Stone, but she could bear it no more. He was out, probably hunting for their supper. Only a man, she thought, as she pulled on her clothes, would worry over his stomach while facing a battle between light and dark, good and evil. Issues of the utmost importance hung in the balance, and her husband sought venison for his evening meal.

She tucked his plaid securely about her shoulders to ward off the chill of the day. The time had come to take the matters into her own hands. Despite his warnings, she knew she must go to the Stone. Titania was a woman, after all. Surely she would listen.

As Laren made her way to the Rocking Stone, an odd tingling filled her limbs. She felt a certain force pulling her along the familiar path. Her heartbeat accelerated. Her blood seemed to flow faster. A ringing sound persisted in her ears. The closer she drew to the spot, the more compelled she felt to continue.

When she finally emerged from the woods in the clearing near the old ruins, she felt an odd squeezing sensation in her temples. In the back of her mind, she heard Struan's pleas as he begged her not to go. The place did seem different. Gone was the familiar comfort she always felt near the ruins. In its place was unease.

The water slapped against the rocks in an eerie cadence. The dew that misted the bluebells lent the earth a damp smell that filled her head like an intoxicating draught. Confused, she picked her way across the marshy clearing to the Stone. The answer must lie there.

To her surprise, the glow that had settled on the Stone in the wake of Nathara's disappearance lingered. A berry bush, one she'd never seen before, had sprouted there. Vaguely, she heard Struan's voice telling her about the berries, but she couldn't seem to latch on to a thought. Her mind felt fogged. She bent to examine the bush, wondering how the plant could have developed and born fruit so quickly. Dread filled her as she thought of what the magic could mean.

The fat, purplish berries looked juicy and sweet. Her tongue felt suddenly dry. She thought of how refreshing the juice would be on her lips.

Her fingers closed on the largest berry when she heard the sound of approaching hoofbeats. With a startled gasp, she dropped the fruit to the ground. A man's voice called her name. Through the fog in her mind, she couldn't identify him. It must be Struan. He would have seen her by the Stone and come for her.

When the hoofbeats ceased, she turned to face him.

Cullen MacEwan sat astride his black gelding, studying her with an odd amber light in his eyes. "So," he said, " 'tis true what Nathara said. You are enchanted."

Laren gasped. The spell that seemed to have held her dissipated like mist before morning sun. Shaken, she looked in horror at the berries. This is what Struan had told her would happen. Because of her own stubborn intent to interfere, despite her promise not to, she'd almost ended his last chance at life. Breath came in restricted gasps as she considered the magnitude of what had almost happened.

And worse, she owed her life, and Struan's, to Cullen MacEwan's arrival.

She wiped a trembling hand over her face, then made herself face Cullen. "Good morning, Cullen."

"Indeed it is," he said. She didn't like the sinister look in his eyes. "Better than I thought it could be."

Laren shuddered. "What brings you here?"

"You."

The way he said the word made her flesh creep. "You can't be wanting anything with me. Struan has spoken with you. You know, by now, that Keith MacLachlan has accepted our marriage."

He shifted in his saddle. "Your marriage is of no importance to me."

"Then what do you want?" she asked, not really wanting to know.

Cullen pointed to the Stone. "I heard a remarkable story about you and this place from a remarkable source. I was reluctant to believe it."

She began to wonder what her best chance of escape would be. Surely Struan would return soon. He'd see her by the Stone with Cullen. Though it meant admitting she'd come here despite his warnings, she'd welcome his arrival. If she could delay long enough, she should be able to find a way from this mess she'd gotten herself into. "You shouldn't believe all that you hear, Cullen. Stories are rarely true."

"Aye, but this one is."

A breeze, cold and ominous, ruffled the skirt of her woolen dress. "Why do you think so?"

"Because one of the faeries came to me and told me I'd find you here today. She told me of that bush." He pointed to the berries. "And that Struan MacLachlan knows where the Seelies have hidden their gold."

"That's silly, Cullen. You cannot believe in something like faeries." The wind blew harder. Laren sent up a silent prayer that Titania would understand her reason for the lie.

"Yesterday, I didn't."

"And now you've changed your mind because of a few berries."

"The bush wasn't there before."

"Of course it was."

"Nay. Yesterday, after the visit, I checked the spot. It's grown and borne fruit in less than a day. I have no reason to doubt the story now."

Where, she wondered, was Struan? Cullen was making her nervous. An odd light had settled in his eyes. It reminded her of the glow that had ringed the Rocking Stone after Nathara's disappearance. "What do you want, Cullen?"

He trotted his horse foreword. "What every man of the Highlands wants. I want Titania's gold."

She swallowed. "Men have sought the faerie gold for centuries. What makes you think you will find it?"

"Because, according to my little visitor, your husband knows where it is."

"He'll never tell you."

Cullen edged his horse nearer to her spot by the Stone. "He will," he promised, "if I have you."

Before she could flee, he'd looped a thick arm around her waist and hauled her onto the saddle. "I suggest you cling." His voice mocked her. "I've always liked that in a woman."

Chapter 5

THE instant he stepped into the cottage, fear filled him. Laren was missing.

His gaze went, instantly, to the Rocking Stone. With dreadful certainty, he knew she'd gone there. It didn't matter that she could be a thousand other places doing a thousand other things. His heart knew she'd gone to the Stone.

He dropped the slain deer onto the table as he mentally fought for control. He must not panic. It could not have happened. He had until moon rise. He'd always had until moon rise.

He drew several deep breaths before he headed for the door. Titania had give him little comfort these last two nights, but she would have told him if there'd been a change. She wanted him to win, after all, she would not allow Nathara to speed the process by cutting short his time.

He hurried along the path, searching for signs of her in every broken twig and small footprint. She had come this way. The muddy trail betrayed her.

When he reached the Stone, fear had become a living thing in him. His blood ran cold when he saw the berry bush. Perched on the Stone, Titania sat watching him. "You are later than I thought."

"Where is she?"

"She is not here."

At the assurance, he breathed again. "Where? It's not moon rise. I have until moon rise."

Titania tilted her head to study him. "You have given up hope, haven't you?"

His hands fisted at his sides as he considered the question. He didn't have time for Titania's game of philosophy. He must find Laren. The ominous presence of the berry bush and, his mind noted, the few fat berries lying on the ground as if they'd been freshly picked, sent terror sluicing through him. He knew better than to rush Titania, however, so he schooled himself to patience. She held the key to what little hope remained. He could not afford to irritate her. "I have resigned myself to what appears to be the reality." He hoped the tactful answer would satisfy her.

"You *have* given up hope. You believe Nathara will win."

"I believe that the sun has never shone in the midnight sky, and that losing what matters to me most is impossible. To do that, I'd have to let Laren die. I cannot." He shrugged his wide shoulders in a gesture of surrender. "So what hope remains?"

"Do you not believe, even a little, in magic?"

"Of course I believe in magic. I owe my existence to it."

"But you doubt its power?"

"I doubt its goodwill." He studied the beautiful little faerie. "I have no reason to do otherwise."

She fluttered her wings in what might have been a sigh. "I see I have failed to properly instruct you."

"Titania, if there is something you aren't telling me, please do so. No one wants this matter solved more than I."

"Struan, for every moment of joy, there must be a moment of sorrow. For light, there is darkness. Comfort follows fear. Love balances hate. This is what governs the faerie world and yours. You cannot have one without the other."

"What has this to do with Laren and me?"

"You have walked a thousand years in fear and darkness for the sake of a great love. Can't you trust the powers of the world to spare you one small miracle in exchange for the sacrifice?"

His heart lurched. "A miracle?"

She gave him a slight smile. "The sun has never, in your lifetime, shone in the midnight sky. 'Tis true. But neither has another man lived a thousand years for the sake of a woman."

"Titania, please." He fell to his knees beside the Stone. "Solve this riddle for me. Tell me there's a way from the curse."

"It's in your heart, Struan. Believe in it. When the time comes, you will know what is right."

His eyes drifted shut in frustration. She had said these words to him so many times, he'd numbed himself to them. "Where is Laren, then? At least tell me that."

"She is in the hands of your enemy."

He glanced at the berry bush. "Nathara has her?" The words chilled his soul.

"Nathara has used the spirit of a mortal."

"Cullen."

"Yes. She went to him in the night and told him you know the secret of our gold."

"Dear God."

"He has taken your Laren because he believes you will trade your knowledge for her life."

He looked at Titania with deadly earnest. "I will."

Instead of the rage he expected, he saw on her lips a contented smile. "I know."

Struan approached Cullen MacEwan's manor with a warlike rage burning in his chest. Astride the new gray mount he'd purchased that morning from Keith MacLachlan, he felt the blood of his warrior ancestors driving him to the mouth of the enemy. If need be, he would kill the bastard. He'd wanted to all those years ago.

"MacEwan," he shouted from the far side of the marsh that protected the manor from intrusion. "Open the gates. It is I, Struan MacLachlan."

Behind the gate, a young man looked at him nervously. "What is your business here, sir?"

"I have come for the woman your lord holds captive within those walls."

The young man cleared his throat. "I think there's been a mistake. Lord MacEwan is not here. There is no woman here, either."

Frustration poured through him. At a tug of the reins, his horse reared, then kicked at the iron gates with his front hooves. The man on the other side fled seconds before the gates tore from their weak hinges and landed inside the wall. Struan rode beneath the arch. "I want the woman." His fingers curled into the man's collar so he could jerk him off the ground. "Where is MacEwan?"

Fear filled the man's eyes as he wagged his head. "I swear to you, I don't know. I'm Lord MacEwan's steward. If there were a woman here, I'd know it. His lordship left early this morning. He hasn't returned. His mount is still missing from the stables."

Struan dropped him to the ground. "I will hunt him myself. If he returns, tell him I will have his head if he harms her."

He charged from the gates, driven by fear and fury as he considered where Cullen could be holding Laren. He had wanted, desperately, to believe Titania's words. His heart ached to believe them. She'd offered him the first glimmer of hope. It gave him an urgent desire to see Laren, safe and whole, to hold her once more. He'd planned to spend the entire day letting her know how much he loved her, giving her something to cling to when he was gone. His trip to fetch the venison from his snare should have been his last venture from the stalker's cottage until moon rise.

Now, Cullen had taken her. With the abduction, he'd stolen the slender thread of control Struan held on his anger at Nathara. If Cullen had harmed Laren, in any way, Struan knew his rage would consume him despite Titania's warnings. A man could only endure so much.

He returned, quickly, to the Stone, where he found Cullen's trail. In his haste, he'd foolishly assumed Cullen would take Laren to the security of his manor. But he was wrong. Instead, he'd have to hunt him like the dog he was.

The day passed too slowly for Laren. A hundred times she imagined the sound of Struan riding up the steep rocks to the cave where Cullen had her hidden. In the adjacent rock chamber, she heard Cullen discussing his strategy with several more men. They had every intention of tricking Struan into revealing the secret of the faerie gold. Privately, she feared no trick would be necessary. Struan seemed almost determined to die on her behalf. If Cullen offered him the choice of her freedom for his knowledge, he'd gladly give the faerie's secret, though it meant his own demise.

She shuddered when she thought of the consequences, particularly when she considered how her own broken promise had created this mess. She should not have gone to the Stone. Struan had given his life the first time because of her, now she'd placed him in an impossible situation once more. She must escape Cullen before he used her to extract the secret of the gold from Struan. It was her only hope.

For hours that seemed like days, she watched the shadows lengthening on the wall of the cave. Several times, Cullen left the damp place. Always, a guard stood at the mouth of her chamber where she sat bound by thick ropes. Still, Struan hadn't come for her. She thanked God for that. If a fight ensued, he'd be badly outnumbered, though perhaps not outmatched. Cullen wouldn't hesitate to kill him, however, and she refused to be the cause of his death.

Finally, when the ropes had begun to cut her wrists and her feet had grown numb from the damp cold in the cave, Cullen appeared at the opening of the chamber. "The moon rises," he said. "It's time."

Struan paced about the Rocking Stone in increasing frustration. He'd located Cullen's cave hours before, but had quickly determined that he could not approach it in secret. The rocky ledge overlooked the ruins and copse of trees that lined Loch Fyne. To reach it, he'd have to ride directly up the boulder-strewn slope. He could not risk Laren's safety. His only choice was to wait until Cullen brought her down to the Stone.

He had no doubt at all that Nathara would have instructed Cullen to bring Laren to the Stone. She knew the location of Titania's gold. She was merely using Cullen to force Struan's betrayal. If he betrayed Titania's secret, he'd surrender his soul to Nathara forever. What better spot than where she'd first laid claim to it.

He paced, feeling anxious and angry. Darkness had begun to fall.

Soon, the moon would rise on his last hours. Throwing back his head, he uttered a pained curse. How could he have imagined it would turn out this way? He'd been so full of hope that day so long ago. Then, he'd blithely promised to find a way from the enchantment. Now, wiser, and so very much older, he realized the folly of his young heart. Love, then, had been simple and uncomplicated. It had filled him with hope and joy. Now, he loved her so much more deeply, so much more fully, it was almost a pain within him.

For the first time, he understood that his sacrifice had not been a choice in vain. He'd given her a full life. In exchange, he'd received what he'd always desired—the knowledge that Laren had, indeed, lived on stolen years.

His eyes drifted shut when he saw the first star twinkle in the darkening sky. The moon had risen. His time was at an end.

"You cannot win, Cullen." Laren followed him down the rocky ledge. From the placement of the moon, she mentally set the time near enough to midnight to mean danger to them both. The days had lengthened with the coming of spring, and the sun set close to ten o'clock at night. Darkness didn't fall until an hour or so later. The moon's clear presence in the partially light sky made her shiver with fear. "Struan won't let you."

"Struan is a weak man. He's let you turn his head." He waited while she climbed over a pile of loose rock. "He will tell me about the gold to save you. In exchange, he'll lose his life to the faeries." His expression was harsh when he glanced at her. "It seems that I'll have you after all."

Laren gritted her teeth. She must find her way free.

Cullen guided her down the hill, through the dense foliage, across the sheep pasture, and on toward the path that led to the Rocking Stone. She trudged behind in anxious silence. With her hands bound behind her, escape would be tricky. At least Cullen had not brought more men with him. He'd left the three men at the cave. His greed, she supposed, had overruled his common sense. He wouldn't want to share the fairies' secret with his companions.

When they finally reached the path, her feet settled onto the familiar trail. She knew every rock, every root, every turn in the lane. She'd walked this way countless times. Her heart knew it so well, she could make the journey blindfolded.

She searched her mind for a means of escape, and finally settled on the place where the road branched. The flat way led directly to the ruins. The high path, steep and difficult to follow, cut through the MacLachlan home woods. She'd followed that way only once, and had been forced to turn back when she'd reached the steep embankment at its edge. Still, Cullen would have a more difficult time following her there, and surely she could find a way down the slope. If she could reach the Stone, she could warn Struan of Cullen's intent.

She wondered at her certain knowledge that she'd find him there. What if he still sought her? What would she do when she reached the Stone?

A buzzing near her ear captured her attention. She turned to find Titania hovering near her. "Follow your heart, Laren," the faerie queen told her. "That is the key. Follow your heart and you will find your way to him."

Like a firefly, Titania's light dimmed, then disappeared. Laren caught her breath as she looked at Cullen's back. He didn't seem to have heard. Gathering her courage and clinging to the sliver of hope, she strained her eyes in the near darkness for a glimpse of the fork in the path. She would flee up it, then trust the faerie's advice. She had no other choice.

When they reached the fork, Cullen still walked in front of her. Laren slowed her pace until he was far enough ahead to give her several seconds lead. Drawing a deep breath, she charged up the path.

She had almost reached the top when she heard Cullen shout her name. Determination mingled with fear as she stumbled past the roots and rocks along the steep embankment.

"Stop." Cullen's voice echoed in the still night. She heard the heavy fall of his footsteps on the path.

"Struan." She used what little breath she had to scream his name. He must know. "Struan, it's a trap."

She plunged into the woods, using the dim light the moon cast through the trees to thread her way through the underbrush. Behind her, Cullen's boots crashed through brambles and fallen leaves. He drew closer.

Ducking beneath a low branch, she darted to the right. The embankment, she knew, loomed ahead. She would have to find a path down or she'd hurt herself. Without the use of her hands, she didn't have the balance she needed to ease her way down.

Cullen cursed as he tangled himself in a thorn bush. Laren used the precious extra moments to weave between the rhododendrons that lined the floor of the forest. "Struan," she called his name again. "I'm here. On the hillside."

She'd reached the edge of the slope. She tried several times to find a way down, but felt panic surge when Cullen's voice sounded close behind her. "You can't get down." He was snarling now.

She glanced over her shoulder once, saw his shadow looming closer. With no time to consider the consequences, she yelled Struan's name a final time, then hurled herself down the mud-slick slope.

Struan raced through the marshy grass toward the embankment. From her first scream, he'd been squeezed with an undeniable panic. The darkness obscured his vision. He could hear Cullen's voice. He could hear the snapping of the forest underbrush. He could hear the determination in Laren's calls. He must reach her.

He'd started running toward the forest when he'd heard her say his name the first time. "Laren, I'm here." The ominous sound of breaking branches met his shout. He plunged forward through the thick grass. It tore at his legs.

"Struan?" Her voice came from the small rivulet at his left. He raced toward it.

"Laren, where are you?"

"I'm here." She stumbled free of the brush. Her hands were bound behind her. Her clothes were torn. Dirt smudged her face. Her hair lay in tangled disarray around her shoulders.

He pulled her sharply to him. "My God, are you all right?"

"It's a trap," she said between sharply indrawn breaths. "He's trying to trick you. You mustn't tell—"

"Laren."

When she shook her head, dirt and leaves rained about her. "Nay. Listen. Cullen has consorted with Nathara. You can't tell him, Struan. You can't."

Cullen emerged from the brush holding a drawn pistol. Instinctively, Struan stepped in front of Laren. "What do you want, Cullen?"

"You know what I want, MacLachlan. You hold the secret to the faerie gold. I want it."

"It won't do you any good to know where they've hidden it. You cannot reach it without magic."

Cullen's laugh was harsh and unpleasant. "What a charming little story. Unfortunately, I don't believe it." He motioned to the ruins with the pistol. "Let's go to that blasted rock. She said we'd find it there."

"Who said?"

Cullen frowned at him. "I'm not in the mood for your trickery, MacLachlan. I know you've consorted with the faeries."

Still Struan hesitated. He kept his gaze carefully fixed on the weapon. "Let Laren go," he said carefully. "She knows nothing of this."

Cullen's lips twisted into a tight little smile. "I am no fool. As long as she lives, you are weak. If she is near, you will sacrifice to protect her. It's why you can't win. You hold the secret to the faerie gold, the secret every man in the Highlands would gladly sell his soul to possess, yet you've given it up for a woman. You're a lovesick fool, MacLachlan. And it'll mean the death of you."

Laren leaned against Struan's back. "Struan, please. It's a trap. Nathara told him you'd give him the gold. You can't do it. You can't."

Struan straightened his shoulders. "I won't tell you until you release her."

"And I won't release her until you tell me." Cullen tilted his head to one side. "What a dilemma." With no warning, he fired a shot.

The bullet lodged itself in Struan's shoulder. When he flinched in pain, Laren screamed. Cullen used the momentary confusion to grab Laren's bound hands and haul her up against him. Clutching his wounded shoulder, Struan made a futile attempt to free her.

Cullen slammed his fist into Struan's wound. Pain lanced down his arm as he staggered back.

"Struan, no." Laren watched him with anguished eyes.

Cullen gave the rope a hard jerk. "That, I think, settles the matter," he said. "Now you'll tell me where the gold lies."

Struan found Laren's gaze. The pain in his arm dimmed compared to the pain in his heart. "Laren, I must."

"No. Don't. Please, don't. You'll die. I can't live if you do."

"Go to Keith. He'll care for you."

"No." She struggled against Cullen's confining grip. "No, I won't do it. If you give him the secret, Nathara will win. Don't you remember? Don't let the hate win. It's what Titania told you. Please, Struan. Don't."

He had but one choice, and he knew it. Lily had given him the dirk as his talisman. It protected him, allowed him to live. If he surrendered it to Cullen, he'd forfeit his soul to Nathara, but she'd allow Laren to live. That was the bargain. His soul for hers. His death so she could live. Nathara had never wanted Laren. She'd wanted to best Titania in the constant struggle for power that ruled the faerie world. She wanted to win. If he allowed her this victory, she would allow Titania a smaller victory of her own.

Light for darkness.

Joy for sorrow.

Long ago, Titania had sworn to him that she would not let him die in vain. She would save Laren if he kept Titania's secret at the cost of his life. Suddenly, it was all that mattered.

In a bitter moment of self-recrimination, he realized that it was selfishness, not love, that had driven him all these years. He'd wanted Laren to live, but he'd wanted it so he could have her for himself. If he'd chosen, he could have made this sacrifice centuries ago and freed her. Even this time, he'd forced her to remember their past. He'd taken her to wife. He'd created a false sense of hope in her that would leave her mourning after his death. His heart felt leaden and sick. Indeed, he was the weakling Cullen had called him. In his own cowardice, he'd forced a thousand years of evil on the woman he claimed to love.

Feeling broken, he looked at Laren. "I'm sorry."

The whisper carried on the breeze. "Struan, no."

He tore his gaze from her to face Cullen. "It's the dirk," he said, reaching for it in his belt. His bloodstained hand closed on the gold hilt. "It will show you the way."

Cullen looked at him dubiously. Laren gasped. "You can't," she said. "Don't give it to him. Please don't give it to him."

Cullen's shrewd eyes studied her for long moments. "There must be something to it, else you wouldn't be so insistent."

She shook her head. "No. Look." She nodded in the direction of the Rocking Stone. It had started to move. A strange glow hovered about its base. "There, by the Stone. That is what you seek."

Still cautious, as if he knew there were forces at work beyond his understanding, Cullen waved the pistol in the direction of the Stone. "You lead, MacLachlan. Take us over there."

"The dirk is all you need," Struan insisted.

"Then it won't matter if we wait a bit longer, will it?"

Struan's eyes drifted shut on a silent prayer. Cullen cocked the revolver. "Let's go."

They walked back to the ruins through the marsh. Struan could practically feel the anxious energy coming from Laren. She trudged behind him, silently begging him not to do what he planned. He was so closely attuned to her, he could almost hear the thoughts pouring from her.

When they reached the Stone, it was rocking in an ominous rhythm. Cullen put his hand on it to still it, but it continued to move, driven by an odd force. "What moves it?"

"Faerie magic," Struan told him. "The gold lies beneath it."

Cullen's expression altered to one of distrust. He pointed the pistol at Laren. "Knock it from the ledge," he commanded.

"You'll still need the dirk. It won't be enough to see beneath the Stone."

"Just do it. Push it from the ledge."

When Laren choked out a final plea, Cullen pointed the pistol at her temple. "Do it," he commanded.

Struan put his good shoulder to the rock and pushed until it tilted off its ledge with a mighty cracking noise. It teetered on end for several long seconds, then tilted to fall with a loud crash into the waters of the Loch.

Beneath it sat the ledge where it had perched for over ten centuries, and an uninspiring piece of earth. Cullen frowned. "There's nothing here."

"You need the dirk," Struan insisted.

As if on command, the earth began to glow. Cullen's eyes widened as he stared at the eerie light. "What's that?"

" 'Tis the hillock of gold." Struan extended the dirk to him once more. He must convince him to take it. Cullen's suspicions would soon win over his greed if Struan couldn't get him to accept the gold charm. He couldn't bring himself to look at Laren, knowing full well he'd crumple if he saw the expression on her face. "Take it," he urged again. "It's my greatest treasure."

Cullen stared at the glowing earth for several more seconds, then reached out a shaking hand for the dirk.

Laren gasped, then plunged forward. "No," she yelled. "No, don't do it."

Startled, Cullen took a hasty step back as the dagger plunged to the ground. It lodged in the earth on its point. Struan reached for Laren. Cullen tripped over the blackberry bush. As he fell, his hand tightened instinctively on the gun. The trigger clicked. A shot pierced the still night.

And Laren fell to the ground.

In horror, Struan looked at the pool of blood that soaked quickly, too quickly, through her dress. "No." His anguished cry sounded as loud as the gun's report. "No!" He dropped to his knees to pull her into his arms.

With frantic hands, he brushed her hair from her whitening face. "No."

From the corner of his eye, he saw Cullen reaching for the dirk. The earth had begun to tremble. An instant before Cullen's fingers closed on the hilt, a burst of light shot from the ground. Titania rode the light like a chariot.

Struan clutched Laren to him and wept. "Titania, it can't end this way," he begged. "Please stop it."

She didn't take her eyes from Cullen. "Twice," she said, "you have tried to take what is rightfully mine. I'll allow it no more."

A burst of red light erupted from the opposite side of the gold dirk. Nathara sat atop it, her expression smug. "You're in no position to allow or disallow anything, Titania. Once again, the mortals have failed you." She pointed to Cullen. "That's what drives them. Greed. Hate. Vengeance. You thought you'd prove to me that there was goodness in their hearts, but you've failed." Angrily, she looked at Struan. "And you thought you could defy me?"

He clung to Laren's limp body. "Titania, please. I beg you."

"Look at him," Nathara mocked. "He is nothing more than a simpering fool."

Titania sat, like the queen she was, on her pillar of light. "He is not the fool, Nathara. 'Tis you."

Nathara grunted in rage. "He would have given the secret. When it mattered, he would have given it."

"But he didn't."

"Only because you interfered."

Struan felt the tears begin to burn at his eyes. While they argued, the life drained from Laren's body. "Please," he whispered again. "You can have whatever you want." He looked at Nathara. "If it's my soul, take it." He found Titania's gaze. "If it's my hope of happiness, it's yours. Just let her live."

In his arms, Laren stirred. He looked at her quickly. Her eyes fluttered open. Her hand lifted slowly to point at the darkening sky. "Don't move. Lie still."

"Look." Her voice was a thready whisper.

He turned to gaze at the sky. A red light was slowly eclipsing the full moon. Laren's fingers tightened on his hand. "The sun. The sun shines in the midnight sky." Her hand touched his face. Tears streamed from his eyes to bathe her fingers. "It is over." She managed a slight smile. "You are free."

"Laren, don't die. My God, please don't die."

"We have ended it." Her expression turned heartbreakingly tender. "Just as you said we would. Live long, my love."

And with a shuddering breath, she died.

Struan felt the anguished cry ripping through him before it reached his lips. He clutched her limp body to him and shouted her name on a gasp of pain.

Nathara uttered an enraged stream of obscenities. Titania rose on her pillar of light. "Take your servant"—she pointed at Cullen—"and leave these shores. You have failed, Nathara."

Struan clung to Laren as he tried to will his life into her body. He no longer cared what the faeries commanded. He no longer cared who had won or lost. He had failed to save her. That was all that mattered to him.

Nathara roared her outrage. "You cannot banish me from here. Without me, you wouldn't exist."

Titania shook her head. "There will always be evil in the world, Nathara. You are not its only source. Leave here. I have won."

In an angry burst of wind, Nathara laid her hand on Cullen's head. From his body, the life seemed to drain into the ground. His body slowly disintegrated, piece by piece, disappearing into the black chasm Nathara had opened. When all that was left of him was a pile of ash, she looked once more at Titania. "You cannot believe this is the end."

"We had a bargain, Nathara. You must keep your part of it. Go."

In a final cry of rage, with a promise to return, Nathara followed Cullen's essence into the earth.

A strange silence remained. Struan met Titania's gaze with tear-filled eyes. "How could you do this? How could you let her die like some kind of pawn in your struggle with your sister? It wasn't necessary."

She regarded him for several seconds. "In all our time together, I have never taught you to trust the magic, Struan."

He wiped at his eyes with the back of his hands. He was so tired of the riddled talk. So tired of the philosophy and hidden meanings. In his arms, Laren lay dead. He no longer had the will to fight Titania. "It doesn't matter," he muttered. "You have what you want. Now leave me to die."

She pointed to the sky where the moon had now gone completely red. "Look, Struan. The miracle is yours. The sun shines in the midnight sky."

He looked at Laren. "And I have lost what I valued most."

"Nay." She flew over to pick up the dirk. "You gave what you valued most. The dirk held your life in its power. You could have chosen to end the enchantment at any time, but you did not. Living was more important to you than freeing Laren."

His body shook. "I cannot bear it. I cannot live knowing I've allowed this to happen."

She laid a tiny comforting hand on his shoulder. "You will not have to."

"Will you take my life after all? I would have betrayed you to Cullen. I would have told him your secret in exchange for Laren's life."

"I know. That is why, now, you have what you sought." With a flutter of her wings, she moved to hover above Laren's face. "Her body seems dead to you, but her soul lives still. She needs nothing more than the touch of your lips to breathe again." She pressed a butterfly kiss to his forehead. "Live long, Struan. You have earned it."

She disappeared then, and he was left cradling Laren. His eyes shut in an anguished prayer that Titania's promise was true. He willed himself to believe it. Trust the magic, she'd urged. Dare he?

Looking at Laren, he realized he had no choice. If she perished, his soul would truly wither. He might live on in years, but his heart would die on this spot. So, half fearful, half hopeful, while his soul whispered a prayer, he bent to lay his lips on hers. For a moment, when he felt nothing, no movement in her, no sign of life, panic flared in his heart.

But then, incredibly, so softly at first, he thought he'd imagined it, she stirred in his arms.

She had loved him for a thousand years. And it explained, she supposed, why the strange feeling of awakening began in the region of her chest. Her heart expanded and grew, while warmth flooded her limbs, and then she realized, at once, that she lay in Struan's arms. Through the miracle of magic, he held her close to his heart. She wrapped her hand around his nape to cradle his head to hers.

And when he lifted his head to gasp a prayer of thanksgiving, she used the sweet breath in her lungs to whisper his name.

 Epilogue

S truan and Laren lived out their days in the small stalker's cottage
by the Loch. They greeted each morning with a prayer of thanksgiving for the remarkable gift they'd received that night at the Rocking
Stone.

Their three sons and two daughters grew to have fine families of their
own, and the legend of the thousand-year slumber, though believed by
few, was cherished by all. When curiosity seekers would come 'round,
they found a small home, filled with an ageless love, and a couple,
usually so absorbed in themselves, they spared little time for those
who wanted to hear of faeries and such.

To this day, Inver Cottage lies across the bay from the ruins of the
old Lachlan Castle. Visitors there have been known to report the sound
of the bagpipes carrying on an evening breeze. The shelf of rock, where
once the Rocking Stone stood, still sits above the dark waters of the
Loch. And there, on a clear night, when the moon is high and the
tide is in, a faint glow can be seen near the edge of the water. Thousands
have tried to explain away the strange phenomenon.

If they lived still, Struan and Laren would share a secret laugh at
the skeptics. For they, like the MacLachlans before them, knew that
the magic of the spot speaks only to those who believe.